MW00774436

Tattooed Souls

Book Two of the Tattooed Duet

A Forever Inked Novel

Sabrina Wagner

Stay Connected!

Want to be the first to learn book news, updates and more?
Sign up for my Newsletter.

https://www.subscribepage.com/sabrinawagnernewsletter

Want to know about my new releases and upcoming sales?
Stay connected on:

Facebook~Instagram~Twitter~TikTok
Goodreads~BookBub~Amazon

I'd love to hear from you.
Visit my website to connect with me.

www.sabrinawagnerauthor.com

Books by Sabrina Wagner

Hearts Trilogy
Hearts on Fire
Shattered Hearts
Reviving my Heart

Wild Hearts Trilogy
Wild Hearts
Secrets of the Heart
Eternal Hearts

Forever Inked Novels
Tattooed Hearts: Tattooed Duet #1
Tattooed Souls: Tattooed Duet #2
Smoke and Mirrors
Regret and Redemption
Sin and Salvation

Vegas Love Series
What Happens in Vegas (Hot Vegas Nights)
Billionaire Bachelor in Vegas

About This Book

Book Two of the Tattooed Duet. Zack and Rissa's story continues...

Everyone I'd ever loved left me.
It was foolish to fall in love with Zack. I knew he'd leave too.
It was only a matter of time.

When he found out I was pregnant and the baby wasn't his, he was gone.
I had no choice but to pack my bags and leave.
Even if I still loved him, I didn't need him.

I grieved for the two men I'd loved and lost. The one who'd cherished me and given me the greatest gift I could ever ask for; and the one who rescued me, then destroyed my heart because of the gift the first had given me.

Being a single mom while starting a music career was never my plan, but I was determined to make a life for my unborn child.
No one was going to save me… I had to save myself.

♥♫♥♪♥

I evicted Rissa my apartment, but I couldn't get her out of my heart.
Nothing was right without her.
Despite the circumstances, I wanted her back.

I was a fool to think she could've been mine. That we could find happiness in my brother's shadow.
His parting gift was complication I wasn't prepared for.

After the things I said and did, I didn't deserve her friendship, let alone her love.
She was determined to make it on her own; she didn't need me.
I was crazy to believe I could live without her… or the baby.

Losing her forever was not a risk I was willing to take.
She'd given up on me, but I hadn't given up on her.
I'd fight to the end for our happily ever after.

She hadn't just tattooed my heart; she'd tattooed my soul.

Table of Contents

Prologue

"Love is a meeting of two souls, fully accepting the dark and the light within each other, bound by the courage to grow through struggle into bliss."

~Jackson Kiddard

Chapter 1
Rissa

The door slammed, and I flinched. I sobbed into my knees. I was curled into the corner like a scared child. I had never seen such rage in my entire life.

If I thought Malcolm was bad, Zack was worse. Much Worse. At least Zack's father never called me nasty names to my face.

Zack wouldn't let me say a word. I never got to explain. He just assumed I had cheated and that hurt. It hurt more than I could have ever imagined.

He'd thrown money at me like a whore because that's what he thought about me. I realized in that moment, how little I meant to him. I had been fooling myself to think that he was anything like his brother, Wes.

I pulled myself to my feet and grabbed some garbage bags from under the kitchen sink. I started emptying my dresser drawers into them without any thought. This was my life. Everything I owned fit into a few boxes and bags.

I stripped the sheets and comforter I'd paid for from the bed, leaving the throw pillows on the bare mattress. I wouldn't take one damn thing from him. I didn't need him or his fucking money. The hurt in my chest was quickly replaced by anger.

How dare he?

I was dumping the contents of the bathroom drawers into my overnight bag when I heard the door open.

"Rissa?" Layla's voice called out.

"I'm in the bathroom," I answered. I grabbed my shampoo from the shower when Layla entered.

"What's going on?" she asked tentatively.

I grabbed my body wash, razor, and shower scrubby and threw them into the bag. "Zack is an asshole," I stated.

"Are you really leaving?"

3

"Not much of a choice. He kicked me out." I pushed past her and strode into Zack's bedroom. I snatched my underwear off the floor and the shoe that sat next to them. Fuck! Where was my other shoe? I looked around the room and then under the bed. There it was, thrown carelessly underneath. I shimmied under the bed and grabbed the shoe, backing out less than gracefully.

Layla grabbed me by the shoulders. "What the hell happened?"

"Nothing I want to relive. It's over between us."

"But last night everything was fine," she said.

"Was it? Why was Gina there? She's been fucking Zack for years. Hell, he's probably there right now," I raged. This wasn't Gina's fault, but I couldn't help putting part of the blame on her anyway.

"Gina?"

"Yeah, Gina. You know, his fuck buddy? Tall, long legs and big tits. She practically shoved it in my face last night. UGH!" I ripped at my hair. "It doesn't even matter. She's not the problem." I swiped the diamond collar off the nightstand and stormed towards my own room.

I threw the collar on my bed and Layla quickly picked it up. "Are these diamonds?" she asked.

"Yeah. It's a dog collar. You want it?"

Layla turned it over in her hands. "Ummm... Zack doesn't have a dog."

"No shit! That was for me. He wanted me to wear it when he fucked me. I should have known then that I was nothing to him. But not me. Nooo... I wore the fucking thing because I wanted to make him happy, prove to him that I loved him. But it meant nothing."

"That's fucked up," Layla mumbled, tossing it back on the bed.

"Yeah, well that's what Zack and I are...fucked up. We were fucked up before we even got together. He's not who I thought he was and I'm definitely not who he thinks I am."

Layla sat on my bed. "I don't understand. You two are great together. I don't think that I've ever seen him happier than he has been the last couple of months."

I blew out a breath and sat next to Layla. She had become my friend since I'd been here. There was no use in keeping everything a secret anymore.

It was bound to come out eventually. Better she heard it from me. "Do you know how Zack and I met?"

She squinted her eyes. "Yeah. You were friends from New York. You two reconnected when he went home for his brother's funeral."

I rubbed my hand over my mouth. "It's a little more complicated than that." I wasn't sure if I should tell her the truth, but figured why the hell not? "I was engaged to Zack's brother. I loved Wes with all my heart. He was my everything and then he died."

Layla's head snapped to attention. "You were with his brother?"

"Yep, for two years. When he died, Zack's dad stripped me of everything, the car, our apartment, and our bank account. I had nothing left. Zack, being Zack, tried to save me. He brought me here to give me a new start. What he didn't know was that Wes left me with one thing their father couldn't take away... his baby. I'm pregnant."

Layla sighed. "Rissa..."

I pushed on. Telling my side of the story felt cathartic. "When Zack found out I was pregnant and that it wasn't his, he assumed I cheated on him. That's why he kicked me out. I tried to tell him the truth, but he wouldn't let me say a word. He thinks I used him for his money, but nothing could be further from the truth. I love Zack, but I won't let him treat me like this. I'll start over, make more money, and then move back home. I don't belong here. I never did."

Layla's eyes were wide from the story I had just told her. "So, he doesn't know it's his brother's baby?"

"Nope."

"And you're not going to tell him?"

"What would be the point? He's already shown me what he thinks of me. He accused me of cheating, of being a money-grubbing whore, of using him. I love him, but I don't need him."

"How long are you staying?"

I shrugged my shoulders. "I'm not sure. A month, maybe two. I need to save some money before I go back to Oklahoma."

"Oklahoma? What about your music?"

"Well, I don't think that's really possible with a baby on the way."

5

Layla reached out and wrapped me in her arms. "I'm going to miss you."

I returned her hug with eagerness. "I'll miss you too," I said honestly, a tear leaking from my eye. I quickly wiped it away. Tears weren't going to solve anything. "Okay, enough of the pity party." I stood from the bed. "I need a plan and I need it fast. First thing I need is a place to live."

"You can stay with me," Layla offered. "It's nothing fancy, but it's roomy."

"That's sweet of you," I said while scrolling through my contacts. "But it's probably not a good idea. You know, conflict of interest and all." I found the number I had been looking for and made the call. I'd seen the sign a few weeks ago and stashed the number in my phone just in case. "Hi. I saw your sign that you had an apartment for rent. Is it still available?"

Luckily, it was.

Layla went with me to check it out. The apartment was only about three blocks from The Locker, so I'd be able to walk to work. We headed into the party store where I'd seen the sign. The owner gave us a key and directed us to the back of the building. In the alley, was a black metal staircase that looked like it had seen better days. I headed up the creaking stairs, carefully holding onto the railing.

"I don't like this, Rissa," Layla said as she followed me up. "It's not safe."

"It's not ideal, but I lived in Brooklyn for three years. Utica is much safer than that." We reached the top of the stairs and stood on the small landing while I slipped the key into the door. The lock was stuck, but with a little jiggling, I was able to open it.

The musty smell when I opened the door nearly knocked me back. "First order of business will be getting some fresh air in here," I said as I held my hand over my nose. I stepped in further and surveyed the room. It was small. There was a ratty looking couch and a scratched coffee table sitting in the room. The tiny kitchen had a two-burner stove, a sink, mini-fridge, and a microwave.

Layla walked around me checking things out. She went into the bathroom and came right back out. "You can't stay here, Rissa. Zack would kill me if he knew I let you live here."

I let out a huff. "Well, Zack doesn't get a say and he doesn't have to know. Yeah, it's dingy and dark and about the size of a shoebox, but I won't be here forever. It's only for a couple of months and the rent is cheap. Utilities are included and look," I said pointing to the couch, "it's fully furnished."

"Rissa, it's awful. You could catch a STD just by sitting on that thing. There's not even a bedroom," she reasoned.

"Meh. Consider it a studio apartment. I'll throw a sheet over the couch and sleep there. Seriously, Layla, my options are limited. I need to get out of Zack's apartment today. This is my best bet."

Layla huffed. "I'll call Chase. He can help us move your things."

Layla was right, this place sucked. It was dreary and drab, but it was a roof over my head. I could make it work for a couple of months. I slapped a smile on my face. "Perfect."

Chapter 2
Zack

I drove and drove, breaking speed limits and weaving in and out of traffic along the expressway. I finally reached a rest area somewhere close to Saginaw. I pulled over and parked in a secluded picnic area. Ripping the helmet from my head, I threw it to the ground. "Fuck her!"

I climbed off my Harley and checked my phone. I expected there to be a message from Clarissa, begging me to come back.

Something.

Anything.

But there was nothing.

That was all I needed to know that things between us were truly over. After what I'd said to her, how could it not be?

I sat on a picnic table and rested my head in my hands. That was when the first wave of emotions hit me. Not the anger I'd been hanging onto the last two hours, but the sadness.

I wanted to hate her so bad, but I couldn't. I just couldn't. The anger had subsided and was replaced with a deep sense of loss. Memories of the time we had spent together took over.

I remembered driving from New York to Michigan and how she'd begged to drive my car.

I remembered our time at the fair and how adorable she'd been with the animals.

I remembered the nights I held her tight in my arms, listening to her soft sounds.

I remembered the night she sang with Bobby and how sinfully sexy her voice was.

That was when it hit me. She'd never been mine to begin with. She belonged to Wes, and this was my punishment for taking what was his. I'd tried to make her mine when she wasn't mine for the taking. I was so fucking stupid to think that we could have made it work.

She'd been lonely, and I filled a need for her. She'd warned me, but I didn't listen. So many times she tried to tell me she wasn't a good person, but I was blinded by.... what? Infatuation? Beauty? Lust? Love?

Yes, I had loved her. I still loved her, but I couldn't forgive her. Ever.

I thought about what I had missed over the past couple of months. All the signs were there, I was just too blind to see them. I couldn't remember her ever having her period. She refused to have a drink, even to celebrate. She'd been tired a lot lately, often slipping upstairs for a mid-day nap.

How could she do this to me?

Why?

Hadn't I given her everything she needed?

Hadn't I taken care of her?

Why wasn't I enough for her?

None of it mattered though. What was done, was done. She couldn't take it back and I couldn't be with her knowing she was carrying another man's baby. It was over.

I choked back the tears, refusing to shed any for her. I laid back on the table and watched the leaves billow in the breeze. I listened to the silence. I let it consume me as I drifted into nothingness.

I don't know how long I laid there, but eventually I got up and hopped back on my bike. I couldn't go home yet. I called the only true friend who had always been there for me. "Are you home?"

"Yeah."

"I'm coming over."

"Okay. See you soon."

I pulled up in front of the tall, red brick condo and walked to the door. I hadn't been here in so long, it felt weird. I knocked hesitantly. It only took a moment for the door to swing open. "Hi."

"Hi."

"I need you," I said.

"I know."

I fell into Gina's arms, and she led me to her couch. She wrapped my hand in hers and waited for me to talk.

9

"Did you know?" I asked her.

She squeezed my hand tighter. "Not until last night. I knew her from Doc Peterson's, but I didn't know she was your girl. I put two and two together pretty fast."

I nodded, accepting what she had to say. "It's not mine."

"I'm so sorry. I suspected, but I wasn't sure."

"I loved her. I still love her. What the fuck is wrong with me? Do I have a big sign above my head that says *I'm an idiot, take advantage of me*?"

Gina held my face in her hands. "No, Zack. You have a huge heart. Anyone would be lucky to have you. You deserve so much better."

"Then why? Why would she do this to me? How could she cheat on me?"

She leaned into my side, comforting me. "I don't know, Zack."

I wrapped my arm around the only woman I could truly trust. "I can't go home tonight. Can I stay here?"

"Of course. Whatever you need, I'm here for you." She gave me an innocent kiss on the cheek, "Do you want a drink?"

"Please. Something strong." After last night, the very last thing I needed was alcohol, but I wanted to forget. I wanted to forget that my heart was broken. I wanted everything to go back to when I was under the illusion that Clarissa loved me. I wanted to drown her out with whiskey.

Gina came back with a rock glass full of amber liquid. I drank it down greedily. "Slow down, baby. Getting plastered isn't going to solve anything."

"It will for tonight."

"And tomorrow?"

"I don't want to think about tomorrow." I tossed back the rest of the whiskey and handed Gina the glass. "I'll take another." I laid back on the couch and stared at Gina as she strode back to the kitchen. She wasn't wearing anything sexy, just sweatpants and a t-shirt, but I appreciated the view. She obviously wasn't wearing a bra, and her nipples poked through the thin material of her shirt. She was gorgeous. Always had been. Long legs, a small waist, and large, luscious tits. My dick perked up as I looked at her.

She returned with another glass of whiskey. I drank down half in one gulp. "I don't know why I even brought her home with me. I should have known better. You and I were good together, Gina. I'm sorry I set you aside

10

for her. It was shitty of me. What we had was a good thing." I finished the glass and set it on the coffee table.

Gina perched on the edge of the couch. "I'll always be here for you, Zack. No one understands me like you do." She ran her hand over my chest in a soothing manner.

My skin came to life under her touch. I shouldn't have been responding to her like I was. "Bring me the bottle, will ya?"

She left and came back carrying a bottle of Jack. She tilted the bottle to her own lips before passing it to me. We continued that way for several minutes, passing the bottle back and forth, not talking but drowning ourselves in booze.

Gina leaned over me and pressed her lips to mine. Our tongues tangled together in a dance of slow seduction. Before I knew it, she was straddling my hips and we were full on making out. It felt good. No pressure. No complications. Just the familiarity of our bodies pressed together.

She ran her hands down my chest to my waist. "I've missed you, Zack."

"I've missed you too." My hands reached up and ran over her hard nipples. She leaned back and let out a gasp, her hips grinding into mine. She rubbed her center over my dick, and it stood at full attention. It felt like home. I closed my eyes and ran my hands through her hair. And then her lips were on mine again. I got lost in the kiss, remembering every minute we spent together; the Ferris wheel, her arms wrapped around me on my Harley, the way her body pressed into mine as we danced.

I opened my eyes, and the picture was all wrong. Instead of blond, silky curls, my hands were wrapped in straight, dark strands. Her eyes weren't blue, but a dark chocolate. I pushed on her shoulders. "Stop. I can't do this."

Gina pulled back. "Zack?"

"I'm sorry, Gina. I just can't. Not tonight. I want you, I do, but I'd be using you to erase her memory and I can't do that to you."

Gina eased off my lap. "It's fine, I get it." The look of hurt on her face was unmistakable. She pulled a blanket off the back of the couch and covered me with it. "Just know I would never hurt you like that."

"I'm sorry."

11

"Don't be. I'm going to bed. I'll see you in the morning." She walked away looking dejected.

"Gina?"

She stopped and looked at me over her shoulder. "Yeah?"

"Thank you. You're the best friend I've ever had."

"Anytime. Get some sleep."

Chapter 3
Rissa

We went back to Zack's, and I got busy packing the rest of my things. Was shoving clothes into garbage bags even considered packing? It was haphazard and disorganized, but I didn't have time to worry about it. The sooner I was out, the better.

Chase began carrying my things down to his truck. It was going to take two trips to get all my things moved. When the truck was loaded, he drove us to my new apartment. Chase grabbed a box out of the back and then stared up at the rickety steps. "You're kidding me, right?"

I grabbed a bag and stood beside him. "They're perfectly safe. Don't be such a big baby."

He raised an eyebrow. "If you say so."

"Come on." I led the way up the stairs and unlocked the door, holding it open for him.

"What the hell is that smell?" he asked, setting the box inside.

"It just needs fresh air," I defended. I walked over to the window and tried to push it up. "I think this thing is stuck."

"Let me try." Chase tugged on the window and after a few tries it slid up. "I'll bring something over to fix that when we come back." Then he looked around the empty space. "Rissa, this place is a dump."

I held up my hand. "Save it, Chase. I already know it's not the Ritz, but it'll have to do for now."

I turned toward the door to get another bag from the truck when Chase stopped me. "Rissa?"

"Yeah?"

"Are we ever going to see you after today?"

I slumped and gave him a sad smile. "I'll still be working at The Locker, but I won't be back to Forever Inked. Zack and I are over, and he fired me."

"It's gonna suck. I kinda got used to you being around. I'm going to miss you."

I stepped to Chase and gave him a big hug. "Oh Chase, I'm going to miss you too. But I'll be around for a while. You can come to the bar anytime you want to see me."

Chase released me. "What does 'a while' mean?"

"I'm not sure quite yet, but I won't leave without saying goodbye. I promise."

After loading up the truck a second time, I asked Layla and Chase to give me a few minutes alone. They went down to wait for me in the shop, while I made one last pass through Zack's apartment.

My room was bare, except for the furniture. I laid the diamond collar on top of the dresser. I fluffed Priss's favorite blanket on the bed and made a little nest. I set my notebook and the Mason jar that held the money I owed Zack on the bed. I hated getting rid of that jar. I'd had it since my dad gave it to me the night I left Oklahoma. I'd fished out the jewelry Wes had given me and put it in my purse. Almost all the money I had was in that jar. After paying my rent, I didn't have much left. I'd need to pick up some extra shifts at the bar. The money Zack had thrown at me was stacked neatly with a sticky note on top. I refused to take anything from him.

Before leaving, I found Priss and cuddled her. "I'm going to miss you, sweet girl." She purred loudly into my ear. I laughed for the first time that day as her whiskers tickled my face. I held her up and rubbed my nose against hers. "I never thought I would like a cat, let alone love one, but you are the exception." Her little pink tongue came out and licked the tip of my nose. "Come on, let's get you fed." I gave her an extra helping of food and topped off her water bowl, setting them on the mat next to the fridge. Miss Priss eagerly delved into the food. I slid down the wall and sat next her, rubbing the soft fur on her back and tail. "Zack will be home soon."

The tears welled in my eyes. I was all out of anger and now only sadness remained. I felt it deep in my chest, an ache that physically hurt. It was like a giant hole had been punched through my heart and the blood was seeping out.

I stood from the floor. I couldn't stay here another minute. It was too painful. I set the keys on the counter and headed to the door. There was nothing left for me here, no reason to delay this. I left the apartment and locked the door behind me.

When I got downstairs, Chase and Layla were talking in hushed tones, no doubt it was about me. "I'm ready."

Chase spun his keys on his finger. "Got everything?"

I shrugged. "I guess. I didn't come here with much. We should get going. I didn't realize how late it was. I'm sure you two have other things to do."

Layla hugged me. "Nah. You're the most important thing we have to do tonight."

I wiped at my eyes again. "Thanks. Thanks for being my friends when I had nobody else. I don't know how I would have done this without you."

"Hey," Chase piped up, "just because you and Zack are over doesn't mean we're not your friends. If you need anything, you can call us."

"Thank you."

Layla wrapped her arm around my shoulder, led me out of the studio and to Chase's truck. We pulled into the back alley, and it was pitch black. Chase looked out the front window of the truck and up at my door. "First thing I'm doing tomorrow is fixing that light. You shouldn't be walking around in the dark."

"I'll be fine," I assured him.

"Maybe so, but I'm still fixing it." He opened the door to the truck, and we started unpacking.

After several trips up and down the rickety stairs, we were finished. I was once again surrounded by boxes and bags. This apartment reminded me so much of the first one I had in Brooklyn. This might even be worse if that was possible.

"Are you hungry?" Layla asked. "I haven't seen you eat a thing all day."

I ran a hand over my stomach. "I kind of forgot. I don't have much of an appetite. But I do live over a party store, so that's a perk."

"Come on," Chase said. "We're taking you to Meijer's. You need to at least have a few basics."

Although I didn't feel like going anywhere, Chase was right. I didn't even have a box of cereal.

15

♫♪♫♪

It was almost eleven o'clock by the time we got back. I said goodbye to Chase and Layla and sat down on one of the boxes. I was finally alone. I was probably the most alone I had ever felt in my life. The silence was deafening.

Zack hadn't called or texted all day. I had half expected him to... I don't know, say something? Anything? But all I had gotten was nothing.

It was hard to believe that it was really over. Yesterday seemed so long ago, a distant memory. Last night we were dancing together. He was holding me tight and telling me he loved me. Tonight, I was sitting alone in a shitty apartment. And who knew where Zack was? I didn't even want to think about him being with Gina, which was a very good possibility.

I needed some sleep. I searched through the garbage bags until I found the sheets I had ripped from my bed. I pulled them out and wrapped the fitted one around the couch. I made myself a nice little bed, then stripped out of my clothes. I laid down on the lumpy couch and tucked my pillow under my head.

This day couldn't have been any worse. I knew telling Zack about the baby was a risk, but I didn't think he would jump to conclusions without giving me a chance to explain. I was worse off now than if I had stayed in Brooklyn. I shouldn't have slept with Zack. I shouldn't have come here with him. I shouldn't have let myself fall in love again.

But I couldn't regret my time with Zack. My time with him had been pretty damn amazing. The only thing I regretted was not being honest with him from the beginning. Now it was just my baby and me. I was a survivor, and I was determined to make a life for us... far away from here.

Chapter 4
Zack

Feeling a little disoriented after sleeping on Gina's couch, I reached for my phone. I had a text from Chase that had come late last night. It was two words: **She's gone.** My heart sank. I hated it, but it was for the best.

I crept from Gina's condo and out to my bike. I felt bad for leading her on last night, but I wasn't ready. I couldn't turn Clarissa off like a light switch. It was going to take time before I was ready to hop back into bed with Gina.

I drove home and parked my Harley out back. My key turned in the door awkwardly. It had been a long time since I had come home early in the morning like this. My shop was quiet. It would be several hours before Chase and Layla showed up for work. I made my way up the stairs and to my apartment. I opened the door to the silence. I'd barely stepped through the door and already I missed her presence. The faint scent of her perfume lingered in the air, but I knew she wasn't there.

I shucked off my coat and threw it on the couch along with my keys. I stood in the middle of the apartment, hands on my hips, and looked around. Nothing seemed out of place. Everything was the same as I had left it.

The piano in the corner mocked me. I stepped to it and ran my hand over the black, lacquered surface. I had no use for it anymore, but it would stay.

I went to the kitchen. Priss's bowl was full of food and her water bowl was topped off. Crap! I hadn't given one thought to Miss Priss, but obviously Clarissa had. She had made sure my baby was fed and watered before she left.

I opened the fridge and peered into it. Clarissa's strawberry-banana yogurt and soy milk sat on the top shelf. I pulled them out and poured everything down the sink, throwing the containers into the trash.

Next was the bathroom. The towels were folded neatly over the racks and the counter had been wiped down. I opened the drawers where her things used to reside. They were empty. Not a toothbrush or bottle of nail polish remained. I slid open the shower door. Her shampoo and body wash were gone, along with the puffy, pink scrubby thing she used. You'd never know that yesterday we shared this bathroom. There wasn't one trace of a woman left.

I hesitantly went to her room. The door was cracked. I pushed it open wide, and my heart sank. The curtains I bought still hung on the window. The furniture stood bare, stripped of any remnants of her. The throw pillows sat on the bare mattress. One of her blankets remained, shaped into a nest on the bed where Priss slept peacefully. She blinked her yellow-green eyes at me and went back to sleep.

I went to her dresser and opened every drawer. They were all empty. The boxes she kept in the corner were gone, along with her guitar. All traces of her were gone.

Everything I had bought her remained; the furniture, the art on the wall, the lamp, the television, and... the diamond collar worth thousands. It was all still there. She didn't take anything I had given her.

I sat down on the mattress and looked at what she left behind. The money I threw at her was stacked neatly in a pile with a note, *I'm not a whore.* I picked up the pile of money and counted it. There was almost five-thousand dollars there. If I had to guess, she hadn't taken a penny of it.

But that wasn't what gutted me most. Her glittery pink notebook sat next to the money, a pink stuffed pig placed on top of it. Homer. I won him for her at the fair and she left it behind. There was also an old Mason jar filled with cash.

I pushed both the pig and the jar to the side and picked up the notebook. I'd seen her writing in this notebook many nights. I had assumed it had been a journal or diary. I couldn't have been more wrong. Folded inside was a note:

Dear Zack~

I'm so sorry for everything. Thank you for taking care of me and loving me. I don't know how I would have survived without you. I always knew what we had had an expiration date. I just never expected it to end like this.

I did lie to you and for that I am sorry, but I never lied to you about how I felt. I loved you with all my heart. You were everything to me. I never wanted to hurt you.

I should have never come here, but I can't regret it. The time I spent with you will be forever engrained as a part of me. You've tattooed my heart.

As soon as I can, I'm moving back to Oklahoma. Home. Maybe someday I'll send you that Christmas card.

I always hoped that we could make this work, but you never believed in me.

Love~ Clarissa Lynne Black

"I did believe in you, Clarissa," I said aloud. That's why this hurt so bad.

I tossed the note aside and looked at the first page of her notebook. It was a long list with dates that continued on for several pages. The first entry read: *July 31~ salad... $5.00.* That was the day I brought her with me to Michigan. It was what she had eaten when we stopped for lunch.

The list went on and on, including everything I had ever bought her. She had written entries for rent and utilities. Next to them was written *estimated cost.* She hadn't missed a single item. There were entries for her ticket to the fair, gas, and food. Even toothpaste was on the list. At the bottom she had written a total.

I picked up the Mason jar and twisted off the top. I dumped the contents onto the bare mattress and started counting. The amount of money inside exactly matched her list of expenses. There was a small slip of paper stuck to the bottom of the jar. I reached my fingers in and pried it out. I unfolded the tiny scrap of paper. The note was simple. *It was never about the money.*

I snatched the jar off the bed and threw it against the brick wall. It smashed into a million pieces that scattered onto the hardwood floor. "God dammit, Clarissa! What was it about?"

The first tears I had allowed myself to cry in years, slipped down my face. I quickly wiped them away. Fuck that! I wouldn't cry over her.

I grabbed Miss Priss off the blanket, left her room and shut the door behind me. I closed everything away behind that door. Out of sight, out of mind.

I set Priss down on the couch and headed to the shower. I stripped off my clothes and stepped into the hot water. I let it scald my skin. I welcomed the pain. When the water started to turn cold, I slid down to the floor and cried the tears I'd been holding back since Wes died.

♫♪♫♪

I pulled myself together and got ready for a day of work. I had a business to run and ultimately it was the most important thing I owned. I wasn't going to let my personal life interfere with that. What I needed most was to get lost in the monotony of inking; the buzz of the gun, the swipe of the needle, the wiping of the ink… wash, rinse, and repeat. I could lose myself for hours.

Shortly after ten, both Layla and Chase showed up, acting a little aloof. I had left them to clean up my mess and I'm sure they were none too happy about it. I dug out the envelopes with the bonuses I had promised them. "I know yesterday sucked, but I appreciate you two helping me out. Did you have any issues?" I held out the envelopes for them to take.

Layla glared at me. "Keep it. I don't want it." She slid past me to her studio.

Chase shook his head. "Me neither."

I retracted the envelopes and followed Chase back to Layla's studio. "Just take the money. You both lost a day's work because of me." The last thing I needed was tension in my shop. "I'm sorry I laid that shit on you."

Layla leaned back against the counter and crossed her arms. "I don't want to be paid for helping a friend. And by friend, I'm not referring to you right now. You have no idea what you did."

"That was harsh, man," Chase piped in. "We did what we had to do, but that doesn't mean we have to like it. Do you even care what happens to her? Because we do, she's still our friend."

I ran my hand over my stubble. "I did what I had to do, too. And honestly, it's none of your business. Either of you." I was pissed that Layla and

Chase were passing judgement on me. They wouldn't be so defensive of Clarissa if they knew what she had done.

Chase who's never stood up to me once in all the years he worked for me, crossed his arms too. "No disrespect, but you made it our business."

I supposed I had, but that didn't really matter. "Here's the deal," I said mirroring their stances. "You can get over it or you can find somewhere else to work."

Layla glared at me again. "You gonna throw us out too? Treat us like trash?"

"That's up to you. This wasn't easy on me." I pointed at the ground sharply. "I loved her and for you to suggest otherwise pisses me off." I pointed that same angry finger at my chest. "I didn't ask to be betrayed. I didn't ask for any of this. I gave her everything! Everything she could have wanted, and it wasn't enough for her!"

Layla softened and stepped to me. "That's ironic because she didn't ask for any of it. She left with nothing. The only thing she wanted from you was your love and your trust. Loving her was easy, but you never trusted her. Now... If I'm not fired, I have a client to prepare for."

"It's easy to defend her when you don't have all the facts," I said.

"Maybe you need to ask yourself if you had all the facts before you crucified her," Layla spoke cryptically.

"What's that supposed to mean?"

"Nothing. Forget I said anything. You've made it perfectly clear that it's none of my business," she answered.

"Damn right it's not!" I turned and stormed away.

The tension was so thick you could have cut it with a knife. I needed Chase and Layla not to quit. They were good enough that they could get a job at any tattoo parlor in the area. I knew that somehow, I needed to make amends. They couldn't be bought, that much was clear.

The only thing I could do was apologize. Around closing, I called both Chase and Layla into the back office. Both of them sat across from my desk looking tense. "Listen, I want to apologize to both of you. I'm sorry I blew up this morning. It's been a really stressful last couple of days. I don't want this to ruin our relationship. I know I'm damn lucky to have both of you not only as employees, but friends. I shouldn't have involved the two of you in my personal business. That was wrong of me, but I'm hoping we can move forward."

Chase cracked first. "Yeah, man. It's all good. It's just… it's not gonna be the same without Rissa here."

I steepled my fingers and rested my head on them. "I know. Trust me… I know. But we were fine before her, and we'll be fine without her here now."

Layla sat up and then leaned forward with her elbows on her knees. "I need you to know that I'm still going to be friends with Rissa. So, if that's going to be a problem you need to tell me now."

I'll be honest, it annoyed me, but it was out of my control. "It won't be a problem," I lied.

She nodded her acceptance. "Then we're good. Business as usual, right?"

"Right."

Chase and Layla left for the night, and I stayed downstairs, doing some cleaning and checking my stock. I needed to keep busy, or else my mind wandered to thoughts of Clarissa.

She and I hadn't spent a day apart in the last two months, and now it had been almost two days since I'd seen her. I knew she was still in town, that much I had gathered from Layla. Most likely she was five minutes down the street, pouring drinks behind the bar.

I couldn't get her out of my head. I had so many questions, but the biggest one was *why?* Why did she come here with me? Why did she pretend everything was good between us when it clearly wasn't? Why did she need someone else? Why wasn't I enough?

The second question that racked my brain, was *who?* Who did she fuck when she was living with me? Who was the father of her baby? And where the fuck was he? I swear, if I ever found out the answer to those questions, I'd probably end up in jail.

She said in her note that she was going back to Oklahoma. When was she leaving? And why would she leave if she was seeing someone here? Nothing made sense to me. I had to be missing something, but what?

Then there was Gina. I left her this morning like a coward. I owed her an apology too.

22

I pulled out my phone and called her. "Hey."

"Hey, Zack. How are you?"

"Meh. I'm fine, I guess. I'm sorry for bailing on you this morning."

"It's okay. I can come over if you need company. I can make you feel better."

I stared out the window. "I know you can, but not tonight. I just need to be alone for a while. I hope you understand."

"Yeah, of course. Call me if you change your mind. I'm here for you. Always." The disappointment in her voice was palpable and I felt guilty as hell. I'd never shut her out like this. We always leaned on each other when things were bad.

But I couldn't do it. Not tonight. My heart was hurting, and no amount of sex was going to make it go away.

I went upstairs and found Priss curled up outside Clarissa's door. I wasn't the only one who missed her.

Chapter 5
Rissa

I slept like shit. Not only was the couch lumpy as hell, but it was eerily quiet. I was scared shitless. Every little creak and rattle had my heart beating harder. I should have been exhausted, but sleep evaded me until the early hours of the morning, and even then, it wasn't peaceful sleep.

I dreamt of the look on Zack's face when I admitted the baby wasn't his. I relived his wrath as he screamed at me. I felt the money he threw at me flutter down around my body.

When I woke up, I felt more exhausted than when I'd gone to bed. I dragged myself to the bathroom and looked at my reflection in the cracked mirror. I had dark circles under my bloodshot eyes and my hair was a tangled mess. I turned on the tiny shower and waited for the water to get hot. After five minutes, it was barely lukewarm. I guessed that was the best I was going to get.

After showering, I had a glass of orange juice and got ready for my doctor's appointment. It was the last place I wanted to go because I was sure Gina would be there to rub my demise in my face.

The grey, drizzly day perfectly matched the way I was feeling. I located my umbrella and headed down the metal staircase. I held onto the railing tightly, afraid of slipping and rolling to the bottom. These stairs were going to be hell when the snow came. What was the chance that my new landlord was going to shovel them off for me? Zero to zilch was my guess.

I walked the couple of blocks to Doctor Peterson's office and shook out my umbrella before heading inside. Gina was sitting behind the receptionist window. I made my way to the counter, signed in, and sat down without ever looking up. Leafing through a magazine, I ran through how I was going to handle Gina. It was going to be impossible to avoid her and I wasn't looking forward to her gloating.

A few minutes later, Gina called my name. I strode past her and to the nurse who weighed me and put me in a room to take my temperature and blood pressure. She frowned when she read the gauge on the cuff. "Your blood pressure is up."

I turned away, afraid I would cry again if I looked at her. "It's been a stressful few days."

"You really need to avoid stress while being pregnant. It's not good for the baby," she said with a smile.

"Easier said than done," I replied. How could I avoid stress when the cause of it was living inside me? If I hadn't been pregnant, Zack and I could have been happy. There wouldn't be anything to hold us back.

I admonished myself for the thought. I loved this baby more than I loved Zack. He or she had been made from pure love and commitment. I cherished the fact that I got to hold onto a small piece of Wes. What Zack and I had together paled in comparison to my time with Wes. Two years compared to two months. It wasn't a competition Zack could win.

It didn't mean that I didn't love Zack. I did, as much as my heart would let me. It was foolish to think that I could replace Wes with his brother.

Zack had shown me his true colors yesterday. He was more like his father than I had realized. I wouldn't apologize for the life growing inside me. The only regret I had was not telling him sooner.

After Doc Peterson checked me out, he did another ultrasound. I could clearly see my baby curled up inside me on the screen. "Can you tell if it's a boy or a girl?" I asked.

Doc Peterson smiled at me. "Not yet. By your next appointment we should be able to tell the gender." He wiped the gel from my belly, and I sat up on the table. "How is everything else?" he asked sincerely. "Your blood pressure is up."

I smoothed my shirt down my front. "Not great, but I'm working on it. I just moved into my own place."

He quirked an eyebrow up at me. "So, you're living alone? What happened to the friend you were staying with?"

"That kind of fell apart," I admitted.

"Hmmm." He didn't say anything, but I knew me living alone concerned him. "Let's try to get your blood pressure down. I want you eating healthy, avoiding salt, and getting plenty of exercise. Sleep would be good too," he said, referencing the dark circles under my eyes.

"I will," I promised. I was pretty sure bar food wasn't what he had in mind. I'd have to get to a grocery store to stock up on some fruit and real food. But since I ate for free at the bar, it would have to do for now.

After my exam, I faced Gina. "Hi, Rissa. How's Zack?" she asked smugly.

I didn't have any fight left in me, "You got what you wanted. You won, Gina. He's all yours."

She huffed. "I didn't do anything. You did this to yourself."

"Yes, I'm quite aware of that, but it's not what you think. How much do I owe?"

She slid the bill over the counter. I pulled out my wallet, counted out the cash and handed it to her. Her fingers grasped mine as she took the money. She lowered her voice to a deep whisper, "You know what I think? I think you're a gold digger. A man like Zack would be a pretty sweet deal for a girl like you. Too bad you were stupid enough to get knocked up by someone else. He deserves better than you."

I was starting to get pissed. "I suppose that means someone like you," I hissed. Any thought I had about keeping this quiet, vanished with her accusations. "First of all, don't pretend like you know anything about me. Second, you don't know what the fuck you're talking about."

Our interaction had caught Doc Peterson's attention. "Is there a problem here?"

I let out a sigh. "No problem. I just want to pay my bill and be on my way."

He eyed Gina who gave nothing away. "Everything is fine."

Doc Peterson nodded and walked away.

"He'll never take you back," Gina said, getting in her final dig.

"I don't expect him to."

I left the office and wandered down the street. The sky had started to clear, and the sun poked through the clouds. I pulled my jacket tightly around me to ward off the cool October air.

I walked past the small boutique I'd shopped in earlier and noticed the *Help Wanted* sign in the corner of the window. I needed another job and quick.

26

I pulled open the door and headed inside, out of the cold. Vintage clothes hung on the racks and decorated the walls. I thumbed through the racks, knowing I couldn't afford to buy anything right now.

An older woman, obviously lost to an era gone by, approached me. "Can I help you?" She had long, straight greying hair and a pretty face. She wore a long, flowing skirt, loose-fitting top, and was adorned by more jewelry than I had ever seen anyone wear at once; bangles that covered her arms, a chunky necklace that hung down her chest, rings on every finger and big hoop earrings. Something about her made me smile.

I pointed to her sign in the window. "I need a job."

And that was how I started working at A Second Chance. Audrey, the owner and my new boss, was kind and wise. She quickly became the motherly presence I had been missing for years.

After a week of working at both A Second Chance and The Locker, Audrey sat me down for a chat, as she liked to call it. "What's your story, Rissa?"

I choked back my surprise at her boldness. "What do you mean?"

She patted my hand, "Oh honey, you can't fool me. I've been there and done that. You're a young, beautiful woman. All you do is work. I've never heard you talk about having any fun, which is what a girl your age should be doing."

"It's complicated and I only made it worse," I answered.

"Well, I've got nothing but time. If I had to guess, I'd bet it had something to do with a man," she said.

I didn't deny it. "Two actually."

"Now, I'm intrigued. Go on," she encouraged me.

I told her the whole story, not leaving out any details this time. I laid out all my dirty laundry for her to hear. I told her about Wes. I told her about Malcolm. I told her about Zack. A barrage of Kincaid men that had irrevocably changed my life. I told her about the day Zack kicked me out of the apartment and the assumptions he made.

When I finished, Audrey was speechless. She sat for a while and contemplated everything I told her, tapping her fingers on the table.

I folded my hands in my lap and stared at them. "Not what you were expecting was it?"

27

She shook her head. "Do you love him?"

"More than anything, but that doesn't really matter anymore."

"Do you think he still loves you?"

"I don't know."

"Don't you think you owe it to yourself to find out?" she asked.

I bit my lip. "I wasn't honest with him. He'll never forgive me."

Audrey clasped my hand over the table. "Honey, the lies he believes are worse than the truth. You didn't do anything wrong but fall in love. Yes, you should have told him from the beginning, but you didn't and that was a mistake. We all make mistakes."

Still holding her hand, I stood from the table. "Some mistakes can't be fixed, no matter how hard we try to erase them."

Chapter 6
Zack

It had been a week and I hadn't heard a word from Clarissa. I thought she'd be back to beg me for forgiveness, to ask for money... anything. But all I got was silence. It was as if she never existed. If it weren't for the piano sitting in my apartment and the room full of furniture she left behind, I might have been able to convince myself that was the truth.

I laid on my bed, arms crossed behind my head and thought about her. I remembered her storming away from the cemetery in her three-inch heels, walking down the road alone. I remembered what she said to me when I tried to help her, *I don't need your help... I've been doing shit alone for a long, long time... I'm not a charity case.* She'd been determined that day to do things on her own, come hell or high water. It was one of the things that attracted me to her in the first place. She had an inner strength that I admired.

When I thought about our time together, I realized that she never asked me to help her, never asked me to spend a single dime on her. I was the one who had insisted. It was the thing that we argued about the most. She'd tried to pay her own way, and I always shut her down. I *wanted* to take care of her. I *wanted* to spoil her.

When everything came crashing down, I threw it in her face like she had taken advantage of me. Then to make it worse, I tried to pay her off like a cheap whore. It wasn't one of my finer moments. God, I was just like my father. I treated her no better than he had. At least my father had given her three days to leave. I gave her one... in a city where she had no family, no friends, and no connections. I was such an asshole.

I hated what she had done, but I couldn't stop loving her. I couldn't stop thinking about her. I couldn't stop worrying about her. I couldn't help but wonder where she was living.

It was almost two in the morning. She would be getting off work soon. I needed to see her. I laced up my boots and threw on my heavy leather jacket, then headed down the stairs and out the back door.

I pulled the collar up on my coat as the wind bit at my skin. It was getting fucking cold at night. I walked toward The Locker, not sure what I was going to say to her or if I was going to say anything. I just needed to see her, to know she was all right.

I was down the block from The Locker when I saw her emerge. She slipped off her heels, dropped them in her bag and replaced them with her Vans. Pulling her coat up around her neck she took off in the opposite direction. I should have called out to her, but my curiosity got the best of me, so instead I followed her like a damn stalker. When she got to the corner, she crossed the street and kept walking. Keeping a decent distance, I followed. It was almost three blocks before she slipped into an alley behind a party store. What the fuck was she doing? This wasn't safe... not by a long shot.

I sped up my pace and turned the corner just in time to see her enter a door at the top of a stairway lit by a single bulb. The darkened window came to life and I saw her shadow moving behind the curtains.

I sat down on the bottom of the steps. They creaked and swayed under my weight. At least now I knew where she was living... and I hated it. I hated that I forced her into this. With the money she'd left behind, she probably didn't have much left.

There wasn't anything I could do, except try to keep her safe. I might have been mad at her, but I didn't want anything to happen to her either.

Every night, for a week, I followed her home. I never saw her with anyone.

Tonight, it was storming outside, but I didn't let it deter me. At two-fifteen she left The Locker, pulled her hood over her head, and started home. She walked faster than usual, occasionally breaking into a slow jog as she hopped over puddles. Lightning flashed, lighting up her silhouette. It was followed closely by a deafening boom of thunder. She stopped and covered her head with her arms. She was frozen in place for a good thirty seconds before she started moving again, quicker this time.

She ducked into the alley, and I followed. When I got to the back, she was standing at the top of the stairs looking down at me. She removed the hood from her head and yelled down. "Are you coming up or are you going to stand out there and get soaked?"

I grabbed the railing and bound up the stairs two at a time as she unlocked the door. She stepped inside and shrugged out of her jacket, hanging it on a hook.

I shook the water from my hair and looked around her apartment. Fucking A. What a fucking dump. The thought of her living here disgusted me.

Then she disappeared, coming back with a towel. She dried her hair and threw it to me. I wiped down my face and ran it over my head. "Is this mine?" I asked.

"Yeah. You want it back? You can have it," she snipped.

I tossed it back to her. "Keep it." This wasn't going well. There was hostility on both our ends.

Setting the damp towel on the back of the couch. She crossed her arms and narrowed her eyes. "You wanna tell me why you've been following me all week?"

I couldn't have been more surprised if I tried. I thought I had been careful, keeping at a distance and staying in the shadows.

"Don't look so shocked, Zack. I lived in Brooklyn for three years. You don't think I know when I'm being followed?"

"What if I'd been an attacker? I could have hurt you."

"More than you already have? I doubt it." Clarissa stripped off her wet clothes and crossed the room in her bra and panties. I openly stared at her. She was a sight for sore eyes as she rifled through a garbage bag for dry clothes. "Stop staring. It's not like you haven't seen me naked before," she scolded.

I averted my eyes. "Sorry." She pulled a shirt over her body, and I continued with my questions. "Seriously, Rissa, what were you going to do? It's not safe walking in the dark alone."

"I know how to take care of myself. I did just fine before you. I don't need you to protect me."

She was so damn stubborn. "How? How are you going to protect yourself?"

She reached in her coat pocket. "With this."

Jesus Christ! "What the fuck are you doing with a gun?" How did I not know she had a gun in my apartment? Two months she'd been there and never mentioned it. Of course, I hadn't been very forthcoming about my arsenal either. Being a Marine, I had more than a few, both upstairs and downstairs.

She set the 9mm on the coffee table and sat down. "Did you really think Wes would let me walk the streets of Brooklyn unprotected? He didn't think my pepper spray was enough. He bought me that gun and taught me how to use it."

Of course, he did. Wes was her knight in shining armor, right up until he overdosed. I ran my hands over my face. "Have you ever shot anyone, Rissa?" It was a rhetorical question. "Because I have. It's not as easy as pulling the trigger."

"Maybe not, but if I had to choose between being raped or shooting someone, I know what I would choose. I'm not helpless, Zack. I can take care of myself," she said with conviction.

I picked up the 9mm from the coffee table and inspected it. It was a good one, a Ruger subcompact. I checked the chamber and pulled out the clip. It was fully loaded. "When's the last time this thing was fired?"

"It's been a few months," she answered.

"You should go to the range and practice."

She took the gun from my hands and set it back on the table. "I'll put it on my list of things to do once I get a car," she said sarcastically. "Why are you really here, Zack? The money I left you wasn't enough?"

"I didn't expect you to leave me money. You need it more than I do," I said. As a matter of fact, if I were any kind of man, I would have returned it to her, but something told me she'd never take it.

"No, you expected me to take your money like a whore. Fuck you, Zack! I pay my debts. After the way you talked to me, I wouldn't take a dime from you if I was starving and living in a cardboard box." Her words were sharp and her tone sharper, confirming my suspicions.

"Don't act like you're the victim in all this," I shot back at her. Yeah, what I'd said was awful, but what she had done was awful too.

"I don't deny I made mistakes."

"Mistakes? A mistake is when you forget to feed the cat. I'd call opening your legs for someone else's dick, more than a mistake."

I saw her temper flaring, but she took a deep breath and calmed herself. "I already know what you think about me. What I don't know is why you're here. Why you've been following me."

"I told you. I was worried about you. Where's the guy?" I asked, looking around the room. There wasn't a trace of a man in this shithole.

She frowned. "What guy?"

"Are we going to play this game? The guy who knocked you up," I said with frustration.

She sighed. "Are we going there?"

"Yeah, we are. I think I deserve that much. So, where is he?"

"Gone."

I nodded my head. "Did he know you were pregnant?"

"Yep."

Her one-word answers were pissing me off. "And he left you alone to deal with it yourself?" I asked with disgust. If she was going to cheat on me, at least she could have picked someone who was going to stick around.

"You could say that," she answered sadly.

I should have felt bad for her, but I couldn't. She'd done this to herself. "Sounds like an asshole. So, what are you going to do?"

"What do you mean?"

"Are you keeping it?"

She rubbed her stomach. "I'm not getting rid of my baby."

"So, you're going to raise it with no father. That's gonna be rough."

"Why the fuck do you care what I do? It's none of your business. You lost that right when you kicked me to the curb!" she yelled. "If you came here to pass judgement on me, then you can leave." She crossed the room and yanked the door open.

I refused to leave like this. I made no move to walk out the door. "Just because we're not together, doesn't mean I don't care about you. It kills me that you're living like this." I motioned to the dump that surrounded me.

"It was the best I could do on short notice. It's only temporary anyway," she said easing the door shut.

"Back to Oklahoma, right? Why?" It didn't make sense to me.

"Why not? That's where I belong. It's where I'm from."

33

"What about your music? You're going to give that up when you finally have a chance to make something of yourself? You're going to give up on your dreams?"

"My priorities have changed. I don't think I can be a single mom and music star," she said.

"So, you're going to give up everything for this baby?"

"Yeah, I am."

I shook my head. "I don't understand you, Rissa. I don't understand any of this. Why? Why wasn't I enough for you? We could have been happy together."

She sat down on the couch next to me. "We were happy." She cupped my face with one hand and pierced me with her blue eyes. "I loved you, Zack. I still love you, but it's better this way. I was never good for you. I told you that from the beginning."

I kissed her palm. "I can't accept that. We were good together. We could have been great."

"Zack…"

"But I can't be with you knowing you're carrying another man's baby. I just can't. You hurt me, Rissa. I gave you everything and you betrayed me. I don't think I'll ever forgive you for that." I stood from the couch and walked to the door.

"I didn't think you would. That's why I have to leave. I can't stay here knowing what I've done. It's better for both of us."

I grasped the door handle. "That's a cop out and you know it. I never pegged you for a quitter. You gave up everything for someone who never gave two shits about you or your baby. I would have done anything for you. You made me promise not to leave you, not to tattoo your heart. But the minute you stepped out of this relationship, you left me. You tattooed *mine*. I'm not leaving you, I'm protecting what's left of my heart, because you'll always own a piece of it."

I opened the door and jogged down the steps into the rain. Walking away from her again was one of the hardest things I've ever done.

Chapter 7
Rissa

I sat back on the couch and sobbed into my hands. It was an ugly cry I was glad had no witnesses. Why did he have to come here and rip me apart again? Seeing him opened all the wounds I had tried to stitch back together.

He'd called me Rissa. He hadn't called me anything but Clarissa since we left New York. It was such a small thing, but it had huge meaning. He was done with me. He may still care, but he'd never let himself love me again. When I told him I loved him, he didn't say it back.

There were no apologies from him, just questions I responded to with the briefest of answers. I couldn't elaborate without revealing the truth, so I let him believe that I cheated. It would be easier if he hated me, because despite it all, I was still pregnant with another man's baby.

He'd made it quite clear that he couldn't be with me, so what difference would the truth have made?

♫♪♫♪

I needed a car. The weather was getting colder, and I couldn't walk everywhere I wanted to go. Grocery shopping at the party store I lived above was damn expensive. And honestly, healthy food wasn't their specialty. My baby deserved better.

I pulled out the money I had left and counted it. Even working two jobs, it wasn't close to enough. I rummaged through my purse to the bottom and extracted the small velvet pouch at the bottom. There was no way I would have left it in this apartment when I wasn't home. I didn't have much, but the contents of this bag were irreplaceable.

I opened the bag and dumped it on the table. I held up each item and inspected it. This was going to kill me. It was a last resort, but I was out of options.

35

I pulled out my phone and dialed Tori. She answered on the first ring. "Hey, girl, how are you holding up?" After Zack kicked me out, I had called and told her everything. We'd talked every few days, and I was thankful to have her shoulder to cry on. We'd met for coffee once, but I hadn't let her see my new apartment. It was too embarrassing. I didn't want her to know how low I had sunk.

"I'm good," I lied. "I need a favor. I looked online and found a couple of cars I think I might be able to afford. I was wondering if you had the time to take me to look at them?"

"No problem. I can be there in an hour."

I let out a sigh of relief. "Thank you. I'll meet you outside The Locker."

Now I needed the money. I gathered up the jewelry on the table and placed it back into the black pouch. I shoved it inside my purse and headed down the stairs. I walked a block until I was standing across from Sid's Silver Exchange. I darted across the street and into the pawn shop. The bell above the door jingled, announcing my arrival. I went to the glass counter and waited for someone to help me.

A tall, tatted up guy with bulging arms strode to the counter and leaned on it. "How can I help you?"

I dumped the contents of the bag on the counter. "How much will you give me for these?"

He quirked up an eyebrow and picked up my engagement ring from Wes, carefully inspecting it. Then he lifted the diamond earrings and diamond pendant, giving them each a once over. "You selling or pawning?" he asked.

"Selling. I need the cash."

He pulled out a monocle, like I'd seen on TV, and relooked at each piece. I waited patiently while he inspected the jewelry. He dropped the eyepiece and gave me a stern glare. "Are these hot?"

"What?" I was taken aback by the question. Did I look like a thief?

"Stolen? Pinched? Pilfered?"

"I know what you meant. And no, I didn't steal them," I answered curtly.

"Makes no difference to me, sugar. I ain't the cops, but I don't want them sniffing around my shop either. If these aren't legit, I got no use for them." He pushed them towards me.

I pushed them back across the counter. "They're mine, I swear. They were gifts."

He looked at me skeptically. "Sure they were. Tell ya what, I'll give ya five grand for all of it."

My heart sank. "Five grand? The ring alone is worth twenty."

He laughed. "This is a pawn shop, sugar. I gotta make a profit. It ain't gonna be easy to sell a ring like that. People that come in here ain't looking to spend that kind of money."

"Six," I bargained with him. "The earrings and pendant are worth at least that much."

He tilted his head back and forth as if contemplating. "Done." Then he eyed me up and down, making me feel uncomfortable. "You look familiar. Where do I know you from?"

"I work at The Locker. Maybe there?" I immediately wanted to smack myself over the head. I shouldn't have told this guy where I worked. *Dumb, dumb, dumb!* Maybe Zack was right. I couldn't take care of myself.

He snapped his fingers and pointed at me. "Yeah, yeah. You're the bartender. Sometimes you sing too."

"That's me." I forced a smile.

"You got a real pretty voice, and you don't skimp when pouring a shot," he said.

I squinted at him. "Thanks. I don't cheat my customers. I give them what they deserve."

He let out a huff. "Listen sugar, this ain't personal. Six is the best I can do and that's stretching it. I'll be saddled with these diamonds for a while. Every day they don't sell, is a day I'm losing money on my investment. Tell ya what, if I sell these within the week, I'll split the difference with you."

"Fine," I agreed, knowing damn well I wouldn't see another dime whether he sold them or not.

The guy counted out my cash and handed it across the counter. I recounted it and stuffed it in my purse. "Nice doin' business with ya, sugar. You come back and see me anytime," he said with a wink.

"I'll be back to check on my investment. You can count on that," I said pointedly.

He gave me a smirk. "I'll be looking forward to it."

I left the pawn shop, letting the door jingle behind me and headed toward The Locker. I still had a half hour to wait for Tori, so I headed inside to talk to Lou.

He was behind the bar, prepping garnishes for the night. "Hey, Rissa. What brings you in so early?"

I parked my ass on a bar stool. "I wanted to ask if I could pick up a few more shifts or sing more or something?"

Lou set down the lime and knife in his hands and wiped them on the towel over his shoulder. "You already work five days a week. And didn't you get another job at A Second Chance?"

"Yeah, but I need the money and let's just say idle time is not my friend." I sighed.

He leaned on the bar. "I take it you and Zack haven't patched things up."

I pulled a straw from off the bar and started twisting it around my finger. "No. I don't think that's gonna happen." I threw the straw on the bar. "I'm moving back to Oklahoma. I gotta get away from here. Away from him. I need money to do it though."

Lou filled a glass with sprite and squeezed a lemon into it. He slid it across the bar to me. "You think running away is gonna solve your problems?"

"I'm not running. I'm going home," I defended.

"From what you've said, it doesn't sound like there's anything there for you. No family. No friends."

"And no Zack," I finished.

"Running," he reiterated.

"Yeah, I guess." I shrugged. I took a sip of my drink. "So about getting more shifts?"

"I can give you one more day, but that's it. And I'll need at least two weeks' notice before you bail. It ain't gonna be easy to replace you."

I stood on the bottom rail of the bar stool, leaned over, and kissed Lou on the cheek. "Thanks, Lou. You're the best."

He wiped his hand across his cheek as if I'd slobbered on him. "I'm kind of attached to you. Things won't be the same without you."

"Don't say goodbye yet, old man. I've still got some time." I glanced out the front window as Tori's car pulled up to the curb. "I gotta go, my ride's here."

"See you tonight, Rissa," he called after me as I jetted out the door.

I pulled open the door of Tori's car and plopped into the front seat. "Thanks for this. You don't know how much I appreciate it."

"It's no problem." Tori waved me off. "Savannah's grandpa is excited to see her."

I swung my head to the back and saw Savannah snuggled into her car seat, kicking her tiny legs. "Crap. I don't know what I was thinking. If you don't have time for this, it's fine."

"Relax, Rissa. I've got time and I know the perfect place to get you a car."

I held up my phone. "I've got a couple of leads. We could start there."

Tori shook her head. "No way. You have no idea the history of the car or if it's going to break down five minutes after you drive away. There's only one person I trust… my dad."

"Your dad?"

"Well technically he's my stepdad, but he's the only dad I've ever known. And yeah, he's a mechanic and has his own shop. I called him, and he said he had a couple of cars you might be interested in. What's your budget?"

I pulled the pile of cash out of my purse. "Six grand."

"Jesus, Rissa! Why the hell are you carrying around that kind of money? Don't you have a checking account?" She placed her hand on top of mine and pushed the money back in my purse.

"I'm a cash kind of girl. I lost almost everything after Wes died and his dad froze our account. So, yeah, cash," I explained.

"How the hell did you even get that much money? Last we talked, you left most of it with Zack," she asked.

"I pawned some jewelry."

"Must have been some nice fucking jewelry to rake in cash like that."

"It was." I sighed. "I pawned my engagement ring from Wes. Some diamond earrings and a pendant too. It killed me, but I was out of options. I can't call you every time I need to go somewhere."

She gave me an exaggerated pout. "I'm sorry. That must have been hard."

I leaned on the door. "You have no idea." I stared out the window and watched the trees fly by.

Ten minutes later we pulled up in front of her dad's shop. Tori unfastened Savannah's car seat from the back, and we headed inside. "Hey, Courtney. Is my dad in his office?'

The blond receptionist pushed away from her desk. "Yes, but don't think you're going in there without letting me see that baby."

Tori sat the carrier on the floor and introduced me to Courtney, then unbuckled Savannah. She lifted her under the arms and pulled her from the seat. "Say hi to your Aunt Courtney."

Savannah smiled and gurgled, kicking her legs. "God, she's getting so big," Courtney exclaimed.

"Is my granddaughter out there?" A deep voice bellowed. A tall, stocky man came around the corner and snatched Savannah out of Tori's hands. He pressed his nose to her belly and shook his head back and forth.

"What am I, chopped liver now?" Tori teased.

"Hi, sweetheart." He kissed Tori on the cheek.

Just then, Savannah took it upon herself to spit up all over the front of her onesie. I scrunched up my nose. It was disgusting, but soon this would be my life. Cleaning up puke and changing diapers were part of being a mom. "Oh jeez, dad. Let me take her." Tori took Savannah back and pulled a cloth from her diaper bag.

Her dad turned to me and held out his hand. "I'm Mike.

I shook his hand. "Rissa."

"I hear you're in need of a car."

I nodded my head. "I am. I'm on a limited budget, but I'd be interested in seeing what you have."

He winked at me. "I'm sure we can work something out. I only have a couple. Sometimes people don't want to spend the money to fix their car and I

40

buy it from them. Doesn't take me much to get them in working order. What did you have in mind?"

I shrugged. "It doesn't have to be pretty. Something to get me from point A to point B. Point B is Oklahoma, so it must be reliable. I don't want to be breaking down somewhere in the middle of a cornfield."

"You're going to drive all the way to Oklahoma by yourself?" he asked in surprise.

"That's the plan. I drove from Oklahoma to New York at eighteen, so I'm not worried about the drive."

He raised his eyebrows. "Got it. Follow me." I trailed behind Mike through a maze of hallways and out a back door.

Three cars sat in the lot, a silver Honda, a sporty red Saturn, and an old Bronco. I immediately walked toward the Bronco. It wasn't pretty. It had a few dents and a scrape where someone had backed into something. I didn't care about any of that. It was big enough to pack all my shit into. That's what mattered. I got down on one knee and inspected the tires. They had good tread and were worn evenly. "How's this one run?"

Mike pulled the keys from his pocket and tossed them to me. "Rebuilt the engine myself. It's a stick shift though."

"Not a problem." I unlocked it and hopped into the driver's seat. It started right away and purred like a kitten. I pulled the lever to pop the hood. "Would it be insulting to ask to see the oil and transmission fluid?"

Mike laughed. "Someone taught you well. It'd only be insulting if I had something to hide."

"That would be my dad. He was a car guy. Taught me how to drive when I was fourteen. Our love of cars, not that we could afford much, was mutual." I hopped out of the truck and opened the hood.

Mike smiled a big toothy grin. "I'm impressed. Let me get a couple of rags and a wrench." He disappeared and came back with what he needed. Mike pulled the dip stick on the oil and cleaned it off before dipping it back in. He pulled it again. The oil was on level and clean. Next, he pulled the plug for the transmission fluid and stuck his finger in the hole. He pulled it out and let me inspect the fluid on his finger. It looked good, no burning. Satisfied with what I'd seen, I closed the hood and leaned against the front of the truck. "How much for this baby?"

Tori joined us, balancing Savannah on her hip. "You really want a stick shift?" she asked.

"I want a car that will get me to Oklahoma and fit all my stuff. This one will do that. She's solid."

"She's ugly," Tori huffed.

Okay, so it was an ugly two-toned brown, with dents and scratches. "I'm not in a position to be picky. I'm more interested in how she runs than what she looks like." I turned my attention back to Mike. "How much?"

Mike scratched the side of his head. "Three grand?"

I about lost my shit. "Are y'all fuckin' with me?"

Mike and Tori burst into laughter. Tori pointed at me. "Shit, that's the first time I've heard you sound like a hick. That was priceless."

I always tried to keep the accent at bay, but it had slipped when Mike told me the price. "Laugh it up. I am a hick, born and raised. So, seriously, how much?"

"Three grand," Mike repeated.

I chewed on that a minute. "I'll need to take her for a drive first."

"I wouldn't expect anything less." He chuckled. "Take her for a ride."

"Pass that baby to your dad, Tori, and get your ass in here." I hopped into the driver's seat and Tori quickly got into the passenger side. I shifted her into first and eased out of the lot.

I drove the Bronco up and down the road, pushing her speed limit. Tori grasped the 'oh shit' bar above her window. "Are you crazy? Slow the fuck down!"

I eased off the gas. "I had to know that she could keep up with me. Seems we're a match made in heaven." I slowly turned back into the drive for Mike's shop and drove around the back.

When I parked, Tori hopped out quickly. "You're nuts!" she exclaimed before she slammed the door.

I strode toward Mike. "Seriously, how much?"

"Haven't we already covered that?" he asked.

"I have the money. I can pay more than three grand."

Mike threw up one hand, while clutching Savannah with the other. "That's all I'm asking. If you don't want it, I'm sure someone else will. Suit yourself." He turned and headed back inside.

"Wait! What if I break down in the middle of Missouri?"

"Then I'll fly out there and fix her for you."

"Seriously?" I asked.

"Seriously," Mike answered. "But I can guarantee it won't be necessary."

"I feel like this is charity, and I'm not a charity case."

"Never said you were. I'm a good man, doing something nice for a good girl. You got a problem with that?"

I let go of my defensiveness and accepted his kindness. "No. I think I don't deserve to have friends like you, but I'm glad I do. I'll take the car."

Mike handed Savannah back to Tori and hugged me. "And if my daughter was in your position, I'd want someone to help her."

My eyes welled, and I fought back the tears, "Thank you."

Chapter 8
Zack

I couldn't resist the urge to continue following Clarissa home. The difference was that now she knew I was doing it. I didn't keep to the shadows and she didn't acknowledge me. We were both stubborn as hell.

She ducked into the alley and, of course, I followed. Instead of being empty, an old, brown Bronco was parked in the back. Her door slammed shut at the top of the stairs. The lights were on in her apartment, if it even qualified as an apartment. Looked like she had company tonight.

Jealousy wound through me. I had no right to that emotion, but it was there just the same. I let her go. She had every right to be with someone else. Looked like she meant it when she said she didn't need me.

I wanted her to need me.

The fact that she didn't, pissed me off.

I was fucked up.

Every day I spent away from Clarissa was torture. I couldn't do anything without thinking of her. She was everywhere. My apartment. My shop. My car. My bike. I couldn't even go to my favorite bar. She had burrowed so far under my skin that she was a part of me.

I stalked back to my studio and pulled the picture I had drawn of Clarissa off the ledge. I ran my fingers over the wings I drew on her back. I guess she wasn't an angel after all.

I took it up to my apartment and stashed it in the back of my closet. I couldn't get rid of it, but I didn't want to look at it every day either. I pulled down the box that contained the few things I took when Wes died. His notebook stared up at me. I hadn't taken the time to read it when I first got back from New York, I'd just thumbed through a few pages.

I sat on the floor of my closet and opened it to the first page. It was definitely a journal. The first pages were written when he was only nineteen. I read over the entries and smiled at the young innocence of them. They were about playing his guitar in the bar and the chicks he was picking up. I didn't realize how much tail my little brother had gotten. He was a regular Casanova.

I skipped forward several pages to the middle.

> *I met the most beautiful girl I've ever seen. She was playing the piano and singing when I walked into the bar. I was instantly mesmerized by her voice. I'm going to take it slow with this one. I think I'm in love.*

The next entry confirmed my suspicions.

> *I've been seeing Rissa for almost a month, but she's holding me at arm's length. I've never spent this much time with a girl without fucking her. But her lips are so soft that I could drown in her kisses. She won't let me take her home at night and it's making me crazy. She shouldn't be going home alone. She's hiding something, I'm just not sure what.*

Seemed that some things hadn't changed. She was stubborn then too. I flipped the page.

> *I followed Rissa last night. Now I know why she wouldn't let me take her home. She lived in a crime-ridden part of town and her apartment was a shithole. No way was I going to let my girl live there. I packed up her shit and moved her in with me. On the upside we finally had sex. It was worth every minute she made me wait. I don't know that I've ever been this happy.*

I had half a mind to go over to her apartment right now and do the same thing. I hated where she was living. She was right back where she had started, and I put her there. Wes had taken her out of a dump, and I put her in one. There was no question that he was a better man than I was. Wes deserved Clarissa. Clearly, I didn't.

> *I introduced Rissa to mom and dad today. Dad hated her. He didn't say it, but he's never had a problem letting people know exactly what he thinks of them. I hate all his snide remarks. I may not have gone to college, but I'm not stupid. I couldn't give two fucks about what he thinks.*

I skipped ahead a few pages.

> *Rissa and I sang together tonight, and it was pure magic. I love this woman. I think I'm going to ask her to marry me. Who would've thought? Me being married is crazy but I don't want to spend one single day without her.*

I knew exactly how he felt. The last couple of weeks had been rough. But she had cheated. I couldn't get past that. How could I when she was carrying the evidence inside her? I fast forwarded to the end of his entries.

> *LA is great and I'm finally getting my record deal, but I fucked up big time! Sam took me to a party last night. I've never been to anything like it before. The drugs and chicks were everywhere, like a fucking candy store. I didn't think one hit would hurt. One line turned into two and two turned into three. I don't know how much blow I did last night. I don't think I fucked that redhead, but I can't remember. Rissa can never know. This would destroy her.*

Now I was intrigued. I had to keep reading.

It was supposed to be a one-time thing, but I can't stop. I tried. Rissa found my stash and we had our first real fight. I promised her I'd quit. I wish I could.

What Clarissa told me during the funeral was true. I hadn't thought that she was lying, but this was proof.

I need to take care of my family. They're depending on me. Rissa deserves better than what I'm giving her, when she's giving me everything I ever wanted. I should be on cloud nine, but all I can think about is my next high and how I'm going to get it. Hiding this from her is killing me.

Why would he feel like he had to take care of our family? My parents had more money than God. It didn't make any sense. There was only one entry left.

I hate myself for doing this to her, but I can't stop. My life is out of control. Somebody please help me.

That was it. There was nothing else. I tossed the book across the room. We used to talk almost every other day. Why hadn't he told me he was in trouble? I would have dropped everything and flown out there. I would have gotten him the help he needed. I could have saved him.

♫♪♫♪

I stopped following her. That Bronco had been parked outside her apartment for days. She'd obviously found someone to replace me.

"Zack, you got a visitor!" Layla called back.

I half thought Clarissa had come back. I dropped the tools I used on my last client into the sterilizer and headed up front. Disappointment filled my chest. Not Clarissa.

"Hey, Sid. What's up? You ready for another tat?"

Sid clasped my hand over the counter. "Not today, man. I got something you might be interested in."

Sid owned the pawn shop a couple of blocks over and I'd done most of his ink. Occasionally something interesting came into his shop and he usually gave me first dibs. "Whatcha got?"

"Your girl came in last week."

"What girl?" I wasn't sure if he was talking about Gina or Clarissa. I couldn't see either one of them stepping into a pawn shop.

"The little blond that works in the bar. Thought I remembered seeing her here last time I was in. You two seemed more than friends," he clarified.

Clarissa. "That's over. She's not my girl." It was one of the biggest lies I had ever told, because whether or not we were together… she was still my girl. I couldn't get her out of my system.

His disappointment was evident and now I was curious. "What'd she buy?"

"Wasn't buying. She was selling."

I crossed my arms. "Fine. What was she selling?" If she stole something of mine and tried to pawn it, it would be one more reason for me to let her go.

Sid pulled a plastic bag out of his front pocket and tossed it on the counter. I opened the bag and dumped it out. My heart sank. I knew exactly where she got these. I'd seen her wearing all of this at the funeral and I hadn't seen them since. I guess I could understand the earrings and the necklace, but how could she get rid of the engagement ring that Wes had given her? "She say why she was selling it?"

He shook his head. "Just that she needed the cash. I thought maybe she stole the shit."

"But you gave her money anyway?" I asked. I'm sure his eyes had popped out when he'd seen the diamonds. No doubt, thoughts of making a quick buck swirled through his tiny brain.

"I'm not the cops."

"She didn't steal any of this. It was hers." I slipped the ring on my pinky and stared at it. "How much did you give her?"

Sid hesitated a second too long, "Ten grand."

It came out more as a question than a statement. "Don't bullshit me, Sid."

He straightened his shoulders. "Fine. Eight."

I glared at him.

"Six. I gave her six grand and that's the honest to God truth. I wanted to give her five, but she bargained for six."

That sounded about right. I'd known Sid for a few years, and I knew how he operated. He always tried to pay as little as possible to pad his bottom line. I didn't blame him. He was in the business to make money, but if I ever had anything to sell, I wouldn't take it to him.

"You ripped her off. We both know this stuff is worth five times that much. I'll buy it all back for the same six," I told him.

"That's not how this works, Zack. You know that. I gotta make a profit."

I called his bluff and pulled the ring off my finger. I put everything back in the bag and set it on the counter. "I don't need any of this. We both know the only reason you came here is because that diamond is going to sit in your case for months, maybe years. Not many people would come to a pawn shop for diamonds like those. You can take my six or you can lose your ass on your investment. Makes no difference to me."

"Seven?" he pressed.

"Six. Take it or leave it." I wasn't going to let him make a profit off Clarissa's desperation. She had to have been desperate to sell this stuff for a few thousand dollars. I had no doubt she knew the value was way more.

"Let me think about it. If I don't sell it in a month, I'll be back. No promises though, I've got a couple of other buyers I'm going to contact." He scooped everything up and shoved the bag in his pocket. He turned to leave and something inside squeezed my heart.

He was full of shit, but I couldn't let that ring walk out the door. That ring belonged to Clarissa and for someone else to have it wasn't right. I had the means to get it back for her. "You're an ass. You know that, Sid?"

"I'm a businessman, Zack. If anyone could relate, I thought it would be you."

"I'll pay the damn seven, but not a penny more. I'll get your money. Go wait in my studio." I wasn't going to do a cash transaction in the lobby of my shop. I went to my safe and pulled out the money. To most people seven grand was a lot. To me it was nothing. But even though I could afford it, I didn't like being exploited. I silently chastised myself for letting Clarissa be my weakness.

I handed him the money and he took his time counting it. When he was finished, he shoved the wad of cash in his pocket and handed me the jewelry. "Pleasure doing business with you, Zack."

I took the bag and gripped it tight in my fist. "The pleasure was all yours. Do me a solid, if she comes back asking about the jewelry, don't tell her you sold it to me."

Sid patted his pocket where my money sat. "What jewelry?"

"Perfect. I'll see you around."

He flashed me a peace sign and left.

I took the jewelry up to my apartment and laid it out on my dresser. I wondered what she needed the money for, and quickly realigned my thinking. What didn't she need the money for? She was living like a pauper, when for the last two years Wes had made sure she wanted for nothing. She wasn't a stranger to living on practically nothing, but it didn't mean I had to like it.

I hated all of it.

♫♪♫♪

I was about to close up shop when Gina strolled in looking sexy in a short skirt and thigh-high boots. Her heels made her look even taller and sexier than usual. She unzipped her coat to reveal a low-cut blouse that showed off her fantastic tits. "You never called."

I ran my hand through my hair. "I know. I've been busy."

She stepped around the counter and laid her hand on my chest. "Too busy for me. That's not the way we work, Zack. We make time for each other."

I picked up her hand and kissed her palm. "I know. I'm sorry. You wanna come upstairs?"

Gina stripped out of her jacket. "I thought you'd never ask."

Layla cleared her throat and glared at Gina without acknowledging her. "We done for the night?"

50

I was holding Gina's hand. "We're good. See you in the morning."

Layla threw her purse over her shoulder. "Chase and I are headed over to The Locker for a drink if you want to join us." She eyed my hand holding Gina's. "Unless you have other plans." She'd never been a fan of Gina's and was intentionally trying to provoke her. I wasn't going to get in the middle of that cat fight.

"I'm going to pass."

"Suit yourself. You've been a moody ass since Rissa left. I liked you better when you were pussy-whipped."

I wanted to point out that Rissa didn't leave, that I had kicked her out, but figured that wouldn't win me any points either. Instead, I gave her a stern warning with one word. "Layla." Sometimes she forgot that I was the boss and signed her paychecks.

She flipped her jet-black hair over her shoulder. "What the fuck ever! I'm going to get my drink on. Go get your dick wet if it makes you happy." She strode out the front door and held her middle finger up over her shoulder. "Good to see you, Gina."

The bell jingled, and I locked the door behind Layla. I was going to have a talk with her tomorrow, and it wouldn't be pleasant.

"Well, that was lovely," Gina said sarcastically.

"Yeah, sorry about that. She's…"

"A bitch," Gina provided.

"I was going to say complicated, but yeah, she has her moments." I led Gina upstairs and she sat at the kitchen island. "You want a drink?" I offered.

"I'll take a vodka and cranberry if you have it." I pulled two glasses out of the cupboard and filled them with ice. I added vodka to both and cranberry juice to hers. Gina took a slow sip. "I've missed you, Zack."

I stared at her tits. I was a fool to not want to get my hands on them, but right now they did nothing for me or my dick. There was something seriously wrong with me. All I could think about were Clarissa's tits… touching them, sucking them, coming all over them. I felt the pressure against my zipper, *Hello, dick. There you are.*

Gina waved her hand in front of my face. "Hello. Earth to Zack." I snapped my eyes to her. "Where'd you go?"

I shook my head. "I don't know." I couldn't very well tell her I was picturing Clarissa's naked tits.

Gina took my hand over the counter. "What's going on, Zack? You show up on my doorstep devastated because some girl cheated on you. You don't call me anymore. I try to come over and you refuse. I've practically offered myself to you on a silver platter and all you do is shoot me down. I'm starting to get a complex."

"Gina…" I really wasn't in the mood to deal with this right now.

She started unbuttoning her blouse and slipped it off her shoulders. She stood from the stool and her skirt came off next. Fuck me! She was gorgeous. Gina was standing in my kitchen wearing a barely-there bra, thong, and thigh-high boots. She came around the counter and rubbed up against me like a cat in heat. I openly stared at her. How could I not?

Gina took my hands and put them on her tits. "These have missed you." Then she lowered one of my hands to between her legs. "And my pussy has missed you."

I ran my hand along the fabric of her panties and slipped one finger inside. She was soaked. It felt wrong. I pulled my hands back and placed them on the counter. "I can't."

Her hands ran along my back as she whispered in my ear. "Yes, you can. Forget about her. She didn't deserve you."

I slammed my hand on the counter and Gina took a step back. "That's the whole fucking problem. I can't forget about her! I've tried. God, I've tried, but I just can't."

Gina stalked back around the counter and shimmied her skirt back into place. "I don't understand you, Zack. She fucking cheated on you and you want her back?"

"No! Yes! No! I don't fucking know!"

She pulled her blouse on and started buttoning it. "Call me when you figure it out. I deserve better than this. I won't play second-string to some cheap whore."

"Don't call her that!"

Gina pulled her hands to her chest, "Oh, excuse me. Is she not pregnant with someone else's baby?"

I dropped my head. Gina was right. "She is."

52

She came back and rested her hands on my shoulders. "I'm sorry she hurt you, but you need to move on. This isn't healthy."

"I don't understand any of this. That's what's holding me back. Where's the guy? And if she wasn't going to be with someone else, why didn't she just lie to me. I would have thought the baby was mine and never been the wiser. She could have lied, but she didn't. Why is that?"

"Maybe it was about the money," Gina suggested.

"It wasn't about the money. She left with nothing. She paid me back every dime I spent on her."

"Then I don't know what it was about. All I know is that I'm in love with you and I can't be here until you're done with her."

I shook my head. "You're not in love with me, Gina. That's not what you and I were ever about. We had an understanding."

"Yeah, I guess you're right." She grabbed her purse off the chair. "I'm gonna leave. Call me if you need anything."

I felt like an ass. "I'll walk you out." We went down the stairs and I walked her out to her car that was parked along the sidewalk. I opened her door for her. "I'm sorry."

"Me too."

I kissed her on the forehead and put her in the car. Gina left without another word. I stood on the sidewalk and watched her taillights disappear.

Chapter 9
Rissa

I watched him kiss Gina and put her in the car. I was a fool to think that we could work things out. I was ready to tell Zack the truth, but it didn't matter. He'd already moved on.

I walked back into the bar after my break. The break, on which I had decided to walk toward Forever Inked. I wasn't planning on telling him tonight. I just wanted to prove to myself that I could stand in front of his building without shattering. I hadn't made it very far when I saw them.

I shattered.

My little experiment failed miserably.

Now I was back behind the bar with Layla and Chase seated in front of me. "So, Zack and Gina are back together," I said. It wasn't a question.

Layla glanced at Chase. He shook his head almost imperceptibly.

"I just saw them together in front of Forever Inked. It's okay. You don't have to lie to me."

"I don't know if they're together or not. She hasn't been around, but she was there when I left," Layla said.

"He kissed her. They're together."

Chase quickly tried to change the subject, "How are you? Do you need anything?"

"No. I'm fine. I bought a car." I gave them a half-hearted smile.

"That's cool. So, you're really okay?" Chase asked. "How's your window working? Giving you any problems?"

"It's sliding up and down perfectly." How sad was it that we had nothing more to talk about than my window?

"Zack's miserable without you," Chase blurted out.

I was shocked by his confession, but it conflicted with what I had just seen. "Didn't look that way to me."

"He's grumpy as fuck. Walks around all day with a scowl on his face." Chase did a disturbingly funny impression of Zack.

I couldn't help the giggle that escaped me. "It can't be that bad."

"It's worse," Layla confirmed. "You two gonna fuck around all day or are you going to do some work. I ain't paying you two to shoot the shit," she grumbled, doing an even funnier impression.

I laughed out loud, and it felt good. "It's nice to know that we're both miserable."

"You should talk to him, maybe you guys can work it out," Chase suggested hopefully.

I put my hand over his. "That's naïve of you Chase. We tried talking and all we did was fight. He ended up storming out of my apartment."

"You let him see your apartment?" Layla questioned.

"Didn't really have a choice. He kept following me home, so I invited him up."

"I'm surprised he didn't drag you out of that dump," Chase interjected. I glared at him. "Sorry, Rissa."

"Trust me, Zack doesn't care where I live. He wants nothing to do with me."

"I wouldn't be so sure of that," Layla mumbled.

♫♪♫♪

The next morning, I was putting out some vintage tees that had arrived by UPS at A Second Chance. I took each one out of the box, priced it, hung it neatly on a hanger and placed it on the rack. If I weren't pregnant, I'd have swiped the Janis Joplin one for myself. But not only would it not fit, but I didn't have cash to be throwing around frivolously.

That was just sad. It was a freaking t-shirt for God's sake. But I was going to be a mom. I needed maternity tops not Janis Joplin t-shirts. What I wanted didn't matter anymore. My whole life was going to revolve around being a mom.

"That's a pretty serious face you've got there, missy." Audrey's voice broke through my thoughts.

I smiled at her. "Just thinking."

"I'm a good listener," she pried.

I held up the shirt. "I was just thinking about how great this would have looked on me if I weren't having a baby in a few months." My belly had really popped in the last week or so. I could still cover it, but when I stood naked in front of the bathroom mirror it was undeniable.

"And what about after you have the baby? It would still look amazing on you."

I placed the shirt back on the rack. "I can't spend money on dumb stuff. Just because I want something doesn't mean I need it."

Audrey frowned. "I'm going to pretend like you didn't just call that shirt dumb. Janis Joplin is timeless. You should have seen her in concert. That woman could really command the stage. When she was singing, she had the audience in the palm of her hand."

"You saw her in concert?" I asked.

"Yep. Woodstock, 1969. I don't remember a lot of that weekend, but I remember her."

I let out a little laugh. "You were a hippy, Audrey? Who knew?"

She gave me a light smack on the arm. "You already knew that. I had a lot of fun back in the day. That was the summer of sex, drugs, and rock 'n roll. I was probably about your age, maybe younger."

I knew what she was getting at. "I've had fun," I defended.

She raised her eyebrows. "Not lately. All you do is work. And you're giving up your dreams on top of it. Trust me, I know regret and it ain't fun."

I went back to hanging the shirts. "My dreams are worth giving up for Wes's baby. It's the only piece of him I have left."

Audrey pulled the shirt out of my hand. "Why does it have to be an either-or situation? Why can't you do both?"

I let out a sigh. "Seriously, Audrey, how am I going to sing and raise a baby by myself. It's not like I have money for a nanny, not that I'd want a nanny raising my child anyway."

"You have friends, and you have me. You don't think I'd be willing to help you take care of this sweet baby?" She put her hand on my belly.

I started to get teary. "I won't throw my responsibilities on other people. Taking care of this baby is my job and if I'm going to be good at anything in this lifetime, I'm going to be a good mom."

Audrey went to the front door, locked it, and turned the sign to *Closed*. She took me by the hand and started dragging me to the backroom. "You and I are having a little chat."

"But the store…" I protested.

"Fuck the store," Audrey said crassly. "You're more important right now." She plopped me into a chair and poured two cups of coffee, setting one down in front of me.

"I can't drink coffee."

"One cup isn't going to kill you and it sure as hell doesn't make you a bad mom."

"Fine," I grumped. I lifted the cup to my lips and took a drink. It wasn't my usual coffee with French vanilla creamer, but God did it taste good. I closed my eyes and savored it.

Audrey sat down across from me with a satisfied smirk on her face. "Well, that's a start. Now, I'm going to ask some questions and I want you to be honest with me."

I nodded my head at her request. "Go for it."

"How old were you when your mama got sick?"

I didn't really understand how this question was relevant to anything, but I answered anyway. "Sixteen."

"And what did you do when she got sick?"

That was easy. "I quit school to take care of her and worked in the diner to help with the bills."

"And then when she passed away, what did you do?"

"I stayed working at the dinner and took care of my daddy. He was lost without my mama, and he needed me."

"And when your daddy died?"

I hadn't told Audrey the grisly details of my father's death. I'd simply said he died. "I got in his truck and drove across the country to New York. I was going to be a star." I laughed at the foolishness of a young girl's dreams.

"And who took care of you when you got there?"

"I did."

"And how long was it before you met Wes?"

"A little over a year." I had no idea where she was going with these questions, but I went along anyway.

"So, for three years you took care of your mom, your dad, and yourself? No one took care of you?"

"I didn't have much choice. There wasn't anyone else."

"But you let Wes take care of you?"

"Not right away, but I guess so." I was starting to understand where she was headed, and I didn't like it.

"And then?" She tapped her fingers on the table baiting me. I wasn't going to do it. I wouldn't take the bait. But she kept tapping and waiting. "And what happened, Rissa?"

Her eyes bored into me as she waited for my answer. I couldn't take the quiet tension any longer and I snapped. "He died! They all died! Everyone who was supposed to be there for me left!" I pointed at my chest. "I'm the only one I can depend on! Me! No one's going to take care of me but me!" I wiped at the tears that were streaming down my face. "And I'm going to take care of this baby too. I never want him or her to feel this way. I'll always be there for my child."

Then Audrey went in for the kill. The real reason for this little chat. "And what about Zack?"

"What about Zack? He left me too. Kicked me out without a second thought."

"And why is that?"

"Because he's an asshole," I said the words, but they lacked conviction.

She shook her head. "Is he? Or did you sabotage it from the beginning? You didn't trust him with the truth. You didn't trust him not to leave you. You figured everyone else had, so why wouldn't he? So, when things fell apart, you didn't fight for him. You let him believe lies instead of giving him the truth. It was a self-fulfilling prophecy."

"I knew it was too good to be true."

"It wasn't too good to be true. You just didn't think you deserved it." She took my hand in hers. "Let me tell you something, missy. You do deserve it. You deserve someone to help you and watch over you. You don't have to do everything by yourself."

I dropped my head in my hands. "I think it's too late. The damage is already done."

"Rissa, it's never too late. Don't give up on your dreams. It would be a waste for you not to share that voice of yours with the world. And if you trust him enough, I think you know a man who would stand by your side while you do it."

Audrey made it all seem so easy. But it wasn't. This was going to be damn hard.

♫♪♫♪

When I got back to my apartment, I listened to the voicemail Daniel McClain left two days ago. I'd been avoiding it like the plague. He'd asked me to come up with some original songs, and I hadn't done a thing. I let everything else get in the way.

If I didn't call him back, he would give up on me and my opportunity would be gone. The chances of me getting another one like this were slim.

I took a deep breath and summoned up my courage before pressing send on my phone. It rang three times before he finally answered. "Well, if it isn't Miss Rissa Black. I was starting to think you were blowing me off."

"Ummm. Hi, Mr. McClain. I wasn't blowing you off, I've just had a lot on my plate lately." I cringed. It sounded lame even to my own ears, but I hoped I hadn't blown my chance.

"It's Daniel," he reminded me. "How are those songs coming?" he asked.

I cringed again. "Slow but sure," I lied. "I'm singing at The Locker in Utica next Friday, maybe you could come and hear for yourself." I mentally smacked myself. A week? I was giving myself a week to come up with something? *Brilliant, Rissa. Just brilliant!*

"I think I'll take you up on that Miss Black," he said skeptically. "I need to know if you're serious about this or if I'm wasting my time."

I straightened my spine even though he couldn't see me. "I assure you, I'm serious. I want this."

"Well then, I'll see you next Friday."

"I'll see you then." I ended the call and slouched back on the couch. What a disaster. I had a week to come up with original songs. I needed two at least and they needed to be great.

There was no better time than the present to get started. I would have to spend every free moment for the next week working on this. I pulled my Gibson from its case. I hadn't done much with it since I'd moved from Zack's. I had sung a few times at the bar, but other than that... nothing. I rooted around in the bottom of a box until I found my lyrics notebook. I had some half-finished songs written, maybe I could do something with one of them.

I opened the notebook and started to think about Zack. I'd get this nailed down first, and then tell him the truth. The worst he could do was hate me, and since I was pretty sure he already did, I didn't have much to lose.

I started jotting down the thoughts that came into my head. After a few lines, I read what I had written:

I'm sitting here drowning in my tears,
And I wonder where you're at.
I'd give anything to see you again,
Cuz I really miss you and your big fluffy cat.

Oh, jeez. What the fuck! I took my pen and scribbled it out. This was going to be more difficult than I thought.

After hours of thinking and writing and scratching out and rewriting, I'd only had marginal success. I was tired and frustrated and desperately needed sleep. I laid down on my lumpy couch, quickly falling asleep.

When I woke, it was as if the fog had cleared. I knew exactly what I had to do and where I needed to go. I took my guitar and hopped in my Bronco, headed for Uptown Sound.

I walked through the door carrying my guitar and immediately I could feel the music surround me. The same guy that helped me before came to the counter. "Can I help you?"

"Yes. I was in here a couple of months ago and bought some guitar strings from you."

Recognition flashed in his eyes. "I remember you. You played the piano. Your boyfriend came back and bought one for you. How does it sound?'

I didn't bother to correct his use of the word boyfriend. "It's wonderful. I have a favor to ask."

"What's that?"

"I'm trying to write some music. I find this store inspirational. Do you think I could just hang out for a while, play my guitar and maybe the piano?"

He shrugged his shoulders. "It's not like we're busy. I don't see a problem with it. Knock yourself out."

"Thanks." I shrugged off my coat and pulled out my notebook. I started with the piano and played the notes that were in my head. I played and replayed, adjusting as I went along, then added the lyrics.

After an hour, I was feeling good about what I'd accomplished. One song was completely finished. The guy from the counter strolled over and leaned on the piano. "My name's Paul, by the way."

"Rissa," I introduced myself. "Are you sure it's okay if I stay here."

"It's totally fine. I'm enjoying it. I have some ideas about your song."

"What's that?" I was up for any suggestions.

"Do you mind if I call my friend, Drew? I think we could add some guitar and drums and it would sound amazing," he offered.

I pulled back in surprise. "That would be awesome. Are you sure?"

"Positively. We've been trying to start a band but haven't found a lead singer. We're down for any chance to jam with someone who has talent."

My mind was churning through the possibilities of this new-found opportunity that was being dropped in my lap. I'd wait to see if they were any good before I presented my offer.

I found out quickly that both Paul and Drew were super talented and played multiple instruments. We perfected my new song and practiced some from my regular set.

I was going to meet again with the guys later in the week, but before I left, my plan for next Friday night was firmly in place.

Chapter 10
Zack

Gina's words replayed in my head, *I'm in love with you.* They were on repeat, like when you got a stupid commercial stuck in your head and couldn't stop singing the jingle.

How had I missed that? Yeah, Gina and I were close, and I cared about her. I cared a lot about her, but love? That wasn't something I had ever considered. I thought we were on the same page, friends with exceptionally hot, freaky benefits.

I hadn't hurt just one woman, I'd hurt two.

The woman I was in love with didn't love me enough to be faithful. In fact, I was pretty sure part of her hated me. I'd made sure of it with the venom I had spit at her. How could she love me after I kicked her out and called her a whore? I'd hate me too.

The woman who was in love with me, had never done me wrong. She had always been there for me when I needed her. She was sweet and kind and gorgeous. We had amazing sexual chemistry. She lit every part of my body on fire, except one… my heart.

It was clear that I'd hurt Gina the other night. I didn't mean to. Honestly, I was shocked when she declared her love for me. I wasn't expecting her confession and then I basically dismissed her. It was callous and cold on my part.

The way I treated Clarissa. The way I treated Gina. I was becoming someone I knew very well… my father. And that, scared the shit out of me.

♫♪♫♪

I'd stayed away from both women all week. I hadn't called Gina and she hadn't called me. I guess we both needed a break from the emotional roller coaster I'd put us on.

I'd tried to put Clarissa out of my mind, but it was impossible with the flyer I held in my hand. I had pulled it off my front window this morning. She was singing tonight at The Locker. *Tonight must be something special*, I thought to myself.

I'd seen her sing plenty of times before. There was absolutely no reason for me to go. None. Zero. Zilch.

I kept myself busy all day. I had a back tattoo of an eagle that took several hours, then I took a couple of walk-ins. Chase had offered to take them, but I needed the distraction. Ink, wipe, repeat. Anything to keep my mind off what was going on down the street tonight.

I finally turned the sign to *Closed*. Layla and Chase left over an hour ago, I didn't need to ask to know what their plans were for the night. I glanced out the front window. There was actually a line to get into The Locker. That rarely ever happened.

I made a snap decision. I could slip in, stand in the back, and she would never know I was there. I lied to myself when I said I wanted to see what the fuss was about. Truth be told, I only wanted to see her. It'd been over two weeks and I fucking missed her face.

I locked up my shop and headed down the street. It wasn't a long line, but I bypassed everyone and went right to the front. The bouncer, Joe, lifted his chin to me as I walked in past the grumbling customers outside. I made my way along the back of the bar and signaled to Lou.

He pulled a rock glass and poured three fingers of bourbon into it. He slid it across the bar to me as I slapped a twenty down. "Haven't seen you in a while."

"Yeah, I've been busy."

Lou gave me a look that said he wasn't buying my bullshit. He twisted his lips to the side. "You here to see Rissa?"

I took a sip of my bourbon. "Maybe. I'm not advertising the fact that I'm here though."

"Don't think she'd be happy to see you?"

"Couldn't say." I gripped the back of my neck. "Not sure I know anything about her anymore."

The bar was slammed. Lou, Sonja, and a bartender I didn't recognize were doing their best to keep up with the crowd. Now wasn't the time for this conversation. Lou tapped on the top of the bar before he walked away. "You know enough."

I took my drink and stood along the back wall, camouflaged by dozens of people celebrating their Friday night. I scanned the bar and saw several people I knew. Chase had his arm wrapped around Becca. Layla and some guy I didn't know shared a table with them. Gina and a bunch of her girlfriends were doing shots. Didn't expect to see her here. Sitting close to the stage were Tori, Chris, Kyla, and Tyler.

Seemed my girl had everyone here tonight.

Not my girl, I reminded myself.

I sent Kyla a quick text. I saw her pick up her phone to read it, then she looked around. I knew when her eyes had landed on me. She left the table and made her way back.

I leaned down and kissed her on the cheek. "You look good, little mama. How are those baby boys?"

"Amazing but exhausting. This is the first night I've had out in six weeks." She scanned me from head to toe. "Why are you hanging out back here? You're welcome to come sit with us."

I shook my head. "Nah. I'm good."

"You don't want Rissa to know you're here," she stated.

"Something like that." Did everyone know my business? "She tell you what happened?"

"No, but she's been talking to Tori, and you know Tor."

I let out a little chuckle. "Yeah, subtle as a damn hurricane."

"Let me just say this. Things might seem really shitty right now, but life can change quickly. Look at Tyler and me. There was a time when I thought we'd never get our shit together and now we couldn't be happier."

I took another sip of my bourbon. "I don't think that's in the cards for us."

"You never know," she said with a wink. "Come sit with us if you change your mind."

"I won't."

She stretched up on her toes to kiss my cheek. "You're so damn stubborn. Give yourself a chance to be happy. You deserve it." Then she turned and went back to her table.

I *was* happy until Clarissa cheated on me. I followed Kyla with my eyes and looked further to the stage. Two guys were setting up equipment, including amps, speakers, a keyboard, and a set of drums. Hmmm. That was different.

A few minutes later, Clarissa hopped up on the stage to join the two guys. I wondered if one of them was *the guy*.

She looked beautiful. Her hair was in soft curls that surrounded her face. Her makeup was a little darker than normal but not overdone. She wore tall, heeled boots, jeans and a black sparkly top that hugged her top curves but flared out at the waist. No doubt she was hiding the fact she was pregnant. It was still a hard concept for me to embrace. I wondered how far along she was. How long was it after I'd brought her here that she had stepped out on me? I decided it couldn't have been long if she was already showing. A week? Maybe two? Was that why she had held me off so long? She'd felt guilty about fucking someone else, even if we weren't officially together?

Shit, it hadn't taken her long to fuck me. Wes's body wasn't even cold in the ground, and we fucked on the bed they used to share. I was as much to blame as she was, but… I guess there wasn't any way to defend it. We'd both been sad and lonely. I should have left her there and been done with it. Called it a mistake and moved on. I'd have been better off.

Clarissa grabbed the mic and let her Oklahoma accent run free. "How y'all doin' tonight?" The crowd erupted with applause and hollering. "I want to thank y'all fer comin' out to support me. And don't forget Lou and all our bartenders here at The Locker. Drink up and tip well." She laughed through another round of applause. One thing about Clarissa, she knew how to work a crowd.

"So, you might have noticed I have some company up here tonight. These two talented guys are Drew and Paul. They're from Uptown Sound in Rochester and have been generous enough to provide all this kickass equipment you see on the stage. I feel really lucky to have them here helpin' me out." More applause erupted as the two guys saluted the crowd. When the noise died down, Clarissa moved to the keyboard. "Let's get this started." She rolled into her first song, the guys joining in on the drums and electric guitar.

"She sounds good. Didn't know she played piano too," came a voice I knew well. Bobby was standing next to me in a ball cap that was pulled down

65

low and dark glasses. If I didn't know him so well, I wouldn't have recognized him.

"What the hell are you doing here? Slumming it for the night?" I asked. Bobby rarely stepped outside his comfort zone, which didn't include local bars. The thought of being recognized and hassled kept him far away from places like The Locker.

"Nah, came to hear your girl sing. My agent's here to check her out, so I tagged along."

Well, that explained the hullabaloo over this show. She was finally taking her chance. I wondered if she was still planning on leaving, not that she would tell me shit. "She's not my girl anymore. That's over."

Bobby scratched at his chin. "Yet, you're still here. What happened?"

I crossed my arms defensively. "Nothing I want to talk about."

Bobby wasn't going to let it go. "Did she fuck up or did you?"

I glared at him. "It sure as hell wasn't me."

Bobby held his hands up in surrender. "All right, man." Then he nodded to the stage. "But I'd think long and hard about giving her up. If you do, someone else will swoop in to take your place. She won't stay single long."

I grumbled an incoherent response into my drink as I downed it.

"Let me get you a refill," Bobby offered. I handed him my empty glass and he disappeared.

Clarissa finished off a couple of songs before her eyes locked on me. There was no hiding now. I gave her a chin jerk of acknowledgment.

She got an evil little smile on her face as she grabbed a hold of the mic. "Looks like I forgot somebody tonight. Y'all see that good-looking, broody guy covered in tattoos by the back wall?"

Heads spun in my direction. I kept my eyes on her. What was she up to?

"That's Zack and he owns Forever Inked just down the street. He gave me my first tattoo." She held up her wrist for the audience to see. "And he gave me the encouragement to start singing again. He's a genius with a tattoo gun, so if you're thinking about getting any ink you should go see him. Underneath all that bad-boy exterior is a really sweet guy. He's helped me a lot." Then she started right into her next song, one I hadn't heard before.

66

I ground my teeth. That was not what I expected out of her. I'd expected some of the venom I'd spewed at her, but there was none. She'd just complimented me and gave me free advertising for my shop.

I listened to the words of the song she was singing. It was basically her life story put to music. She sang about being on her own, picking herself up when she'd fallen and having no one to depend on but herself. Clarissa had obviously written this song and it was sad but captivating. It ended with words about letting herself trust again and second chances.

Bobby was back, handing me my drink. "Looks like she hasn't given up on you. Have you given up on her?"

"I don't know," I growled.

"Think about it," he said. "I'm going to go sit with Daniel for a while. I'll catch ya later."

"Later, man. Thanks for the drink."

I scanned the crowd and caught Kyla's stare. She motioned to the empty chair at their table.

It wasn't like Clarissa didn't know I was here, so I headed over and plopped into the empty chair. Her description of me being broody was dead-on accurate right now.

Kyla bumped me with her shoulder. "So much for hiding, huh?"

If I didn't like her so much, I would have flipped her the bird. But Kyla was not the kind of girl you flipped off, even in jest. Instead, I gave her a harsh glare.

"Boy, someone needs to get laid," Tori piped up. Now her, I could flip off no problem, but I restrained myself.

Chris interjected on my behalf. "Give the guy a break. He just got called out in the middle of a bar."

"Women can make you crazy," Tyler said, getting harsh looks from both girls. "What? It's true. You two are a handful." He tipped his beer bottle at them.

"Keep digging asshole. Pretty soon that hole will be big enough for you to crawl into," Tori warned.

"You two wouldn't trade us for anything. Life would be boring without us," Kyla added.

67

Maybe sitting with them wasn't the best idea, but no matter how much they bantered I knew they all cared about each other. They'd been friends forever.

Chris wrapped his arm around Tori and whispered something in her ear that had her smiling. Tyler planted a soft kiss on Kyla's head.

"I'm feeling like a fifth wheel. Maybe I should go sit at the bar."

Kyla put her hand on top of mine. "Stay."

After a few more songs, Clarissa and the guys took a short break. She didn't come to our table, instead she went over to talk to Daniel. I watched her intently. She gave Bobby a kiss on the cheek and shook Daniel's hand. Whatever they were talking about must have been going well. Her face was lit up and she was glowing. A month ago, I would have been there beside her. Now I was the fifth person at a four-person table.

I bought a round of drinks and made the best of it. It was better than standing in the back by myself being pissed off. I tried to make a conscious effort to not be an asshole. It wasn't anyone's fault that I was on edge. The only person to blame was the cute little blond climbing back onto the stage.

I looked away from Clarissa just in time to catch Gina staring at me. She quickly looked away, focusing back on her friends and the drink in her hand. Guess she was still pissed at me too.

"Ugh," Tori sounded in disgust. "Please tell me you haven't been screwing her again."

I lifted a pierced eyebrow at her. "No. She's a friend. What's your problem with her?"

"You mean besides the fact that she's been nasty as hell to Rissa? Nothing."

Now my curiosity was peaked. "What do you mean?"

"Rissa didn't say anything?" she asked.

"We haven't exactly been talking, so no. What happened?"

"I probably shouldn't have said anything. If Rissa wanted you to know, she'd have told you."

Chris squeezed Tori's arm. "You already threw it out, you kind of have to tell him now."

Tori shook her head. "Me and my big fucking mouth." I motioned for her to continue. "The night of your party, Gina trapped Rissa in the bathroom and threatened her. She told Rissa about all the wild sex you two had and that Rissa would never be able to keep you. That you would run back to her. She also made a scene at the doctor's office, accusing Rissa of being a gold-digger. She told Rissa you two were back together."

I dropped my head into my hands. "Fuck! How in the hell did this become my life?"

Tyler pushed my drink in front of me. "Nothing worse than a woman scorned. I can attest to that."

"All I wanted was uncomplicated. Is that too much to ask?"

Chris drained his beer. "How could you ever think life with a woman was uncomplicated? Two women? That's twice the complications."

"Sometimes complications are what make the relationship stronger. Realizing what you've lost, only makes you appreciate it more," Kyla said.

Tyler wrapped his arm around her. "My girl's smart. You should listen to her."

The music started again and all I could focus on was Clarissa. I'd hurt her, and she'd hurt me. We'd hurt each other and there was no coming back from that.

I couldn't deny that I was still in love with her, but I also couldn't see a way for us to be together. There was too much between us that couldn't be fixed. I needed to leave. I needed to put her out of my head for good.

I threw a pile of cash on the table. "Night's on me. I gotta get out of here." I said my goodbyes and headed toward the door.

That's when I heard it. I had one hand on the door and froze in place. This was a new song, and it was about me. I stepped back inside and leaned against the wall. Clarissa's eyes locked with mine and then she looked away. I closed my eyes and listened to her sexy, sultry voice as she sang the lyrics.

I knew from the beginning,
I knew it couldn't last.
I knew that our future,
Would be colored by my past.

I wish things could be different,
I wish I hadn't lied.
I wish you hadn't walked away,

But you were worth every tear I cried.

You've left a mark no one else can see,
And without you, I'm just falling apart.
You'll forever be a part of me,
'Cuz you've tattooed my heart.

You didn't believe in me,
You thought you knew it all.
But you were missing pieces,
And for that I took the fall.

I've never felt so alone,
Drowning in a sea of tears.
I want your arms around me,
Quieting all my silent fears.

I wonder if I'll see you again,
I wonder where you're at.
All I know is you're not here with me,
And I'm not okay with that.

You've left a mark no one else can see,
And without you, I'm just falling apart.
You'll forever be a part of me,
'Cuz you've tattooed my heart.

If you had just listened to me,
I would have told you the truth.
You'd have seen the honesty in my eyes,
When I said it's always been you.

If you give me just one more chance,
I'll give you the world.
I'll promise you my heart,
And be eternally your girl.

If you'd let me inside your walls,
You'd see how much I love you.
I know somewhere deep inside,

That you love me too.
You can deny it all you want,
But I know it's true.

I've left a mark no one else can see,
And without me, you're falling apart.
I'll forever be a part of you,
'Cuz I've tattooed your heart.

The song was about us and it was beautiful, but it left me with more questions than answers. The pain in my chest intensified. It was the tattoo she had given me that hadn't quite healed yet.

"Good night, y'all. Thanks fer comin'. Drive safe and come back again real soon." Whistles and catcalls erupted through the bar, mixed with the thunderous applause. Clarissa blew a kiss to the audience and headed off the stage. She drank down a bottle of water and then started helping the guys clean up the equipment.

We weren't finished yet, not by a long shot. There was something she wasn't telling me, a hidden message in that song and I was going to find out what it was. I was done waiting for her to come to me.

I stalked to where she was winding a cord. I wrapped my fingers around her arm and spun her around to face me. "What the hell was that?"

Clarissa glared at where my fingers bit into her skin a little too harshly. "Can you remove your hand? You're hurting me," she said calmly. Shit! I didn't want to hurt her. I just wanted her full attention. I released her, and she rubbed the red marks on her arm. "What are you talking about?"

I ran my hands through my hair. "That song, Clarissa. What did it mean?"

"It's just a song, Zack. It didn't mean anything."

I might have believed her if she could have looked me in the eye. Her refusal to answer frustrated the fuck out of me. "It was about us and you know it. I call bullshit!"

One of the guys, maybe Paul, came over. "Everything all right, Rissa?"

"Everything is fine," I snapped at him.

71

"It's all good, Drew." He didn't look convinced. "It's fine. I promise," she reiterated. He backed away and continued to pack up the equipment, keeping one eye on us. "This isn't the time or the place," she hissed.

"When is the time?" I asked with frustration.

"Not now. I've got to talk to Daniel and help pack up. I'll be a while."

"When?" I asked again.

"You wanna talk, or yell at me?"

I wasn't going to get anywhere with her if I acted like the asshole she thought I was. I softened my tone. "No yelling, just talking."

"And you'll listen to me?"

"I'll listen," I agreed.

"I get off work at five. I can see you then. I don't have to be back here until seven, so I'll have time."

"You're working a double?"

She shook her head. "No, I'm working two jobs. I need the money."

Of course, she was. Clarissa was a survivor and she'd do whatever was necessary to make ends meet. She'd been on her own for over a month. She didn't need me. That much was clear. The question was... did she want me?

Chapter 11
Rissa

"Fine. I'll meet you at your apartment. But I want the truth, Clarissa. We're going to clear this shit between us."

"Then I'll see you tomorrow," I said swallowing down the lump in my throat.

"Tomorrow," he said gruffly. "I want answers."

"Tomorrow," I repeated.

Zack shoved his hands in his pockets and stalked away. I let out a sigh of relief. I hadn't expected him to confront me like that, but I shouldn't have been surprised. Zack was passionate in more ways than one.

"You all right, Rissa? That was intense. Who was that guy?" Drew asked.

"I'm fine," I assured him. "That was my ex-boyfriend. He might seem like a hard-ass, but he would never hurt me. I gotta go talk to Daniel for a minute. I'll be back to help with all this."

"Don't worry about it. Paul and I got this. Great show tonight, Rissa. I hope everything works out for you."

"We'll find out. I appreciate all your help. I couldn't have done it without you two. I'll get you guys your cash before we leave," I said. I had promised the guys a cut from what Lou was paying me tonight. I couldn't and wouldn't expect them to do it for free, even though they had offered.

"No hurry. Go do your thing." Drew smiled.

Daniel held out his hand to me as I approached. "That was quite the show you put on, Miss Black. I loved the new songs. I want to get you in the studio, soon, so we can cut a demo. My instincts about you were right. You're going to be big."

I felt the blush creeping up my cheeks. "This is more than I ever expected. I can't thank you enough." I looked around the bar. "Where's Bobby?"

"Snuck out like a thief in the night. This isn't really his scene, but he wanted to support you. He's got a soft spot for you and I can see why."

"That's sweet. Thank him for me when you see him."

"Will do. I'll be talking to you soon. Can't wait to get you in a studio." Daniel walked away, leaving me alone with my dreams. Dreams that seemed closer and closer to becoming a reality.

Who would have thought this little town would be where it happened? I'd lived in New York for three years and hadn't gotten this close. Wes had, but not me. The plan had been for him to go to LA, get the record deal, and then he'd pull me along. We were going to make our dreams come true. Together. When Wes died, my dreams had died along with him.

It was ironic that the person who had gotten me here, was the one person who hadn't been able to look at me for the last month. If Zack hadn't introduced me to Bobby, none of this would be happening. I owed him so much, and the truth was a start.

He might still be disgusted with me after he learned the truth, but at least he would know I hadn't cheated on him.

Chapter 12
Zack

The waiting was killing me. All I could think about was that song last night. The glimpses of things that were not what they seemed. I didn't want glimpses. I wanted the whole fucking picture. I wanted to fill in the missing pieces of the puzzle.

Maybe once I had my answers, I would be able to move forward. Whatever that looked like, had to be better than the feeling of being stuck. I couldn't go back, and I couldn't move on.

I looked at the clock again. Quarter to five. I'd give her a few minutes to settle in after work, but then I was getting my answers.

The bell jingled over the door and Gina walked in wearing her pink scrubs. I wasn't in the mood to deal with her today.

She hesitated and then walked to the counter where I was standing. "Hey."

I barely gave her a second look. "I'm not thrilled with you right now. You had no right to harass Rissa like you did."

She stared at the floor. "Did she tattle on me?"

I shook my head. "She didn't say a thing. She wouldn't."

She raised her head. "I'm sorry. Do you still love her?"

I grabbed at the back of my neck. "I don't know. I don't know anything anymore."

Gina hiked her purse up on her shoulder. "I saw the way she looked at you last night. She still loves you."

"Gina…" I started to interrupt, but she held her hand out to stop me.

"I saw the way you looked at her. You've never looked at me like that. It was written all over your face… you love her too."

I didn't know what to say. "I'm sorry, Gina." It seemed a lame response.

"It's okay. I always knew I was in deeper than you. I just hoped that maybe one day you'd change your mind about me."

I came around the counter and wrapped her in a hug. "You know I care about you, right?" I led her back to my studio and shut the door.

Gina sat on the chair. "I care about you too." She dug in her purse and pulled out a folded piece of paper. "Some of the things Rissa has said to me didn't add up, so I did some digging."

"Dammit, Gina, you can't keep interfering." I had about one nerve left, and she was tap dancing all over it.

My admonishing didn't stop her. She held the paper out for me to take. "This is the original form she filled out for Doc Peterson. You should read it."

I snatched the paper out of her hands and unfolded it. It was Clarissa's patient information form. I scanned through it. The top had all her personal information: name, phone number, address. She'd written the address for Forever Inked.

I looked further to her medical information. When I got to the female only section I paused.

First day of your last period: *June 10th*

Are you pregnant: *Yes*

Date of conception: *June 24th?*

Name of father: *Deceased*

I slumped back against the counter and slid to the floor. *No fucking way!* I held up the paper. "Is this legit? No bullshit?"

Gina nodded. "I'm sorry. She didn't cheat on you. She was already pregnant when you two got together."

It couldn't be possible. "I saw her naked every day. How could I not know?"

Gina cringed. "She was only three months along. I've seen women who were five months, and you could barely tell. Everyone's different. You didn't see any signs?"

I rested my arms on my knees and dropped my head. "Her hips had filled out and she was curvier, but I just thought she was getting past the devastation of Wes dying. I thought it was because she was happy." After I said it, it sounded stupid even to my own ears. It was such an ignorant guy thing to say.

"Was she close with Wes?" Gina asked, cocking her head to the side.

I had never filled Gina in on how Clarissa and I met. It wasn't anyone's business at the time, but now it was relevant. "They were engaged. She was his fiancé."

"Wow," she said softly. Gina moved to the floor next to me and wrapped her arm around my shoulders. "You're the uncle. That baby is going to be your niece or nephew."

The gravity of what she said hit me in waves. "I fucked her while she was carrying my brother's baby. I think I'm gonna be sick." I rushed to the sink and hung my head over it until the nausea passed.

Gina rubbed my back soothingly. "It's not your fault. You didn't know. At least now you know she didn't cheat. That's worth something, right?"

I nodded, unable to form any words. Knowing didn't ease the tension inside me like I thought it would. She still lied to me, and I wanted to know why. "I need some time alone to process."

"Of course." Gina picked up her purse from the chair. "If you need me, I'll be there… as a friend, no strings attached."

"Thanks," I mumbled.

Gina quietly slipped out of the room and left me with the thoughts racing through my brain. I cuffed a pregnant woman to my bed. I fucked her. Hard. Repeatedly. I could have hurt her or the baby. My own blood.

Another wave of nausea washed over me, and I choked it down. I had to get out of here. I had to see her. I folded up the paper and shoved it in my back pocket.

I wander back into the shop to find Layla. She was in her studio cleaning up from her last appointment. "I gotta get out of here for a while. Can you cover while I'm gone?"

"Sure, no problem." She crinkled her eyes at me. "Are you feeling okay? You don't look so good."

"I gotta go see Clarissa." I started to turn away when I remembered something Layla had said to me, *you need to ask yourself if you had all the facts before you crucified her.* I dismissed it at the time because I was so pissed. I faced Layla again. "Did you know?"

"Know what?" she asked in confusion.

I took a deep breath. "About Clarissa? About the baby? About Wes?"

Her faced paled and she nodded. "You told me it was none of my business."

I had told her that. "Why didn't she tell me?"

Layla shrugged. "She said she tried but you wouldn't listen to her. I think when you threw money at her and called her a whore, it sealed the deal for her. She had already lost you, so it didn't really matter."

I ground my teeth. "It mattered. She lied to me."

"But not in the way you thought."

"She should have told me from the beginning," I growled.

"She should have, but she was scared."

"Of what?" I roared.

"If you really have to ask, you don't know her at all."

That wasn't an acceptable answer. None of this was acceptable by any standard. Clarissa owed me answers, and I was going to fucking get them. I stormed out the back door and started up my Harley.

I pulled up to the back of her apartment and parked next to that damn Bronco. *She better not have fucking company right now.* I didn't think I could trust myself not to lay some punk out on her floor.

I stormed up the steps and pounded on her door with my fist. "Open the fucking door, Clarissa! Right the fuck now!"

The door swung open, and Clarissa stood on the other side, one hand cocked on her hip. "What the hell is your problem?" She didn't cower, like the first time I yelled at her. She stood tall and resolute.

I barged through the door and scanned the apartment. "Who's fucking truck is that?"

"Mine!"

I swung back to her. "Where the fuck did you get money for a truck? I thought you were broke."

"I sold some shit."

The jewelry. Sid had ripped her off and no doubt she got a bum deal on the car too. "How do you know it's any good? How do you know you didn't get ripped off?"

"I checked it out. I'm not an idiot, Zack. Is that why you wanted to come over? To ask me about a goddamned truck?"

I'd gotten so far from my purpose of coming over and I needed to focus. I was here for answers, and I wasn't leaving without them. "No." I pulled the folded paper from my back pocket and thrust it at her. "Is this true?"

She opened the paper and started to read it. "Where did you get this? It was supposed to be confidential."

"It doesn't matter. Is it true?"

She wadded up the paper and threw it at my face. "Did you fuck Gina for that?"

"No!"

"Come on, Zack. She hasn't exactly been hiding the fact that you two are sleeping together. You ran to her the minute you left me."

She was trying to turn this whole thing around on me. "I'm not sleeping with her. Now answer my question. Is it true?"

"I don't believe you. And you know what? I don't care. You're free to fuck whoever you want." She held open the door. "You can leave."

I shoved the door closed and locked it. "I'm not leaving until you answer my questions." I calmed myself and spoke distinctly, "Are you pregnant with Wes's baby?"

"Yes."

Finally! "So, you didn't cheat on me?"

"I told you I didn't. You didn't want to listen to me. You were too intent on assuming I was a whore and throwing cash at me. You never bothered to ask *who* the father was." Her eyes were teary, but she was fighting like hell not to let them fall.

I did all of that. Everything she said was true. I was such a fucking idiot. I sat on the couch and held my head in my hands. "I asked you *where* the father was."

"And I told you. Gone. I didn't lie about it."

"You weren't exactly forthcoming either. Why? Why would you let me believe you cheated on me?"

She let out a huff and sat on the edge of the coffee table in front of me. "The question is, why would you assume I had? You hurt me when you assumed the worst. You'd already made up your mind about me. I figured it would be easier to leave if you hated me."

"I'm sorry about how I treated you, Clarissa. I never hated you."

"I wanted you to. You didn't deserve the mess I brought to your door."

"That was my choice to make, not yours. I loved you, Clarissa. I would have done anything for you. Despite everything, I still love you. Do you still love me?"

"I'm not sure that really matters anymore."

"It matters to me." I reached forward and took her hands in mine. "Why didn't you tell me from the beginning you were pregnant?"

She swallowed down the lump in her throat. "When we slept together that first time, I figured I'd never see you again. You'd be here, and I'd be in New York. You'd never know, and it wouldn't matter. But then you were still there in the morning. You offered me something I couldn't pass up, a fresh start. I was desperate to get away from your father. It didn't hurt that I was insanely attracted to you when I shouldn't have been. I thought if you knew, you would change your mind. So, I pretended I wasn't pregnant. But I couldn't fool myself. I was so torn between you and my feelings for Wes. He was gone, but I still felt like I was cheating. I felt dirty. Every day that I didn't tell you about the baby, it got harder."

I squeezed her hands. "You had two months, Clarissa. You should have told me. Why didn't you trust me?"

"I thought you would be disgusted by me, knowing I let you fuck me while I was carrying his baby. I knew you would leave me. Everyone I've ever cared about has left me. I was in love with you, and I wasn't ready for you to leave. I wanted to hold onto you as long as I could." The tears flowed down her cheeks.

"I already knew you had slept with Wes. I mean, you two were engaged. I struggled with it too. I tried not to think about the fact that my dick was where his had already been. I shouldn't have wanted you, but I did. I fell in love with you from the very beginning."

"But being pregnant… it changes things. You told me you didn't want kids anytime soon. I couldn't burden you with that responsibility. I couldn't tell you. I did this. It's my responsibility."

Everything she was saying made perfect sense. This was the most honest conversation we'd ever had. "So, you got yourself pregnant? I may have dropped out of Yale, but I'm pretty sure it takes two."

"Yeah, but one of us is gone. That makes it my responsibility. I knew I had to tell you, but I was scared." She wiped at her eyes. "And then I got this crazy idea. I thought maybe we were strong enough that," she paused and looked at the ceiling, "that you could love both of us. That maybe the three of us could be our own little family. I just thought, who would love this baby more than his uncle? It was so silly."

I wasn't sure what to say. She had a point, but I wasn't sure I was ready for that type of commitment. It wasn't my kid. "It wasn't silly. It was hopeful." I reached forward and rubbed my hand along her stomach. I could feel the small baby bump hidden beneath her clothes. "Is it a boy?"

"I don't know yet. I'll know at my next appointment."

"Can I come? You shouldn't have to do all this on your own."

"You don't owe me anything, Zack."

"I know that, but I want to be there for you." I wasn't going to abandon her. The least I could do was go to a doctor's appointment. "Wes knew you were pregnant, didn't he?"

She nodded. "I told him when he got back from LA. He was happy about it. We were going to move the wedding date up."

I clenched my fists. "I can't even tell you how pissed I am at him." I remembered everything I read in his journal. It made sense now.

"He had a problem, Zack. I was pissed at him too, but he had a problem. I just wish he would have asked for help."

"Me too. I would have helped him."

Clarissa patted my hand. "I know you would have. I really think he thought he had it under control."

I'd read his journal. He knew he didn't have it under control. "Don't defend him. There's no excuse for choosing drugs over your family."

"It's neither here nor there at this point." Clarissa got up and rubbed her hands on her pants. "So... where does this leave us?"

"I don't know. This was a lot to take in. I'm still processing everything."

"Friends?" she asked.

I smiled at her. "Friends definitely." I stood up and took her face in my hands. "I love you, sweetheart."

"I love you too," she said.

"Why don't we pack your stuff, and you can move back into my apartment. I hate you living here."

She shook her head. "No. I need to stand on my own two feet for a while. And despite everything, I'm still pregnant with another man's baby. If I live with you, it will only complicate things. You need time to think without me around."

"I don't like it, but I respect your decision. Do you need anything? Money?" I offered.

She stuck her hands in her back pockets. "Nope. I'm good."

"You're stubborn is what you are." I tapped her on the nose.

She walked me to the door. "You can do one thing for me. Think you can take me for a ride on your bike before I'm too big to fit on the back of it?"

I laughed. "I think I can do that." I leaned down and pressed my lips to hers. She wrapped her arms around my neck. "I've missed you."

"I've missed you too."

I kissed her like we were teenagers making out in the back seat of a car. My tongue tangled with hers. She tasted so damn sweet I could have devoured her all night, but I pulled back. "I better stop before the friend lines get too blurry."

"I think they're already blurry." She tapped me on the ass. "Go on. Get out of here."

I bounced down the steps and out to my bike. Clarissa watched me as I pushed up the kickstand and drove away. I had a lot to think about. But at least we were back on speaking terms and that was a start. If it weren't for Wes's baby growing inside her, it would have been a no-brainer. There was no doubt that I wanted Clarissa. I just didn't know if I could be a father to her baby.

It wasn't a decision I should have had to make. Damn Wes. I was so pissed at him and I needed to tell him in person.

When I got back to the shop, I checked the airlines for tickets to JFK Airport. There was a plane leaving at 8:30 and I was going to be on it.

I quickly packed my backpack, fed Miss Priss, and had Chase and Layla cover all my appointments. It took me less than fifteen minutes to be on the road.

♫♪♫♪

82

I stood in front of Wes's grave, the moon my only light. It hadn't been hard to find. The Kincaids had their own section in this cemetery. Only the best, even when we were dead. The ground was still soft where the dirt had been piled over Wes's casket.

I shoved my hands in my pockets. "I'm so pissed at you. You should have fucking told me. I would have helped you." I hadn't planned out this little speech, but I had plenty to say.

"I was mad when I thought you had just left Clarissa behind. I felt guilty for being with her. Felt like I was betraying you. But you betrayed her. Do you have any idea the mess you left behind? You left her and the baby, for what? A high? You knew she was fucking pregnant. You're a selfish bastard! How the hell did you think she was going to raise a kid on her own?"

I thought this would make me feel better, but it didn't. Not one little bit. I threw my hands into the air. "What the fuck am I supposed to do? You want me to be daddy to your kid? That's not fair. This was your responsibility, not mine!"

"She's so damn stubborn too! She won't even let me give her money. She's determined to do this on her own. She's working like a dog and living in a fucking shithole, and there's not a damn thing I can do about it. The least you could have done was set her up. Made sure she had money and a place to live, but all you were thinking about was your goddamn self!"

I sat down on the damp grass and dropped my head between my knees. "You know what the worst part is? I love her. So fucking much. But I don't know if I can be a dad to your kid. If it was our kid, sure. But it's not. I'll always know it's not mine."

"I don't even know if she's staying. She was going to move home to Oklahoma, give up on her dreams." I stared up at the stars. "God, you should have heard her sing last night. She's the most beautiful thing I've ever seen in my life. And now I may have to give her up because you fucked up. If you hadn't OD'd, I would have never fallen in love with her. She wouldn't have broken my heart. And I wouldn't be in this position. Fuck you, Wes. Just fuck you!"

"I'll tell you this though… Clarissa may not let me take care of her, but I will take care of that baby. My niece or nephew won't want for anything. That, I'll make sure of."

I don't know how long I sat there talking to Wes. When I left, I didn't feel any better and I didn't have any answers. I was still confused as hell.

In the morning I called the one person in my family I could talk to. Ronnie met me for breakfast at a local diner just outside Forest Hills. I was already seated when she walked in wearing a black power suit and her red-soled Louboutin heels. She looked like a million bucks, and she was worth many, many times that. Ronnie stuck out like a sore thumb in this restaurant, but you'd never be able to tell if she was uncomfortable from the smile on her face. She was used to meeting me at out-of-the-way places.

I stood when my sister approached the table, wrapping her in a warm hug and kissing her cheek.

"Well, look what the cat dragged in," she teased. "It's not often I get to see my big brother twice within a few months. What brings you to town?" She sat down across from me as the waitress poured our coffee.

"Wes. Rissa."

Ronnie held up her hand. "Please don't say her name in front of me. I knew there was something fishy with her. You dodged a bullet with that one. Little slut tried to trap you while she was out messing around. Did she move back to Oklahoma yet? Thank God, she never officially became part of this family. You can dress up the trash, but underneath the designer clothes and expensive jewelry she's still trash." Ronnie paused in her tirade to take sip a of her coffee.

I held my tongue but glared at her. She set her cup down and lifted a freshly-waxed eyebrow at me. "Zack, please tell me you're not still in love with her."

I leaned my elbows on the table. "She was going to be Wes's wife, your sister-in-law. After he died, how many times did you call to talk to her or check on her?"

She waved her hand in the air. "None. We weren't that close."

"What about mom?" I asked.

"I doubt she called her at all. What are you getting at, Zack?"

I leaned back in my chair. "I'm just trying to figure this out. Wes was with her for two years, brought her to dinners and family events. She was going to be part of this family in a few months, and when she was kicked out of her home and left penniless, no one bothered to check on her?"

Ronnie stared into her coffee cup to avoid my questioning.

"You knew she had no family, right? You're the one who told me that."

Ronnie straightened her shoulders. "I don't understand this line of questioning. What were we supposed to do, take her in like an orphan off the street?"

"No, but a little basic decency would have been nice."

I hit a nerve with my sister. She leaned forward on her elbows. "Why are you being so defensive of her? She cheated on you."

I shook my head. "She didn't cheat on me. And when I kicked her out, she paid back every dime I gave her."

"How honorable," she said with sarcasm.

"You might want to rethink her status in this family. She's pregnant with your niece or nephew," I said.

Her jaw dropped, and she was rendered speechless. When she pulled it together, Ronnie stared daggers at me. "I can't believe this! How could you have been so careless?"

My jaw twitched. "Wrong brother."

Her hand came up to cover her mouth. "Oh. My. God!"

"That's right. So, no matter how you feel about her, she will be connected to this family."

Ronnie's eyes narrowed. "What does she want? Money?"

"Better watch yourself," I warned her. "You've been spending too much time with our father. You sound just like him. I thought you were better than that."

She threw her hands in the air. "What am I supposed to think, Zack?"

"I just found out yesterday. Do you know why she didn't tell anyone? Because she says it's her responsibility. She won't take anything from me."

Ronnie tapped her chin with her red manicured nail. "What if it's not Wes's? What if she cheated on him? What if this is all a ploy?"

85

I answered all three of her questions in rapid succession. "It is. She didn't. It's not."

"How do you know?"

"I just know, okay? I believe her. She's not asking for anything, but that doesn't mean she doesn't deserve something."

"You still love her, don't you? Are you going to step up and play daddy?"

I ran my hand over my scruffy chin. "Yes. I still love her. I'm miserable without her, but I don't know what I'm going to do. I don't know if I can do it."

Ronnie reached over the table and took my hand. "It's not your responsibility, Zack," she said softly.

I banged my fist on the table. "It's all of our responsibility. It's our blood she's carrying."

Ronnie looked around to see if anyone was watching us. "Quit making a scene."

"It's all about the image, isn't it? You forgot I stopped caring what people thought about me a long time ago." I threw my napkin down. "It was a mistake coming here. Out of everyone, I expected more from you. But I can see now that you've been sucked so far down the rabbit hole that you can't see your way out."

This didn't go at all the way I thought it would. I expected compassion from my sister, and I got none. I stood to leave, and she grasped my arm. "You're not being fair, Zack."

"Life's not fair. If it was, Wes would still be here." I walked out of the restaurant, got in my rental, and drove straight to the airport.

.

Chapter 13
Rissa

I had a lightness in my step, I hadn't felt in weeks. I had no commitments from Zack and no promises, but at least I had my friend back. And that was worth everything to me.

We loved each other, but I didn't know if we would ever be a couple again. I didn't expect him to jump in and be my baby's daddy. I was hoping he would want the job, but even if he didn't take it, he would be an awesome uncle. Zack would fill some of the void Wes had left.

"Audrey, how long has that car been parked across the street?" I asked her while wiping down the front window.

She looked over my shoulder. "Which car?"

"That black sedan. I've never seen it before." It had blacked out windows and looked out of place in this neighborhood.

Audrey placed her hand on my shoulder. "Don't know. Why?"

I shrugged my shoulders. "Just seems weird is all."

She waved me off. "Weird is all around us. Forget about it."

"I guess." I gave the window one last wipe and told Audrey my news. "I talked to Zack."

She stopped sorting the jewelry she had bought off eBay. "When?"

I skipped over to the counter where she was working. "Two days ago."

"You look like the cat that ate the canary. Spill it, missy."

I pulled a stool from behind the counter and plopped onto it. "I told him the baby is Wes's."

"And?"

"We're not back together, but at least we're talking. He was shocked and relieved. I know he still loves me but…" I shrugged.

She reached across the counter and pushed my hair over my ear. It was such a mom thing to do. I was so thankful for Audrey. She came into my life when I needed her most. "Give him time. He'll come around."

I shrugged again. "Maybe, maybe not. But at least we're friends again. I don't want to pressure him into anything."

"Are you moving back in with him?" she asked.

"Not anytime soon. I need to stand on my own two feet." I played with the tangled chains on the counter. "Wes took care of me for so long, I kind of forgot what that feels like."

"He took care of you, or you took care of each other?"

"He had way more money than me. He definitely took care of me," I said as I pulled one of the chains free from the knot on the counter.

"Oh honey, there's so much more than money to consider. Relationships are a give and take. You may not have had a lot of money, but I'm sure you took care of him in other ways."

I tossed the rest of the tangled chains on the counter. "I don't know. I just feel like I need to do this on my own. I don't want to owe anyone."

"Did Zack make you feel like you owed him?" she asked.

"Never. He always tried to pay for everything."

"Did you ever think that maybe he wanted to take care of you? It's a primitive instinct, you know? Men want to take care of their women. It makes them feel like they're doing their job."

I laughed. "Well, that is primitive. Haven't they heard of the Sexual Revolution?"

She winked at me. "It takes men a while to catch up. But while you're waiting, there's nothing wrong with letting a man dote on you."

I gave her the stink eye.

"What? There's got to be some advantages to being a woman. I wouldn't mind some man wining and dining me. And I sure as hell wouldn't mind a man taking care of some other things for me, if you know what I mean." She waggled her eyebrows.

"Oh my God, Audrey! Are you talking about sex?"

Audrey slapped me on the arm playfully. "Don't look so scandalized. Women have needs, even women my age."

I buried my head in my hands. "I'm going to pretend we're not talking about this."

"How is Zack in bed anyway?" she continued.

"Audrey!"

"Come on, indulge an old woman. Do you know how long it's been since I had sex?"

I held up one finger. "First of all, you're not old." I held up another finger. "Second of all, I won't kiss and tell. But I will tell you this, he's intense. It's the best I've ever had, and Wes was no slacker."

♩♪♩♪

I parked my Bronco in the lot behind Zack's shop. I was thankful that he was letting me use his washer and dryer. Lugging my stuff to the laundromat really sucked. I pulled the garbage bag from the back seat and carried it through the back door. I dropped it at the bottom of the stairs and made my way into his shop.

I went right to his studio and popped my head in the open door. "Thanks for letting me do my laundry here. I really appreciate it."

Zack looked up from the tattoo he was doing. "Anything for you, sweetheart. Make yourself at home. The door is unlocked."

I winked at him. "Thanks."

I carted my clothes up the stairs and dropped them in front of the washer. I started sorting the lights from the darks when I felt softness rub against my leg. "Priss." I picked her up and snuggled her to my chest. I couldn't believe I'd wanted nothing to do with her when I first came here, because I had missed her horribly over the last month. I checked her food and water and topped them both off before starting my first load.

I stood with my hands on my hips and looked around the apartment. The urge to snoop overwhelmed me. I shouldn't have but figured a little wouldn't hurt. This had once been my home and I was curious what Zack had done with my old room. He had probably turned it back into his art studio.

I went to the closed door and put my hand on the knob. It wasn't my business to know, but I needed to. I slowly turned the knob and pushed the door open. Relief filled my chest. It was exactly how I had left it. The furniture stood empty with only the diamond collar adorning the top of the dresser. The mattress was bare, except for the throw pillows, Priss's nest, my notebook, and a stack of money. I wonder what had happened to the Mason Jar. I crept further into the room and got my answer when I rounded the bed. Shards of glass covered the floor. "Oh crap,"

I had a choice to make. I could either leave and shut the door like I'd never seen it, or I could get a broom and sweep it up. Priss jumped up on the bed and watched me. She made my decision. It would kill me if she wandered in here and cut her paws.

I scooped her off the bed and set her safely outside the room, while I pulled the broom and dustpan from the laundry closet. I carefully swept the glass from the floor, making sure to sweep in all the corners and under the bed. When I was positive I had gotten it all, I dumped the glass into the trash and returned the broom to the closet.

I closed the door to the bedroom and went to the bathroom. I opened the drawers where I had stored my things and found them empty. I slid open the shower door and peeked inside. The shelf where I had kept my shampoo and body wash were also empty.

The piano stood in the corner of the front room, covered by a white sheet. Zack didn't know how to play it and I wondered why he kept it. It was an expensive instrument he could have returned or sold.

Zack hadn't changed anything. It was as if time had frozen, and he was waiting for me to come back.

I wanted to come back more than anything. I hated my crappy apartment, but I wouldn't complicate our lives any further by moving back here. I had to know that he wanted me *and* my baby. We were a package deal.

I pushed the thought of us together out of my head. Agonizing over it wouldn't change anything.

I had a lot of time to kill while waiting for my laundry to be finished. I wandered through the kitchen and opened the pantry. He still had the ingredients from the last time I baked cookies. I started pulling them out and setting everything on the counter. Zack loved my cookies and making him a batch would be the perfect way to thank him.

I grabbed a big bowl from the cabinet under the sink, along with the cookie sheets. I started mixing the butter and eggs together then carefully measured the flour and sugar. I was surprised when I moved in here to find that he had an electric mixer. What single guy has an electric mixer? I was

90

glad he did though, because it had allowed me to make him treats at least once a week.

I scooped spoonfuls of dough onto the cookie sheet and popped the first tray into the oven. I set the timer as the washer stopped. I took the load out of the washer and put it in the dryer, then put my next load in.

I wandered into Zack's room out of habit and sat on the bed. I shouldn't have been in there. It wasn't my place anymore. I couldn't help it though. Sitting on the firm mattress reminded me how awful my current *bed* was. I scanned the room, remembering all the nights I spent on this bed, even when he was just holding me.

I zeroed in on Zack's hamper that was overflowing with dirty clothes. It had been my habit to wash his clothes while I was doing laundry, but now it almost felt like a violation of privacy. It wasn't like I wasn't intimately acquainted with his underwear. I had pulled them off with my teeth, right before I had… I pushed the memory from my mind. He wasn't mine anymore. He was doing me a favor by letting me use his washer.

I took one last look at his hamper and decided that doing one load wouldn't be so awful. He might even appreciate it. I separated out his clothes, most of which fell into the dark pile, and carried it to the washer. I still had time to wait until my clothes were finished.

The piano called to me. I went to it and pulled the sheet from the top. Except for my time at Uptown Sound, I hadn't played for enjoyment in a month. I sat down on the bench and played "*My Immortal*" by Evanescence. When I played it after Wes's death, it was for him. He had left me alone and I didn't know how to cope. But as my fingers flew over the keys, I realized I wasn't playing for Wes anymore. I was playing for Zack.

This strange limbo we were in was destroying me. I wanted him to accept me and my baby, but I knew I couldn't force the issue. Seeing him and knowing we were only friends was killing me. I wondered if it would be better if I left and returned to Oklahoma, but I owed it to myself to see if I could make a future with my music. The downside was that staying would always remind me of what could have been with Zack. I couldn't and wouldn't deny that I was undeniably and irrevocably in love with him.

It seemed like no matter what choice I made I wouldn't truly be happy.

♫♪♫♪

Bartending was the last thing I wanted to do tonight, but I had to work. Money was money and every penny counted. It was relatively slow for a Wednesday. A half-dozen tables were filled with patrons and another half dozen sat at the bar.

I approached the guy in the suit seated at the end of the bar. "What can I get you?"

"How about you?" he said trying to be smooth.

I rolled my eyes as I placed a napkin in front of him. "I'm not on the menu. What else?"

He frowned. "How about Macallan? Straight up."

I let out a little laugh. "I don't know where you think you are, but that's a little above our pay grade. I've got Dewar's. That's the best you're going to get."

"Then Dewar's it is."

I pulled a glass and poured two fingers worth into it. I slid the glass across the bar and placed it in front of him.

He grabbed my wrist. "What are you doing later?"

I wrenched my arm away. "Nothing with you. I have to wash my hair or maybe watch paint dry. Either one would be a more attractive option than what you're proposing. This isn't that type of bar."

He mocked a gasp. "Oh, you're breaking my heart, sweetheart."

I backed away from the bar, stumbling over my own feet. "Don't call me that." Zack was the only one who had ever called me sweetheart and this guy was creeping me out.

"Hey, Relax. No harm. No foul," he said while taking a sip of his scotch. "Just testing the waters." He pulled out his phone and started texting, as if I didn't exist.

I was relieved. Rarely did a customer give me the creep factor, but this guy did. When he finished his scotch, he placed a fifty on the bar and left as if nothing had happened. I grabbed the money off the bar and cashed him out, pocketing the tip. It was a good one. The guy obviously had money. I don't know what made me uneasy about him. It wasn't the first time I'd been propositioned, but the way he looked at me was weird. Like I was up for grabs and he wanted his chance. No way in hell!

I finished my shift and helped Lou put all the chairs on top of the tables. One of the chairs Lou put up slid off the table and crashed to the floor. I jumped in surprise and clasped my hand to my chest.

"What's up with you?" Lou asked. "You've been jumpy all night."

"I don't know. There was this one guy tonight that gave me the heebie- jeebies." I waved a hand in front of my face. "I'm just overreacting."

"You walk to work tonight?" Lou asked.

"Yeah."

"I can drive you home. It's not a problem."

I tried to ground myself. I was being ridiculous. It was one guy. One overweight, middle-aged guy who was overzealous and thought I would be an easy lay. But then again, I had learned to follow my instincts and my instincts told me the guy was bad news. "Would you mind?"

"Absolutely not. Give me fifteen minutes and then we can leave," Lou told me.

Fifteen minutes later I was sitting in his F-150, giving him directions to my apartment. Lou pulled around the back of the party store and parked next to my Bronco. The light above my door was out again.

"Seriously, Rissa? I try not to get involved, but really?" he asked.

"What?" I countered like I had no idea what he was talking about.

"Zack is okay with you living here? I know you're not together, but Jesus Christ!"

I straightened my shoulders. "Zack doesn't tell me what to do."

"So, he's not okay with you living here?" Lou questioned.

I slumped back in the seat. "Not really. But we're not together and I'm not going to live at his place. My options are limited."

Lou leaned against his door. "I'm not going to pry, Rissa, but you're like a daughter to me and I don't want to see anything happen to you. This is not where I'd want my daughter living. Let me at least walk you up."

I agreed without any argument. The way that guy at the bar made me feel, I was glad for the extra company. Lou walked me to the top of the stairs and waited patiently while I jiggled the key in the door.

"Do you have any lightbulbs?" Lou asked.

"I might." I scurried inside and turned on the light in the kitchen. I looked under the sink but found nothing. "Looks like I'm out." That damn bulb blew every few days and I'd already gone through half a dozen.

He scowled at me. "I'll be back in the morning with a whole box. I wish I didn't know that you lived here. Lock the door behind me and don't open it for anyone."

I kissed him on the cheek. "I won't. Thank you, Lou. I appreciate it."

"Anytime. You might want to think about driving to work. It's getting colder and honestly, I've never been comfortable with you walking home. You can park in the alley behind the bar. Once the snow comes, you'll be thankful I suggested it."

I felt like if I said yes, I'd be giving in to both Zack and Lou. I hated doing something because a man suggested it. On the other hand, Creepy McCreeperton made me nervous tonight. Walking home from The Locker wasn't like walking home in Brooklyn. In Brooklyn, the streets were always busy at night, walking home here I doubted anyone would even hear me if I screamed.

I tapped my finger on my lips. "I'll think about it."

Chapter 14
Zack

Knowing that Clarissa was upstairs earlier today was pure torture. I could occasionally hear the soft sound of the piano coming through the vents. I'd missed hearing it over the past month, and I found the sound soothing. It was like a piece of my life that was missing had been returned to its proper place.

When I'd gone upstairs at the end of the night, Clarissa was long gone. She had to bartend, so she scooted out as soon as her laundry was done. But when I opened the door there was no question that she had been there. I smelled the chocolate chip cookies immediately. The woman knew how to get to me.

I went immediately to the kitchen counter and lifted the foil off the plate. I snatched a cookie off the plate and popped it in my mouth. The chocolate melted on my tongue. It was heavenly. I stole another and picked up the plate to put it on top of the fridge where Priss couldn't reach.

Under the plate was a five-dollar bill with a sticky note on top. *Thank you. Please take this and don't make a big deal about it. ~Rissa* She drew a little heart over the i, just like she had done when the girl in the bar asked for her autograph. I never expected her to pay to do her laundry here. Knowing she was in my apartment was payment enough for me.

I wished she would agree to move back in. I hated where she was living, but we needed to take this slow. She was smart to tell me no. After all, I hadn't made any decisions as to what type of relationship I wanted with Clarissa.

Did I love her? *Yes.*

Did I have an overwhelming urge to take care of her? *More than anything.*

Did she make my life feel complete? *Undeniably.*

Did I want to kiss her repeatedly? *Hell, yes.*

95

Did I want to fuck her? *Absolutely.*

Was I ready to be a father to my brother's kid? *I wasn't sure.*

It was like a checklist with one box left unchecked. My mind continually wavered between checking yes or no.

I stumbled into my room, ready to call it a night. I stopped when I flicked on the light. The laundry that had filled my hamper was clean and folded on my bed. Miss Priss was curled up on top on my shirts. The fissure in my chest widened and became a gaping hole.

Why? Why had she done any of this? Why was she so damned intent on taking care of me when I had treated her so awfully?

I tried to rationalize everything. It was only cookies. It was only laundry. None of it was reason enough to make a life-changing decision.

I had a business to run. Employees who I supported with regular work and paychecks. Clients who depended on me. How the hell would a baby fit into my world?

I was making excuses. Because if I was being honest with myself, it wasn't the baby that was throwing me off. Hell, I'd been happy when I thought the baby was mine. It was the fact that the baby was Wes's.

I tried to ignore the fact that Wes had been fucking her for the last two years. I had hoped that over time she wouldn't see Wes when she looked at me. I didn't want to be the link to her past. I wanted to be her future. I wanted her to love me for me. I thought, given time, that it would be possible. But if I helped her raise his child, Wes would always be a part of our life.

It was an awful thought. Wes was my brother, and I didn't want to erase him, but I didn't want him to be the third person in our relationship either.

I should have thought about that before I fucked her. Before I let her weave herself into my life and ingrain herself into my soul. Before I fell in love with her. Before I gave her my heart.

I had no one to blame but myself.

♫♪♫♪

I strolled into the bar after my last client left. I could have called Clarissa, but I rejected that option in favor of seeing her in person. She looked

96

just as beautiful as ever as she pulled beer from the tap. I liked seeing her in her element when she didn't know I was watching.

Some people would be critical of her being a bartender, namely my family, but there was no shame in hard work. Clarissa busted her ass for every dime she made. She was a stubborn woman and she made me crazy.

I sat at the end of the bar and watched as Clarissa tended to her other customers. It only took her a moment to notice me. "Hey. What are you doing here?" She pulled a rock glass from the shelf and poured me a Jim Beam.

"Just checking on you," I answered.

She eyed me skeptically. "I'm doing fine. Tired, but that's to be expected."

I nodded, wishing she didn't have to work so hard. "I wanted to know when your next doctor's appointment is. I want to go, if it's okay with you."

She swallowed down the lump in her throat before she answered. "You don't have to, Zack. It's not your responsibility. I'm fine going by myself."

"I know you are, but wouldn't it be nice to have someone with you?" I asked.

"Gina will be there. Won't that be weird for you? I mean, you two are… what are you exactly?" she asked, cocking her head to the side.

She and I hadn't really addressed my relationship with Gina. All she knew was what Gina had told her. "I think you know what we were. It was never serious between us. But I promise you, Clarissa, we haven't been together since you moved here. Yes, I did go to see her when we broke up, but nothing happened. We're friends, nothing more."

She wrung her hands together nervously. "Friends with benefits."

"At one time, yes. But not anymore. Not until we figure out what this is between you and me. I wouldn't do that to you."

"She's in love with you."

"I don't love her. I never have. She knows that."

Clarissa looked over her shoulder at the other customers sitting around the bar. "I have to get back to work. My appointment is tomorrow morning at 9 o'clock. I'll understand if you change your mind." She turned her back on me and started towards the other end of the bar.

"Can I walk you home?" I shouted.

She glanced my way one more time. "I drove."

Those words made the tension in my chest subside. I hated her walking home. I finished my drink, leaving a healthy tip on the bar. If she wouldn't let me give her money, the least I could do was tip her well.

♫♪♫♪

I stood outside Doc Peterson's office, shuffling from foot to foot while I waited for Clarissa. I'd never been to this type of appointment before. Actually, I stayed away from the doctor's office as much as possible. I had insurance because I'd be a shit boss if I didn't provide it for my employees, but I rarely used it on myself. I'd been patched up plenty while I was in the Marines but since then, except the time I had the flu, I hadn't needed a doctor.

I saw Clarissa coming down the sidewalk, her coat zipped up tight and a scarf wrapped around her neck. It was fucking cold today, and I was glad to see she had a proper coat. It was hard to believe that it was almost Thanksgiving. Time was flying by and every day I spent away from her was killing me.

Clarissa approached me, sheepishly. There was no hello. "You don't have to be here."

"I want to be here," I assured her with a kiss on the cheek.

"Let's go." She opened the door and walked towards Gina to check in. She didn't make eye contact, just signed her name, and came back to sit next to me.

I took her hand in mine. "Are you nervous?"

"Every time I come here, I'm a nervous wreck. It gets more real with every visit."

I knew exactly what she meant, because up until this moment, Clarissa being pregnant had been abstract to me. Obviously, I knew what pregnancy was. I was a twenty-eight-year-old man, not a kid. But this was personal.

When Megan got pregnant, I'd watched her body change and grow, thinking it was my baby inside her. I loved Megan, but I wasn't ready to be a father. I always made excuses for not going with her to the doctor. However, I did love her, and I provided for her. The truth about her betrayals crushed me and I detached myself from the situation without a second thought. I would not

98

be used again. That night I got inked again. The heart with a dagger through it was a reminder to guard my heart. When you gave it away, there was always a risk that someone could destroy it.

Clarissa was different. Both our hearts had been shattered, but not by our own betrayals. It was a shit set of circumstances neither of us had asked for. As much as I tried, I couldn't detach. We were connected by more than the blood that ran through her baby.

Gina called Clarissa's name. When we walked back Gina bit her lip and nodded her head. It was an acceptance of me being there and I appreciated it. This wasn't easy for her either.

Clarissa stepped on the scale and then we were led to a private room. The nurse took her blood pressure. "Your numbers are down. That's good." She gave Clarissa instructions to undress from the waist down and left.

I hadn't thought about this part of her appointment. "Do you want me to wait outside?"

"No. Just turn away. I know you've seen me before, but this is different," she answered.

"I've done more than just see you, Clarissa. But I get it. We're not together."

"Thank you."

I turned and stared at the pregnancy poster on the wall that showed the development of a baby at different stages. I wondered where exactly Clarissa fit on this timeline.

"You can turn around now." Clarissa sat on the table with a sheet covering her waist and legs. "If this is too weird for you, you don't have to stay."

Again, she was giving me an out. There was no way I was taking it. I sat in the chair next to her and threaded my fingers through hers. "No way, sweetheart." I kissed the top of her hand. "What did the nurse mean about your numbers being down?"

Clarissa sighed. "Last time I was here was the day after our falling out. My blood pressure was up."

I frowned as the guilt weighed down on me. "I'm sorry." *Falling Out?* That was a euphemism if I'd ever heard one.

Before she could say anything, there was a knock and Doc Peterson entered. "Good morning, Rissa." His eyes glanced at me, but he kept his focus on Clarissa. "You have company today."

I held out my hand. "I'm Zack.

He shook my hand. "Oh, I know who you are. You've got a reputation for being the best tattoo artist in the area. Had a little ink done myself back in the day." He winked at me. "Soooo... you're here as Rissa's...?" His question hung in the air.

"Friend," she supplied before I had a chance. That stung. It was what we agreed to, but it sounded all wrong.

"How are you feeling today?"

She kicked her legs nervously under the sheet. "A little tired but other than that good."

"Still working at the bar?" he asked.

"Yeah, and I'm working at A Second Chance."

"Rissa," he tsked. "You need to be careful not to overdo it. No wonder you're tired. Are you still living alone?"

"MmmHmm."

Doc Peterson turned to me. "Will you please try to talk some sense into this woman. She needs to be careful. The next few months are critical."

"Have you met her?" I asked. "She's stubborn as hell, but I'll try."

"Listen to your body, Rissa, and rest when you need to," he instructed. "Now let's see what's going on. Lay back for me."

Rissa did as she was told. I backed up and stood by her head, holding her hand as Doc Peterson completed his exam. Then he rolled over the ultrasound machine as Rissa put her legs down.

"Let's see this baby," he said as he smoothed gel over her stomach. Clarissa had a definite baby bump that she did a good job hiding under her clothes. He rubbed the wand over her belly and a picture appeared on the screen. I gasped at what I saw. I could clearly see a head, body, and tiny legs. It looked like the baby was sucking its thumb. My heart seized in my chest.

A tear rolled down Rissa's cheek. "Can you tell if it's a boy or a girl?"

"Are you sure you want to know?" the doc asked.

"Yes, please."

He moved the wand around to the side of her belly. "It's a girl."

Clarissa's hand came up to cover her mouth as she let out a soft sob. *We're having a girl.* I squeezed her hand as I processed the information. She looked at me. "I'm having a daughter," she whispered.

And just like that, I felt crushed. Clarissa was having a daughter. Not us. Her. There was no us. I pushed my own feelings to the side and smiled down on her. "Congratulations, sweetheart."

Chapter 15
Rissa

Zack was quiet when we left Doc Peterson's office. I shouldn't have let him come with me today. It was too much, too real. I saw it on his face during the ultrasound. My hope that he would change his mind and we could be a family was gone. He didn't have to tell me his decision, I already knew what it was.

I didn't want to admit to myself that I'd been holding on to that little bit of hope like it was a life vest, keeping me from drowning in my own sadness and fear. But I had. Every day that passed, I worried how I was going to support myself and my daughter. I'd be out of work for at least a few weeks. I wouldn't be able to afford six weeks like most women. If I asked, Zack would give me the money, but that would make me exactly what everyone thought I was... a money-grubber, a gold-digger, a freeloader. I refused to be any of those. I would have to find a way. I just didn't know what that was yet.

♫♪♫♪

A few days later I was at Bobby's house. It was tucked back off the road in a wealthy area I didn't even know existed. I drove up to the gate in my old Bronco, feeling very out of place. My car stood out like a sore thumb in this neighborhood where people drove BMWs, Audis, Jaguars and Porsches. I rang the buzzer and the gate slid open.

I drove up the long driveway that led to a beautiful mansion that rivaled Malcolm Kincaid's. I felt as insignificant here as I did there. Memories of being called trash floated through my mind. I didn't belong here. This wasn't my world.

I almost turned my Bronco around and drove away. If Daniel hadn't been outside waiting for me, I would have. Instead, I pushed down my insecurities and got out of my car with my guitar. This might be my only chance to provide for my daughter and I had to take it.

He reached out his hand to shake mine. "Did you find it all right?"

I nodded and took in the sprawling estate in front of me. "This is where Bobby lives?" It was a stupid question. I already knew he lived here. I just couldn't reconcile the man I knew with the house in front of me. Bobby wasn't flashy. If anything, he was rough around the edges. Hell, I'd met him in a tattoo parlor. Maybe that was why I had always felt comfortable around him.

"Crazy, isn't it?" Daniel answered.

"A little. He has a recording studio in there?" I asked, pointing at the house.

"Yep, and he's agreed to let us use it. He believes in you."

I took a deep breath and straightened my spine. "Let's get started then."

Daniel led me through the house to an elevator. *Bobby had a freaking elevator in his house!* It descended to the basement. When the doors opened, we stood in an actual recording studio, complete with a staff at my disposal. It was surreal.

Daniel made the introductions and then shuffled me into the soundproof room where I would record my demo. My nerves kicked up ten notches. I set down my guitar and ran my hand along the beautiful piano that took up a corner of the room. I faced Daniel and asked him the question that had been burning through my mind. "Who's paying for all this? I can't afford any of this." I waved my hand around the room to emphasize my point.

Daniel laughed. "Lucky for you, we're not paying for studio time. If I'm your agent, I'll get paid when you get paid. My standard is ten percent. Do you want to go over the paperwork first?"

Paperwork. Contracts. I hadn't thought about any of it. All I had focused on was making money to support my daughter. How could I have been so clueless? "I think maybe we should," I said.

Daniel pulled a thick folder from his briefcase. We sat down on the couch, and he started going over the legalese with me. It might as well have been in a foreign language because I didn't understand half of it. I'd heard of artists getting taken advantage of and never making a penny from their music. I started to panic. I wasn't stupid, but I only had a tenth-grade education. I had never felt the weight of my shortcomings as much as I did right now. I was a hick from Oklahoma, and nothing was going to change that.

"So, what do you think?" Daniel asked.

My brain raced to find something intelligent to say. I could only think of one thing. "Is Bobby here?"

"He's upstairs. He wanted to give you space. He thought him being here would make you nervous," Daniel answered.

He thought he would make me nervous? The opposite was true. I needed him. "Can you call him for me? I'd really like to talk to him."

Daniel pulled out his phone and made the call. Five minutes later, Bobby entered the studio. I stood and went to him with the stack of papers in my hand. "Can I talk to you? In private?"

"Of course."

He led me down a hallway and into a private office. I threw the papers on his desk. "I don't understand any of this. I'm freaking out. I know I should have a lawyer look over this contract, but I don't have the time or the money."

"Hello to you too," he said with humor in his voice.

"I'm sorry," I said as I started pacing the room. "All of this is so overwhelming. I don't know who to trust, but I trust you. How well do you know Daniel?"

Bobby gripped me by the shoulders to stop my pacing. "Breathe, Rissa. I've known Daniel for ten years and he's never steered me wrong. You can trust him, I promise you."

"I don't know what the fuck I'm doing. I'm so out of my element. What if I make a mistake?" I asked.

"Rissa, stop. I'll fax this to my lawyer, and you'll have your answer within the hour."

I bit the side of my thumb. "I can't pay for that."

Bobby pulled my thumb from my mouth. "You don't have to. I have him on retainer. Let me do this for you."

It was another piece of charity I didn't deserve, but my choices were limited. I swallowed my pride. "Okay."

Bobby turned me towards the door. "Go. Do what you do best. Make music. Let me handle this."

An hour later, after many stumbles and a lot of restarts, I'd recorded three songs. Daniel had been patient with me, even after I didn't sign his fancy contract. When I finished the last song, Bobby returned carrying the stack of papers I left on his desk. He said two words to me. "Sign it."

I picked up the pen and scrawled *Clarissa Lynne Black* on the last page, hoping I wasn't making a deal with the devil. It was a risk I had no choice but to take.

I drove home feeling apprehension and excitement. I'd signed a document I didn't understand, and I recorded three songs that Daniel was going to submit to the biggest recording labels in the country. Whatever happened from this point forward was out of my control. I could only hope that I had made the right decisions. My daughter was depending on me.

I pulled around the back of my apartment and started up the stairs. I had to be at work in two hours and was hoping I could get a quick nap in first. The metal mailbox beneath my sporadically working porch light held a large envelope. I rarely got mail. I hadn't changed my address from Forever Inked and anything I got usually came courtesy of Layla. I pulled out the envelope and jiggled my key in the door, opening it after a few tries.

I plopped down on my couch slash bed and sank back into the lumps. I didn't care how uncomfortable it was, all I wanted to do was sleep. I wanted to close my eyes, but instead I picked up the envelope I'd tossed onto the coffee table.

My full name was printed on the outside, along with this address. The return label was from a law office in New York. *Oh. My. God. Wes had left me something.* It had to be from his lawyers, who else could it be from? *We were going to be okay. Thank God!*

I quickly ripped open the envelope and dumped the contents on the table. Two smaller envelopes fell out of the larger envelope. I opened the letter-sized one first, excitement coursing through me.

I read the first two lines of the letter inside and every bit of excitement drained from me, replaced with pure rage. *What. The. Fuck!!!!!* I finished the letter and opened the second envelope, pulling out the contents. Nothing could have prepared me for the pictures that were inside. I flipped through them one by one, my anger grew with each one. *How could this have happened?*

My greatest fears had materialized right before my eyes and there was only one person to blame. Only one person who knew the truth and had this kind of reach.

I shoved everything back into the envelope and ran down the steps to my Bronco. I'd felt betrayed before, but nothing... nothing could compare to this. It took me less than three minutes to pull up onto the curb. I did a shit job parking, but it was the least of my worries.

I stormed through the front door of a place that used to be my home. "Where the fuck is he?" I screamed.

.

Chapter 16
Zack

Clarissa's voice carried through my shop. I'd recognize it anywhere. "Where the fuck is he?"

I didn't have to wait long before she burst into my studio. I stopped my tattooing and made silent apologies to my client.

"You fucking bastard!" she yelled. I'd never seen such rage in her. "You were supposed to be my friend! I should have never trusted you! I should have known better than to trust a Kincaid! How could you fucking do this to me? I hate you!"

I snapped my gloves off. "Layla," I yelled. "I'm so sorry," I said to my client. Layla quickly came to my rescue and led my client out of the room.

I shut the door behind them and faced Clarissa. I was pissed that she would barge in here and make a scene. "What the hell? This is my business, Clarissa!"

Her chest heaved up and down. "And this is my fucking life! It wasn't enough for the Kincaids to take my money and my apartment? Now you want my baby? I fucking hate you!"

I scrunched up my eyebrows. "What the hell are you talking about?"

She held up an envelope. "This! I might be white trash, but I won't give up my baby! You can't have her! None of you! I can't believe I trusted you! I can't believe I actually fell in love with you! I'm leaving tonight, and you'll never find me! You can count on that!"

Nothing she said made sense to me. I ripped the envelope from her hand and opened it, trying to contain my anger and figure out what this was about. I pulled out a letter from my father's lawyer. I quickly skimmed it. It was a court order requiring a paternity test on Clarissa's baby, via amniocentesis. It further proclaimed her an unfit mother, citing drug abuse and financial instability. Pending the results of the paternity test, my father was seeking custody of her child. No wonder she was pissed.

I opened the second envelope to find pictures of her. The first showed her leaning over the bar, her cleavage the focus. I flipped to the next. Clarissa hauling a garbage bag from the back of her car. The next... the inside of her apartment. Each picture showcased her in a less than flattering light.

There was only one person to blame for this. My father. I tapped on the pictures. "I didn't do this."

"Oh, fucking save it, Zack! How did he even know I was pregnant? You're the only connection. Why the fuck do you think I was so anxious to leave New York?"

I shoved everything back into the envelope. "I didn't say shit to my father!"

"Then how does he know? Because I sure as fuck didn't tell him! Explain that to me! Explain to me how he got pictures of the inside of my apartment!" And then she broke, collapsing into a heap on the floor. Full force sobs racked her chest. "They can't have her," she cried. "She's all I have left."

I scooped her up from the floor and held her to my chest. Her hands gripped the front of my shirt, her tears soaking it as I caressed the back of her head. Seeing her like this killed me. "I didn't do this, Clarissa. I think you know me better than that."

"I don't... know... what... to think," she hiccupped. "How do they know? How can he take my baby? Is this even legal?"

She had so many questions and I didn't have any answers. Well, that was a lie. I had one answer. I didn't like it, and neither would she. "My sister. The day you told me, I went to New York. I needed to talk to someone, and I thought I could trust her."

Clarissa pulled back from me. "You told Veronica? She works for your father." I could see the wheels spinning in her head. "I have to leave. I have to pack tonight and go." She quickly shoved all the paperwork in the envelope and turned in a frantic attempt to escape.

I put my hand on the door to keep her from running. "You can't leave. Do you really think that will help? My father is resourceful, no matter where you go, he'll find you."

"I have to at least try. What other choice do I have?"

Her fingers tried to pry my hand from the door. I spun her around and gripped her by the shoulders. "You stay and fight. You don't let him win."

Her eyes met mine and I saw something in them I'd never seen before. Fear. "How? I can't win against him. I don't have money for a lawyer."

"Let me talk to my sister. I'll see what I can do. Maybe I can talk some sense into her. She has a lot of pull with my father."

Her throat bobbed, as she nodded. "Fix this, Zack," she pleaded. "If you ever cared about me at all, fix this."

I'd known Clarissa for three and a half months, but I didn't know the woman who stood before me now. Desperate was the only word that could be used to describe her.

"I'll try," I promised.

She wiped at her eyes. "Thank you. I'm sorry I barged in here like this. It was a gut reaction. I should have known you wouldn't do this."

I hugged her tight. "It's okay. I'll let you know what I find out." I kissed her on the head. "Don't worry. No one will take your baby from you," I promised, having no idea if I could keep it or not.

Clarissa opened the door and left my shop looking forlorn. I watched her drive away and back to her apartment, where no doubt she would continue to cry and worry.

This was my fault. If it weren't for me, Ronnie would have never known, and neither would my father.

Chase clapped me on the shoulder. "You all right, man?"

There was no sense in denying that things were a mess. Both Chase and Layla had just witnessed it firsthand, along with a few clients. "I need a few minutes to make some calls."

"Do what you need to do. We've got it handled here," Chase assured me.

"Thanks. I won't be long."

I took the stairs two at a time up to my apartment and pulled my phone from my pocket. I was furious with Ronnie. This was her retaliation for the things I said the last time I saw her. I was sure of it. When had she changed so much?

I listened to the line ring. After what seemed like an eternity, she answered, "Veronica Kincaid."

So that was how we were going to play this. "Cut the crap, Ronnie."

"Is that you, Zack? It's hard to hear you from down here in the rabbit hole." I could imagine the smug look on her face.

"Ronnie, please."

"What do you want, Zack?"

"I want to know why you told Malcolm about the baby. I trusted you," I said.

"I didn't know it was a secret. Why does it matter?" she asked.

She was either playing dumb or she really didn't know what he had done. "Did you know he's fighting Clarissa for custody of the baby?"

"Oh that," she said nonchalantly. "That was a family decision. We got together and decided you were right. Our family has a responsibility towards Wes's baby. If it is his child, that is."

"And your solution is to try to take Wes's daughter away from her mother? That's shitty, Ronnie. You know that's not what I meant by taking responsibility."

"Oh, it's a girl? Mom will be so excited."

I kicked myself for giving her more information. "Mom knows about this and she's okay with it?" I asked.

"We're all concerned. This is in the baby's best interest. You know Rissa can't provide for a child like we can."

"And what about Rissa? What's she supposed to do? She's just supposed to give up her baby?" I asked, getting more frustrated by the second.

"Rissa isn't our concern. She's not family. Did you know they found cocaine in her apartment? Do you really want a drug addict raising your niece?"

I growled, "She's not a drug addict. That shit was Wes's. You know that!"

"Do I? For all I know, she's the one who got him hooked. As a matter of fact, she's probably the reason he's dead," Ronnie declared.

"You're ridiculous! He got hooked when he went to LA, she didn't have anything to do with it," I defended.

"Is that what she told you?"

I almost told her about the journal but decided better than to share that information. "It's what I know. Why are you doing this to her?"

"Technically, I'm not doing anything. Malcolm is doing what he always does, protecting this family. You'd know that, if you hadn't walked away from us."

Now I was pissed, "You know why I left. You're not being fair!"

"Yeah, well life isn't fair. If it were, Wes would still be alive." She threw my own words back in my face and disconnected the call.

I threw my phone down on the couch. I didn't even know my own sister anymore. Veronica had been so corrupted by our father that I wasn't sure Ronnie even existed.

I picked up my phone and called my mom. Surely, she would listen to reason. There was no way she could be all right with this.

"Hi, honey."

"Hi, Mom. Do you have a minute to talk?" I ran my hand through my hair, hoping she was clueless about all of this.

"Sure. What's on your mind?"

"Have you talked to Ronnie lately?" I asked.

"I talked to her yesterday. Why?"

"Did she tell you about Rissa?" I sat down on the couch and hung my head.

"No. How is she doing? I felt so bad for her. Are you two still hanging out?"

Obviously, my mom was oblivious to what was happening here. Ronnie hadn't told her anything. My mom knew I had brought Clarissa to Michigan to start over, but I hadn't told her that we were together. "I'm in love with her, Mom."

"Oh, I see."

"There's more," I hesitated. "She's pregnant."

"I'm going to be a grandma?" she gasped excitedly.

"Yeah, you're going to be a grandma. But... I'm not the father. Wes is."

"Well, fuck a duck!" she exclaimed.

I couldn't help but laugh. My mom was usually so prim and proper and hearing her swear was an oddity. "You could say that. But there's more."

"More? Are you trying to give me a heart attack?" she asked. "What else?"

111

I took a deep breath. "This is so complicated, Mom. I'm not used to talking to you about this kind of stuff."

"Zack, you're my first born. You were always so headstrong, and I didn't want to pry into your life, but I'm still your mom. You can talk to me. I won't judge you."

A lump formed in my throat. "God, I miss you."

"I miss you too, honey," she sniffed.

I told her the whole story, from the time Wes died until I went with Clarissa for her ultrasound. I didn't leave out any of the gory details. When I finished, she only had one question. "Do you love her?"

"More than anything. Is it wrong?"

"Oh honey, you can't help who you fall in love with. Does she love you?"

"Yeah. But I don't know if I can be a father to Wes's baby. Won't that be weird?" I asked.

"It's unconventional, but not weird. Would you rather some stranger help raise your niece?"

Who? "What do you mean?"

"Zack, she's a beautiful girl. Eventually she'll meet someone. She won't stay single forever."

I ran my hand through my hair again. "I hadn't thought about it. I just assumed if I didn't step up, she'd raise the baby by herself."

"That's naïve, Zack. She's a young woman. It wouldn't be fair to expect her to be alone forever. The question is, can you accept the consequences if you let her go? Are you worried about what other people will think? No one even needs to know it's not your baby. It's no one's business."

"Someone else already does know. I told Ronnie and she told Malcolm. He sent Rissa a letter from his lawyer, demanding a paternity test and seeking custody of her baby."

"He what?"

"He wants to take her baby away and Ronnie is in on it with him," I added.

"Why in the world?" My mom left her question hanging.

"Because he thinks she's trash. He doesn't want her raising a Kincaid."

"So typical," she fumed. "I'll find out what I can, but I'm not going to confront him. I'll have to be stealthy about this. He's gone too far this time. Get that girl a lawyer and fast. She's going to need it."

My mom didn't always agree with my father, but she usually defended him. It was something I never understood. "Thanks, Mom. You have no idea how much this means to me."

"I love you, Zack. I'm sorry I haven't been there for you."

"I haven't made it easy," I admitted.

"You haven't, but that's no excuse on my part. And one more thing... if you love Rissa, make sure she knows."

"I will, Mom. Love you."

"Love you too. I'll keep you posted."

When I hung up with my mom, most of the tension had eased from my chest. Finally, I felt like I had an ally. I hadn't felt that way since my grandfather had died. My mom gave me hope that we could beat Malcolm at his own game.

I had one more call to make. My lawyer was going to earn his money on this one.

Chapter 17
Rissa

After another cry when I got home and a miraculous makeup job, I went to work. Zack said not to worry, but how could I not? I tried to figure out how Malcolm had gotten those pictures and I kept coming up blank. Someone must have broken into my apartment. Surely even Malcolm couldn't get away with breaking and entering. But how would I prove it?

I hadn't heard from Zack since I'd barged into his shop like a crazy person. I had lost it. The thought of someone taking my daughter away from me was enough to push me over the edge I'd been standing on.

I'd listen to what Zack had found out and then I'd make my decision. I racked my brain to think of somewhere Malcolm wouldn't find me. I couldn't go back to Oklahoma. It was the first place he would look.

I was making a Long Island Iced Tea when my phone buzzed in my back pocket. I put down the bottle of tequila and pulled it from my pocket. *Zack. Thank God.* "Hey."

"Hey. I'm coming over."

I scrunched up my nose. "I'm at work. I don't get off until after two."

"Why are you at work?" he asked, sounding exasperated.

"Ummm. Because I have a job and I'm supposed to be here," I answered.

"I figured after what happened you'd take the night off."

"I can't do that, Zack. You know I need the money, now more than ever." My customer that had ordered the Long Island was giving me the evil eye across the bar. "I gotta go. I can come by after work if that's okay."

"I'll see you then."

I looked at the drink I was making and couldn't remember what I had already put in it. Fuck it. I dumped the whole thing down the sink and started over. I handed it to the customer and apologized for being distracted.

114

I looked at the clock over the bar. It was only eight. It was going to be a long night.

Lou bumped me with his shoulder. "You all right?"

"Yeah, just tired."

"Why don't you go take a break. I've got this covered."

I rarely took breaks. "Are you sure?"

"Absolutely. Go."

I gave Lou's arm a light squeeze. "Thanks. I won't be gone long." I threw my towel on the bar and headed back to the breakroom. I laid down on the old turquoise vinyl couch. It was uncomfortable as hell, but right now I didn't care. I just needed to close my eyes for ten minutes.

Chapter 18
Zack

Getting a call from Lou was not what I expected. He was drying glasses behind the bar when I walked in. He motioned to the breakroom, and I headed in that direction.

I quietly pushed open the door. Clarissa was fast asleep on the couch. She was curled up tightly, snoring softly. Her hair was fanned out around her head. She looked so peaceful, I hated to wake her.

I sat on the edge of the couch and gently shook her. "Sweetheart, wake up." She was out cold. "Clarissa, sweetheart, you need to get up."

Her eyes fluttered open. "Zack? How did you get in here?"

I smiled at her confusion. She was so damn cute when she was tired. "You're at work. Lou called me."

Her eyes popped fully open, and she bolted upright. "What time is it?"

"It's after midnight."

"Shit, shit, shit! I've been asleep for..." she mentally calculated "...four hours? Holy hell! Lou is gonna kill me."

I rubbed her back. "Relax. Lou isn't going to kill you. He said you were dead on your feet. He didn't have the heart to wake you, so he called me."

She rubbed her temples. "I can't do stuff like this. I have to get it together."

"Sweetheart, how many hours a week have you been working?"

"I don't know, like seventy."

I growled. "Seventy hours? That's ridiculous, Clarissa."

She glared at me. "I don't have a choice. I have to save up for when I have the baby. I won't be able to work for a few weeks and I'm going to need things. I can't afford the luxury of a forty-hour work week."

I let out a sigh and stood up. "Come on, I'm taking you home."

She hiked her thumb over her shoulder. "I have my car out back."

116

I grabbed her hand and pulled her up. "Leave your car here. I'm taking you to my place tonight."

"I don't think that's a good idea," she protested.

"It's one night. Besides, we have stuff to talk about," I insisted.

"I don't have pajamas or a toothbrush."

I laughed at her. "Now you're just making excuses. Let's go or I'll throw you over my shoulder and carry you out."

She glared at me. "You wouldn't."

"Wanna test me?" I leaned down and wrapped my arms around her waist.

"Okay, okay. I'll come over, but only for tonight!"

I held her hand and swung it between us as we walked back to Forever Inked. It felt right to be with her like this again. Perfect. She was perfect.

I thought about what my mom had said. If I wanted to keep her, I needed to make a decision and fast. I didn't want to risk her being with someone else.

I was lost in my own thoughts and so was she as we walked in a comfortable silence. Suddenly she stopped and turned her head towards the sky. "Oh, my God. It's snowing."

Sure enough, tiny flakes, barely big enough to see, floated through the air.

She let go of my hand, threw her arms out and turned in a circle, "I love the first snow."

I couldn't help but smile at her. She looked like an angel as the light from the lampposts glowed around her. "You don't get snow in Oklahoma, do you?" I asked.

"We get some. Maybe a couple of times a year, but nothing like New York. I love when everything is covered in a fresh blanket of white. The world is so quiet and peaceful."

I reached for her hand, and we made our way back to my apartment. I wished it were *our* apartment, and maybe with some time we'd be back there. I thought a lot about what my mom said. It would be torturous to watch her with someone else because I'd been too chickenshit to step up to the plate. I wasn't there yet, but I was getting closer.

Having her in my apartment was a step in the right direction. This is where she belonged, not in some dumpy craphole. She deserved better and I could give it to her. Now, I had to convince her.

She pulled off her high-heeled boots and dropped them by the front door. Her bare feet padded across the floor to the kitchen where she perched on a stool. "I hate to ask this, but what do you have to eat? I'm famished."

"I can make you scrambled eggs," I offered.

"Mmmm. That sounds divine. Are you sure it's not too much work?"

"It's scrambled eggs, not a five-course meal." I smirked at her. "When's the last time you ate?"

She tapped her finger against her lips. "I had cereal for breakfast."

"That's it? You have to do better than that. You're eating for two and that little girl needs food." She should have been taking better care of herself.

"I know. I just got busy and then I lost my appetite when I got the letter from Malcolm."

I appreciated that she called him Malcolm and not my *father*. I always called him father because he was never a dad to me. But even father was more than he deserved. I hated him before, but now I despised him.

"What were you doing that you didn't have time to eat? Doesn't Audrey give you breaks?" I asked as I cracked a couple of eggs in a bowl.

"I didn't work for Audrey this morning." She took a deep breath and picked at her nails. "I was with Bobby."

She was with Bobby? I'd seen the way he looked at her when she sang last week. I pretty much told him that it was over between us. I gave him the green light without even realizing it. If she ended up with Bobby... my heart sank. I didn't want to picture what that looked like. He could make all her dreams come true and could provide for her even better than I could. And I would have no one to blame but myself.

"What were you doing with Bobby?" I asked, trying to keep the jealousy out of my voice and concentrating on the eggs frying in the pan.

"Daniel wanted to record a demo. Bobby offered for us to use his private recording studio."

"That's cool," I said. Maybe it was all innocent.

"It was, until Daniel asked me to sign a contract to officially make him my agent. He shoved all these papers at me, and I freaked out. I didn't understand any of it. So, I asked Bobby what to do. He faxed them to his lawyer for me. He was a lifesaver. I don't know what I would have done without him."

If I hadn't been such a jerk, she would have asked me to go with her. I could have been her lifesaver, instead of Bobby. "Did you sign the contract?"

"Yeah. Bobby assured me it was on the up and up. I recorded three songs." She shrugged her shoulders. "I guess we'll see what happens. I really need this, otherwise I don't know how I'll be able to take care of us," she said rubbing her tummy.

I slid the eggs out of the pan onto a plate and placed them in front of Clarissa with a fork. "You shouldn't worry so much. Everything will work out."

She dug in and a look of complete contentment crossed her face. "God, Zack, these are so good. Thank you."

"It's just eggs, Clarissa. And I better not find a five-dollar bill after you leave."

"All I have is singles, so you won't." She smirked.

"Having you here is all I need," I said. "I want you to move back in." There. I'd thrown it out there. Now I needed her to grab a hold of it.

She dropped the fork on her plate. "I can't do that, Zack. It wouldn't be right."

"Why not?"

"Because I refuse to take advantage of you. I need to do this on my own." She picked her fork back up and pushed the eggs around on her plate. "I'm sorry I said I hate you. I don't hate you."

I leaned on the counter in front of her. "I know, sweetheart. You were just lashing out. I was an easy target and honestly, I can understand why you did."

"What am I going to do, Zack? I can't lose my baby." Tears filled her eyes and threatened to spill over.

I took her hand in mine. "You won't. My sister is a lost cause, but I talked to my mom. She's going to try to help us. And I called my lawyer. He's going to meet with us in the morning."

"Zack, I can't afford a lawyer. And I have to work in the morning." She dropped her head on the counter. "This is hopeless."

119

I lifted her chin and met her eyes. "It's not hopeless. It's my fault for telling my sister. Don't worry about the lawyer, I've got it covered. And I talked to Audrey. You don't have to go in until eleven. We'll have plenty of time."

I expected her to balk at me paying for the lawyer, but she didn't. She had resigned herself to the fact that she didn't have any choices left. "You talked to your mom? Does she know... everything?"

"She knows. She's the one who suggested I get you a lawyer."

"She thinks I'm trash," Clarissa said turning to the side.

I held her chin and turned her head back to me. "My mom doesn't think you're trash. And she was pretty damn excited to find out she's going to have a grandchild. I think you should give her a chance. I've never seen my mom go against Malcolm, so the fact that she wants to help, speaks volumes."

"I'm sorry. I just don't know who to trust anymore."

"Trust me. I'm going to be by your side through all of this. We're going to fight him and we're going to win."

"Promise?"

"I promise we'll find a way."

Clarissa finished her eggs and pushed her plate away. "I need to go to bed. Can I borrow a t-shirt?"

I threw her plate in the sink. "Of course. I'll get you a toothbrush too."

I got what she needed, and Clarissa headed to the bathroom. She came out a few minutes later in my t-shirt that hit her mid-thigh. I could see her baby bump beneath my shirt and all I wanted to do was rub my hand over it. Her body was changing, but she was beautiful.

Clarissa went to my room, grabbed a pillow and blanket, and settled in on the couch.

"What do you think you're doing?" I asked, standing before her.

"Going to sleep. I'm exhausted."

"You're not sleeping on the couch." I scooped her up in my arms and took her to my room. I gently placed her on her side of the bed. "This is where you belong."

"It's not a good idea, Zack," she protested.

"It's a perfect idea. There's plenty of room. We did it before. We can do it again," I insisted.

"I forgot how comfortable this bed is," she said as she snuggled under the blankets sleepily. "Just for tonight and no hanky-panky."

"Absolutely none," I chuckled.

She was sound asleep before I even turned off the light. I stripped down to my boxer briefs and crawled into my side of the bed. I crossed my arms behind my head and stared at the ceiling. My mom's words kept running through my head. If I didn't make a decision soon, I would lose her. Having Clarissa in my bed again reinforced how much I loved her. I couldn't lose her.

I was starting to drift off into sleep when her warm body wrapped around me and her head snuggled into my chest. "I love you," she muttered.

I looked down at her. She was dead to the world. I wrapped my arms around her. "I love you too, Clarissa Lynne," I whispered back.

Chapter 19
Rissa

The next morning, Zack's lawyer met with us. Jeff Masterson was a little older, probably in his late thirties. He was dressed casually, wearing jeans and a button-down shirt with the sleeves rolled up. I saw the edge of a tattoo peeking out under his sleeve.

He set me at ease right away. "Let's see what we're dealing with here. Do you have the letter?"

I handed him the envelope from inside my purse and he started to read it. "This is complete bullshit," he said pointing to the letter. "How in the hell did he find a judge to sign a court order for an amnio? It's practically unheard of."

"Doesn't surprise me a bit," Zack scoffed. "He probably has the judge in his back pocket along with a handful of politicians."

"The first thing we're going to do is rebut this order with a letter from your doctor, citing it as unsafe for you and the baby. No judge would go against the health of the mother." Jeff focused on me next. "Don't take this the wrong way, but I need full disclosure. Is there any chance the baby isn't Wes's?"

The question pissed me off, but I understood the need for it. "Absolutely not. He's the only one."

"Next question, about the drugs…"

"She doesn't do drugs," Zack interjected.

I appreciated Zack's support, but I need to confirm it myself. "I smoked a little pot when I was younger, but I've never done hard drugs. I'm not worried."

Jeff let out a sigh of relief. "That's good. We'll get your doctor to write a letter and do a hair follicle drug test. That should put to rest the accusation of being a drug addict and by putting off the paternity test, it gives us time to formulate a plan. Basically, it takes away their advantage. They won't have anything to act on until the paternity test is done."

"What about the pictures?" I asked.

Jeff pulled the pictures out of the envelope and scanned through them. "They've obviously had someone following you. Think, Rissa. Do you remember anyone or anything that seemed off?"

I took back the pictures and studied each one. One of them was me cleaning the front window at A Second Chance. I stared at it and the outfit I was wearing. Suddenly a light bulb went on. I pointed at the picture. "I remember this day. There was a black sedan parked across the street with dark windows. I asked Audrey about it."

"When was that?" Jeff asked. I told him the date and he scribbled it down on the notepad. "Anything else?"

I looked through the pictures again. The one taken at the bar caught my attention. "This was taken the next day. This guy came in and grabbed me by the wrist, trying to get me to go out with him. He creeped me out. I had Lou drive me home that night. That's when I decided to start driving to work."

Zack's lips twisted to the side. "Why didn't you tell me some creep was hitting on you?"

I glared at him. "You know why. Besides, I thought I was just being paranoid, but he was persistent."

"He probably wanted to prove that you were easy. Do you remember what he looked like?"

I gave Jeff the best description I could, and he wrote it all down. "He was creepy, but that's not what bothers me the most. How did they get pictures of the inside of my apartment? That's breaking and entering. Can they do that?"

"Absolutely not. They were probably looking for something incriminating but came up empty. The only thing they could do was show your living conditions. I'll be questioning the source of the picture. Maybe we can prove a pattern of harassment."

"Can they take my baby away based on my employment and apartment?" I asked.

"I can't make any promises. Usually I'd say no, but it seems like Malcolm has a lot of pull. I'm not sure what he can get away with. What are your plans for employment once the baby is born?"

I let out a huff. "I don't know. I don't really have any skills. Bartending is the only thing I know how to do."

"That's not true," Zack said. "She sings. Clarissa just made a demo of her music, and her agent is sending it out."

"It's not a sure thing," I countered.

"It's something," Jeff said. "We'll start with your doctor. I want you to change the locks on your apartment and be aware of your surroundings. Call me if anything is suspicious. If that guy comes back into the bar, try to get a picture of him."

I felt a little better by the time Jeff left. Maybe there was hope.

I liked spending time with Zack. We were a good team, but it wasn't just about the two of us anymore. Really it never was. I had just fooled myself into thinking he would accept my baby. Zack wasn't ready for a family, especially one where he wasn't the biological father. The sooner I accepted that, the better off I'd be. We could be friends, but that was where it had to end.

It meant no more kissing. No moving into his apartment. No sleeping in his bed. No taking advantage of his generosity, except for the lawyer. Him telling his sister about the baby was a loophole I'd gladly jump through.

And definitely, no sex.

I'd be lying if I said my body didn't crave him. I missed the way he looked at me like I was his favorite dessert and then devoured me as if to prove I was. I missed how he caressed my body and worshipped me. I missed the repeated orgasms he gave me without giving me a chance to come down. I missed the way our bodies fit together and the closeness we shared.

Most of all, I just missed him.

♪♪♪♪

I walked into A Second Chance and apologized to Audrey for coming in late.

"No need to apologize, Rissa. When Zack called, I assumed you two were working it out."

"We're not," I huffed. "I mean, we sort of are. We're friends again, but that's it." I told her about the letter from Malcolm and what happened yesterday. "He's helping me, but I think it's mostly out of guilt. It's also a big 'fuck you' to his father."

"So, you don't think he's in love with you? Because he sounded smitten when I talked to him on the phone."

"He loves me, but I don't think he's *in* love with me. Besides, he's got to love both of us," I rubbed my belly, "and I don't think he's capable of that. He doesn't want kids yet."

"How do you know?" she asked.

"He's made it pretty clear. When he went to my ultrasound appointment, he seemed freaked out afterwards. I'm not going to try to push him into something he doesn't want."

"Sometimes men don't know what they want. It takes a good woman to show them," Audrey said.

I'm sure she was trying to make me feel better, but she didn't know Zack the way I did. "Zack's not that kind of guy. He knows exactly what he wants and being a dad is not at the top of his list."

She frowned at me.

"It's okay, Audrey. Do I love him? Yes. Do I want him? Yes. Do I need him? No. I'm a strong, independent woman. I don't need a man to make me complete. And who knows, maybe one day I'll find someone who wants both of us. Until then, I'm fine being alone."

It was one of the biggest lies I had ever told. But maybe if I told it to myself long enough, I'd eventually believe it. I had to. There wasn't any other choice.

♪♪♪♪

When I got home from work, Zack was waiting outside my apartment sitting on the steps. I parked my Bronco next to his Chevelle and got out. "What are you doing here?"

He held up a bag from the hardware store. "I came to change your lock and fix your light."

I shook my head. "You didn't have to do that. It was on my list of things to do tomorrow."

"Now you don't have to. I'll have everything fixed before you go to work tonight." He kissed my temple in a friendly manner and followed me up the stairs.

I stuck my key in the lock and jiggled it open. "How much do I owe you?"

He followed me inside, shutting the door behind us. "Nothing."

"That's not the way this works, Zack." I tossed my purse on the couch.

"It was ten bucks. It's not a big deal."

I squinted at him. "You're an awful liar."

He threw his hands up. "Fine. Twenty."

I continued to glare at him.

"Twenty and not a penny more. I swear." He held up the scout's honor sign.

"I already know you weren't a boy scout, you big liar," I accused. I fished a twenty-dollar bill out of my purse. "I don't have time to fight with you. I have to take a shower and get ready for work." I slapped the twenty into his hand. "Thank you."

I pulled a shirt and jeans from my pile of clothes on the floor and headed to the bathroom. Zack being here when I got home totally threw me off. I didn't expect to see him for at least a couple of days.

I turned on the water in my tiny shower and let it get lukewarm, which was the best I ever got. I stepped under the spray and ran my hand through my hair. I wished I could get Zack out of my head, but it was impossible lately. I washed and conditioned my hair and then soaped up my pink body puff with my dollar store body wash. I scrubbed my skin clean and then rubbed between my legs.

As it ran over my clit, a wave of want and need ran through me. It was so wrong. While Zack was out there fixing my lock and light, I was standing in the shower thinking about the way he made me come.

I didn't want to want him, but I did. I rubbed a little more, making small circles with my fingers over my clit. I remembered all the things he'd

126

done to my body. The way he kissed me and licked me and made me feel like I was the only thing that mattered in those moments. I felt the stirring of an orgasm and couldn't force myself to stop. I kept going, chasing the feelings that Zack gave me.

My breaths came faster, and my muscles clenched tighter until I was on the edge. *Fuck me, Zack* was all I could think. I slumped back into the wall as the orgasm took over my body and wave after wave of pleasure racked my body. God, it felt so good. It was a pleasure I had denied myself since he'd left me. I basked in the afterglow, allowing myself to enjoy it while it lasted.

I turned off the shower, dried myself and got dressed. My jeans were too tight. Uncomfortably so. I would have to put shopping on my list of things to do. It was another expense I couldn't afford but was unavoidable.

I took a towel and wiped the steam off the mirror, so I could do my makeup and hair. Once I had pulled myself together, I checked on Zack's progress.

He handed me a new key. "This lock is better and more secure. Also, the light at the top of the stairs is triggered by a motion sensor. It should turn on automatically as soon as you pull up."

"Thank you." I switched out my keys. "You didn't have to do this."

"Yeah, I did. If you won't move back in with me, the least I can do is try to make sure you're safe."

My safety. That was what he cared about. It was something you would do for any friend. He cared about me as a friend. I silently kicked myself for getting lost in his memory while in the shower. Zack and I wouldn't ever be together like that again. It was stupid. I was stupid for daydreaming about something more. More was something I didn't deserve.

Maybe someday someone would want me regardless of the baggage I carried. Today was not that day. Nor was tomorrow. But someday maybe someone would want all of me, including my daughter. *Dare to dream* I told myself.

Zack left, and I headed off for work. I parked out back and came in through the rear entrance. I owed Lou an apology. A huge one. I went to his office and knocked on the open door.

Lou looked up from the papers in front of him on the desk and pulled his old man glasses off. "Hey, Rissa. How are you feeling?"

I stepped into his office and shut the door. "I'm sorry about last night. It won't happen again."

"It's no big deal. You were wiped out and obviously needed the sleep."

"It's more than that, Lou. I don't know how much longer I can work here."

He dropped his glasses on the desk and rubbed his hand over his grey beard. "Is this your two weeks' notice? Are you moving back to Oklahoma?"

I shook my head. "I'm not moving anytime soon, but I haven't been honest with you."

Lou quirked his eyebrow curiously. "Okay. What's this about? Are you in trouble?"

I let out a sarcastic laugh. "Trouble? My whole life has been trouble. I'm pregnant, Lou. I've been pregnant since before you hired me. I should have told you from the beginning, but I was afraid you wouldn't want a pregnant girl behind the bar, and I really needed the job."

"I see," he said tapping his fingers over his lips. "Is Zack the father?"

I knew this question would come. People would just assume it was his baby. I was done lying, "No. I got pregnant before Zack and I were together. The father died. I didn't tell Zack about it and that's why we broke up. I wasn't honest with him."

"He still loves you. I see the way he is with you."

I didn't really expect to be discussing my love life with Lou, but since he opened the door, I walked through it. "He might love me, but he doesn't love this," I said motioning to my belly. "We're a package deal, so although Zack and I care about each other, the most we'll ever be is friends."

Lou rocked back in his chair. "But you still love him?"

I shrugged my shoulders. "It doesn't really matter. He's not ready to be a dad and I can't hold that against him, even if I'd hoped he'd want the job." We'd talked enough about my personal life. That wasn't why I had come in here. I straightened in my chair. "So, about my job?"

"What about it?"

"I get it if you don't want me to work here anymore. I'm starting to show. I won't be able to hide it much longer."

128

He let out a little laugh. "You're the best bartender I've ever had. I don't give a shit if you're pregnant. You can work here as long as you feel up to it. You just have to promise you'll take breaks when you need them and not overdo it."

"What about your customers? Don't you think it'll weird them out?" I asked.

"If they don't like it, they can go somewhere else. Honestly, I don't think anyone will care. It's not like your sitting behind the bar drinking Tequila Sunrises."

"No danger of that." I got up, walked around the desk, and kissed Lou on the cheek. "Thanks, old man. You're the best."

"Yeah, well this old man is instituting mandatory breaks for you. Every two hours on the dot. More, if I think you're overdoing it. It's a condition of your employment, so no squawking," he insisted.

"I wouldn't squawk. I'm just happy you're not letting me go."

"The customers love you. They'd have my head if I fired you, so consider it self-preservation."

I laughed. "That's okay, Lou." I gave him a wink. "Don't worry. I won't tell anyone that underneath all the gruffness you exude is a man with a huge heart. It'll be our secret." I pretended to lock my lips and throw away the key.

He chuckled. "Get out of here and get to work."

I saluted him as I left his office. At least I wasn't going to lose my job.

Chapter 20
Zack

By the end of the week, Clarissa had a letter from Doc Peterson stating that the amnio would be dangerous to her health and the health of the baby. She also had the drug test results that cleared her of any drug use for the past ninety days.

Jeff got busy filing the proper paperwork to stop the court order. There was nothing my father could legally do until paternity was confirmed. That gave us some time to come up with a legal plan.

It also gave me time to come up with a plan of my own. I called my mom to see if she had found anything out.

"Hey, honey."

"Hi, Mom. I wanted to give you an update. I got Clarissa a lawyer."

"Clarissa? I thought her name was Rissa?" my mom said with confusion.

"It is, but her full name is Clarissa. No one ever calls her that because she was embarrassed of her Oklahoma roots. She didn't want people calling her Clarissa Lynne, so she shortened it to Rissa. She thought Rissa would be better for New York, but she's Clarissa to me," I explained.

"Clarissa is a pretty name. Has she thought about names for my granddaughter yet?"

That was a good question, but I had no answer. "I don't know. She hasn't said."

"Did you ask her?"

"No," I said sheepishly.

"Zack, have you talked to her at all about the baby?" she asked.

"Not really. I don't know what to say, except that I don't want Malcolm to get custody."

"You haven't told her yet, have you?"

"She knows I love her," I said.

"Does she?"

"Yes. It's just," I stumbled for the words. "I don't think I can be a father. Not to Wes's kid anyway. She loved him. I don't doubt that. But every time she looks at that baby she'll think of Wes. I can't be a replacement for what she lost. I can't compete with a ghost."

"I see. Well, you need to do what's right for you. You'll make a great uncle."

I wasn't sure, but I thought my mom was doing some reverse psychology on me. My mom may have always played second fiddle to my father, but she was in no way inferior. She graduated from Harvard with a degree in business. She was a shrewd businesswoman whose skills had been used primarily to plan charity functions that cast Kincaid Industries in the best light possible. She was not to be underestimated.

Malcolm had always undervalued my mother. He saw her kind heart as a weakness. He was so wrong. It was her greatest strength.

She always supported Wes, Ronnie, and me. When I went into the Marines, she cried and told me to stay safe. She wrote me letters every week and sent me care packages, I was sure Malcolm knew nothing about. I never told her, but her support was what got me through some of my hardest times.

When I came home three years later, I let Malcolm put a wedge between my mom and me. I couldn't understand how she let him control her. Somewhere along the line, my mom had lost her way. I guess I gave up on thinking we could have a normal relationship. I hated him, and I resented her for being his pawn.

"I'm thinking of coming for a visit," my mom said.

She couldn't have shocked me more if she had tried. "You're coming here? Why? You've never come here."

My mom let out a big sigh. "I know. I haven't made much of an effort to be part of your life and I want to change that. I want to know my son again. I've let your father keep us apart and I'm done with that. I didn't take the time to do it with Wes and now I'll never get that chance. Do you know that I never saw him perform? Not even once?"

I could hear the sadness and regret in her voice. "He knew you loved him, Mom."

131

"Maybe, but I could have and should have done more. I'm not going to let that happen to us. I want to know what makes you happy. I want to know who you are when you're not so angry with your father."

"When are you coming?" I asked, still shocked that she was actually coming here.

"The end of the week?"

"What about Malcolm? What does he have to say about this?"

"Your father will barely know I'm gone. He's too busy trying to make people's lives miserable. I'll tell him I'm going to a spa or something."

"Mom, what's going on? Are you and him fighting?" I asked suspiciously.

"We don't fight, Zack. We barely talk, but enough about him. Is Friday okay?"

"It's fine. Send me your flight information and I'll pick you up from the airport." I couldn't believe my mom was coming here. "Do you want to stay with me or are you going to stay in a hotel?"

"I'd like to stay with you if that's all right," she answered.

"It's fine, but you do realize I live over a tattoo parlor, right? It's not the Four Seasons," I reminded her.

"I said I wanted to get to know my son again. I don't care where I stay, as long as I get to be with you." She paused and then sounding unsure asked, "Do you think I could see Rissa while I'm there? Do you think she'd forgive me?"

"Forgive you for what?" As far as I knew Clarissa's hate was for Malcolm, not my mom.

"I should have stood up for her. I should have made more of an effort to make her part of this family. Now she's having my grandchild and I need to make amends. I want to be there for her now, even if I wasn't before."

"I think she'd like that, Mom." I smiled even though she couldn't see me.

♫♪♫♪

I'd barely seen Clarissa all week. If I didn't know better, I'd think she was avoiding me.

Gina came in on Wednesday. She'd kept things platonic, like she promised she would. There were no more sexy outfits or impromptu stripteases.

We sat in my studio while she was on her lunch break. "Is your father really trying to get custody of Rissa's baby?" she asked.

"Yeah. Did Doc Peterson tell you that?" I asked. I assumed Clarissa wouldn't have volunteered that information to Gina.

"No. I overheard them talking. I wasn't eavesdropping. I swear."

"It's fine. I got her a lawyer. I'll do whatever I can to help her."

Gina nodded. "I don't hate her," she blurted out. "I was just jealous, I guess. She seems really sweet. I wouldn't wish this on her, even if I wasn't her biggest fan."

"She is sweet," I confirmed.

"Are you two together? You came with her to her appointment, so I wasn't sure," she asked.

"We're not together. I don't know what we are right now. She's my friend and I'm helping her is all."

I heard a light knock on the door and Clarissa peeked her head in. She looked between Gina and me. "I'm sorry to interrupt. I was going to do my laundry, if that's all right."

Her hair was pulled up on top of her head, the curls sticking out in all directions. "It's fine. I left the door open for you."

She gave me a weak smile. "Thanks." She shut the door and was gone.

Gina stared at me and shook her head. "You should see your face right now."

I frowned at her. "What do you mean?"

"Every time you look at her you just seem… happy. You get this little twinkle in your eyes."

"I don't fucking get a twinkle in my eyes," I protested at her ridiculousness.

She laughed. "Yeah, you do. What are you afraid of?"

I contemplate my answer. Was I afraid? I didn't know. Instead of giving her a real answered I lied. "Nothing. We're just friends. Nothing more."

133

Chapter 21
Rissa

It shouldn't have bothered me, but it did. I heard Zack and Gina talking before I interrupted them. *We're not together. I don't know what we are right now. She's my friend and I'm helping her is all.*

I left my five dollars on the counter and left as soon as I could. Next time I would use the crappy laundromat down the street.

I loaded my clothes back into my Bronco. It was super cold out today. I had on one of Wes's old sweatshirts because it was cozy and nothing else fit. I couldn't continue to walk around with the top button of my jeans undone just because they were too tight. I needed to get some maternity clothes that fit properly.

When I got back to my apartment and unloaded my car, I called Tori. She would know where to go shopping. I could hear a bunch of commotion in the background when she picked up. "Hey, Rissa. How are you?"

"Fine. I need to go shopping for maternity clothes. I was wondering if you had any suggestions."

I heard a door click and the noise in the background died down. "You know, I have a bunch of stuff you could borrow. We're about the same size."

"Oh, no. I couldn't. If you could just point me in the right direction, I'd appreciate it."

"Rissa, don't be stubborn. It's not like I'll be wearing them anytime soon. What are you doing tonight?" she asked.

"I actually have the night off."

"Great! Kyla and I are taking you to dinner. She and Tyler are here now, and the guys can handle the kids. We need a girls' night."

"Are you sure? I don't want to impose."

"Are you kidding? You'll be doing us a favor. Do you remember where P.F. Chang's is?"

"I can find it," I assured her.

134

"Great! We'll meet you in an hour."

I hung up feeling a little bit better. Maybe girl time was what I needed to get me out of my funk.

I sat back on my couch and brainstormed where I could get some extra money without dipping into my savings. I stared at the boxes that sat in the corner of my apartment. God, I was so stupid. I worked at a resale shop. Some of those boxes were filled with stuff that could sustain me for weeks.

I got off the couch and started riffling through the boxes. I pulled out the Chanel and Louis Vuitton bags Wes had bought me. They were in pristine condition. I continued to go through the boxes, removing shoes and expensive dresses I no longer had use for. Before I went to dinner, I had a substantial pile of clothes I would take with me to A Second Chance tomorrow. I was sure Audrey would be okay with me selling my stuff at her boutique.

♫♪♫♪

I waited outside for the girls to get there. I didn't have to wait long before Tori and Kyla met me. When I first met Kyla, I thought I would hate her, but I actually liked her a lot. She and Tori had become my closest girlfriends next to Layla.

When our appetizers arrived, Tori popped a green bean into her mouth and got down to business. "So, what's up with you and Zack?"

"Nothing. I think he's seeing Gina." I shrugged my shoulders. "We're back to being friends."

Kyla took a sip of her Captain and diet Coke. "He's an idiot."

I laughed at her. "I thought you two were close."

"We are, but that doesn't mean he's not an idiot. He has no idea what he has, and he's letting it slip away," she said.

I sipped on my Sprite, wishing it were a mixed drink. "He's not ready to be a dad. I can't fault him for that. If anything, he should be pissed at me. I'm the one who lied."

Tori smirked at Kyla. "Does this feel like déjà vu to you?"

I looked between the two of them who obviously shared a secret. "What's going on?"

"Let me tell you a story," Kyla started.

135

By the end of our dinner, I had a new appreciation for Kyla. She'd been through hell and back and she survived. She not only survived, but she was happy. She got the guy, the family, and the life she always wanted.

I wished I could feel some comfort by it, but I couldn't. Things may have worked out for her, but it didn't mean they would for me.

After dinner we did some shopping and I left with a few things to tide me over until I could afford more. Tori had also given me a bag full of maternity clothes. I would be set for a while, and it was a relief.

When I got home, I tried to call Daniel to see if he had heard anything about my demo yet. The line rang and rang, then finally went to voicemail. I left a brief message. It'd been almost two weeks. If I hadn't heard anything yet, chances were, I wouldn't.

♫♪♫♪

The next morning, I walked into A Second Chance with my arms loaded full of expensive clothes and accessories. I dropped everything on the counter.

"What's all this?" Audrey asked.

"Shit to sell," I answered.

Audrey pulled a Chanel bag from the pile and inspected it. "Where the hell did you get this stuff?"

"Wes bought it for me. I don't have anywhere to wear it, so I'm selling it."

She pulled a black sequined dress from the pile and held it up. "Are you sure?"

"Yep. He bought that for me for a fundraiser we attended. I doubt I'll ever need it again."

"Rissa, this is expensive. You said Wes had money, but damn girl," she whistled.

"He was a millionaire. Money didn't mean that much to him, and he always spoiled me," I admitted.

"So…" Audrey tapped her finger on her chin. "Does that mean that Zack has money too?"

"Yep. A boatload I'm guessing."

136

Audrey started pulling everything from the pile, inspecting each item. "I had no idea. He doesn't seem the type. I mean, I knew he had a successful business, but shit."

"So, can I sell this stuff here?"

"Absolutely. Why don't you change the window display? This stuff is sure to bring in some business."

I spent the rest of the morning steaming the dresses and creating a stunning window display. What didn't fit in the window was placed strategically throughout the store. Audrey looked everything up online and determined what we should price each item for. If I sold even half of my things, it would help tremendously.

Chapter 22
Zack

My mom coming to visit shouldn't have made me nervous, but it did. She was going to see what my life was like. Not the privileged upbringing I had, but the real me.

I went and bought all new bedding for Clarissa's old room. I hesitated outside the door. I hadn't been in this room since the day she left. The day I kicked her out. Since then, the door had remained closed. I didn't need the memories flooding me every time I walked by.

I pushed the door open and placed the freshly washed sheets on the bed. Her scent filled my senses. If I closed my eyes, I could picture her here. The pile of cash she left was still there, along with her notebook and that stupid pig.

I glanced at the wall where I had thrown the jar and smashed it into a million pieces. It was time to move forward and clean up the mess that was my life. I laid across the bare mattress and stared at the floor.

The glass that should have been there was gone. I scrambled off the bed and searched the floor. Every last bit of evidence of my anger had been swept away. I knew my cleaning lady, Linda, hadn't done it. I banned her from this room. That only left Clarissa. She was the only one who would have cleaned up my mess.

She'd never said a word about it, but I wasn't surprised. That was the way Clarissa was. She had always taken care of me. I missed it.

I moved what was left of her things to my room and tucked them away in the bottom drawer of my dresser, along with the diamond collar I bought her. The memories of the time we'd spent together invaded my mind. I tried so hard to push them away, but they just wouldn't go. Everything reminded me of her.

I went back to Clarissa's room and made the bed with the clean sheets. Then I prepared the rest of my apartment for my mom's arrival. She was going to hate it here. I was sure of it.

♫♪♫♪

I met my mom by baggage claim. She was dressed as I would have expected. She wore cashmere pants and an expensive trench coat. Heeled boots adorned her feet, and I could see her signature pearls peeking out from the top of her coat. My mom was a beautiful woman, but she looked tired.

I approached her in my black jeans and black leather jacket. I hadn't removed any of my piercings. If she wanted to see me, this is who I was.

When her eyes met mine, she smiled. I leaned down to hug her, and she wrapped her arms tightly around me. "I'm so happy to see you, Zack."

"Me too." I kissed her cheek.

We waited for her luggage, and I pulled it off the revolving conveyor belt. I wheeled her suitcase to the curb. "Wait here and I'll get the car," I said.

"Nonsense. I can walk," she insisted. I led her to my Chevelle and opened the door for her. After I put her luggage in the trunk, I jumped into the driver's seat.

My mom looked around the inside of my vehicle. She was taking in every little detail of the muscle car that was my pride and joy. I chuckled. "It's not a Mercedes."

"No, but I like it. It suits you."

We drove the forty-five minutes to my shop in relative silence. The trip from the airport to home wasn't the prettiest. We passed some burned out houses and even a few hookers, Detroit's finest. I saw the panic in my mom's eyes, thinking this is where I lived.

By the time we reached the suburbs, she had relaxed back into her seat. It wasn't fancy, but it was safe and clean. I pulled around the back of my shop. "This is it," I said.

"This is where you work?" she asked.

"I own the building. My shop is on the bottom and my apartment is above it," I explained.

139

"Well, let's see it." She opened her door, and I quickly grabbed her suitcase from the trunk.

We went in through the back door and I could hear the rock music pouring through the speakers. I opened the door to the right that led to my apartment. "After you."

My mom held onto the railing as she ascended the stairs. I unlocked the door for her and led us inside. She walked in and looked around. A slow smile spread across her face. "This is really nice, Zack."

"It's not much, but it's all I need and it's home."

Priss came out of hiding and rubbed on my mom's ankles. My mom picked her up and snuggled her. "How come I didn't know you had a cat?"

I shrugged my shoulders. "I guess it never came up. That's Miss Priss. She's a sweetheart." I rolled her suitcase towards Clarissa's old room. "This is where you'll be staying, unless you change your mind and want to stay in a hotel."

My mom untied the belt on her coat. "No, this is perfect."

She followed me into the bedroom and laid her coat on the bed. She took in the light-colored furniture and the feminine touches of the room, the colorful throw pillows, and flowing curtains. "Was this Rissa's room?"

"Yeah. It used to be my art studio, but when she came here, I changed it." I shrugged. "I wanted her to be happy."

"And was she?"

"She was, until I kicked her out. Now she lives a couple of blocks over in the shittiest apartment I've ever seen. I asked her to move back, but she won't. She's stubborn as hell."

"I don't think it's stubbornness. I have a feeling it's pride."

I rolled my eyes. "Trust me, where she's living isn't something to be proud of."

"But she's surviving on her own? Has her own apartment, her own car, works hard to support herself?"

"She works like a dog. Two jobs and seventy hours a week. It borders on ridiculous, Mom. She won't take a dime from me. When she does laundry here, she leaves five bucks on the counter."

My mom laughed. "Okay, maybe she's a little stubborn. But you need to remember, the Kincaid men have had a big impact on her life. Your father is fighting her for custody, your brother died on her, and you kicked her out. I wouldn't blame her for having trust issues."

I sat on the bed. "Thanks for reminding me."

She sat next to me and put her hand on my leg. "Hey, I'm not judging. I wasn't any better. I should have stood up for her and I didn't. We can't go back, but we sure as hell can move forward. We have to earn her trust again."

I knew she was right, even if I didn't like it. "You want a drink? I want one." I stood from the bed and went to the kitchen, my mom following behind. "I bought you a bottle of wine. It's a Cabernet from Napa Valley."

"Sounds good," she said, settling herself on the bar stool.

I pulled two rock glasses from the cupboard. I poured Jim Beam into mine and filled hers with wine. "Sorry. I don't have any wine glasses."

She waved me off. "I'm not a snob, Zack. Wine is wine no matter what I drink it out of."

I laughed. This was the mom I remembered from my youth. We sat and talked and got to know each other again, enjoying each other's company. Before we both got too tipsy, we decided to get something to eat. It was almost eight o'clock and neither of us had eaten in a while. I suggested a couple of places within walking distance, but she wanted to go to The Locker since Clarissa was singing tonight.

"Did you bring jeans?" I asked. "This place isn't fancy, Mom. It's a bar."

She held up a finger. "I bought a pair just for this trip. I haven't worn jeans in forever, so I hope they're all right. Will this shirt be okay?"

I looked at her silk blouse that cost more than Clarissa's rent. "I have an idea. I'll be right back." I ran down to the shop and pulled out a black woman's t-shirt with Forever Inked scrawled across the front in cursive. I took it back upstairs and handed it to her. "Try this."

She inspected the shirt. "Is this your business?"

"Yep."

She straightened her shoulders. "Then I'll wear it proudly." She went to Clarissa's room and shut the door.

I wasn't sure who this woman was, but I liked her. A lot. Malcolm had stifled my mom for years. Being here, she was like a butterfly that had broken free of its cocoon, and her wings were beautiful.

She opened the door a few minutes later and smoothed her hands down her jeans. "Does this look okay?"

I took in my mom from her black t-shirt down to her black high-heeled boots. "You look hot, Mom," I said with a smirk. "Don't be surprised if you get hit on tonight."

She lifted her chin and strode towards the door. "I'll take that as a compliment."

I took Clarissa's black leather coat from behind the door and helped my mom into it. My mom checked out my shop as we walked through to the front door. "I want you to show me around down here tomorrow," she insisted.

"Will do." I smiled at her.

We walked the half block to The Locker and went right to the bar where Lou was pouring drinks. He saw us and came over, slinging his towel over his shoulder. "Hey, Zack." He motioned with his chin to my mom. "Who's the hot chick?"

My mom giggled. Yeah, actually giggled as she reached her hand over the bar. "I'm Zack's mom, Catherine."

Lou took her hand and kissed the back of it while I rolled my eyes. "Well, it's easy to see where Zack got his good looks. It's a pleasure to meet you, Catherine," Lou flirted.

I pulled my mom's hand back from his grasp. "Hands off, old man. I'll have a Jim on the rocks and red wine for my mom."

"Actually," my mom piped up. "I'll have a Grey Goose martini, two olives." She wiggled her eyebrows. "Make it extra dirty."

Lou stared at her for a moment and then tapped on the bar. "Whatever the lady wants." Lou quickly made our drinks and slid them across to us.

We found a table and sat down. "You were flirting with Lou," I scolded her.

My mom brought a hand to her chest. "Was I?"

"Yes," I hissed. "What's gotten into you? First, you surprise me by coming here to visit. Next thing I know, you're wearing jeans, ordering martinis, and flirting with Lou."

My mom set her drink on the table and pinned me with green eyes that mirrored mine. "I wasn't going to tell you this until later, but I'm divorcing your father."

I leaned back in my chair absorbing the words she had just told me. "Wow." I let the information sink in for a moment. "What does he have to say about this?"

She reached for her pearls that were no longer at her neck. "He doesn't know yet, but I suspect he's going to put up a fight. It'll tarnish the Kincaid image."

"How long have you been planning this?" I asked. I was shocked because I never thought my mom would leave Malcolm, but relieved because she deserved so much better. I'd watched her identity disappear over the years and she'd become a shell of her former self.

"Since your brother died. The way he handled everything was so callous and cold. And then his fight with you practically broke my heart."

"You don't have to do this for us, mom."

She took a sip of her martini. "I'm not. I'm doing it for me. We haven't loved each other in years. What we have is more of a business arrangement than a marriage. I'm pretty sure he's been cheating on me. We haven't had sex in months."

I held my hands up. "Too much information. I don't need to know that."

She gave her shoulders a little lift. "I'm lonely. I don't want to spend the rest of my life with a miserable man in a loveless marriage."

"Did you ever love him?" I asked out of curiosity.

"Very much so. He was handsome, driven, and quite charming when he was younger. He was quite the catch." She smiled coyly. "But over time he became power hungry and all he cared about was status and money. His relationship with you should have been my first clue. I tried to tell myself that it was because you were both hard-headed, but it was always deeper than that."

"I was a disappointment to him, and he never let me forget it. Nothing I did was ever good enough. He wanted me to share his love of Kincaid Industries, but I had my own dreams and he hated that. One of the reasons I dropped out of Yale was because I was afraid of turning into him," I admitted.

My mom cupped my cheek. "You never had to worry about that. Your heart is too pure."

143

"You should have seen the way I treated Clarissa," I huffed. "The apple didn't fall far from the tree. I was awful to her. I'm amazed she even talks to me at all."

"The fact that you feel bad about it, proves that you're not cut from the same cloth. Your father doesn't feel guilty about anything, including trying to get custody of Rissa's baby. It was the last straw for me."

My mom and I ordered bar burgers and fries. She said she hadn't had a greasy bar burger since college, and she devoured every last bite. We were just finishing our dinner when Clarissa took the stage. She was wearing something similar to what she wore the last time I saw her perform and she looked just as beautiful. She was glowing.

She had no idea that my mom and I were here. As a matter of fact, I hadn't told her my mom was visiting.

She grabbed the mic. "Hey, y'all. Thanks fer comin' out tonight. I've got a couple of new ones for you and a surprise I think you're going to love." She sat on the barstool and adjusted her guitar on her lap. "This first one has been my inspiration lately to pick myself up and start over."

Clarissa started playing a song I didn't know but immediately hated it. She was telling me she was done. My mom leaned over and whispered in my ear. "I love Sara Evans. "*A Little Bit Stronger*" is one of my favorite songs." She hummed along with the tune, but all I heard was the finality of the words. Clarissa had given up on me.

Each song she sang cut me a little deeper. There was definitely a theme to tonight's show. I felt like it was the "Fuck Zack" show. Her voice was strong and sexy, just like her. She was lost in the music barely seeing the crowd shrouded in darkness that adored her. I wanted her to see me. I wanted her to... fuck I didn't even know what I wanted.

Lou personally brought another round of drinks to our table. He chatted and flirted with my mom, and she giggled like a schoolgirl. This night couldn't have been any weirder if I had planned it. Or so I thought.

Clarissa grabbed the mic again and started addressing the crowd. "I told y'all that I had a surprise for you. So, will you please help me in welcoming someone who needs no introduction." She motioned to the side of the stage and Bobby walked up to join her. Everyone in the bar went crazy.

"You've got to be fucking kidding me," I mumbled.

144

Bobby kissed Clarissa on the cheek then took ahold of the mic. "I don't usually sing in bars anymore, but when Rissa called and asked me to join her, I just couldn't say no."

"What's wrong?" my mom asked. "You look like you're going to kill someone."

I waved my hand at the stage. "Him. He's trying to steal my girl. I knew it, I just knew it."

"I thought you decided you didn't want to be in a relationship with her. I thought you were just friends."

I scowled. "We are. But just because Clarissa and I aren't together doesn't mean he can swoop in and try to steal her."

"You can't have it both ways, Zack. I warned you this might happen."

"Yeah, well it sucks."

I watched as they did the song she had done at his concert. Memories of that night filled my head. The way she laughed when someone asked for her autograph. The way she danced with me. The way we made love that night. The way I held her tight to my chest as she rode me up and down. It was one of the best nights of my life and now it was being tarnished by Bobby.

"You have to let her go, Zack."

"I don't want to. She's mine," I insisted.

"She needs someone who's going to love her *and* the baby. If you can't do that, then you have to let her go. Even if it hurts."

I turned away from my mom. I knew she was right, but I didn't want to hear it.

Bobby and Clarissa sang a few upbeat songs together and then they ended the show singing a lovey dovey duet.

I hated it.

I hated seeing them together.

I hated that she looked happy.

I hated that she was happy without me.

When the lights came up Bobby kissed Clarissa on the cheek again and then headed towards the bar. He was immediately flocked by fans. He stopped and took photos and signed some autographs.

When Bobby got to the bar, I pushed my chair back leaving my mom at the table. I sidled up next to him. "What are you doing here?"

145

"Hey, Zack. Thought I might see you here. What's up?" He held up his fist for me to bump.

I ignored the gesture. "What are you doing here, Bobby?"

Lou placed a drink in front of him and he knocked it back. "I'm sensing some tension here. What's the problem?"

I motioned to the stage. "You and Clarissa."

He shrugged his shoulders. "She asked me to sing with her and I said yes. What's the problem?"

"She's mine, that's the problem," I growled.

"Is she? Because last I heard, you gave her up."

I glared at him. "She's pregnant."

"Yeah, I know."

"And that doesn't bother you?" I asked.

"Why should it? It doesn't change anything about who she is. She's a sweet girl who deserves a break. I'm just trying to help her right now and be a friend. If it turns into something more…"

"It's not going to turn into something more," I growled again.

"That's not really your decision. It's ours."

"You'll never love her the way I do." I poked him in the chest.

He held up his empty glass and Lou brought him a refill. "Maybe you should tell her that, instead of me."

Chapter 23
Rissa

I looked up from the stage and saw someone I never thought I'd see again. What was she doing here? I recognized her face, but the clothes had me second guessing myself.

I walked toward the table and her green eyes, so much like Wes's, met mine. "Catherine?"

She stood up and held her arms out. I don't know why but I walked right into them. After a tight hug she released me. "What are you doing here?" I asked.

She motioned to the bar where Zack was talking with Bobby. "I came to see my son and the mother of my granddaughter." She held my hands, and we sat down. "I need to apologize to you, Rissa. I'm so sorry that I didn't stand up for you. I wasn't strong enough, but I am now, and I want to make it right."

Her words shocked me. "I don't know what to say." It was the truth. I was lost for words.

"Say you'll forgive me for being weak." She reached for her neck but dropped her hand. "I'm divorcing Malcolm."

I leaned back in the chair. "Wow. What does Malcolm think of that? I can't imagine he'd allow that to happen without a fight."

She let out a little laugh. "You sound just like Zack. He said the exact same thing. To answer your question, Malcolm doesn't know yet. It's going to be ugly." She got a little tear in her eye and wiped it away. "So, tell me about you. I didn't know you could sing like that. You have a beautiful voice."

"Wes and I used to sing together all the time. When I came here, Zack encouraged me to start again. Bobby is helping me try to get a recording contract. I did a demo, but I haven't heard anything back yet."

"That's so exciting for you. I think you've got a good chance. When you become a big star, will you still let me see my granddaughter?" she asked.

I laughed. "I doubt very seriously that I'll ever be famous, but if you want to see your granddaughter, I'd never keep her from you. She should have at least one grandma."

Catherine nodded to my stomach. "May I?"

"Of course."

She lightly rubbed her hand over my protruding belly. "When are you due?"

"Not until March."

"Did Wes know you were pregnant?"

I nodded. "He did. We were really happy about it. But then…"

Zack returned to the table with a scowl on his face. His voice was harsh when he addressed me. "Nice show."

I smiled weakly. "Thanks."

Then he focused on Catherine. "I'll be waiting outside when you're ready." And with that he abruptly left.

I watched him walk out the door. "What's up his ass?" I asked.

"Never mind him. I think he's getting a dose of reality."

I didn't know what that meant, but I was getting used to Zack's Jekyll and Hyde antics. I must have pissed him off again, but about what, I had no idea.

Catherine grabbed my hand and commanded my attention. "I'd like to take you to lunch tomorrow, if that's okay."

I didn't know what to make of this sudden change in Catherine, but I agreed anyway. I couldn't see that it would hurt. "Sure, but it'll have to be more of an early dinner. I don't get off from my other job until three and then I have to be back here at six. I can meet you at Zack's shop if you like."

Her face lit up, "That would be wonderful." She stood and gave me another hug, "I should get going, before he wears a hole in the sidewalk pacing. I'll see you tomorrow."

I watched Catherine leave wearing jeans and a Forever Inked t-shirt. I internally laughed. I never thought I'd see the day she looked more like a barfly than a wealthy socialite. I tapped my fingers on the table, wondering what the catch was.

When I was with Wes, Catherine was always kind to me, but she never went out of her way to include me in anything. After he died, I never heard from her. She had to have known I came here with Zack, but yet no one seemed to care. It was as if I didn't exist.

Honestly, it hadn't really bothered me. I was nothing to the Kincaids. I was almost relieved to be rid of them and their hoity-toity ways. I wasn't sure how Wes and Zack had escaped their pretentiousness, but I hadn't questioned it.

To trust Catherine or not? That was the question. All of a sudden, she cared about me? It was hard to believe. There had to be an ulterior motive, I just wasn't sure what it was.

I was going to dinner with her tomorrow, and I would kill her with kindness. I was a hick for sure, but I wasn't stupid. *Keep your friends close, and your enemies closer.* Wasn't that what they said? I was going to figure this out and I decided... I didn't trust her. Not one little bit.

I was mulling everything over when Bobby sat down next to me. "Don't look so serious."

"Sorry. Weird night," I said shaking myself out of my thoughts.

"You're telling me," he responded. "Zack just flipped the fuck out on me."

I pulled back in surprise. "Really? What about?"

Bobby let out a low laugh. "You."

"Me?" I clasped my chest. "What about me?"

Bobby laughed again. "He thinks I'm trying to steal you away from him. That guy is so in love with you, it's damn near pathetic."

I shook my head. "He's ridiculous. I gave him a chance. I made it known that I loved him, and he's made it known to everyone that we're just *friends*," I finger-quoted. "He might love me, but he doesn't want to be with me or this baby." I patted my stomach.

"Seems he doesn't want anyone else to be with you either. He poked me in the chest and told me I would never love you like he does."

"Well, flippin' flapjacks. What am I supposed to do with that?" I asked with exasperation. "What's he going to do, chase off anyone who shows interest in me?"

Bobby picked up my hand. "He doesn't scare me."

"No?" I asked.

"Nope," he said with a devious smile.

149

"Just what are you proposing?"

He tapped on his chin, "I'm not sure yet, but jealousy is an evil bitch."

♫♪♫♪

I changed into a nice pair of slacks and a cute long-sleeved blouse Tori had given me. I steamed them in the backroom of A Second Chance and changed from my work clothes.

"You look nice." Audrey admired me through the mirror I stood in front of.

I let out a little sigh. "I'm meeting Zack's mom for dinner. She's classy and I don't want to look like a bumpkin from Oklahoma."

Audrey stepped behind me and grasped my shoulders. "No one sees you like that. It's all in your head."

I had always felt scrutinized by Malcolm. He made me feel small and insignificant and trashy. His not so subtle digs at my upbringing and his perceived notion of my intentions were thinly veiled insults. It pissed him off that he had never chased me away. I wouldn't let him do that, instead it had fueled my hate of him.

Catherine had stood beside him and watched it all, never intervening.

"Well, I haven't talked to Catherine since Wes's funeral. She seems to want a relationship with me, but I don't trust her. The timing is too coincidental. First, I get a letter from Malcolm threatening to take away my baby and then Zack's mom just shows up out of the blue. Something smells fishy."

"Maybe it's caviar and it'll be divine," Audrey encouraged.

"It could be, but maybe it's a Mississippi mud catfish with whiskers and beady eyes." I rubbed at my neck. "I wish I had the necklace and earrings Wes gave me. They would give this outfit the little extra it needs."

"Wait here," Audrey instructed. She returned carrying a sapphire pendant and earrings that matched my blouse perfectly. "Try these."

I held them up to the light. "Are these real? They're gorgeous."

Audrey shrugged her shoulders. "I doubt it. I got them on eBay for a song, but they look real enough for tonight."

150

I fastened the clasp around my neck and slipped the earrings in. "Thank you, Audrey."

She winked at me. "Just bring them back tomorrow."

"I will." I pulled on my coat and grabbed my purse. "Wish me luck."

"Remember, you're a strong, independent woman. Don't let anyone make you feel like less." Audrey hugged me as I walked out the door towards Forever Inked.

I pulled my coat tightly around me, trying to fend off the cold November breeze. When I arrived at Zack's shop, I took a deep breath and reached for the handle. *I'm a strong, independent woman,* I repeated Audrey's words to myself. The door jingled as I opened it, announcing my arrival.

Layla stepped out from her studio and smiled at me. "Hey, girl. Where've you been?"

I strode over and gave her a warm hug. "I've been busy working and trying to get this music thing off the ground."

"I've missed you. We need to do lunch or coffee. Hanging around here, I need some serious girl time."

I let out a little laugh. "I would love that. Where's Mr. Broody Pants?"

Layla huffed. "Skulking around here somewhere. Seriously, Rissa, you should just fuck him or blow him or something. He's like a miserable little gremlin." She held up her hands in claws and growled to emphasize her point.

I couldn't help but laugh at her imitation of him.

Zack emerged from his studio with a scowl that I had become accustomed to. "I can hear you, you know?"

Layla quickly pulled her hands behind her back and stared at the ceiling innocently. "Hear what?" she asked.

He glared at her with his arms crossed over his chest. "Remember that raise I promised you? It's in serious jeopardy."

Layla leaned in close to me. "See what I mean?"

I pulled my hand over my mouth to hide my amusement. "Where's Catherine?" I asked.

"You don't say hello to me anymore?" He continued to scowl.

I swayed over to him and kissed his pouty lips. "Hello."

I felt his lips turn upward and his hands grasped my hips. "Hi."

151

"It's just like Sleeping Beauty," Layla gasped, grabbing her chest. "One kiss and he's Prince Charming again."

Zack flipped her the bird. "Fuck off." Then his lips pressed against mine to continue the kiss.

"And back to a gremlin, just like that." Layla snapped her fingers. "Seriously, Rissa, help a woman out."

"Sorry. You're on your own." I winked at her.

Layla let out a frustrated huff and stomped into her studio.

I took a step back from Zack and shoved my hands in my coat pockets. *No kissing*, I reminded myself.

He looked disappointed that I created the space between us. But, if this wasn't going to be real and lasting, I had to protect myself. It would be too easy to slip back into the comfort of his arms. I had to ignore the little flutter in my heart his touch gave me.

Last night he'd been so grouchy and short with me. Today he was acting like he wanted nothing more than to hold me tight and kiss me senseless. His mixed messages made my head spin. Maybe that was what I should call my next song, *Mixed Messages*. The words were already forming in my mind.

"You look nice," he said, reaching for my hand.

"I wanted to be at my best for your mom," I admitted, unbuttoning my coat. I wasn't sure if it was Zack or hormones or nerves over having dinner with his mom, but suddenly I was feeling too warm in my wool coat.

Zack took me in from head to toe. My baby bump was becoming more prominent and harder to hide. His eyes stopped on my belly, and I saw the panic in them. Disappointment surged through me, but I held it at bay pulling my coat over my bump.

His eyes returned to my face, then locked on the pendant around my neck. His fingers gently ran over the faux sapphire as if it were real. "This is new. I haven't seen you wear this before."

I cast my eyes downward. "It was given to me by a friend."

"Must be some friend," he scoffed. *And here we go again*, I thought.

"Definitely someone special," I admitted. Audrey had become my biggest cheerleader and source of support in the past couple of months.

"My mom is waiting upstairs. She's anxious to see you," he said dismissively.

I met his eyes. "Why? I don't understand."

He pursed his lips and crossed his arms over his chest. "You're carrying the child of her dead son. I would think it was obvious."

What the hell?

His words cut deep. Not only my heart, but my soul, felt like it had been carved open by his cruelty. The stabbing pain almost brought me to my knees. I didn't know the man standing before me. He was a stranger in every sense of the word.

Tears filled my eyes. "This was a mistake." I turned and darted out the door, not caring about the dinner I was skipping out on. My feet couldn't carry me fast enough. I ran in my high-heeled boots. Away from Zack. Away from his mother. Away from everything.

I hated him. He wasn't the man I fell in love with. He was someone else entirely.

I was almost a block away when my legs finally gave out. I made it around the corner and into the alley behind an office building. I kneeled on the rough pavement and sobbed, holding my stomach in my arms. The first wave of nausea hit with vengeance. I leaned to the side and threw up next to the dumpster.

My breath was ragged, coming in short bursts. The next wave came without warning, and I threw up again, this time more violently. My body was shaking and sweat dotted my forehead, chills invaded every part of me.

I wiped my mouth with the back of my hand and sat back against the building. I let the tears fall down my face without trying to stop them.

I used my other hand to wipe my face. Black smudges covered my skin from the makeup that had run down my cheeks.

Finally, I found the will to stand, and blurry-eyed, made my way home through the back alleys. I was defeated. This was not the life I had planned. But then again, when had any of my plans ever turned out the way I had hoped?

Back inside the safety of my own apartment, I broke again. I cried for the two men I'd loved and lost. The one who had cherished me and had given me the greatest gift I could ever ask for. And the one who had saved me, then destroyed my heart because of the gift the first had left me.

Although I wasn't religious, I dropped to my knees in my tiny apartment and prayed to a God who I barely believed in, for the strength to save myself. But I knew it was useless. God had forgotten about me a long time ago.

Chapter 24
Zack

I smashed my hand into the brick wall. "What the fuck is wrong with me?" I yelled. My knuckles were split open, and blood ran down my hand. I stalked back into my studio and slammed the door. Sinking down to the ground, I dropped my head between my knees and let the blood drip onto the floor.

The door creaked open, and Layla stood there with a first-aid kit in her hands. She cautiously walked over like I would bite her head off and kneeled before me. I wanted to lash out, but Layla didn't deserve it. She opened the kit and pulled out some gauze and peroxide. Picking up my hand, she silently began to clean the gashes on my knuckles. It stung like a bitch, and I hissed at the pain.

"I think you might need stitches," she said quietly, dabbing the gashes.

I yanked my hand back. "I don't need stitches. I need a brain transplant." I stared at the ceiling and calmed my spinning head.

Why would I say that to Clarissa? She looked so pretty, dressed up for dinner with my mom. And what did I do? I ripped her apart with my words.

I saw that necklace around her neck that I was sure was a gift from Bobby. Jealousy had reared its ugly head. I wanted her to hurt as much as I was hurting.

By the way she ran out of here, I'd say I succeeded.

My mom walked into my studio, dressed for dinner. She took one look at me and hurried to my side. "What happened?"

"His hand met a brick wall," Layla explained.

I glared at her. She held her hands up in surrender, quietly backing towards the door and leaning on the frame.

My mom grabbed my hand and inspected the open wounds. She silently began bandaging my knuckles. "Layla," she called, "can you get some ice?"

155

"Sure thing." Layla scurried away.

She came back with a bag of ice wrapped in a towel and handed it to my mom. She placed the ice on the back of my knuckles and used my other hand to hold it in place. In full mom mode, she grabbed some paper towel and began to wipe the blood from the floor.

"Leave it," I snapped. "I'll get it later."

She dropped the paper towel on the floor. "What happened?" she asked. "Where's Rissa?"

"She left because I'm an asshole," I barked.

My mom let out a sigh. "What'd you do?"

"She came in here looking all pretty. She kissed me and for a moment, everything was perfect. Then I let jealousy take over and I…" I couldn't admit to my mom what I'd said.

"You what, Zack?" she prodded.

"I said something really nasty to her." I slammed my head back into the cabinet. "God, I don't even know who I am anymore. I can't believe the things that come out of my mouth."

My mom sat on the floor next to me. "Maybe you need to take a break for a while. Take some time to decide what you really want. You two might not be able to be friends. You might have to separate completely."

I swallowed the lump in my throat. The thought of never seeing Clarissa again made my chest ache. "I can't do that."

"Then you've got a serious problem. This isn't healthy for either one of you. Rissa loves you. She's just waiting for you to decide you love her too. She won't wait forever."

"Doesn't seem like she's waiting at all. I didn't ask for this. I gave her everything and she…" I shook my head.

"What did she do, Zack? All of this happened before she ever got together with you. Do you think she planned it? Do you think this is what she wanted? Do you think she wanted to be pregnant and alone?" my mom asked.

"No, but she could have been honest with me," I defended.

"So, if you knew she was pregnant you wouldn't have fallen for her?"

I pulled at my hair. "I don't know and now I never will."

She patted my leg. "You can't change the past."

I pulled the towel from my hand and flexed my fingers. Thank God, I hadn't broken my hand. I'd have been hard pressed to tattoo with a cast. "I'm sorry I ruined your dinner. If you still want to see Rissa, she works at six. I'm sure she'd talk to you."

My mom stood and ran her hands down her pants. "I might just do that. I could use another martini."

"Wanna get a pizza first? I'm buying." I smiled at her. I had been skeptical about my mom coming here, but I was glad she did. We'd connected in a way we hadn't in years. I finally had my mom back.

I ordered us a pizza and we ate in my studio. My mom left at six-thirty to see Clarissa. I prayed that her meeting would go better than my interaction with her. I was afraid I had turned her against my mom. I didn't want that for either one of them.

Chapter 25
Rissa

I arrived at work promptly at six o'clock. I couldn't let my personal life affect my job. I had cried for a good hour and then forced myself to pull it together.

I was done with Zack. Completely. I couldn't handle the highs and the lows. The highs were so good, but the lows practically destroyed me. There was no balance and self-preservation told me to be done with all of it.

Shortly after I started my shift, Catherine strode into the bar looking like a million bucks. I didn't want to wait on her. I didn't want to see her at all. However, since I ran out on our dinner date, she deserved an explanation.

I tentatively approached her. "Hey, Catherine. What can I get you?"

"A martini. Two olives, extra dirty," she said.

I grabbed the Grey Goose off the shelf and shook her a killer martini, adding the olives and the juice. I placed her drink on the bar. "Sorry about our dinner. Something came up," I explained.

"Something like a brick wall and my son's hand?" she asked, peering over the top of her glass.

"I wouldn't know. I left before anything like that happened. One minute he's kissing me, the next he's hurling insults at me. I don't even know who he is anymore," I admitted.

I wished the bar was busy, but it was early, and the crowd wouldn't pick up for another hour or so. That left me face to face with Zack's mom, trying to explain the complicated relationship we had.

"He's confused," she said sipping her martini.

"That's great. I don't have the time or patience to deal with his emotions. I have enough of my own to deal with, and I'm done. I thought he was a good guy. Now, I'm not so sure. Coming here was a mistake. I just wish I had the means to leave tonight."

"Are you sure about that?" she asked.

I let out a sigh. "You and I have never been close, but can I confide in you?"

"Of course. One of my biggest regrets is not getting to know you better. You have no idea what it's like to live with Malcolm, but I won't let him control me anymore. I want to get to know you, Rissa."

Tears filled my eyes, and I felt the sincerity pouring from the woman in front of me. "Kincaid men are complicated."

She held up her martini. "I'll drink to that."

I let out a nervous laugh. "I loved Wes. I really did. He was my everything, but toward the end I felt like he was someone else. He loved the cocaine more than he loved me. He knew I was pregnant, yet he wouldn't stop. I begged him, for me and our baby. I guess we weren't enough."

Catherine took my hand. "It was the drugs, it wasn't you. I'm his mother. I should have seen how he was struggling."

"He didn't want you to know. He tried to hide it, but it happened so fast and got out of control."

"I'm sorry. I wish I had seen the signs."

"When Wes left me, I felt like my whole world fell apart. And then Zack showed up. He was kind and acted like he actually gave a shit about me. It was easy to fall for him, even if I knew it was wrong."

Catherine set her almost empty drink on the bar. "You can't help who you fall in love with. Do you know how honored I am that you fell for both of my sons?"

I shook my head in disbelief. "You should be pissed, not honored."

"No. It means that I did something right with both of them. They both became good men, despite their father."

I had a hard time believing her words. She should have thought I was a terrible person. "It doesn't matter. I may love Zack, but there's too much hurt between us. I can't go on like this."

"I'm not asking you to. I told Zack that if he can't commit, then he might need to let go."

I nodded. "Wise words from a wise woman." I turned to walk away.

Catherine grabbed my wrist. "But, Rissa, if you have any feelings for Zack, forgive him."

159

I wrenched my wrist free. "I can't this time. He's hurt me beyond repair. I need to think about me for a change."

Catherine pushed her empty glass across the bar. "I understand." She left some cash on the bar and walked out without any further words. I was left again with only my emotions.

I continued to work the bar. The night got busy and so did I. I appreciated the distraction, even if I couldn't get Zack out of my head.

Around midnight the bar was packed. It was Saturday and the tips were piling up. I barely saw the faces of my customers as I pulled beer and mixed drinks. It was going to be a good tip night and I needed as many of those as possible.

A familiar brooding, tattooed guy sat at the end of the bar. I hesitantly walked towards him. "What can I get you?"

"You," he said simply. He reached over the bar to hold my hand. His large hand was covered in bandages that hadn't been there earlier. Despite the bandages, the warmth of his touch felt nice. "I'm so sorry, Clarissa. You make me crazy. Can you forgive me?"

I pulled my hand back and sighed. "Not this time. I've tried, but I'm done. You want to crucify me for my decisions? That's fine. I got your message loud and clear tonight. You want to hurt me? Mission accomplished. You want me gone? I am. I'm done with trying to make something out of what we had." I passed him an envelope across the bar. "I called your lawyer. This should cover the costs incurred. I'm done fighting. I told him to stop all activity on the case. Whatever happens, happens. I'm trusting my gut and it tells me to cut ties. I can't be your friend, Zack. I can't let you continue to rip me apart."

I walked away feeling a sense of strength. I didn't need Zack to make me feel whole. All I needed was me. Being on my own wasn't a new feeling, just one I hadn't felt since before Wes. I could do this.

"Clarissa," he pleaded.

He still hadn't said the one thing I needed to hear. The one thing that could make everything better. "I'm done. I don't need to be saved. Find another pet project." I walked away and left him at the end of the bar. Maybe he thought I would never walk away for good, but I did have something resembling self-respect. I couldn't deal with his ups and downs. Walking away was difficult at best, but as I remembered his words, it got easier.

Zack left without a word, leaving me a generous tip. It was so like him, but money couldn't heal the wounds he had inflicted on my heart.

I would do this on my own. No Wes. No Zack. Just me and my determination.

Chapter 26
Zack

I walked home knowing I had blown it. There was no chance of us ever reconciling. I didn't hate her. I missed her like crazy, but tonight I pushed beyond her limits. It was too much, and I had no one to blame but myself and my big mouth.

A deep sense of loss flowed through me. Up until tonight, I thought we would be able to work it out no matter what. But the envelope in my hand told me otherwise. I knew she couldn't afford to pay Jeff's fees, but she was willing to leave herself short just to be rid of me.

I opened the envelope and let out a low chuckle. Two hundred bucks? Was that really what she thought it cost?

I called Jeff on his line reserved for emergencies. We had laughed when I called it his Bat Phone, but right now was an emergency for me. The line rang and rang until he finally answered. "Jeff?"

"Hey. What's up Zack? This is outside of my office hours, so this better be an emergency," he said, sounding annoyed.

"Did you talk to Rissa?" I asked, ignoring his irritation at me calling so late.

"Yeah."

"Did you tell her what your fees were?"

He hemmed and hawed. "Sort of?" His answer was more of a question.

"What does that mean?" I prodded, tapping the envelope in my hand.

"Look, Zack, she wanted to pay you back. I knew she didn't have that kind of money, so I told her some ridiculously low number. Are you pissed?"

"Not at all. And between us, this isn't done. We're not closing the case. Let her think what she wants, but this isn't over." No matter how mad Clarissa was at me, I wouldn't let Malcolm take her baby without a fight.

162

"Understood. Now, I have a wife who's a little sexually frustrated with the interruption. Anything else?"

"Sorry, man. Get back to your woman. I'll talk to you soon." I laughed again at the two hundred bucks in the envelope. She was so damn cute.

And stubborn.

And determined.

And pissed.

I had to find a way to change her mind. Not having Clarissa in my life was not an option. Maybe after we spent some time apart, she'd be willing to forgive me.

My mom came from her room wrapping her robe around herself. "How'd it go?"

I let out a sigh. "Not good. She's really mad at me." I sat down on the couch and leaned my head back. "She wouldn't accept my apology."

My mom perched on the chair across from me. "Did you really think it would be that easy? You hurt her deeply and this isn't the first time. She's in self-preservation mode."

I pushed the heels of my hands into my eyes. "I know. I need to stop being an asshole."

My mom let out a little laugh. "Well, yes, that would help. But you also need to decide what kind of relationship you want with her. If you only want to be her friend, then you need to accept that she might date someone else and be her friend. If you want more, then you need to tell her that. Part of the problem is she doesn't know where you stand."

"I want to help her. I want to make sure she's okay. I hate watching her struggle. She tried to pay me back for my lawyer." I handed my mom the envelope.

She opened it, pulled out the money and smiled. "She doesn't have a clue, does she?"

"Nope. Jeff told her two hundred and she believed him. I won't tell her she's wrong. I'll do whatever I have to, to make sure Malcolm stays far away from her daughter. I can at least save her from that miserable bastard."

My mom nodded. "Agreed. But I think you're missing the most important thing about Rissa, or any woman for that matter. She doesn't need someone to swoop in to save her. That's not what she wants."

"Then please enlighten me because I have no idea what she wants anymore. All I know is she doesn't want me."

"The key to a woman's heart isn't that mysterious, Zack. She doesn't want to be saved. She wants to be loved."

"I do love her. She knows that."

My mom shook her head. "No, Zack. She wants to be loved completely. She wants someone who will love all of her, including the baby. Anything less won't ever be enough. And, honestly, she shouldn't settle for anything less."

"I will love her baby," I defended myself.

"Like an uncle or like a dad?" she questioned.

"I'm not the dad," I pointed out.

"No. Your brother is, but he's not here. You are. That baby will never know her real father, but she will know who loves her. That's all that's going to matter. Biology won't determine who her daddy is. Love will. And biologically speaking, you and your brother shared at least fifty percent of the same DNA. So, no matter what, that little girl is going to share at least twenty-five percent of your DNA, maybe more."

I squinted my eyes at my mom. She sounded like she was quoting from a medical journal. "How in the hell do you know all of that? You weren't a biology major."

She squared her shoulders. "I looked it up," she said proudly. "You can find anything using Google."

I laughed. "Yeah, I guess you can. Maybe it can tell me how not to be a jerk."

She smiled at me. "You don't need Google for that. Everything you need is right here." She placed her hand on my chest. "If you follow your heart, you'll win her back. It won't be easy, and she'll fight you every step of the way, but if you really love her, it'll be worth it. Is that what you want? Do you love her completely?"

I rubbed my lips together and ran my battered and bruised hand over my chin. "Yeah, I think I do." It was almost a relief to finally admit it to

164

myself. I couldn't live without Clarissa. The thought of some other man taking my place and playing daddy, killed me. I loved her. All of her. Heart and soul.

My mom clapped her hands together giddily. "I'm so excited! Let's come up with a plan to win her back. Go get a notepad, we're going to write this down."

I laughed at her. "Really, Mom?"

"We're not leaving anything to chance. Go get the notepad," she instructed.

"It's one o'clock in the morning. Aren't you tired?" I questioned.

She kissed me on the cheek. "Nope. My son's having a baby. There's nothing more important to me."

"Mom?"

"Hmmm?

"Thanks for coming here. I really needed you. You're going to make a great grandma," I told her.

♫♪♫♪

Step one: Flowers.

I don't know why I hadn't ever thought of it before. I'd never bought her flowers, even when we lived together. It was such a simple gesture, but my mom assured me she would like it.

Flowers alone weren't going to win her back, it was going to take a hell of a lot more, but it was a start. I'd fucked up big time. This wasn't a sprint; it was a marathon. It was going to be long and grueling, but I wouldn't lose sight of the prize at the end of it. I was willing to put in every bit of effort needed to have Clarissa back in my arms again. Anything else wasn't an option. She may have been stubborn, but I was determined. It would be a war of wills and I had every intention of winning.

I wasn't good at this romance stuff. I'd never actively pursued a girl; they usually pursued me. I took my mom's lead and Googled *romantic gestures*.

The next morning, my mom went with me to the florist. I suggested ordering online and my mom frowned at me. She said if Clarissa was that important to me, she was worth the effort. A handwritten note would mean

165

more than an impersonal typed message from some clerk. Of course, she was right.

I put in a week's worth of orders. Clarissa would have flowers covering every surface by the time I was done. I ordered roses, wildflowers, daisies, and tulips. I wasn't sure what she liked, so I made every bouquet different.

After writing a message for each, I handed my credit card across the counter. The clerk smiled at me. "She's either really special or you messed up big time."

"Both. She's having my baby." I smiled back. It was the first time I had said it aloud and I liked the way it sounded.

Now, I just had to convince Clarissa it was true.

Chapter 27
Rissa

I woke up the next morning with a new mindset. I'd been hanging onto the thought of Zack coming around to accepting me for me. That he would be willing to be part of a family of three.

Giving up on the delusion was freeing. I couldn't forgive him for the callous words he'd said to me. I believed he was sorry, but it was hindsight. I'd forgiven him for his initial reaction to finding out I was pregnant. I shared the blame by not telling him the truth from the beginning.

I had thought that maybe we were finally moving past all the hurt, but he hurt me deeper this time. The knife he stabbed into my heart, left a gaping hole. Shoving Wes's death in my face was cruel. It proved Zack would never see me as more than a vessel for his brother's baby. And it wasn't just his words, it was his tone, the anger and disgust behind them that cut the deepest. I didn't do anything wrong this time. The thing that he was mad about, was out of my control and even if I could change it, I wouldn't. If he couldn't accept my baby, then there was no hope.

My focus was me, my music, and making a life for my daughter and myself.

♫♪♫♪

Sunday nights were always slow at The Locker. I looked around at the nearly empty bar and was glad we closed at midnight on Sundays. Nights like tonight, didn't pay much in tips, but I had to take my share of slow nights, so the other bartenders didn't have animosity towards me for all the prime nights I made good money.

"What are you doing for Thanksgiving?" Lou asked, as I pulled glasses from the automatic washer and dried them.

"Nothing." I'd honestly forgot that Thursday was Thanksgiving. I had no family to spend it with and any friends I did have would be spending it with their own families. My Thanksgiving would consist of a frozen turkey dinner I nuked in the microwave.

Lou frowned. "What about Zack? You're not going to see him?"

"Nope."

"So, what are you going to do?"

I shrugged. "I don't get many days off, so I'm going to sleep in late, stay in my pajamas, and watch Netflix. I can't think of anything better," I lied.

"You can't spend it alone," Lou insisted. "Do you want to come with me to my sister's house? It's crazy there with all her grandkids running around, but the food is good."

"That's sweet of you to offer, but I'm going to pass. Being alone really doesn't bother me." I hadn't had a real Thanksgiving since before my mom got sick. When Wes and I were together, we had gone to his parent's house the first year. It was strained and uncomfortable as Malcolm made snide remarks through the entire dinner.

It was cold and formal, lacking all the lightness that I'd experienced when I was little. There was no football on TV. There was no sneaking into the kitchen to sample the turkey before it was served. No one even said what they were thankful for.

Drinks were served in the sitting room and dinner in the formal dining room. A waitstaff had brought out the food which was eaten on the finest china. Conversation revolved around Kincaid Industries, to which I had nothing to contribute. Much to Catherine's dismay, we left before dessert.

After that, I sent Wes to every holiday on his own. He never stayed long. He made his appearance and came home to me. We'd lay in bed naked. He'd apologize for leaving me alone and make long, slow, sensual love to me. Then we'd turn on a movie and eat ice cream cuddled together under the covers. I never minded being alone and Wes always more than made up for it.

"I don't like it," Lou huffed as he took the glasses I'd dried and placed them on the shelf under the bar.

I shrugged. "I like the downtime. I might even download a smutty book and read it while eating ice cream." It was the closest thing I would get to being with Wes.

Lou shook his head, looking unconvinced.

A cute, young guy walked to the bar carrying a big white box. "I'm looking for..." he glanced at the name on his paperwork, "...Clarissa Lynne Black."

"That's me," I piped up.

"I have a delivery for you." He set the box on the edge of the bar and turned to walk away.

"Wait," I called. "I need to give you a tip."

He held his hand up. "It's already been handled. Have a great day."

I stared at the box curiously. From the blue writing on the outside, it was obviously from a florist.

"You just going to stare at it or are you going to open it?" Lou asked.

"I don't know." Zack had never sent me flowers before, but who else could it be from? "If it's from Zack, I don't want it."

Lou rolled his eyes and grabbed a knife. He cut the plastic ties holding the box together and lifted off the top. I gasped. It was a beautiful bouquet of red and white roses. I studied them carefully. There were at least two dozen.

"There's a card," Lou said as he pulled a tiny envelope from a plastic holder in the middle of the bouquet. He tried to hand it to me, but I backed away.

"You open it," I told Lou.

He sighed heavily and opened the envelope. Lou pulled his glasses off his head and read the card silently.

"What's it say?"

"*There's a rose for every time I've thought of you since last night. I'm so sorry. Love Always~ Zack.*" Lou placed his glasses back on top of his head. "You guys have a fight?"

"No. It wasn't a fight. It was... it was worse than that. It was an ending."

"Hmmm," Lou said shoving the card into my hand. "Sounds like he's not finished yet."

I looked down at the card that was in his neat, scripted writing. I shoved it into my back pocket. "He doesn't get to decide this time." I wasn't sure why I kept the card. I should have thrown it into the trash along with the

169

flowers, but I couldn't find the will to do it. "Do you have a lady friend, Lou?" I asked.

"Nope." Then he scratched his bearded chin. "How long is Zack's mom in town?"

I raised an eyebrow at that. "She's leaving today."

"Hmmm. Pretty lady," he mused.

I giggled. "Yeah, she is. She lives in New York, but… she is getting a divorce. She might be around more."

"Yeah?"

"Mmmhmm," I hummed with a silly grin. "You like her, don't you?"

"Let's just say I wouldn't mind her being around more," he said. "Catherine? Pretty name too."

It was cute that Lou had a crush on Zack's mom. They were totally different types of people, but I had a feeling Catherine was ready for different.

"What should I do with these?" I asked pointing at the roses.

"Take them home," he said.

"I'm not taking them home. I don't want them," I insisted.

"Then leave them on the bar. Everyone can enjoy them."

And that's exactly what I did. I left the crystal vase sitting on the end of the bar when I went home for the night.

♫♪♫♪

"Delivery for Clarissa Lynne Black," the same cute guy from yesterday announced as he walked into A Second Chance.

"Put them on the counter," I instructed. "Tip?"

"Handled," he said as he walked out.

"Somebody's sending you flowers?" Audrey asked.

I huffed. "They're from Zack."

"How do you know?" she asked as she pulled a pair of scissors from the drawer.

"Because he sent roses to the bar yesterday." I stared at the box. It was bigger than the last one. Audrey tried to hand me the scissors, but I shook my head.

"Really? A man sends you flowers, and you don't want to open them?" she said with disapproval.

"They're out of guilt. He was shitty to me, and he knows it."

"Then I'll do it. No one sends me flowers." She cut the plastic straps and pulled the top off the box. "Wow," Audrey gasped.

I was expecting roses, but I was wrong. It was a bouquet of wildflowers in bright pinks and purples and yellows. It was over the top and gorgeous. "Is there a card?" I asked.

Audrey pulled a small envelope from the center, "Yep. Right here."

"Can you read it?"

Audrey pulled the card from the envelope and read it aloud. *"These flowers are nowhere near as beautiful as you. Please forgive me. Love Always~ Zack"* Audrey handed me the card. "Sounds like somebody misses you."

I examined the card. It was written in the same carefully scripted letters. I stuffed it in my back pocket. "They're just words, Audrey. Words are cheap. He'll forget about me soon enough. Out of sight, out of mind."

I left them on the counter when I went home.

♫♪♫♪

The next day, I parked behind my apartment, anxious to get in a quick meal between jobs. I hopped out of my Bronco and a white van pulled up. Same guy, another box.

"Seriously? This is getting ridiculous," I huffed at the guy.

"Just doing my job," he said. "Someone must really like you."

"He thinks he does. He doesn't know what he wants," I said off-handedly.

I went to grab the box, but he pulled it back. "I was instructed to carry them up for you." He looked at my pregnant belly and the black wrought-iron stairs leading to my apartment. "It's a good idea."

"Fine." I led him up the stairs and stuck my key in the door. I stepped inside, and he handed me the box.

"Have a great day. See you tomorrow." He jogged back down the steps and to his van.

171

I set the box on my tiny kitchen counter and used a knife to cut through the straps. I pulled the top from the box. Daisies in every color and shade of the rainbow; oranges, yellows, pinks, reds, and purples. I smiled despite myself. They were pretty after all.

I pulled the card and giggled. *"Life is not the same without you. We miss you. Love Always~ Zack"* In the corner of the card he had drawn a picture of himself and Priss. "What a goofball," I muttered to myself. I opened the kitchen drawer and placed the card inside with the others.

♫♪♫♪

Every day that week, I received another bouquet, even on Thanksgiving. It was a fall arrangement with a little stuffed turkey in the middle of it. When you pressed its belly, it made a funny gobbling sound that made me laugh. The card attached was the lamest yet. *"If we were together today, I'd gobble you up. Happy Thanksgiving! Love Always~ Zack"*

I stuck the card in the drawer with the rest and set the little turkey on my coffee table. I snuggled in my pajamas under a blanket as I watched Netflix on my phone and ate Chunky Monkey ice cream. Every once in a while, I pushed on the belly of the turkey and listened to him gobble. It was a ridiculously annoying sound, but I kind of loved it.

Chapter 28
Zack

Step Two: Remind her of all the good times.

I hadn't heard a word from Clarissa, but I hadn't expected to. She wasn't going to give in easily. She was going to make me work for it and I was more than willing.

Before we opened on Saturday, I called Chase and Layla into my office. "Team meeting," I announced.

They both sauntered in and collapsed into the chairs opposite my desk. "Are we in trouble?" Chase asked.

I lifted a pierced brow at him. "Did you do something to be in trouble?"

He gazed at the ceiling as if thinking. "I don't think so."

Layla rolled her eyes at him. "We're not in trouble, you idiot. Does he look mad to you?"

Chase looked me up and down as I rested my hands under my chin. "Naw. He actually looks kind of...happy? I'm not sure. It's been a while."

I chuckled and focused on Layla. "Anything to report?"

She sat up in her chair. "I talked to Rissa yesterday. She mentioned the flowers and said, and I quote, *He's up to something, but I'm not sure what.* She's intrigued but doesn't know what to make of it."

"That's okay. I knew this wouldn't be easy," I admitted. "At least I've gotten her attention."

"You fucked up royally," Layla reminded me.

I didn't disagree. "Yes, I did, but I'm going to get her back."

"What's the next step?" Chase asked.

"The flowers were good, but it has to be better," Layla added.

I rubbed my temples. "I want to remind her of the great times we had together. It's brainstorming time. Any ideas?"

"Oh!" Layla perked up. "She used to make you cookies all the time. What if you made her a batch and I could deliver them to her?"

I tapped my pen on the desk and then pointed it at her. "That's good." I wrote it down. "What else you got?"

"What about a pair of handcuffs?" Chase suggested.

Layla and I both stared at him questioningly.

"I mean, the sex was good, right?" he clarified.

Layla picked up an invoice from the desk, crumpled it up, and threw it at his head. "He's looking for romantic ideas, not kinky shit. Besides, she already remembers the sex was good."

"She does?" I questioned.

"Of course. Women don't forget stuff like that."

I smirked. "Good to know."

"Fine." Chase held up his hands. "I remember my mom saying that she had a boyfriend that used to make her mixed tapes back in high school. She's still talking about it, so it must have meant something to her."

I pointed the pen at him, "Much better. I like it."

We brainstormed for the better part of an hour and we had come up with some really good ideas. The best thing about having Chase and Layla work for me wasn't that they were kickass artists, it was that they were friends I could depend on.

♫♪♫♪

My kitchen looked like a bomb had gone off in it. When Clarissa made cookies, it never looked like this. She made it look so easy.

Flour and sugar covered the countertop. Batter was splashed across the cabinets from accidently lifting the mixer out of the bowl while it was running. And I may or may not have dropped a couple of eggs while trying to juggle them like I'd seen once on a cooking show.

If I really wanted to get her back, I should have videotaped this debacle and sent it to her. Maybe she would have taken me back out of pure pity.

Miss Priss sat on the bar stool watching me curiously. I pet her on the head. "Don't judge. If we get her back, you'll never have to see this again. Cross your paws that all of this works."

I finished scooping little rounded mounds of dough on the cookie sheet and popped the first tray into the oven as my phone rang. I wiped my hands on my flour-cover jeans and picked it up "Hey, Mom."

"How's it going, honey? Any progress?"

"I'm not sure, but I think so. I'm making her chocolate chip cookies right now," I said proudly.

"You know how to bake?"

"Not a bit. The kitchen is destroyed, but she's worth it."

"She'll love it. It's very thoughtful and so much better than store bought. Anyone can buy cookies, but a man who bakes is something special," she said.

"Honestly, Mom, what do you think the chances are that she'll forgive me?"

"It's only been a week. I told you it wouldn't be easy, but if you keep at it, I don't see how she couldn't."

"I'm not giving up." I hated what I asked next, but I had to. "How are things at home? Was he pissed you were gone?"

"He was fine, Zack. I saw my attorney today and filed the divorce papers."

I walked to the couch and sat down. She said she was going to, but part of me hadn't believed it. "Are you okay?"

She sighed. "I'm sad. I didn't want my marriage to end, but I couldn't stay either. Malcolm's not the same man I married. I deserve more."

"I'm proud of you mom. I know it wasn't easy, but you do deserve more. I've always thought so. When will he find out?" I asked.

"He'll be served the papers by the end of the week. I'm a little scared. He's going to be so mad."

"Where will you live? Have you found an apartment?" I asked. I hated that she was so far away. For the first time ever, I wished I hadn't left New York."

"My attorney advised me to stay in the house. There's plenty of room, so I'll move my things to another bedroom."

It sounded miserable. "You can always come here if you need to get away," I offered. "I loved having you here."

"I might have to take you up on that," she said wistfully.

It would be nice to have her here permanently, but it was a discussion for another day. I worried about her. Malcolm wouldn't hurt her physically, that wasn't his forte. He was more of an expert in mental torture. "Be safe, Mom."

"I will be. Now, enough about me. How did your cookies turn out?"

"Oh crap!" I hopped up off the couch and opened the oven door. Smoke poured out and I waved it away with a padded mitt. I pulled out the rack and sighed at the little black mounds on the tray. "I guess next time I should set the timer."

She laughed. "That would probably be a good idea."

Chapter 29
Rissa

Sunday, I expected another bouquet of flowers, but my new friend, Phil, never showed up. I hated to admit that I waited all day for him. As the clock ticked past six, I decided he wasn't coming.

"What's the sad look for?" Lou asked me.

I shrugged my shoulders. "I was just expecting something that didn't happen." I couldn't blame Zack for giving up on me. He's sent me seven bouquets of flowers and not once did I pick up the phone to call him. I could have shot him a quick text, but I didn't even do that.

I had known that he would eventually forget about me and move on, I just didn't like it. I had told myself I didn't care, that I didn't need or want him. The worst lies, were the ones you told yourself, because you couldn't deny them. Deep inside you always knew the truth and the truth led to hurt and disappointment. You couldn't ever truly fool yourself.

And even though I was disappointed, I shouldn't have been. He still hadn't said the words I needed to hear. The words that would have changed everything.

"Oh shoot! Something came for you earlier. I darn near forgot." Lou hurried from behind the bar and went to his office.

Maybe Zack did send me flowers today, I thought. I let a little flutter take up residence inside as I waited for him. But when Lou returned, he wasn't carrying a big white box. He had a small heart-shaped tin in his hands. "Layla brought this by earlier," he said.

My heart dropped, and the fluttering ceased. It wasn't from Zack. "Thanks," I said through my disappointment.

I opened the tin. There was a note on top of the tissue paper inside. I pulled out the note and read:

Hey Sweetheart,

My kitchen is destroyed, but I made these myself. There would have been more, but I burned the first tray. Guess I should have set the timer.

I tried one and they're pretty good, but nothing compares to how sweet you are. I'm missing my dessert. Please come back to me.

Love Always~ Zack

I let out a little laugh, as I remembered the notes I would leave Zack when I made him treats. I pulled back the tissue paper to reveal the chocolate chip cookies inside. I took one from the tin and took a small bite. Mmmm. He'd done good. I ate the rest of the cookie, and I should have offered one to Lou, but these were just for me.

♫♪♫♪

The next morning, I headed to work at A Second Chance. It was freezing out and a light coat of frost covered my stairs. I grabbed the railing and carefully made my way down. I hated these fucking stairs. No wonder this apartment had been empty for so long. That, and the fact that it was a craphole.

The sky was grey, covered in thick clouds. We were supposed to get our first real snow today. I wasn't looking forward to it. I didn't have a ton of experience driving in snow, but at least I had the right car for it.

I could see from the stairs, that my windshield was covered in frost. Great! I would have to let it run for a while until the ice melted and I could see.

As I got closer to my Bronco, I noticed a small white box wrapped in a red bow sitting on the hood. Next to the box was a snow brush with a scraper on the end. *How did he know I didn't have one of those? Because he knows you.*

I unlocked my car and started the engine. Grabbing the box off the hood, I set it on the seat while I scraped the windows. After clearing the frost, I hopped into the front seat. Even though I had on gloves, my fingers were freezing. I pulled them off and breathed into my hands to warm them.

I picked up the small box, wondering what could be inside. I had no idea what he could have gotten me. I pulled the ends of the red ribbon and peeled it away, then lifted the top off. Inside was a small matchbox-sized replica of his Chevelle. It was painted cherry red with black racing stripes, just like the real thing.

God, I missed that car. I missed how he held my hand over the console, and I rested my head on his shoulder. I remembered the first time he let me drive it. I remembered how excited I had been and how I had scared the crap out of him. All of it made me smile despite myself.

There was a handwritten note tucked inside:

Clarissa~

I bought you this car because you drive me crazy, but it's my kind of crazy. I may not have driven in a straight line and I got lost along the way. I took a lot of detours and misread the signs, but all roads lead to you. You are my final destination, please tell me I'm yours. There's no one I'd rather make this journey with than you.

Love Always~ Zack

I wiped the tears from my eyes. I wanted to believe him so bad, but I was scared. What if he let me down again? I didn't think my heart could take it and I had to think of more than myself. I needed stability and someone I could depend on. I stuffed everything back in the box and tossed it on the seat next to me.

When I walked into work, Audrey was anxiously awaiting my arrival. She clapped her hands excitedly. "I've got good news."

"You won the lottery, and you want to adopt me?" I asked jokingly, although it wasn't a half bad thought.

She swatted at me. "I wish." She reached under the counter and pulled out an envelope. "This is even better, because it's real."

"What is it?"

"I sold almost all your stuff." She handed me the envelope and I peeked at the money inside.

I couldn't believe my ears. "What? How?"

"A group of young girls came in looking for holiday dresses. Your window display caught their attention. All that's left is a couple pairs of shoes and a purse," she said.

I opened the envelope and counted the money. There was over six hundred bucks inside. I pulled out a fifty and handed it to Audrey.

She took a step back. "I don't want your money, Rissa."

"Please take it, Audrey. I wouldn't have been able to sell my clothes without you." I shoved it at her.

"No way, missy. You take that and save it for that sweet baby of yours."

I stuck the fifty back in the envelope. "Thank you."

"You're more than welcome."

"Sooo…. any more flowers?" she asked coyly, waiting for me to tell her the sordid details of my non-existent love life.

"No more flowers, but he did bake me cookies and he left a gift on top of my car this morning," I said nonchalantly as I hung my coat and purse in the backroom.

"That's good, right?" she asked, following behind me. "What kind of gift?"

"It was a snowbrush," I said.

Audrey wrinkled up her nose. "Not very romantic."

"Not everything can be roses. I needed one, so I guess it's a win," I answered. "There was more. He gave me this little car, that looks just like his and there was a note." I pulled the note from my purse and handed it to Audrey. "What do you think this means?"

Audrey silently read the note. "I think he's admitting his mistakes. He wants you back. The question is, do you want him?"

I threw my hands up in the air. "I don't know. I mean, I do. I would love for us to be together again, but I don't know if I can trust him. He hurt me! How can I trust him not to do it again? What if this is all him just missing what he's lost? What if it's not real?" I expelled all my fears and frustrations on her. "What if I give him a chance and he leaves me again? I don't think I could survive it." I sank down in a chair more confused now than ever before.

Audrey kneeled before me. "Rissa, look at me. Do you love him?"

I nodded as a tear fell down my cheek. "I miss him so much it hurts."

"Oh, sweet girl, love is about trust. He admittedly lost his way, but he's working like hell to show you he's found it in you."

"I need more time," I said. "I need to be able to take care of myself. I don't want to depend on him."

"Depending on him doesn't make you weak, missy. Loving someone, missing someone, needing someone… it all makes you human.

180

♫♪♫♪

The snow came down hard and furious. I looked out my apartment window at the flakes that had been coming down since last night. The snow covered my car and the small parking lot behind the party store. It was peaceful, but somewhat unfulfilling. I had always enjoyed watching the snow fall, but today I had no one to enjoy it with. It just looked cold and wet and uninviting.

It didn't stop the delivery guy from trodding up my steps. I answered the door in my oversized sweatshirt, leggings, and fluffy socks. I honestly didn't care what I looked like. I was in hibernation mode until I had to work at the bar tonight. He brought me another gift from Zack. This time it was a fancy cookie bouquet. I swore he was trying to make me fat.

Too late. I was already getting big, and it had nothing to do with food. It seemed I got bigger by the week.

I opened the package and inside was a basket with several cookies stuck into foam with long sticks. The outside cookies were shaped as cows and horses but the one in the middle was a big, fat, pink pig. I laughed at the pig's silly face.

And, of course there was a note:

My Sweet Little Pig Whisperer~

Please come home to me. Homer and I miss you.

There is so much I want to tell you. I want to start again. I want to be the man you need, the man you can depend on and the man you trust.

Love Always~ Zack

I wasn't sure if the words were saying what I thought they were saying or not. If they were, this was what I'd wanted. Maybe he was ready to fully commit, but I didn't want to jump to conclusions. I contemplated texting him or calling him or going to see him. But if I was wrong, I'd be crushed again.

I held my phone in my hand, my thumb hovering over his name, when it started to buzz. It was Daniel. I hadn't heard from him in so long.

I took a deep breath and answered, "Hello."

"Rissa, I've got great news. They want to meet you. The music executives I sent your demo to want us in LA tomorrow."

I nearly dropped my phone from the shock. "Tomorrow?"

"Yeah. I'll have a car come pick you up to bring you to the airport. We'll fly to LA, have our meeting, I'll take you to dinner, and we'll be back the next day. How does that sound?"

"Ummm. Quick. Does it have to be tomorrow? I'm not ready," I insisted.

"You were born ready, darling. I know it's last minute, but that's how these things work. I'll send a car around seven."

A nervous chill ran through my body. "Okay. What do I need to bring? How should I dress?" I asked.

"You just be you. You're beautiful the way you are. Bring your guitar, I've got your demo. We'll have time to change at the hotel before our meeting, so dress comfortably."

I nodded my head even though he couldn't see me. "I'll be ready," I assured him.

When I hung up, nerves racked my body. This was it. My chance to provide for myself and my daughter. I couldn't mess it up.

I had so much to do. I had to pack. I needed to practice my songs. I had to let Lou know I would be MIA tomorrow night.

And I needed to talk to Zack.

A phone call wasn't going to do it. I needed to look in his eyes to know if the words he had written were true. Everything he was offering was so tempting, but I'd be a fool to fall for it all again without proof. I wanted to believe him, but part of me couldn't. A recording contract and a man who loved me completely; it all seemed too good to be true.

Chapter 30
Zack

I snapped off my gloves and sent the guy who'd had a portrait of his daughter tattooed on his arm on his way. The devotion he had shown was heart wrenching. I hoped I had done his daughter justice with the ink I permanently etched into his skin.

While doing his tat, my mind wandered. I wondered what Clarissa's baby would look like. What our daughter, if Clarissa would have me, would look like.

I still hadn't heard a word from her, and I started to worry that it was too late. Maybe I'd been an asshole one too many times. Maybe Bobby had stolen her away from me. She hadn't told me to fuck off yet, so I considered myself still in the running for her heart.

The front door jingled. I left my studio and headed to the reception area. My eyes hadn't seen something so beautiful in a long time.

Clarissa stood there in her big white winter coat. She had a fluffy scarf wrapped around her neck and a hat pulled down over her soft curls. She was an angel standing amidst sin and everything that wasn't worthy of her, including me.

I broke the silence. "Hi."

She looked everywhere except at me. When our eyes met, she gave me a small smile. "Hi."

It was a start. I had so much to make up for. It was like starting at square one. A blank page in my sketch book. A new beginning. One where she didn't keep secrets and I didn't act like a total fuckwad.

I stuck my hands in my pockets to keep from wrapping them around her hips. She needed to lead this. I'd poured out my heart in the letters I wrote her. Now, it was her turn.

"We need to talk," she said.

"I'd like that. Wanna come upstairs?"

Her gaze shot to the door that hid the steps to my apartment. "Sure."

I let out a breath of relief. I motioned for her to lead the way as we headed upstairs.

She removed her furry boots at the door and hung her coat, scarf and hat on the hook. She looked damn cute in a big sweatshirt and fluffy pink socks. Miss Priss rubbed at her ankles and Clarissa picked her up immediately. She hugged Priss to her chest and headed for the bar stools. She carefully stroked Priss's fur and whispered in her ear.

I stood on the other side of the counter, putting the space between us. "Do you want some hot chocolate?" I asked.

A smile graced her lips. "I'd love some." She tapped her fingers nervously on the counter. This wasn't easy for either of us.

I filled a pan with water and set it on the stove to boil. It wouldn't be gourmet, but I knew she would still like it.

"Soooo..." she started. "I got the flowers and all your little gifts." She tapped her fingers more nervously. "And your notes."

I reached over the counter to hold her nervous hands. "I meant every word."

She closed her eyes and sighed heavily. "I want to believe you. I really do. But I trusted you before and we both know how that turned out. I can't go through that again."

"You won't have to," I assured her.

"Words, Zack. All they are is words. I can't take the tongue lashings when you get jealous or pissed. You're like Jekyll and Hyde lately. I don't know which is the real you. I have to think about more than myself."

I had scarred her. I made her doubt my intentions. "You don't have to take me back now or ever if that's what you decide. I want you to trust me. Let me prove myself to you," I pleaded.

The water on the stove began to boil. I let go of her hand to make two cups of hot chocolate. I poured the packets into the mugs and added the hot water. I stirred both until all the powder was dissolved. Then I went to the pantry for my secret ingredient, the tiny marshmallows I had bought especially for her. I topped both mugs with the little white sugary treats and passed a mug across the counter to her.

"I love marshmallows," she said softly.

I checked a box in the "win" column.

I had to ask her the one question that wouldn't stop nagging at me. "I need to ask this, so forgive me. Are you dating Bobby?"

She shook her head. "It's not like that with us. He's helped me so much and I don't know how I'll ever thank him, but we're only friends."

I swallowed the lump in my throat and nodded, trying to accept what she was saying. "Did he give you the necklace you had on last week?"

She cocked her head to the side. "What necklace?"

"The blue sapphire," I clarified.

She brought a hand over her mouth and started to laugh.

"It's a serious question, Clarissa. A man doesn't give a woman jewelry like that unless he wants more than a friendship."

She held her hands out in front of her. "I'm sorry. No, he didn't give that to me. It wasn't even real. Audrey loaned it to me for my dinner with your mom. I wanted to look nice and not like a piece of white trash."

I breathed out a sigh of relief. I had fretted over nothing. And I lashed out at her for no reason. "Sweetheart, you couldn't look like white trash if you tried. You're a classy, beautiful woman."

She took a sip of her hot chocolate and licked her luscious lips. "Your father doesn't think so. He thinks I'm so trashy that I deserve to have my baby taken away from me."

"Who cares what he thinks? Malcolm is an asshole. Even my mom would tell you that. She's finally divorcing the selfish bastard."

"I know. She told me."

"She did?" I didn't know that. I wondered what else they had talked about.

"Uh huh. She seemed different when she was here. More... I don't know, just different," she said.

I smiled. "My mom was always there for us as kids. She was my biggest supporter growing up. Over the years, Malcolm beat her down, turned her into a shell of herself. She has a lot of regret since Wes died. She said she wasn't going to make the same mistake twice and wanted us to have a relationship again. Her leaving my dad is a big step, but the right one. I feel like I finally have my mom back. You should give her a chance, not just for yourself but for the baby."

185

"So, she wasn't here to spy on me?"

"Hell no! She wants to have a relationship with you and the baby."

Her shoulders sagged. "I'm sorry. Her being here was unexpected. I don't know who to trust."

I tucked a strand of her curls over her ear, "If you can trust anyone, it's my mom. She's pretty great."

"I liked her better this time. She was always nice to me, but she kept me at arm's length. I didn't really think she liked me," Clarissa said sadly.

"Trust me, she likes you. She actually thinks you're amazing," I said.

"She barely knows me."

"She knows enough." It was the truth. If it wasn't, my mom wouldn't have helped me get her back. My mom saw the strength in Clarissa, she wished she'd had herself. She admired her courage and tenacity. But what my mom loved best about Clarissa, was that she made me happy... and she had made my brother happy. A woman who had captured the hearts of both her sons had to be something special.

Clarissa pushed away from the counter and sauntered over to the piano draped in a white sheet. She pulled it off and sat on the bench. "May I?"

"Of course. It's yours."

Her fingers danced over the keys, and she began to sing. It was the call of a siren, sucking me in and lulling me into a trance. Her voice was so sultry and sexy, I wanted to be selfish and keep it just for me.

You thought I was an angel,
And I proved you wrong.
You saw what you wanted to see,
I fooled you all along.

I want to be your angel,
But I can't fly with broken wings.
Our anger got the best of us,
We said some awful things.
I need you to come back to me,
Only you can heal my broken wings.

She finished the song, so evidently written about us, and I had tears in my eyes. I rubbed them on my shoulder. "Is that new?" I asked.

186

"Yeah. It's called…"

"Broken Wings," I finished for her.

She nodded. "I'm going to LA tomorrow. Do you think I should play it?"

I gulped down the lump in my throat, "You're going to LA? By yourself?" It was my worst fear. She was leaving for good. It was everything she dreamed of, to make something with her music and her dream was coming true. I wanted nothing more for her, but at the same time I wanted to keep her here with me.

She shook her head. "With Daniel. I have a meeting with a music exec. Do you think he'll like the song?"

"He'll love it. It's beautiful, sweetheart. When are you coming back? You're coming back, right?" I held my breath as I waited for her answer.

"I'll only be gone overnight. I told Lou I would only miss one night of work."

I let out a breath of relief. She was coming back. I still had more time. "Do you need a ride to the airport?"

"No. Daniel's sending a car to pick me up. That's all I know."

I hated myself for asking, "Is Bobby going?"

She shrugged. "I don't think so. Daniel didn't say he was."

Again, relief flooded me. "Do you have a suitcase?" I didn't remember seeing one when we packed her up in New York.

"No. I've never needed one. I've never flown before. I'm just going to pack a duffle bag."

"You need something better than that for an airplane. Wait here just a second." I raced to my room and pulled out the black suitcase from my closet.

I was still supposed to be on Step Two, but circumstances had changed. I needed to move to Step Three immediately: Speak her language.

I unzipped the suitcase and carefully put the portable CD player I had bought into the inside pocket. I attached a note that said, *Listen to me on the plane.*

Then I grabbed the plastic bag from my top drawer and emptied the contents into my hand. I closed my fist tightly and carried the suitcase out of my room. I placed it by the front door and crossed back to Clarissa.

My heart was tight in my chest as I sat next to her on the bench. "I have something for you."

"More?" she asked with a smile. "I think you've given me enough."

"It'll never be enough," I told her. "I want you to wear these for your meeting." I opened her hand and dropped the jewelry into it. "Wes would be so proud of you. You need to have him with you tomorrow."

Clarissa stared at the diamond pendant and earrings. Her eyes filled with tears, and one silently fell down her cheek. "How? I sold these to buy my car."

"I have my ways. I couldn't let you lose them." I took the necklace from her palm and fastened it around her neck. I ran my fingers over the pendant, "You never wore this when we were together. I don't want you to pretend he didn't exist for my benefit. We were both lucky to have had you."

"I didn't want to hurt you," she sniffled.

"I know." I ran my hand along the side of her face. "I'll be here waiting for you. Promise to call me when you get back?"

"I will. I promise."

Chapter 31
Rissa

The car Daniel sent arrived promptly at seven a.m. I hadn't gotten much sleep. I spent most of the night tossing and turning. The nerves in my stomach had brought up my dinner more than once. Not only was I meeting with a music exec, but I was flying for the first time.

I was all packed and ready to go when the driver knocked on my apartment door. "Miss Black?"

"That's me," I said nervously.

"Let me take your bag." He quickly took my suitcase, headed down the stairs and placed it in the trunk of the black sedan. I cautiously walked down the stairs I'd swept off with a broom, with my purse slung over my shoulder and my guitar in my hand. The driver opened the back door for me. "My name's Charlie and I'm at your service today."

I slid into the backseat. "Thank you, Charlie." He carefully shut the door and we were on our way. The sky was still dark, and we sped down the expressway with all the people racing to get to work on time. "Will this be your first time in LA?" Charlie asked while looking at me through the rearview mirror.

"Yes, I've never flown before. Have you been to LA?" I asked.

"Born and raised there."

"What's it like? Is it like on TV, with crazy traffic and eternal sunshine?"

Charlie laughed. "Pretty much. It's a different pace of life for sure, but there are some beautiful beaches along the shore."

"I've never been to the beach either. I grew up in Oklahoma, moved to New York and now I'm here. I won't be there long enough to go to the beach though." The thought bummed me out. I wanted to know what it was like to walk in the waves with my toes buried in the sand.

"Maybe next time." After a long silence, Charlie pulled down a winding road and soon a few planes came into sight, but nothing like what I expected.

"This is the airport?" I asked.

"It's a private airstrip. You're going first class today." He drove towards a large metal building and pulled up outside.

Daniel was waiting for us as Charlie opened my door. "Daniel, what is this?"

He opened his arms wide. "Courtesy of Bobby. He's already in LA and will be flying home with us."

"Oh, I didn't know that." I thought back to telling Zack that Bobby wasn't going to be there. Technically, I didn't lie.

Charlie grabbed my guitar and suitcase from the car and headed towards a private jet setting not more than fifty yards from us. I watched him as he took my bags aboard.

"Shall we?" Daniel motioned with his arm.

"I've never been on an airplane," I said.

"Then you're in for a treat. This is so much better than flying commercial. You can kick back and relax. There's nothing to be nervous about."

I nodded and walked towards the plane. How did this become my life? I'd gone from never flying to boarding a private jet. It was overwhelming. I hoped Daniel and Bobby didn't regret spending this money on me. What if it didn't work out? But it had to. This was my chance to finally be financially independent while living my dream.

I sank down in the cream-colored leather seat. It was soft and comfortable, nothing like what I imagined flying on a plane would be like. I looked out the window at the sun that was just peeking over the horizon. The morning sky was a beautiful shade of pink, dotted with a few clouds.

"Are you all right?" Daniel asked, pulling my attention back to the here and now.

"Yeah. Just nervous."

"Don't be. Take off your coat and relax. You'll have to buckle up for takeoff, but after that they'll bring us some breakfast and you can kick back."

I took my coat off and set it on the seat next to me. Then I strapped myself in, fastening the belt under my ever-growing belly. It pulled my shirt tight and made my stomach look more prominent.

I saw Daniel's gaze drift down to the tiny beach ball hiding under my clothes. "When are you due?"

I rubbed my tummy. "Not until the middle of March. I really need this to work out."

He leaned over and patted my knee. "It will. I don't know how they could resist you."

"Daniel, why are you taking such a big chance on me? Surely, you have other clients who need you."

He cocked his head to the side. "You really don't know, do you, Rissa?"

I shook my head.

"You have one of the most beautiful voices I've ever heard. It can be soft and sultry or strong and powerful. Either way, I've watched you bring audiences to tears. You can't fake that. You're the real deal. If I didn't scoop you up, someone else would. My intentions are purely selfish." He winked at me.

"Hmph! I sang in New York for three years and no one was interested. All they wanted was my fiancé. Everybody loved him."

"What was his name?" Daniel asked. We had never talked about my past before or who the daddy of my baby was. We were always strictly business.

"Wes Kincaid. He was somewhat of a local celebrity in Brooklyn. Got a record deal and everything, but he died before recording a single track," I reminisced.

Daniel sat up straighter. "I saw that guy perform in bars a few times. Wicked talented and the ladies loved him."

I smiled. "That, they did."

"I tried to get him to sign with me, but he had already signed with an agent. He died of heart issues or something like that."

I stared back out the window. "Something like that."

He took my hand. "I'm sorry, Rissa. I didn't know. Is he...?" Daniel nodded to my belly.

"My baby daddy? Yeah. Now it's just the two of us," I said sadly.

"Huh. I guess I just assumed Zack was the father," Daniel said. "You two seemed so in love at the concert."

"We were, but it's a long story. I thought he might want the job, now I'm not sure if that's going to happen. It's a lot to ask of someone."

Charlie wandered into the cabin. "We're just about to take off," he informed us, then left without another word.

I closed my eyes as we taxied down the runway. I held onto the armrests with a death grip, my fingers sinking into the soft leather. My stomach lurched into my throat when I felt the plane lift into the air. "Fuck, fuck, fuck, fuck," I murmured to myself. *Breathe in, breathe out, breathe in, breathe out, breathe in, breathe out.*

"You gonna make it?" Daniel asked.

"Yep." A one-word answer was all I was capable of. Anything else would have distracted me from my carefully controlled breathing.

What seemed like forever, but in reality, was probably only a few minutes, Charlie returned. "You can take off your seatbelts now. Can I get you something to drink or eat?"

Daniel requested a coffee. "Water for me. I don't think I should eat anything right now," I responded.

"No problem. It's over a four-hour flight, so let me know if you change your mind," Charlie smiled.

Daniel was immersed in his laptop, typing away furiously. I eyed the couch across the aisle. "Is it okay if I lay down? I didn't sleep well last night."

He glanced at me over his reading glasses. "Of course. I'll get you a blanket and a pillow."

I moved over to the couch and sank into the buttery soft leather. Daniel handed me a pillow and warm blanket. "Thank you." I reached into my purse and pulled out the CD player I'd found in the suitcase Zack gave me. Leave it to him to slip me another unexpected gift. He was a sneaky one. I adjusted the pillow and popped the earbuds into my ears. I laid down and covered myself with the blanket, then hit play.

A soft, distinctly seventies groove filled the silence. "Baby Come Back". *You can blame it all on me...* I smiled at the words, because I loved this song. Who didn't? I had no idea who sang it, so I pulled out my phone and typed it into Google. "Player" popped up on my screen. Never heard of them, but I knew the song. Everyone did, it was a classic.

As the song faded, my curiosity was peaked as to what would be next. Chris Daughtry's "It's Not Over" started. He was a true success story, along with Carrie Underwood. Two people who took a chance by trying out for *American Idol*. Now they were both famous and successful beyond their wildest dreams. I wondered if that would ever be me.

My eyes started to get heavy, and I could feel myself drifting off. The song playing, "On Bended Knee" by Boyz II Men, lulled me into a peaceful state. Everything but the words of the song left my frazzled mind. They soothed my heart and soul. It was the last thing I remembered before I faded off into nothingness.

♫♪♫♪

I felt rested and rejuvenated when Daniel and I exited the elevator on the fifty-first floor of a fancy high-rise in downtown LA. I had changed into a pair of jeans Tori loaned me that fit surprisingly well and didn't make me feel like a cow. I paired it with a black short-sleeved top adorned with silver sparkly hearts. It wasn't form fitting and helped to hide my growing bump. My black high-heeled boots clicked on the shiny marble floor as we headed towards the receptionist.

I let Daniel do the talking and we were asked to take a seat. Mr. Riley would be with us shortly. "Do I look all right?" I whispered to Daniel.

He winked at me. "Gorgeous."

I wiped my sweaty palms on my jeans. This was the most important meeting I'd ever had. It could be life changing. I grasped the necklace that hung around my neck and sent up a special request to Wes. *Baby, wherever you are, please help me. Send me your strength and watch over us. We need you so much right now. I'm going to make you proud.* I brought the pendant to my lips and kissed it.

The pretty red-headed receptionist called us over. "Mr. Riley will see you now." We stood and followed her to a corner office that had the most amazing view of LA. Off in the distance I could see the famous Hollywood sign perched high on the side of a mountain. I couldn't believe I was here. I wondered if Wes had felt these same things on his visit. They had offered him a full recording contract. I felt the excitement fill me at the prospect of being offered the same.

"Mr. McClain, Miss Black, it's a pleasure to meet you both." Mr. Riley extended his hand.

I reached for it, hoping my palm wasn't too sweaty. "It's Rissa." I smiled. "And the pleasure is all mine. Thank you for this opportunity."

He motioned to the chairs in front of his desk. Daniel and I took our seats and waited for Mr. Riley to begin. He leaned back in his chair and steepled his fingers, "I've heard your demo and I'm highly impressed with what I've heard. How much of that is real and how much is the magic of a recording studio?"

Daniel sat up straight. "I assure you, Rissa's voice is pure. There's nothing a recording studio could do to improve it."

Mr. Riley looked skeptical. "I highly doubt that. I've been in this business a long time."

"I can sing something for you," I offered. Daniel had told me to let him do the talking, but I couldn't sit by idly and let them talk about me as if I wasn't there.

"Be my guest," Mr. Riley said smugly, as if he knew something I didn't.

I bit my bottom lip and reached for my guitar. No. I spied the baby grand sitting in the corner and quickly made my decision. I had prepared for a different song, but my heart was telling me otherwise. The piano was my true passion. The place I could get lost in the music and the words.

I tentatively walked to the piano and sat down on the bench. Taking a deep breath, I began to play Broken Wings. My fingers flew over the keys. I didn't think, I just felt. I let the music consume me and unleashed my voice. This song was written on emotion alone, and I let it pour through me with every note I sang. The soft verses tugged at my heart and the powerful chorus gave me strength. I closed my eyes and saw the two men that loved me and changed my life. My past and my future tied together by an unbreakable bond. When I finished the song, I wiped away the tear that fell down my cheek.

The room was silent.

I swallowed down the lump in my throat. There was nothing more I could do. I gave it everything I had.

"Oh. My. God." Mr. Riley leaned forward on his desk, "That was... I'm rarely left without words, but right now I have none."

I crossed the room and sat back down next to Daniel. He quickly grabbed my hand and gave it a squeeze of encouragement. "Beautiful," he whispered as he kissed my cheek.

We waited patiently for Mr. Riley to say something. Anything. The silence was killing me.

He leaned back in his chair. "That was magical. It was money in the bank. We could do great things together."

I sat up straighter, the hope building in my chest. I had done it. I was going to finally make something of myself. I hoped my mom and dad were watching. I hoped Wes was watching. I wanted them to know that I had finally made it. The poor girl from Oklahoma had actually made something of herself. I needed it for me and for my daughter. I wouldn't have to depend on anyone else. I could depend on me. It was liberating.

"However," Mr. Riley continued, "I can't ignore the elephant in the room."

And just like that, my heart dropped out of my chest.

"You're pregnant. When are you due?"

"March," I croaked out.

"My wife and I have three children. I know the changes you're going to face. The next few months are tough. There's no way you could handle the recording schedule, the promotional work or the public appearances that are necessary when launching a new artist. Right now, you're unmarketable. No one wants to see a pregnant woman at a concert. Even if we could photoshop the pictures, we wouldn't be able to hide it."

"But, but I can..." I stuttered.

"Mr. Riley, I assure you, Rissa is one hundred percent committed to this. You're making a mistake," Daniel argued.

He held up his hand to silence the both of us. "I love you, Rissa. You've got the look and the talent, but I have to say not now. Come see me in six or seven months, we'll talk again. That's the best I can offer you."

I held it together. I stood and thrust my hand over his desk. "Thank you for the opportunity. We'll be in touch."

He gently shook my hand in both of his. "I'm sorry, Rissa. Good luck with the rest of your pregnancy. Even if you don't understand it, I'm doing you a favor. I look forward to working with you in the future."

I nodded, picked up my guitar and turned on my heel with only one destination. Anywhere that wasn't here. I didn't hear the rest of the conversation between Daniel and Mr. Riley. It didn't matter what was said. I'd heard enough.

It was a no. No recording contract. No albums. No concerts. No money. No way to support my daughter.

I made it to the elevator without breaking down and stabbed at the call button. *Come on, come on.* I waited impatiently, tapping my foot on the marble. *Hurry the fuck up!* I could feel the pressure building behind my eyes. If this damn elevator didn't get here soon, I was going to fall apart right here in the reception area.

The doors finally opened, and I quickly stepped inside, frantically pushing the button for the lobby. The doors were almost closed when a hand shot between them. "Stop, Rissa!"

The door slid back open, and Daniel stepped in next to me. "I don't want to talk about it," I said over the lump in my throat.

"Rissa, it's not as bad as you think. He didn't say no. He said not right now. He loved you..."

"Stop! I said I don't want to talk about it. Later doesn't help me now. You don't know how badly I needed this, so stop trying to make me feel better." I stared at the numbers above the door and willed them to move faster.

The ride down seemed to take forever. Daniel stayed silent. Charlie opened the door of the waiting car. I slid in and scooted over. Daniel slipped in next to me. "Should I assume dinner is cancelled?" he asked.

"I want to go home. If you can't make that happen, then take me to LAX. I'll figure it out from there." Home? Where was home? Oklahoma? New York? Michigan? None of them felt like home to me.

"Let me make a few calls. Charlie take us to the hotel, please."

I stared out the window and watched as the lights of the city flew by. Tears streamed down my face. I couldn't hold them in any longer. I started to sob uncontrollably. The pain in my chest got worse and worse. My stomach churned, and I could feel the contents of my lunch making a reappearance. "Pull over!" I shouted.

Charlie quickly pulled to the side of the road. The car had barely stopped before I thrust the door open, and I heaved my entire lunch onto the concrete. Daniel rubbed my back gently. "Are you all right?"

I wiped my mouth with the back of my hand. "I don't know."

He ran his hand over my neck and forehead. "You're burning up."

"I'm fine," I snapped.

Daniel handed me a bottle of water. "Charlie, the hotel. Quickly."

I faced Daniel, embarrassed by my outburst. He didn't deserve my attitude. "I'm sorry. I know you did your best. I wish I could have been a better client. I'm sorry I disappointed you."

He wrapped his arm around my shoulder and pulled me into his side. I rested my head on his shoulder. "You have nothing to be sorry for. When we go back, and we are going back, we're going to slay them. This isn't the end, Rissa. It's a speedbump, that's all."

I wanted to believe him, but all I could see right now was a future where I had no way to support my child.

♫♪♫♪

Back on the plane I curled up on the couch and huddled in the corner of it. I felt like shit both physically and emotionally. I'd let the hope fill so much of me that now that it was gone there was nothing left. I was completely empty. Void of any feelings except despair and disappointment.

Bobby came over and wrapped his arm around me. He'd cancelled his evening plans, so I could get home tonight. I didn't deserve to have a friend like him, but I was glad I did. He pulled me into his side, and I leaned into his warm body. "It's going to be okay, Rissa," he whispered into my hair.

"It's not going to be okay," I whispered back. I didn't want to tell him all my fears. He'd think I was a bigger charity case than I already was. Instead, I let him hold me as I cried.

"This isn't over, Rissa. You keep writing and making music. When you go back in a few months, you'll have a whole album to present. When you take off, you're going to soar," he encouraged.

"To the moon," I said lifelessly.

"To the stars," he said shooting his hand into the air like a rocket. "You'll get there, of that, I have no doubt."

"Thanks, Bobby. I'm gonna try to get some rest." I untangled myself from him and pulled the CD player from my purse. I put in my earbuds and closed my eyes. Zack's selection of songs was well thought out and sweet. They held an overwhelmingly clear message: he wanted me back.

Before this trip I was leaning towards giving us another chance. But now... if it didn't work out, I didn't think my heart could take one more disappointment. What was the point in trying anymore? My life had become a series of highs and God they were good, but the continual crashes of the lows were destroying me, tearing away at me one little piece at a time until eventually there would be nothing left.

Almost everything I had, had already been taken from me. The only thing left was the little girl growing inside me and I had nothing to give her.

I dozed on and off but by the time we touched down, I was still exhausted. My body ached, and I had the chills. Bobby offered to ride home with me, but I politely declined. I just wanted to be alone.

I slid into the back of the town car and let Charlie drive me back to my shamble of a life.

Chapter 32
Zack

I waited all day for Rissa to call me. She had to be back in town by now, she was supposed to be working at The Locker.

When I closed the shop, I trudged out into the snow that was falling heavily and walked the half block to the bar. Once inside, I spotted Lou immediately but no Clarissa. Lou was hustling around like a crazy person. Thursday was Ladies' Night, and the place was packed.

I waved to Lou to grab his attention. As Lou started walking my way I called out, "Is she here?"

"Rissa called in sick." He grabbed two glasses from under the bar, filled them with ice and started pouring liquor into them. "Said she wasn't feeling well. Nothing else."

I tapped on the bar. "Thanks." I walked back towards my shop with a bad feeling in my gut. As long as I'd known Clarissa she'd never called into work. I tried calling her, but it went immediately to voicemail. My text went unanswered too. If she was sleeping, I didn't want to bother her.

The next day I still hadn't heard from her. She was either ignoring me or something was terribly wrong. She called into work again as well. My calls and texts all continued to go unanswered.

The nagging feeling inside of me wouldn't go away. I wished I had Daniel's number, surely, he knew something.

I scrolled through my contacts and found the one I needed. It rang and rang. I was about to give up, when Bobby answered, "What's up, Zack?"

"Did you go to LA with Rissa?"

"Nope. I was already there for my own meetings," he said in a clipped tone.

Being an ass was not going to get me the answers I needed. "Did you see her? Do you know what happened?"

"Shouldn't you be asking Rissa?"

199

"Listen, Bobby, I know I've acted like a prick, but I really need your help. She was supposed to be home yesterday. She called into work two days in a row, and she refuses to answer her phone. I'm worried."

"Fuck. I shouldn't be the one telling you this," he said.

"Telling me what?" I prodded.

"Daniel said they loved her. She nailed it, singing some new song."

"That's good, right?"

"It's great, except they wouldn't sign her. They told her she was unmarketable because she was pregnant, and they were worried she wouldn't be able to handle the obligations. They want her to come back in six months or so."

My heart dropped out of my chest. "Fuck! How'd she take it?"

Bobby sighed. "Not well. She wanted to come home right away. I cancelled my plans, and we all came home on my jet that night. She barely said two words."

I blew out a breath. "So, she's been home since Wednesday night?"

"Yep."

"Thanks, man. Listen, I'm sorry for getting in your face before. It's just that..."

"You're so in love with her, you couldn't help yourself?" he interrupted.

I ran my hand through my hair. "Yeah. It's made me act like a crazy person."

"She's just a friend, man. I'm not trying to move in on your girl. I'm not that guy."

"I know you're not. Thanks for taking care of her and getting her home safe. Are we cool?" I didn't want to lose Bobby as a client or a friend.

"Yeah, we're cool. Go get your girl, she needs you."

"I will."

I pulled my keys out of my pocket and headed to the garage. I wouldn't let her ignore me if she was hurting. I'd be there for her, whether she wanted me to or not.

When I pulled behind her building, her car was there covered in six inches of snow. The steps were covered too. Her damn landlord hadn't even cleared the steps for her. I hated her in this apartment.

I knocked on her door, waiting impatiently. When she didn't answer, I knocked again, louder this time. "Clarissa, open the door, sweetheart," I called out.

Still nothing.

I looked for the key on my ring from when I installed her new lock. I slipped it in and turned the knob. It was eerily quiet and cold inside. She was nowhere in sight. The only sign of life was the light that shown under the bathroom door.

I knocked on it gently, "Clarissa?"

"Go away. I want to be alone," she said hoarsely.

"No can do, sweetheart," I said from outside the closed door.

"Please. Just go away, Zack." I could barely hear her quiet voice.

I turned the knob and slowly pushed it open. She sat on the bathroom floor, eyes red, skin pale and looking exhausted. She had on sweats with a scarf wrapped around her neck. Her hair was tied up and sticking out in every direction. She was beautiful.

I crouched down in front of her. "Are you okay?"

She let out a little chuckle, but her eyes held no humor. "Is that a trick question? Because by now I'd think you'd know I'm a total train wreck." Then she dashed to her knees and leaned over the toilet, throwing up nothing but water. I rubbed her back as she continued with dry heaving. When she finished, she sat back down and took a sip from the almost empty water bottle next to her. Leaning her head back against the wall, she closed her eyes. "You shouldn't be here," she said weakly.

I put my hand on her forehead. She was burning up. "How long have you been like this?"

"Two days. I think I have the flu."

"Why didn't you call me?" I asked softly.

She shrugged her shoulders. "I'm not your problem anymore."

I hated she felt that way. I ran the back of my hand down her soft face. "No, you're my heart. I'll always take care of you."

Her eyes filled with tears. "You don't have to."

"Don't you know how much I love you?"

She shook her head and she started to sob. I pulled her into my arms. "Oh, sweetheart." I pulled Clarissa to her feet, and led her to the couch. "We're going to get you feeling better, okay?"

"I don't have medical insurance," she whispered.

"Don't you worry about that." I grabbed her boots from the front door and stuck her feet into them. Then I helped her into her coat that barely zipped up the front anymore. I looked around the room. "Where's your purse?" I asked.

"Under the bathroom counter, in the back." I went in search of it. Sure enough, hidden back behind the towels was her purse and a jar full of money. I shook my head. I had to get her out of this goddamn apartment. It wasn't safe, and the heat was barely working.

I helped Clarissa out to my car, making sure she didn't fall down the fucking stairs that no one had bothered to clear. I opened her door and set her inside buckling the seat belt over her belly. "Let me know if you need me to pull over, okay?"

She nodded. "I'll be fine."

I drove us to Troy Beaumont Hospital, pulling up in front of the ER. I led her inside and set her in a chair. I went directly to the check-in desk.

The curly-haired older lady glanced up at me in less than an interested manner. "How can I help you?"

"My girlfriend has the flu."

The lady let out a huff.

I didn't let it deter me. "She's got a fever, she's throwing up, and she's six months pregnant."

That got her attention. "Are you the father?"

"Yes," I said without hesitation.

She handed me some papers over the counter. "Fill these out and we'll get her in immediately."

"Thank you." I took the clipboard and sat next to Clarissa. "How are you holding up?"

She rubbed her hand over her stomach. "I think I'm going to throw up again."

I scanned the waiting room and spotted a small garbage can. I grabbed it and placed it next to her, then I got to work on her forms. I filled in her name, address, and phone number. Birth date? Embarrassingly enough, I didn't know when her birthday was. How could I not know that? I pulled out her driver's license to search for the information. My heart sank. I was such a jerk. Yesterday. Her birthday was yesterday, and I didn't even wish her a happy birthday.

Just then, they called us back and into a private room. The nurse took her temperature and raised her eyebrows. She patted Clarissa on the hand. "I'm going to get a doctor, sweetie."

Within the hour, Clarissa was admitted to the hospital. I pulled some strings, namely waving money at them, and got her a private room. In addition to the 102 fever, Clarissa was suffering from extreme exhaustion and dehydration. She was hooked to an IV drip, as well as a fetal monitor.

Clarissa had barely talked. She stared blankly out the window as I held her hand. "I'm sorry I missed your birthday," I whispered.

She continued to stare out the window.

"And I'm sorry your trip to LA didn't go well."

More silence.

"And I'm sorry I've been such an ass. I'm going to do better."

Nothing.

I rubbed my fingers lightly along the back of her hand with no response. We sat like that for over an hour. Me trying to coax something out of her. Clarissa staring blankly out the window. I wished I knew what she was thinking, but her silence gave me no clue.

When she spoke, it was so soft at first, I had to lean in closer. "I'm selfish. Malcolm was right. I can't take care of myself, let alone a daughter. I want her to have everything I didn't have growing up. I want her to have a good life. She deserves better than what I can give her."

"Clarissa…" I started.

"No, Zack," she turned to me. "I have no business raising a baby. Look at me. I can't do this. I'm single, I don't have insurance, I live in a shithole and I work in a bar. Stellar credentials for being a mother. I'm going to sign the paperwork. It's the right thing to do."

"You're wrong," I said.

"I'm not wrong," she insisted.

"Well, you're not doing anything today. Let's worry about getting you better first." I wasn't sure if it was the fever talking or if she was really thinking about giving up her baby. Our baby. There was no way in hell I was letting that happen.

I stood up. "I need some coffee. Do you want anything?"

She stared back out the window. "I want to go back to being 15, before my mom got sick and everything fell apart."

My heart clenched. Clarissa was so strong, sometimes I forgot everything she had been through. "If I could give you that, I would. Anything else?"

"You can go home. You don't have to stay with me."

"I'm not going anywhere. I'll be back in a few minutes."

She was slipping away. Not just from me, but from everything. I'd never seen her like this before. I went down to the bottom floor to grab a coffee. I called both Lou and Audrey to let them know Clarissa was in the hospital.

Next, I called Chase. I was getting her out of that damn apartment if it was the last thing I did. Tonight. Chase and Layla agreed to meet me in an hour to get the keys. Goodbye shithole.

♫♪♫♪

I stayed with her all night, sleeping in the chair. My neck was crinked and my back ached. But none of that mattered. Clarissa slept soundly. I watched the fetal monitor as it registered my daughter's heartbeat. She was strong, just like her mom.

By the time morning came, color had returned to her cheeks, but her eyes were still dull. No life whatsoever had returned to them. The nurse came in and checked her vitals. Her fever had broken.

Despite my attempts to talk to her, Clarissa barely said a word. My worry over her mental state increased. The only thing she had said was, "Why are you still here?"

"Because you're my heart," I repeated. I would say it as many times as necessary until she believed it.

The doctor signed her release papers mid-afternoon. The nurse removed the IV and the fetal monitor. I took her clothes out of the bag they were in and handed them to her.

"Can you give me some privacy?" she asked.

"Sure, sweetheart." I stepped into the hallway and let her change. After a few minutes, I went back in. She sat on the edge of the bed staring at the floor.

The nurse came in with a wheelchair. Clarissa sat down without a word. "I bet you're glad to be going home, sweetie," the nurse said.

"I am."

I pulled the car up front and tucked her inside. I drove us the ten minutes back to my apartment and pulled around back.

She looked around. "What are we doing here? Why is my car here?"

"You're home," I said.

"Zack, take me back to my apartment," she said.

I put my hand on her knee. "All of your things are here. This is where you belong." Chase and Layla had moved all of Clarissa's things here last night, including her car. It was a risky move on my part, but well worth it. At least here, I knew she was safe. I could take care of her.

Clarissa exited the car silently. She'd been practically mute since we checked in at the hospital yesterday. She headed up the stairs and let herself into my apartment. Our apartment.

Layla touched me on the shoulder. "How is she?"

I shook my head. "Physically, she's fine. But mentally, I'm not so sure."

"Let me know what I can do," she said.

"You've done plenty. Thank you for moving her things last night."

"It was our pleasure. Chase and I hated her living there as much as you did. This is better."

"Yeah, it is."

I headed upstairs and found Clarissa sitting on her neatly made bed, staring out the window again. "Do you want something to eat? I can make you some soup or a grilled cheese."

"I'm not hungry."

"You have to eat, sweetheart."

205

"I said I'm not hungry. I just want to sleep," she said sharply.

Priss slipped through the door and hopped up onto the bed next to Clarissa. She tentatively stepped onto my girl's lap and curled up. Clarissa absentmindedly rubbed Priss's back.

"I bet a hot shower would make you feel better," I suggested.

"I doubt it," she said. "But I probably stink. Where is my stuff?"

"You don't stink," I assured her. "Layla put everything you need in the bathroom."

She nodded and headed off to shower. When I heard the water start to run, I called my mom.

"Hi, honey. How did Rissa's trip to LA go?"

"Not well. They turned her down because she's pregnant. She came home early. When I didn't hear from her, I went to check on her and she was sick with the flu. She spent last night in the hospital."

"Oh, Zack! How is she feeling? How's the baby?" she asked with concern.

I stepped into the hallway, just in case she could hear me. "The baby is fine, but I'm worried, Mom. She's barely said anything to me. Her eyes are vacant. She's just...gone. She's thinking about giving up the baby." Just saying the words hurt more than I ever thought they would. Two months ago, I couldn't imagine being a father, but now it was the only thing I wanted. I wanted to be the one that little girl depended on. The one she ran to when she scraped her knee and the one who held her tightly when she had bad dreams.

"She's in a low place right now, Zack. All her dreams just shattered. Give her time. Take care of her."

"I'm trying. I had Chase and Layla move her things here. She's in the shower right now."

"That's good, honey. She'll come around. We're not letting her give up the baby. Put that idea out of your head, right now."

"Okay, Mom. I'm going to go check on her. I'll talk to you later."

"Okay. Love you, honey."

"Love you too, Mom." I went back in and put some water on the stove to boil and thought about how I was going to break Clarissa out of her funk. *Give her time.* I could do that.

The bathroom door opened, and Clarissa came out with her robe wrapped tight around her. She went to her room leaving the door open just a crack.

I made her a cup of hot chocolate and knocked on her door. When she didn't answer, I tentatively opened the door. She was laying on top of the covers, curled up on her side. Her pink pajamas had little white kittens all over them.

I sat down on the edge of her bed, placing the mug on her nightstand. "These are cute," I said running my hand down her side.

"Wes bought them for me," she said.

I laughed. "My brother bought cat pajamas for the woman who hated cats."

She shrugged. "I guess."

"I brought you some hot chocolate." I motioned to the cup on her nightstand.

"You don't have to babysit me. I'm fine by myself."

I ran my hand through her wet hair. "I know you are. But you want to know a secret? I'm not fine without you."

Chapter 33
Rissa

I felt dead inside.

I'd failed, and I had nothing to offer the baby growing inside me.

Nothingness. That's all I felt.

My guitar stood in the corner, mocking me. I had no desire to pick it up. No desire to play a single chord. No desire to sing. No desire to make music. I moved it to my closet and shoved it far into the back out of my sight.

It wasn't even my closet. I was like a leech taking up space in Zack's apartment.

The only bonus of being here was the bed. It was soft and warm. The perfect place to do nothing but sleep.

Every morning, Zack brought me breakfast and a glass of orange juice. Sometimes it was scrambled eggs, sometimes a cut up apple with peanut butter, and sometimes it was a bowl of oatmeal. I always pretended I was asleep when he came in. It was easier than talking to him.

For days, it went on like this. I had no hope for a future with my baby and all I could think about was the way it was supposed to be. Wes and me. Me and Wes. We made this baby together and now I was alone. He wouldn't be in the delivery room with me holding my hand. He would never hold our baby.

Miss Priss had become my best friend. She always curled up next to me. I would pet her soft fur and she'd purr loudly. She was good company. She didn't try to talk to me. She didn't tell me to eat. And she didn't look at me with pity in her eyes.

Sometimes in the middle of the night, when I knew Zack was asleep, I would bundle up in my coat and sneak up to the rooftop. I'd stare at the moon and the stars and absorb the peaceful, quiet night. The world looked different from up there. Everything was blanketed in white, looking pure and innocent, even if I knew otherwise. I'd inhale the fresh air and watch my breath as I exhaled. I craved the cold, because lately it was the only thing that made me feel alive.

♫♪♫♪

The covers were ripped from my head and I was startled awake. "What the fuck?"

"It's time to get up," Zack pronounced.

I ripped the blanket from his hand and pulled it back over my head. "I'm sleeping. Leave me alone."

Zack pulled the blanket off me again. "Gina called. You missed your doctor's appointment."

I huffed out my disgust. "My appointment isn't until Thursday."

"And today is Friday. I made you a new appointment. We're leaving in an hour."

I sat up with wide eyes, shocked at what he had said. "Today is Friday? How?"

Zack sat on the side of my bed. "You've done nothing but sleep for a week. I was fine with giving you space and letting you get the rest you needed, but I'm not fine with you missing your appointment. I know you're sad and disappointed, but you need to get back on track. And that starts with showering, having a good breakfast, and letting me take you to your appointment."

I stared down at my hands that were folded in my lap. How could I have lost track of so much time? How could I have forgotten the most important thing I had to do? "You don't have to go with me," I said. "I'll go. I won't flake out."

Zack twined his fingers with mine. "I know you won't, but I'm still going. You're not alone in this. I'm going to be with you every step of the way."

"Why?"

"Because you're my heart." Zack stood from the bed. "Go get in the shower. I'll make you breakfast."

"Okay." I trudged off to the bathroom and locked the door. I took off my pajamas and tossed them on the floor, then looked at my naked body in the mirror. *You're my heart.* He'd said it more than once over the last week. I rubbed my hand over my growing belly. He'd change his mind when all of this became a reality. The crying, the diaper changing, the sleepless nights... he didn't sign up for any of that. It wasn't his responsibility.

I stood under the hot spray of water. Zack had a great shower. The water pressure was divine, and the temperature was better than lukewarm. I spent a few extra minutes letting the warmth sink into my skin. I'd have to thank Layla for organizing all my things and making sure I had what I needed. I shaved my legs and some places down below that I'd been ignoring. Even if I wasn't sleeping with Zack, it made me feel better. Sexier. I let out a little huff. There was nothing sexy about my body right now.

I wondered what Zack saw when he looked at me. Did he see me, or did he only see Wes's baby growing inside me? He was being sweet. He had put up with more than any man should, especially for a woman carrying another man's baby. He was going to make a great uncle, of that, I was sure.

I dried off and wrapped my robe around me. Then I scurried off to my room to get dressed. I opened my drawers. Inside were all my clothes, neatly folded. I'd worn nothing but pajamas for... a week, apparently. I pulled out a pair of jeans and then headed to my closet where all my shirts hung. Tori hadn't been this big in the winter, but there were a few cute long-sleeved shirts. I pulled one off the hanger and got dressed.

Next, I tackled my hair and make-up. Even if I didn't want to admit it, I did feel better. I went sheepishly to the kitchen. I was embarrassed that I had let it get so bad. Zack stood at the stove, flipping pancakes. "Hi."

He turned and smiled at me. "There's my girl. How do you feel?"

"Better," I admitted. I sipped the glass of orange juice sitting on the counter. "Thanks for taking care of me. I'm sorry I was such a pain in the ass."

Zack leaned on the counter facing me. "I love taking care of you and you were only a teeny tiny bit a pain in the ass," he said holding his thumb and forefinger barely an inch apart. Zack returned to the gridle and placed a couple of pancakes on a plate for me. He set the butter and syrup down. "We need to talk about some things."

My shoulders drooped. "Like what?"

He took a deep breath. "Like work. I'm fine if you don't want to go back, but you need to talk to Lou and Audrey."

"Shit." I hadn't been to either job in over a week and I hadn't even called in. I'd been so self-consumed with my pity party that I'd forgot about everything else. "I'm probably fired."

Zack shook his head. "You're not fired. I've been keeping in contact. Both Lou and Audrey agreed that you've been working too much. You just need to decide what you want to do and let them know."

"You called my bosses?" I asked incredulously.

Zack nodded. "How about we come up with a more reasonable schedule today?"

"I need to work, Zack. I can't give up my jobs." I needed the money, and he knew that. I wouldn't be a freeloader.

"I know you do. I'm not suggesting you quit, maybe just cut back a little," he reasoned.

"I'll think about it. I think I should work as much as I can while I feel good," I said. "Because when I have this baby, I'm not going to be able to work for a while."

Zack frowned. "I don't want you to worry about that. We'll make it work. All I want you to focus on is you and having a healthy baby. Nothing else matters. Now, finish up your breakfast, we're leaving in fifteen minutes."

"You really don't have to come, Zack."

"I really do," he answered.

♫♪♫♪

I sat on the table in Doc Peterson's office. I was only getting an ultrasound today. The door opened, and he walked in. Doc Peterson tapped the chart in his hand. "I missed you yesterday."

"Ummm. I kind of slept through my appointment." He didn't need to know the truth and the excuse seemed plausible.

"I see," he said, raising his eyebrows. He looked down at the chart again. "You haven't gained any weight since your last appointment. As a matter of fact, you lost a pound."

Zack squeezed my hand, giving me courage. "I went through a bout of depression, but I'm back on track. I promise."

"I hope so. You need to take better care of yourself," he scolded.

211

"I will. I got the flu and ended up in the hospital, but I'm better now. Zack's been taking good care of me." If nothing else, I hoped it would make Doc Peterson ease off the guilt trip.

"I'll give you a pass," he said with a smile. "How's our baby. Has she been kicking?"

I shook my head. "Not really. I mean, sometimes I have discomfort, but it's more like a nudge than a kick."

"Lie back," he instructed. "We're going to get this baby kicking."

"Can we listen to the heartbeat?" Zack piped up. "I haven't got to hear it yet."

Doc Peterson smiled. "I think we can do that."

I pulled my shirt up and bared my belly. Zack hadn't seen me this big and round. I stole a glance at him to gage his reaction. He didn't look disgusted. He looked awed. I bit my lip and focused on the ultrasound machine.

Doc Peterson rubbed the gel over my tummy and then the wand. My baby filled the screen. Her perfect little body was curled up tight inside me. And she was sucking her thumb or at least it looked that way. He turned on the sound and the glorious beating filled the room. It was steady and strong. "Let's get her moving."

Doc Peterson pressed hard on the side of my stomach. I felt a kick as her little leg moved on the screen. "Do you want to feel it?" I asked Zack.

"I'd love that," he said. I placed his hand on my stomach and Doc Peterson pushed again. She kicked harder this time. "That's amazing."

Doc Peterson wiped my belly off and pulled my shirt down. "Everything looks good, but you need to gain some weight, young lady."

I nodded. "I will."

When we left the office, Zack grabbed a hold of my hand. We walked that way back to his apartment. I felt warm inside, despite the cold weather. I wasn't sure what the feeling was, but it felt a little bit like hope.

Chapter 34
Zack

.

Clarissa started a slow climb back to normal. She went to see both Lou and Audrey. Much to my disapproval, she continued working both jobs. Lou cut back her hours, letting her come in later when the tips were better. At least her shifts were shorter which meant less time on her feet. She kept working at A Second Chance on her regular schedule, but there she wasn't on her feet all day. Audrey was like a mother hen and promised me she wouldn't let Clarissa overdo it. If anyone could talk sense into Clarissa it was Audrey.

It was the time when Clarissa wasn't at work that worried me the most. She locked herself away in our apartment. When she was home, she sat in her room with the door closed. I never heard the television. I never heard her guitar. I never heard anything.

I never saw her smile.

She didn't come down to my shop. She didn't talk to Layla. She didn't talk to Chase. Kyla hadn't heard from her and neither had Tori. She isolated herself.

I went back to walking her home from the bar at night. She said it was too close to drive and I didn't want her walking by herself. I held her hand as we walked in silence.

The holidays were quickly approaching. The small downtown area was transformed into a Christmas scene out of a book. Wreathes hung from every lamppost, and colorful lights were strung on every building. The Fire and Ice Festival was this weekend, and I was taking Clarissa whether she wanted to go or not. I needed to break her out of her depression.

Saturday morning, I knocked on her door. "Come in," she answered.

I opened the door. She closed the notebook on her lap and slipped it into the nightstand. "What are you doing?" I asked.

"Thinking," she said.

I sat down next to her. "About what?"

213

"Just stuff," she answered vaguely. "Did you need something?"

"Yep. I need a date for the Fire and Ice Festival, and that's you," I said bumping her shoulder with mine.

"I don't think so," she answered scrunching up her nose.

I made a buzzing noise. "Wrong answer. The only thing I want to hear from you is *Yes, Zack. I'd love to go with you.*"

Clarissa gave me a weak smile. "Why don't you take Gina? I'm sure she'd love it."

I shook my head. "I don't want to take Gina. I want to take you. You're my heart."

"You keep saying that, but what does that even mean?" she asked.

I put her hand on my heart. "It means that you fill this space right here. I feel empty without you. I know you don't believe me, but I'm going to prove it to you. I'm going to make you trust me again."

"And what happens when you change your mind?"

"I'm not changing my mind, Clarissa. Walking away from you would be like walking away from my destiny." I pulled her hand to my lips and kissed her palm. "I'm smarter than that. I went to Yale, remember?" I said, giving her a wink.

"You mean you dropped out of Yale," she said with a smirk.

"Oh, you've got jokes now? You think you're funny?" I pulled her back on the bed with me and tickled her. She laughed, and it was like music to my ears. "I've missed you, Clarissa."

She got tears in her eyes. "I've missed you too, Zack. I really, really have."

I wiped the moisture from her face. "You're a hormonal mess, aren't you? One minute you're laughing, the next you're crying."

She bit her lip and nodded.

"Can you try with me?" I asked. "I know that things didn't go how you planned in LA. I know you think you can't do this. I know you thought Wes would be here with you through your pregnancy and he's not. I know you think you're alone, but I'm right here. I love you and I'm not walking away from you again. I want this, Clarissa. Can we start over?"

"I'm scared," she whispered.

214

"I know you are, sweetheart. But you don't have to be. Everything's going be okay. We'll take it slow if you need to," I promised her. I wanted to kiss her so badly, but now wasn't the time.

She scrunched up her nose again. "So, what's the Fire and Ice Festival?"

I sat up and clapped my hands together. "Well, there's lots of food, overflowing hot chocolate, bonfires, music, and ice sculptures. It's a big community event. It'll be fun." I wiggled my eyebrows at her. "Trust me."

She smiled. "Okay. It's a date. Give me twenty minutes to pull myself together."

"Take your time."

Clarissa went off to lock herself in the bathroom. This was good. I'd remind her of how it was when we were together. I couldn't fail, it wasn't an option for me.

I stared at the nightstand where she had shoved her notebook. The last time she was writing in a notebook, she was making a list of everything she owed me. That wasn't happening again.

Even though I shouldn't have, I opened her nightstand and pulled out the notebook. I opened it to the first page.

It wasn't a list.

Dear Alexandria~

I want you to know how much I love you. Giving you up was the hardest decision I've ever made. It was a choice I made out of love. I grew up poor and I wanted so much more for you. When your father died, my whole world fell apart. I thought I could do it on my own, but that was just selfish. I had nothing to offer you except love. So, I made the decision that I thought was best. I wanted you to have a better life than me. I wanted you to have everything your heart desired.

Don't think for a moment that I abandoned you or that I didn't love you, because you are the best thing that ever happened to me.

Love Always~
Your Mom

I swallowed down the lump in my throat and flipped to the next page.

Dear Alexandria~

I want to tell you about your father. His name was Wesley Alexander Kincaid. You were named after him. He wanted to name you Nicole. I knew as soon as he died, that if you were a girl, you would be Alexandria.

I met him when I was nineteen and he was twenty-one. I was playing the piano and he was sitting at the bar. We bonded instantly over music. He was amazingly talented. He could play any instrument and his voice was like silky smooth chocolate. The ladies loved him because he was a looker. But I was lucky, and he chose me. We lived happily together for two years.

I wish you could have met him. He would have loved you so much. He had bright green eyes and blond hair that sometimes fell over his eyes. He was the type of man that brought home ice cream just because he thought you needed it and danced with you in the middle of the kitchen. Your father was one in a million.

He was a sweet man, who would bring me flowers for no reason. We were so happy when we found out you would be ours. I love you!

Love Always~
Your Mom

I choked down the emotion that welled in my chest and flipped the page.

Dear Alexandria~

I'm sure you're wondering why I let your grandfather raise you. Let me tell you a story.

I was born in Oklahoma. Your grandparents, my mom and dad, were the best and they would have loved you so much. My mom died when I was seventeen. My dad died when I was eighteen. They taught me how to play the piano and the guitar. They taught me to love music. They never got to meet you, but they would have been over the moon with love for you.

I was on my own at eighteen and moved to New York, trying to be a musician. That was when I met your dad. I tried really hard to make a life for you, a life for us. I failed you. I couldn't support you and for that I will eternally be sorry. Please forgive me.

Love Always~
Your Mom

Clarissa was already preparing to give up her daughter. Every word I read, cut away at a little part of my heart. I felt the desperation in her words.

Dear Alexandria~

I need to tell you something so important. I don't know if you know your Uncle Zack or not, but you need to know about him. I was so alone, and he helped me so much. He was like your dad, but better. When your dad died, your Uncle Zack lifted me up. He helped me to go on even if I was heartbroken.

He's a great man. You were lucky to have both of them love you before you were born. I hope you get to know him, because he's wonderful. He helped when I thought I was alone. He was the light in my darkness.

Love Always~
Your Mom

Dear Alexandria~

My days with you are numbered. I think I have ninety left, but maybe you'll come early, and I'll have even less. I'll cherish every moment with you. You're my heart. That's what your Uncle Zack always says.

I Love You. Forever and Always~

217

I was pissed that she was preparing to give up our daughter.

I was shattered she felt this was her only choice.

I was pained that she didn't think of me as an option.

"What are you doing?" Clarissa's voice cut through my haze.

"You're not giving up your daughter," I said sternly, while tapping the notebook in my hand.

She stalked toward me and yanked it from my fingers. "That was private. You had no right!"

I pulled it back and ripped the pages out. I shredded them into tiny pieces. "She won't need any of this because you're her mom and you're not giving her up. You're not letting them take her away from you. You're not letting them take her away from me!" I shouted.

She dropped to the ground and began picking up the pieces. "She needs to know! I need to tell her everything!" Sobs racked her as she scrambled to put the pieces back together.

"Stop!" I knelt before her and grabbed a hold of her shoulders. "Stop, Clarissa! She's not just yours. She's ours! She's my baby too!"

"You don't know what you're talking about!" she yelled. "I can't. I can't let her grow up like me. She deserves better!" She clutched the pieces in her hands, holding them like they were all she had left.

I pried her fingers apart and let the pieces fall to the floor. "I love you, Clarissa. I want to be her daddy. I want to help you raise our daughter. I may not be her biological father, but no one, and I mean no one will love her more than me. Give me a chance."

"You... you don't know what you're saying," she stuttered.

I took her hands in mine. "I do. I know exactly what I'm saying and what I'm committing to. I've thought about this long and hard. This little girl," I put my hand on Clarissa's belly, "is mine. I'm going to be here. Forever, Clarissa. Just like you, she's my heart. Maybe I haven't made this clear, but I want both of you. I want to be the man that both of you can depend on. I want us to be a family."

"Why?" she asked through her tears.

"Isn't it obvious?" I took her face in my hands and stared into her bright blue eyes. "I love you, Clarissa. From the first night we were together, I've loved you. Even when I thought I shouldn't, I couldn't stop. You've completely captured my heart and I don't ever want you to let it go."

"I love you, too," she sniffed. "Even when I shouldn't have, I couldn't stop either. I love you so much, Zack."

I wrapped my arms around Clarissa and pulled her to my chest. She held me back and we kneeled there on the floor just holding each other. Never letting go. I ran my hand through her hair. "Will you let me be Alexandria's daddy?"

She nodded her head against my chest. "Yes. She'll be the luckiest little girl in the world to have you for a daddy."

"And you for a mamma," I added. "No one will love her like us." I pulled back to kiss her on the forehead, the tip of her nose and finally her lips that I had missed so much.

She let out a little gasp and I slipped my tongue inside. I'd missed kissing her so much. Our tongues tangled together, and she gripped my shoulders tightly. I drowned in her touch. Lost myself to her. Let her consume me in the very best way.

"I missed you so much," I told her.

"I missed you too."

"I need to be inside you."

She dropped her head and shook it. "I don't want you to see me. I'm too big."

"You're beautiful. There isn't a single inch of you that isn't. Every curve of your body is beautiful, Clarissa. Let me show you."

I lifted her from the floor and into my arms. She wrapped hers around my neck as I carried her to my room. I gently set her on the edge of the bed. She sat quietly and watched me. I pulled one fluffy sock from her foot and then the other. Clarissa wiggled her red toenails as I freed her feet. I kissed the arch of each soft foot.

I grasped the bottom of her sweatshirt. She pulled it down tighter over her stomach. Without saying a word, I removed her hands and lifted her shirt over her head. Her tits filled her bra and overflowed. Her tummy was big and round, carrying our baby. I reached behind her back and undid the clasp of her bra, pulling it away from her body. "You're beautiful, Clarissa," I whispered. I ran my hands over her full breasts, rubbing my thumbs over her nipples. She moaned, and they hardened under my touch.

"Zack," she whispered.

My hands continued their exploration of her body, caressing her firm baby bump where our child rested. "Beautiful," I said again. My fingers sank into the sides of her leggings. She lifted her hips and I pulled them down her legs. "Lay back for me, sweetheart."

She laid down and I spread her legs apart. I kneeled between them, ready to worship her body. I lifted one leg, kissing her behind the knee and up towards the apex of her thigh. I put her leg over my shoulder and started kissing up her other one. With both legs over my shoulders, I slid my fingers over her wetness. "I've missed this. I've missed the way you taste."

She let out a soft whimper as I licked her pussy. Her essence covered my tongue and I had forgotten how good she tasted. How much I loved eating her out. That would never happen again.

"Make me come, Zack," she whispered. "I need you to make me come."

I licked up through her folds until I reached her clit. I ran my tongue over the little bundle of nerves and then sucked her between my lips. Two fingers sank deep inside her wet pussy, searching for the spot that would make her fall apart. I felt her walls fluttering against my fingers and I sucked harder, running my tongue over her. Clarissa's breath hitched, and her hands grabbed at the comforter as her back arched up off the bed. "Oh my God, oh my God, oh my…" She shattered beneath me into a million beautiful pieces.

Her hands flew to her stomach. "Are you okay?" I panicked.

She smiled. "Somebody else liked that too." She reached for my hand and put it on her stomach. I felt the little kicks against my palm. "I didn't know that's what it would take to make her move."

I smiled down on Clarissa. "It's amazing. We'll have to do that more often." I reached behind my head and pulled my shirt off, then stripped off my jeans and boxers in one motion.

Clarissa stared at my hard cock as I slowly jacked it. "I've really missed you. All of you."

"You won't ever have to again." I leaned over her and kissed her lips. I kissed down her neck to her tits and sucked one luscious nipple into my mouth. She arched up into me and I gave her other breast the same attention. I kissed down her body and placed several kisses along her round belly.

I stood and lifted her hips, nudging my head against her opening. "Let me know if I hurt you." I slowly slid inside her. She was so tight and wet. She felt spectacular around my cock. I slid in and out at a leisurely pace, savoring the feel of her. It felt like home, the only place I wanted to be. Clarissa made all those soft little sounds that I loved and missed. "Look at me, sweetheart. I want you to look at me while I make love to you."

She arched into me, wrapping her legs around my waist, pulling us together. We couldn't get close enough. We moved together in a rhythm that we had perfected months ago. "I'm gonna come, Zack. Please fuck me harder," she whispered.

"I don't want to hurt you."

"You won't. I need to feel you deeper."

My fingers dug into her hips as I sped up my pace, pushing harder and deeper. She closed her eyes and her pussy started to squeeze my dick. "Open your eyes."

She did and then fell apart, quaking around me. I pumped harder and faster. I felt the sparks zipping through me, starting at the base of my spine. My balls pulled tight and then I released. I came deep inside her, the only place I wanted to be. I collapsed over the top of Clarissa holding myself up with my forearms and twining our fingers together, careful not to crush her beautiful body. I kissed her forehead. "Are you okay?"

She got a satisfied smile on her face. "I'm more than okay. Will you lay with me?"

"I'm not going anywhere." I used my t-shirt to wipe us both off. I pulled back the covers and we slid in side by side. I curled on my side and pulled her back against my chest. My hand rested on her round belly. "I want you in my bed at night. No more sleeping separately. I need to feel you next to me."

"I'd like that," she whispered. She snuggled back against me. "I'm so tired."

"Sleep, my love. I told you, I'm not going anywhere."

♫♪♫♪

Later that day, I took her to the Fire and Ice Festival. We were dressed warmly for the cold December day. Snowflakes fell lightly around us, creating a magical winter wonderland. We ate hotdogs, drank hot chocolate and warmed our cold hands by the fire.

Finally, I pulled Clarissa across the street to the skating rink. "Oh, no. I don't know how to ice skate," she protested.

"I'll help you," I told her. "I'll never let you fall, whether on this rink or in life, I'll always be there to catch you. I promise, sweetheart."

She smiled up at me sweetly. "I'm trusting you, Zack. Not just with this, but everything. Are you sure this is what you want?"

"I've never wanted anything more in my entire life." It was the most honest thing I had ever said. The woman before me was my present, my future... my everything.

We traded our boots for skates, and I held her hand as we made our way onto the rink. I skated backwards and held both her hands as I pulled her along. "I'm shocked," she said. "You're really good. How did you learn to skate?"

I winked at her. "My mom taught me when I was a kid. Every winter, she'd take the three of us to Rockefeller Center. I loved those days. We'd take the subway like normal people and just be. My father hated the subway, so he never came, and that was all right with me. He always had work to do, there was never any time for fun with him."

"That's sad," she said.

I shrugged. "My mom tried to make up for it. She did a pretty good job too." I let go of one of her hands and skated beside her. She began to get comfortable and skated effortlessly beside me. "I thought you never ice skated before?"

"I haven't." She smiled up at me. "But I have roller skated. It's not that different." She let go of my hand and skated ahead of me.

I followed behind her, afraid she was going to fall. I snuck up behind her and wrapped my arms around her waist. "Thank you for taking a chance with me," I whispered in her ear. "I promise I won't let you down."

"I trust you."

Chapter 35

Rissa

I felt lighter. I no longer felt alone. I could do this. With Zack by my side, I felt like I had a chance at happiness. Not just for now, but for always.

His heat kept me warm at night. I couldn't snuggle up to him like I used to, my belly was too big. Instead, Zack held me from behind and wrapped himself around me. He'd kiss my temple and tell me he loved me.

Tonight, I couldn't sleep though. I was restless under the sheets. Everything was too perfect. I slipped out of Zack's arms and wrapped my robe around me. I crept out to the front room, closing the bedroom door behind me.

The piano called to me. I hadn't played anything since LA, I hadn't had it in me. But tonight, I needed it. I pulled the sheet from the black lacquer and let it fall to the floor. I sat on the bench, letting my fingers touch the keys. I pressed down my index finger and listened to the sound. I did it with each finger, absorbing the sounds of the individual notes.

Then I closed my eyes and started to play. The music wrapped around me, enveloping me in its warm embrace. I felt the peace and serenity it provided. It wasn't a song I had played before. It was something new. I heard the music in my head before it reached my fingers, and they echoed the sounds of my mind. Music wasn't something I did. It was something I felt. It was a part of me.

"You're playing again." Zack stood leaning against the doorway of our bedroom, with his arms crossed over his chest.

"The time felt right. I'm sorry I woke you."

He walked over and sat on the bench next to me. "Don't ever be sorry for doing what you love. What are you playing?"

"Nothing and everything. It's all in my head. It's not anything yet," I whispered. I didn't know why I was talking so softly, except that it seemed I should as we sat in the dark, the only light coming from the moon and the snow falling outside the window.

"It's beautiful, just like you." He placed his fingers under my chin and turned my head to kiss him. "Come back to bed, sweetheart. I can't sleep without you."

"Are we really going to sleep?" I asked coyly.

"Eventually." Zack took my hand and led me back to bed.

I let my robe drop to the floor, crawled into bed, and laid on my side. Zack laid behind me and wrapped his hand around my thigh. "Give me your leg. Open for me." He pulled my leg back over his hip. "I love you, Clarissa Lynne. I can't get enough of you." He slid inside me, slow and deep. He made love to me, and his fingers rubbed gently over every sensitive part of me until I fell apart.

I was pretty sure I had gone to heaven and I never wanted to come back. I felt like I was flying. Maybe I was an angel after all.

♫♪♫♪

I started writing music again. I remembered Bobby's words, *When you take off, you're going to soar*. With Zack to help me, I could do it all. I could be a mom and a musician. Nothing would stop me.

Or at least I thought that was true, until a certified letter came in the mail. It was from Malcolm's attorney. I ran down the stairs to find Zack. "Where is he?" I asked Layla.

"Hi to you too," she quipped.

"I'm sorry. I really need to talk to him."

"He ran out for a few. He had some errands to do. He'll be back shortly," she assured me.

"What do you know about going to court," I asked her.

Layla took a step back and her face paled. "More than I should. My dad's an attorney."

There was something else there, but I couldn't find it in myself to ask her about it now. I shoved the letter at her. "What does this mean?"

Layla read the letter and rubbed her lips together. "It's a summons for Kings County Family Court. It's a preliminary show cause hearing to determine your ability to care for your child. Malcolm will have to prove why you're an unfit parent and you'll have to prove why you are. Nothing is usually decided, it's a way for the judge to collect information about the case."

I bit the side of my thumb. "What if I don't go?"

Layla handed me back the paperwork. "You have to go, or else all the judge will hear is Malcolm's side. You'll be in contempt."

"Shit. So, I have to be in New York on January 10th?"

"Yes. And you need an attorney. Didn't Zack set you up with one?" she asked.

I blew out a ragged breath. "I fired him. I told him I didn't need help."

"You better call him back. You're going to need him," Layla said emphatically.

I waited an hour for Zack to return. He kissed me and assured me everything would be okay. He told me Jeff was still on the case. I wanted to believe him, but really nothing had changed. I had a better living arrangement, but I was still single, I still had no insurance, and I still worked in a bar. I was still the white trash Malcolm saw me as.

Christmas was in seven days. Merry Christmas to me.

♪♪♪♪

I tried to relax and put the court date out of my mind. Zack took me out to get a Christmas tree for our apartment. We spent the day buying lights and ornaments and finding the perfect tree.

I opened the door for Zack as he carried the tree inside. "Since I moved here, I've never had a Christmas tree," he said as he leaned it in the corner.

"Never?" I asked. "How could you not have a Christmas tree? That's like sacrilege."

"I never had anyone to share it with." He kissed me. "Seeing the smile it puts on your face, makes carrying that heavy ass tree up the stairs worth it."

"I kind of love Christmas. I love sitting in the dark with only the tree lit and watching stupid, sappy movies with predictable endings."

He cupped my face in his hands. "Then after we get this set up, that's exactly what we'll do. Consider *Lifetime* my new favorite channel."

"Will you make me hot chocolate too?"

He pretended to think it over. "That depends. Are you willing to negotiate?"

"What did you have in mind?"

"I'll make you hot chocolate if you make me a batch of your chocolate chip cookies tomorrow."

I smiled up at him. "You drive a hard bargain, but it's a deal."

We got to work setting up the tree. Zack about had a fit when I stood on a chair to put the lights on, but I wanted our first tree together to be perfect. When we had hung the last ornaments, I stood back and admired our work. "We're a good team," I said.

Zack wrapped his arm around my waist. "Do you know how happy you make me? You're the best thing that's ever happened to me."

We spent the rest of the night with only the light from the tree, watching *Lifetime* movies while cuddled under a blanket on the couch. In this moment, everything seemed perfect.

· ♪♪♪♪

I had a show at The Locker on December 23rd. It was a Christmas celebration before the bar shut down for the holiday. I was busy writing some new music and rehearsing my favorites. Zack bought me my own keyboard, so I could expand my set on stage. I hated him spending money on me, but I gave up trying to change his mind. It made him happy and that made me happy. I quit fighting him and finally let him take care of me.

Catherine called to let us know she'd be here for Christmas. She needed to finish the holiday charity event for Kincaid Industries and then she'd be on a plane for Michigan. She was coming in on the day of my show.

Lou was giddy over her return. For a hard ass, he was so damn cute when it came to Catherine. I was thankful that he had come into my life. He'd been there for me more than I deserved. Catherine could do worse than finding happiness with Lou.

Chapter 36
Zack

I was on my way to pick up my mom from the airport. Clarissa had been a wreck all week, making sure that everything in our apartment was perfect. She wanted to make a good impression on my mom. She was also concerned about us sleeping together while my mom was there. It was ridiculous. I assured her my mom already knew we were sleeping together. It wasn't like we were teenagers; we were grown adults.

I was ecstatic to have my mom here for Christmas. I hadn't spent the holidays with her in years. It wasn't going to be fancy or elegant, but it would be real. Clarissa had gone shopping and was planning a big dinner. I invited Chase and Layla to join us. Chase declined to spend time with his own family, but Layla accepted since she had no family here. I even invited Audrey and Lou, both of which graciously accepted.

When I saw my mom by baggage claim, she walked quickly to me and wrapped her arms around me. I picked her up, giving her a tight hug. "I'm so glad you're here."

"Me too," she said wiping at her eyes. "I don't know how I went so long before without seeing you."

I grabbed her luggage, and we walked out to my car. I opened the door for her, placed her things in the trunk and hopped in the driver's seat. "How is the divorce going?" If I knew Malcolm, he was making her life a living hell.

She blew out a breath. "I don't know what I was expecting, but I guess I thought he'd give a shit, maybe ask me to stay. But he doesn't care. We're two strangers living in the same house. It's been that way for years, I just chose to ignore it."

"What about Ronnie?"

"I love your sister, but she's always been daddy's little girl. He walks on water as far as she's concerned. We talk, but it's strained," she admitted.

"I'm sorry, mom. I wish I could make it better for you."

She placed her hand over mine. "Being here makes it better. I'm glad to be out of that cold shell of a house. When you kids were little, it was full of life, there was music and laughter and happiness. Since you've all grown up and moved away, it's just empty. Your father isn't any company and I'm lonely."

"Clarissa is nervous about you being here, especially now that we're living together," I said.

She scrunched up her nose. "Why?"

"She wants you to like her. She's really hung up on the fact that she was with Wes before me. She thinks it's awkward."

"Well, I'm not hung up on it. I love her. I'll do my best to set her at ease," she assured me.

"Thanks, Mom."

♫♪♫♪

The Locker was packed. All our friends were here, I'd made sure of it. Kyla, Tyler, Tori, and Chris sat at a table towards the front. Gina was sitting with some guy I'd never seen before. Chase and Layla sat at a table with a few other friends and Audrey sat at the bar. Almost every table was full, except for the one reserved up front for us. I took my mom to the bar to grab some drinks before finding our seats.

Lou's smile overtook his face as we approached. He immediately started shaking my mom's martini and pouring my whisky. He placed the martini, extra dirty with two olives, in front of my mom. "It's nice to see you again, Catherine."

She took a sip of her drink and smiled at him. "It's good to be back." And then she winked.

This side of my mom was going to take some getting used to. I could barely contain the laugh inside me from creeping out. I put my hand on her back, "I think we should find our table."

"You go on and go," she insisted. "I'm going to chat with Lou for a minute. I'll meet you over there."

I rolled my eyes and took the opportunity to go see my girl. She got here an hour ago to attend to any last details since we'd set up her equipment

229

this morning. She was sitting on the old vinyl couch in the breakroom with her guitar on her lap. I knocked on the doorframe and walked in. "You all set?"

"I don't know why I get nervous. I've done this dozens of times." She was wearing her leather cuff around her wrist that matched the one she bought me. I hadn't worn mine in a while, but since we'd reconciled, I wore it all the time.

I laced our fingers and pressed our wrists together. "You've got nothing to be nervous about. This crowd loves you."

"I know. I'll be fine once I get started. Honestly, the crowd doesn't even exist once I start playing." She stood from the couch and did a little spin. "Does this make me look too big?" she asked referring to her outfit.

I pressed my lips to hers. "You look gorgeous as always. You worry too much."

Clarissa wrapped her arms around my neck. "Have I told you lately how much I love you?"

I pushed her hair behind her ear. "Only every day." I loved this feeling between us. I had felt like half my heart was missing when we had split, but with her I felt complete. Happy. Fulfilled. This was the way it was supposed to be. I knew it from the first night we had been together. The circumstances might have been wrong, but the feelings I had for her that night were real. The best thing I ever did was ask her to come home with me. I couldn't imagine living my life without this woman by my side.

She looked at the clock on the wall. "It's time. I better get out there."

"I'd say good luck, but you don't need it. Just do your thing."

She nodded as I walked her out to the stage. My mom was sitting at the table already and Bobby was by her side. I don't think she had a clue who he was, but they were chatting like old friends.

I held out my fist for him to bump. "Thanks for being here, man. It means a lot to me."

He knocked his knuckles with mine. "I wouldn't miss it for the world. You guys are two of my favorite people, even if your shit was fucked up for a while."

I cringed and glanced at my mom. She held up her hands. "Really, Zack? You act like I've never heard swear words before. I've heard the word 'fuck'. As a matter of fact, fuck your father." She held up her martini and took a long drink.

I let out a loud laugh and clinked my glass with hers. "I'll drink to that. Fuck that asshole." We both took another long drink.

"Your mom is pretty cool." Bobby laughed.

"She's the best," I agreed.

Clarissa took the stage and all eyes turned toward her as she grabbed the mic. "Wow! We've got a full house here tonight. Thank y'all for coming out." She turned sideways and rubbed her hand over her stomach, "This might be my last show for a while. This little pumpkin is due in March, so we'll have to see how she treats me." Hoots and hollers came from the crowd, encouraging her to go on. "Remember to treat your bartenders well and have one for me. I haven't had a drink in over six months. Should we get this show started?"

The audience was eating out of the palm of her hand. She had a way with the crowd that couldn't easily be replicated. Their applause was her answer. She started in on a much loved cover song that the audience knew well. I looked around at the crowd. They adored her. Everyone was having a good time.

Clarissa played a good hour before taking a break. She was on fire tonight. I stood to help her off the stage and over to our table. She kissed Bobby on the cheek, and surprisingly I didn't feel even a hint of jealousy. Then she faced my mom. "Hi Catherine. I'm so glad you're here." I could tell she was nervous.

My mom opened her arms wide and wrapped Clarissa in a huge hug. "I'm so happy to be here. Your singing is phenomenal."

"Thank you."

Lou brought Clarissa an ice water with lemon and placed it on the table. He winked at my mom. "You want to come up to the bar for a while? Keep me company?"

"I'd love to," she said. She followed Lou to the bar, leaving us alone with Bobby.

"What's gotten into your mom?" she asked.

I shook my head. "I don't have a clue, but it's nice to see her having fun."

Bobby cleared his throat. "It's nice to see you found your voice again. I was worried about you."

Clarissa cast her eyes downward. "I was worried about me too, but Zack helped pull me out of my funk. Thanks for helping me in LA. I was a mess."

"Don't even think about it. I know this industry. I got shot down a lot when I first started. Now, I just give them all the big ol' middle finger, because I can buy and sell them all," he said.

We all laughed because there was a lot of truth to what Bobby was saying.

Soon enough it was time for Clarissa to hop back on stage. "Y'all ready for my next set?" Again, the crowd went wild. "Before we get started, I have a few people I need to thank tonight. First, my girls Kyla and Tori. They pulled me into their girl posse, when I didn't even know I needed one. Next, my boss, Lou, and also the owner of this fine establishment. He gave me a job when I moved here, gave me a chance to perform, and gave me fatherly advice I desperately needed. Love you, Lou" She blew him a kiss from the stage.

"I also need to thank my friend, Bobby. He gave me the confidence to perform by inviting me to sing at one of his shows. He's given me opportunities and guidance no one else could have given me. And lastly, my broody man, Zack." Our eyes met, and we smiled at each other, "He saved me, in more ways than one, when no one else could. He showed me what it was like to love and trust again. I love you, baby." I blew her a kiss, and she blew one back to me.

Clarissa was well into her last set of the night, and I knew it was getting close to the time. I tapped my fingers nervously on the table. I hadn't done this in forever, not since my days in New York. Bobby pressed his palm down over my twitchy fingers. "Dude, you got this."

I nodded, too nervous to speak.

Clarissa finished her last song. "Thank y'all for coming out and have a great night."

I stood and stepped up on the stage grabbing the mic. "Wait up a minute. We've got one more song for you."

Clarissa stared at me with wide eyes. "We do?"

"Yes, sweetheart, we do." Bobby handed me my guitar that he'd kept beside his chair all night. Then, he passed up a bar stool. I sat down on it and settled my guitar on my lap. I winked at Clarissa. "You can join in at any point."

She was in shock when I started strumming my guitar and singing "*Collide*" by Kid Rock. My voice was steady and strong thanks to Bobby's coaching. She smiled at me with love in her eyes and began singing. We swayed to the music and our voices melded in perfect harmony. Our connection was pure magic. Everything else faded away as we focused on each other. *So, let's roll the dice, one more time. Take a chance on love, again tonight. Risk it all, lay it on the line.* We continued to sing the lyrics, knowing they had special meaning to us. We'd both been hurt by others. Hell, we'd hurt each other, but we were both willing to take this chance to be together.

When we finished the song, Clarissa had tears in her eyes. Our friends were clapping like crazy, knowing everything we'd been through. I slid off my stool and got down on one knee before her. I pulled the ring from my pocket and took her hand in mine. "Clarissa, sweetheart, I love you more than words can say. Will you do me the honor of being my wife? Will you have my baby?"

She nodded as the tears streamed down her cheeks. "Yes, baby. Yes!" She launched herself into my arms. We held each other as everything around us erupted.

We pulled apart and I slid the ring on her finger. I had taken Wes's engagement ring and had it reworked. I had a new center stone put in to represent me. On the sides of it were two more stones. The first was the stone that Wes had given her. The second was a matching stone for Alexandria. It was unconventional, but we would all be tied together for the rest of our lives and I was surprisingly okay with that. I didn't think Clarissa could cry any harder, but when I explained the meaning of the ring she broke down.

"You'll never know how much this means to me," she cried. "It practically destroyed me to sell this ring, but to know that you bought it and made it even better, proves to me that we were meant to be. Thank you for being so thoughtful, so perfect, so you!"

I pressed my lips to hers. "Merry Christmas, sweetheart."

We finally left the stage and made our way back to our table. Bobby had a satisfied smirk on his face. "Congratulations, you two. I expect to be invited to the wedding."

Clarissa wiped at her eyes again. "Without a doubt."

My mom wrapped us both in a tight hug. "Why don't you two head home? I'm going to hang out with Lou for a while. He said he'd walk me home."

I looked at her skeptically. "Are you sure?"

She nodded. "I think you two could use some alone time."

I thanked my mom and handed her a key. I was sure Lou would make sure she got home safely.

Clarissa and I were out the door in a flash. We practically ran the half block home. Everything was out in the open now. Clarissa knew my full intentions and our life together could finally begin.

My mom wouldn't be home until after two, when Lou could close the bar, so we had some time. I carried Clarissa up the stairs and placed her on the bed. I knelt down in front of her. "I love you, Clarissa Lynne Black."

"I love you too, Zackary Michael Kincaid. I can't wait to spend the rest of my life with you."

I stripped her shirt off in one fluid movement. "I need to be inside my fiancé."

Clarissa grabbed my wrist. "Wait. Do you still have the diamond collar?"

I quirked an eyebrow at her. "Yes."

"I want to wear it tonight," she said.

I was so confused. I thought she hated that thing. "Why?"

She stroked her neck. "Because you bought it for me and I. Am. Yours. In every way."

"Are you sure? You don't have to," I asked, caressing her face.

"I'm sure. I want everything you can give tonight." Her voice was raspy and full of lust.

It made my dick stand at full attention. "I don't want to hurt you." I'd be lying if I said I only wanted to make slow sweet love to my girl. The truth was I wanted to fuck her. Hard. I'd resisted and kept myself under control, but what she was offering was so damn tempting.

234

"I'll tell you if it's too much," she promised. "I'm not going to break."

I turned to my dresser and took out the long black box that hadn't been opened in months. I removed the collar and fastened it around her neck. Once in its proper place, I ran my fingers over the diamonds. "This looks beautiful on you," I told her. "It makes me want to fuck you."

"It makes me want you to fuck me," she answered.

"That can definitely be arranged. What else do you want?" She was going to lead the show tonight, not me. She twirled the ring on her finger nervously and stared at her hands. I lifted her chin with one finger and looked deep into her eyes. "You don't have to be embarrassed."

She sighed deeply, working up the courage to talk to me. "It's just… well, before you, I never did any of this stuff. It's… awkward. When we were together before, I let you lead."

"I'm going to be your husband and you're going to be my wife. We like what we like. What we do is nobody else's business. You never have to be embarrassed to tell me what you want. I promise I'll never pass judgement on your needs or wants. I'll do everything I can to always please you."

"That's the thing," she said. "I want to be everything you want me to be. I don't feel like I can do that now that I'm so big."

I kneeled before her. "Listen to me, Clarissa. You are everything I want." We never talked about our last night together before everything fell to shit. I'd been avoiding it because what I did to her that night was wrong. I'd let the darkness take over and I refused to do that with her again. I swallowed down the lump in my throat. "Is this about the night of my birthday?"

She shrugged. "Maybe. I don't know. I felt like I was a disappointment to you. I don't want to disappoint you."

"Oh, sweetheart, you've never been a disappointment to me. That night was messed up on so many levels. I fucked up. I took it too far and I'm sorry."

"I fucked up too. I let Gina get in my head," she admitted.

"So, we both fucked up. It's the past, let's leave it there."

"But parts of it were sooo good. I'd be lying to say I didn't like it."

"So, we keep the good parts and forget the rest. What do you want, Clarissa?" I asked her again.

"I liked the scarves. I like not knowing what you're going to do to me. I liked being tied to the bed. I like letting you have complete control," she said shyly. Clarissa hesitated and swallowed nervously. "And I liked the vibrator."

I smiled. "I like all that too. I like having you at my mercy. But I won't handcuff you again until after you have our baby. I won't ever take the chance that I could hurt you. Do you trust me?"

"Completely."

"Do you want me to fuck you, Clarissa?" Just saying the words got me hard again.

"Yes, Zack. I want you to fuck me."

I returned to the dresser and pulled out two black scarves. Changing my mind, I took one and threw it aside. "I'm going to blindfold you, but I want your hands free. I want you to be able to touch me. I want your hands all over my body tonight." I tied the scarf over her eyes. Then I stripped my shirt off and placed her hands on my chest. "Touch me, Clarissa."

She stood from the bed and felt her way across my chest. Her hands rubbed over my shoulders and down my back. She kissed my chest and down my stomach to the waist of my jeans. She dropped to her knees before me, slowly undoing my button and zipper. I ran my hands through her hair and piled it on top of her head. Before I knew it, my jeans were at my ankles and her hand was wrapped around my cock, stroking me up and down. I let out a growl. "That feels so good, Clarissa. Suck me. I want to come in your mouth."

She didn't need to be asked twice. Her soft lips surrounded me, her tongue working its way up and down my shaft. It was heaven. After she'd worked me over with her tongue, she sank down deep. Her mouth and hand worked in perfect rhythm. She squeezed tighter and sucked harder. I grabbed the sides of her head and guided her up and down my cock. She placed one hand on my ass and pulled me in closer. I couldn't help myself, I started fucking her mouth. She took every inch of me and her other hand tugged gently on my balls. "God, just like that. I'm gonna come. Right. Now." Everything pulled tight and I released into her mouth. Clarissa swallowed everything down and gently released me with a pop of her lips. "Fuck, that was amazing, baby."

"I like making you feel good," she said softly.

"Now it's your turn," I lifted her up and kicked out of my jeans. I quickly got to work on Clarissa's pants and had her completely naked in seconds. I laid her back on the bed and tongued her pussy and clit. She was a chorus of moans and whimpers and soft sighs as I devoured her. I knew how to please my girl and she let me know it. I continued the sweet torture with my tongue as I pushed two fingers deep inside her. Clarissa began to writhe on the bed, grabbing at the comforter with one hand and pushing on my head with the other. I refused to stop until she had at least two orgasms. I wanted her dripping wet for me.

"Oh God, Zack," she panted. "I'm gonna come so hard... fuck!" Clarissa fell apart, her head thrashing from side to side.

I smiled up at her from between her legs. "Are you ready for me to fuck you now?"

"Please," she begged.

I lifted her higher on the bed. "Get on your hands and knees for me, sweetheart." Clarissa quickly did as I asked, and I placed a pillow under her belly to make her more comfortable. "Do you want me to get the vibrator? Do you want me to play with your pussy and your ass?"

I watched her body visibly shiver. "I want everything," she whispered.

I went to my bottom dresser drawer to get the vibrator and the lube. "Tell me if it's too much." I didn't know what her body could take at this stage of her pregnancy and I sure as hell didn't want to hurt her. The thought of hurting her, kept my dark side in check. There was no way I would lose control. I ran my hand down her spine. "You okay, sweetheart?"

She nodded her head. "Yes. I want you inside me so bad."

I whispered in her ear. "I will be. I can't wait to have your sweet pussy wrapped around my cock."

I turned the vibrator on and slipped it between her legs, running it through her wetness and over her clit. Clarissa let out a loud moan and fell to her elbows, sticking her ass high in the air. I ran a hand over the perfection in front of me and between her cheeks. My fingers plunged inside of her pussy and pulled her wetness up her ass to the place I planned on putting that vibrator. I slipped the tip of one finger inside her and felt her tense. "Relax, Clarissa. I promise to go slow."

"I trust you."

I knew she didn't trust easily, and I had broken it the last time we did this. I made a vow to make this as pleasurable for her as it was for me. I dripped some lube down her ass and then onto the vibrator. Slowly I breached her ring of muscle and slid the vibrator inside.

"Oh God, Zack," she panted as I fucked her slowly with the vibrator.

"Are you ready for my cock? Do you want me to fill you up completely?" I growled.

"Please. Please put your cock inside me," she begged. I loved when she told me exactly what she wanted.

I slowly slid the head of my cock into her pussy and then slipped all the way in. Between the vibrations and the tightness of her pussy, I wasn't going to last long. I gripped her hips in both hands and fucked her slowly. "I love watching my dick disappear into this tight little pussy of yours. We fit together so perfectly. I was made for fucking you, Clarissa."

"I love you, Zack. Fuck me harder. Give me everything," she pleaded.

"I could fuck you all night long, sweetheart." I pumped into her harder. "One day I'm going to fuck this sweet little ass of yours."

It was a good thing we were alone, because those soft little sounds I loved, were nowhere to be found as I fucked her from behind. She screamed out my name as she came around my cock and I roared out my own release when her pussy clamped down on me.

After both having earth-shattering orgasms, we collapsed on the bed together wrapped in each other's arms. Being with Clarissa was complete bliss.

Chapter 37
Rissa

Christmas came and went. Every day that passed was another day closer to my court date. Our attorney, Jeff, met with us to go over the details. I was glad Catherine was there to ask the questions Zack and I hadn't thought of.

"So, that's the plan," Jeff finalized. "I'm surprised the judge is even entertaining this case."

"I'm sure Malcolm didn't leave him much choice," Catherine said.

Malcolm was a cold-hearted, power-hungry prick. I hated him more and more every day. There was one thing I had that Malcolm would never have... an unconditional love for my child. It was my trump card, and I was holding onto it tightly.

"One more question," Jeff said. "When are you planning to get married?"

Zack and I looked at each other. With everything going on we hadn't discussed dates. I guess I assumed we would wait until after the baby was born. We weren't in any hurry, being engaged was enough for now.

"We haven't decided," Zack answered. "Why?"

"I'm thinking, sooner would be better than later. We need something solid to present the judge if he's on the fence. Having a date will solidify your engagement," Jeff answered.

It made sense, but I didn't want to rush Zack into committing to a date. We'd just gotten our shit figured out. I was afraid it was going to be too much reality for him at one time.

Zack took a hold of my hand, calming my fears. "We'll come up with a date. That's not a problem."

Catherine smiled at us across the table. "My son is finally getting married and I'm going to be a grandma. You two have made me so happy."

Jeff stuck all his papers into a folder and stuffed them into his briefcase. "So, I guess I'll see you on January 9th. Send me the flight information and I'll meet you at the airport."

Zack shook Jeff's hand and thanked him for his help.

Jeff looked at me. "Keep your head up, Rissa. You've got this. I won't let you down."

I gave him a half-hearted smile. I wanted to believe Jeff, but there was a shadow of doubt hanging over me that I couldn't shake. It all sounded too easy. If I knew Malcolm, he was going to make this anything but easy.

After Jeff left, Zack kissed me on the forehead. "Don't worry." He left me alone with Catherine as he went down to his shop for an appointment.

Catherine clapped her hands together. "I think we need a girls' day. Let's go get manicures and pedicures, and then we're going shopping. I want to buy you a new outfit. When you walk into that courtroom, I want you to feel as classy and beautiful as you are."

I scrunched up my nose. "You don't have to buy me anything. I have money saved."

"I'm sure you do, but you're going to be my daughter-in-law. I have a lot of making up to do for how I treated you before. I made a lot of mistakes with Wes. I'm not going to do that again. You're my family now and I want to treat you as such."

I swallowed down the lump in my throat. "It's been a long time since I've had a family."

Catherine reached for my hand. "I'm not trying to replace your mom, but I'd like to be the mom-figure in your life, if you'll let me."

My eyes filled with tears and I nodded. "I'd like that."

Then her eyes filled with tears. "Do you have any idea how happy you've made my sons?" She used the plural and it felt... I don't know, it just felt strange.

I'd asked her this before, but I needed to do it again. "Is this weird for you Catherine? The fact that I was with Wes and now I'm with Zack?"

She looked at the ceiling before answering. "If I still had Wes, I know you would have been by his side, but I probably would have never gotten to know you like I have. Now that Wes is gone, I'm glad that you and Zack have found happiness. I've never seen him look at anyone the way he looks at you. Are you happy, Rissa?"

I twisted the ring on my finger. "Yeah, I am. I was in love with Wes and then my life shattered. Zack saved me and taught me how to love again. You're a good mom, Catherine. You raised two men who were loving, kind, and generous. They both captured my heart in different ways. They've both made me happy."

Catherine spent the day spoiling me. First, we went to the salon to get manicures and pedicures. Then she took me shopping at Nordstrom. She bought me a blue dress that matched my eyes. It was classy, and it made me feel confident. Paired with a set of amazing heels we'd picked out, I was far from the white trash Malcolm believed me to be. I was Rissa Black, future music star and kick-ass mom.

♫♪♫♪

"Are you sure you want to do this?" I asked Zack, while the clerk prepared our paperwork.

"I've never been more sure of anything in my life," he answered, squeezing my hand.

The clerk slid the papers across the counter, and we signed our names. She stamped them and handed the papers back to us. "Congratulations."

"You can still change your mind," I reminded Zack.

"Not a chance in hell, sweetheart."

We stepped into the elevator and pressed the button for the third floor. My heart was beating out of my chest. When the doors opened, Jeff and Catherine greeted us.

"You ready to do this?" Jeff asked.

I took a deep breath. "Not really, but I'll be glad when it's over."

Catherine wrapped me in a warm hug and kissed my cheek before we walked into the courtroom. Months ago, I thought I would be doing this alone and now I had a solid support group. I had people who believed in me. People who loved me. I was no longer alone.

Jeff and I walked to the front and sat at the table on the left side of the courtroom. Catherine and Zack sat behind us.

Malcolm sat at the table on the right with his attorney. Ronnie sat behind him.

I had divided this family over the custody of my child. I should have felt guilty about it, but I couldn't. This family had been in trouble way before I ever entered the picture. It was funny. I always thought that if I had money, it would solve all my problems. Looking at the broken family surrounding me, I knew money couldn't fix everything. Without love, money meant nothing.

The judge walked in, and everyone stood. Zack grasped my hand and gave it a little squeeze in support before letting go.

"You may be seated." The judge sat and all of us followed suit.

The judge put on his reading glasses and read over the papers in front of him. "We're here today to determine the ability of Miss Clarissa Black to be a suitable parent for her unborn child. Mr. Malcolm Kincaid, the alleged grandfather of said child, is petitioning the court for custody." The judge scanned over both sides of the courtroom. "I have to say that this is an unusual request, but I am ready to hear your arguments."

Malcolm's attorney stood, straightening his coat and buttoning it. "Your honor, it is my client's position that Miss Black is in no way capable of raising a child. She is pregnant with the child of Mr. Kincaid's late son, Wesley Alexander Kincaid. Since his death, Miss Black has moved to Michigan without consulting the family. She is a single woman, who works as a bartender, and lacks the insurance and resources to adequately care for a child. She lives in a tiny run-down apartment and drives a vehicle that is unsafe. According to our records she is barely supporting herself. It is our contention that she would not be able to properly support, care for, or raise a child."

After ripping apart my credibility, Malcolm's attorney proceeded to sing Malcolm's praise. "Mr. Kincaid is an established member of the community, residing in Forrest Hills Gardens. He is the CEO of the business that was started by his grandfather, Kincaid Industries. He has the means to support his grandchild, providing the best housing, medical, childcare and schooling available. Mr. Kincaid is petitioning the court for full custody upon the completion of a paternity test. We believe that Mr. Kincaid having custody would be in the very best interest of the child."

Malcolm's attorney sat down looking smug.

242

Jeff stood up adjusting his own suit jacket. I held my breath as he began to speak. "Miss Black is more than just a bartender. She is an aspiring musician and performs locally on a regular basis. She is also employed at a clothing store. Miss Black has established her life in Utica, Michigan where she plans to raise her child. She has recently become engaged to Mr. Kincaid's other son, Zackary Kincaid. The two are now living together in a very suitable apartment in the building Mr. Kincaid owns. Mr. Kincaid is a successful business owner and is wealthy in his own right. When Miss Black and Mr. Kincaid are married, Miss Black will have full medical insurance for herself and her child. Mr. Zackary Kincaid has agreed to take on the responsibility of being the child's father, including full financial support."

I felt like crap. Everything that was said made Zack sound like the perfect choice as a parent but did nothing to boost my own credibility.

The judge tapped his fingers on the bench. "It seems we have a family dispute much further reaching than the custody of this child." The judge addressed Malcolm. "Mr. Kincaid, do you feel that your son is a responsible and acceptable father figure for your grandchild?"

Malcolm stood up. "Absolutely not. He's irresponsible. He abandoned his family responsibilities by dropping out of college and joining the Marines. He left our family to open a tattoo shop in some hick town. He's nothing but a disappointment." Malcolm sat down without even a glance at his son.

The judge turned back to us. "Miss Black, I'd like to hear from you. What do you have to say about all of this."

Jeff gave me a nod. I stood and smoothed my dress over my stomach. I ran my fingers over Wes's pendant around my neck and then began to speak. "Your Honor, I was born in Oklahoma. Both of my parents were deceased by the time I was eighteen. I drove my daddy's truck across the country to New York, with little more than my guitar. I lived in New York on my own for over a year before I met Wes Kincaid. We dated for two years and became engaged. I had just found out I was pregnant when Wes died of heart complications. Malcolm subsequently stripped me of all assets. He had Wes's car impounded, our bank accounts frozen, and gave me three days to vacate our apartment. I'll admit that I was young and naïve. I should have insisted that we put my name on our assets, but I trusted Wes and never worried. I didn't know that it was Malcolm I had to worry about."

I took a deep breath. "I became acquainted with Zack at the funeral, from which I was banned. Zack made sure I was able to properly pay my respects to Wes. He stood by my side the entire time and for that I will be eternally grateful. When I was faced with being homeless, Zack offered me a place to live and a chance to start over. I accepted his generosity and over time, Zack and I became more than friends. We are now engaged."

"I am more than an aspiring musician. I have been offered a recording contract once my baby is born. This will provide me financial stability beyond what Zack is willing to provide. Malcolm Kincaid may have the upper hand financially; however, he will never be able to provide the love and emotional support that I can. No one loves this baby more than I do."

The judge smiled at me, and I took that as a good sign. "Thank you, Miss Black."

He then focused back on Malcolm. "Mr. Kincaid, your response."

Malcolm stood back up. "I see that I'm going to be painted as the villain here, but nothing could be further than the truth. I did what I had to do for the protection of my family. Miss Black was with my son for his money, and I put a stop to it. She's nothing, but a gold digger."

"Mr. Kincaid…" the judge cautioned Malcolm.

"My son, Zackary, is just like his brother, falling for a pretty face and thinking with the wrong head. How do we even know this engagement will last? How do we know she won't take his money and move on to someone else who can offer her more?"

The judge was visibly irritated with Malcolm's rant. "Mr. Kincaid, I'm warning you that your disrespect of Miss Black is wearing my patience thin." Then the judge faced me. "Miss Black, do you have a date set for the wedding or is this an open-ended engagement? Is it a ploy to appease the court?"

I stood. "Your Honor…"

Zack interrupted and stepped forward. "Your Honor, my name is Zackary Kincaid and I'd like the opportunity to speak on my own behalf."

The judge waved his hand in our direction. "By all means, please."

Zack stepped up next to me and grasped my hand. "Miss Black and I fully intend to be married. I think we can put an end to all this speculation very easily. We've already secured a marriage license. We would like to do this now. Would you do us the honor of marrying us? Right here. Right now."

244

The judge's eyes went wide. "Miss Black?"

I squeezed Zack's hand. "It's what we want. We want to start our life and begin being a family, without any questions about our commitment to each other or our child. She will be born knowing that her mother and father love her unconditionally."

"This is bullshit!" Malcolm roared. "He's not even the father!"

Zack turned towards Malcolm. "I'll be more of a father to this child than you ever were to me. I don't need a paternity test. I know this is Wes's child, but she has my blood, my DNA, and will have my name. I love her. She's my child in every way that matters."

Malcolm yelled at the judge. "Are you just going to sit there and allow this? What the fuck is wrong with you?"

The judge banged his gavel on the bench. "Mr. Kincaid, you are in contempt. I won't allow this type of behavior in my courtroom!"

"I'm in contempt?" he yelled. "I'm not going to sit here and watch my son throw his life away!" Malcolm stormed from the courtroom.

I watched as Malcolm made his exit, my breath shallow in my chest. Then my eyes focused on Ronnie as she watched her father.

Zack was focused on her too. "Ronnie, will you stay for my wedding?" he asked her.

Ronnie had tears in her eyes. "I'm so sorry, Zack. This is my fault. I didn't know."

Zack left my side and approached his sister. "Do you want to be part of our life? Do you want to know your niece?"

Ronnie nodded her head with tears in her eyes. "I do. I'm so sorry, Zack." They hugged tightly. I wanted to forgive her, but I couldn't. Not yet. Maybe in time, but not now. I was here because of her.

Zack walked his sister over to our side of the courtroom. Ronnie held out her arms to me, asking for forgiveness. I gave her a quick hug and whispered in her ear, "I don't forgive you. Forgiveness is something you'll have to earn."

She nodded at me, accepting my words.

The judge cleared his throat. "Well, this was unexpected. Do you still want to get married?"

Zack and I looked at each and then at the judge. "We do," we said in unison.

He called us to the front of the courtroom. We didn't have rings. We hadn't decided to get married until this morning. I didn't have a wedding dress and Zack wasn't wearing a tuxedo. We were totally unprepared. Catherine, Ronnie, and Jeff stepped forward as our witnesses.

Zack leaned into me. "We can do this again, the right way. I'm sorry this is probably not what you imagined for your wedding."

I grabbed ahold of his bicep. "It doesn't matter. All that matters is us. I love you."

The judge came down from behind his bench and stood before us. "We are gathered here today..."

Chapter 38
Zack

We went to New York single and came home married. It should have scared me. I should have been terrified. But I wasn't. I was the happiest I'd ever been. Clarissa was my wife. Her baby was going to be my child.

This wasn't the wedding she wanted though. She didn't say a word, but what woman would want to be married in a courtroom when she was there fighting for custody of her child. It wasn't what any woman would want.

It didn't matter to me, but I knew it mattered to her. Clarissa had been cheated out of so many things, I wouldn't cheat her out of a wedding. I gave Kyla and Tori the go ahead to plan the perfect wedding for us. Money was no object. I just wanted my girl to have something that she could remember with happiness. My only requirement was that it had to happen before Alexandria was born.

My daughter. I'd gotten really comfortable with that phrase. I'd been with Clarissa, on and off since she was only a month pregnant. Our start wasn't conventional. As a matter of fact, it was awful. I was an asshole, and she didn't tell me the truth. But as I looked back, I realized that we wouldn't be where we were now if we hadn't gone through the shit it took to get here.

I wasn't ready before to be a father and she needed someone who was fully committed. I was ready now. I couldn't imagine my life without Clarissa. She made me happy. She made everything better. I may have not been there for her in the beginning, but I was now. I made myself into the man she could depend on.

I began thinking about a house for us. I didn't want to raise my daughter above a tattoo parlor. It would be fine while Alexandria was an infant, but I wanted her to have a yard to run in and trees to climb. I wanted room to grow our family. Because now that Alexandria was almost ready to make her debut, I pictured more with Clarissa. I wanted at least three. Three was a good number.

I called my friend Draven from New York. I was going to need to take some time off. Once this baby was born, I didn't want to be committed to be at Forever Inked at all hours. Plus, if Clarissa did get the recording contract, I wanted to be free to travel with her. I needed someone I could trust who was a great artist. Draven fit the bill. Once we found a house, he could move right into the apartment upstairs. It would be the perfect arrangement.

Kyla came in to drop off some drawings for me. Her shit was beautiful. Our female clientele loved her stuff and when I was at a loss, the first person I called was Kyla.

"So, what's the status?" I asked her. "This has got to be done before our baby is born."

Kyla took my hand in hers. "Don't worry. What do you think about Coach Insignia atop the Renaissance Center in downtown Detroit?"

I thought about it for half a second. It was classy, with a great view of the downtown area and the Ambassador Bridge to Canada. "It's perfect," I said.

"How about March 2nd? Tyler can pull some strings with his connections from football. It pays to be married to one of the Detroit Lions." She smirked.

"It's great." I pulled Kyla in and gave her a kiss on the cheek. I may have hated Tyler in the past, but I'd take every advantage of his celebrity status. "We need to get the invites out ASAP. "

"On it," Kyla answered.

"You girls are going to have to kidnap Clarissa. She's going to know something is up."

Kyla tapped her finger on her lips. "Oh, you underestimate the power of a girl posse. Trust me, we have it covered."

"And a dress?"

"Done," Kyla said.

"What else do I have to do, besides give you unlimited access to my credit card?" I was half joking, but I wanted this to be perfect for her.

"Just show up and be as handsome as you always are. I'm so happy for you, Zack. You deserve this."

♫♪♫♪

"I don't want to go out tonight, Zack. I'm as big as a house. My feet hurt, and this baby is constantly kicking my bladder. Do you have any idea what that's like?" Clarissa complained.

So, maybe this wasn't the best idea I'd ever had. Maybe I should have waited until after Alexandria was born. "Come on, sweetheart. I made us reservations. I want to take you out tonight. I want it to be special. One night together before our life changes," I pleaded.

If we didn't show up for our own wedding, that would be bad. How would I explain to everyone why we didn't show up?

Clarissa let out a little huff. "Fine. If you weren't so darn cute, I'd stay in my pajamas and curl up on the couch with Priss, but I can't resist those damn puppy dog eyes you give me."

I gave her an exaggerated pout and fluttered my eyes at her like a sappy lovesick fool.

"Okay, that's too much." She laughed. "What time is our reservation?"

"Six o'clock." We had to get her there early enough for Kyla and Tori to work their magic. Their plan was to transform Clarissa into the princess she deserved to be for our wedding.

By the time we parked and rode the elevator up seventy-one floors, my nerves were getting the best of me. What if she hated this idea? What if she was pissed that I had blindsided her?

When the elevator doors opened, Kyla and Tori were standing there waiting for us. Clarissa looked at me and then her two friends. "What is going on here?"

Tori wasted no time as we stepped out, taking Clarissa's hand in hers. "Come with us, Rissa. We have a surprise for you."

Clarissa looked over her shoulder at me as the girls pulled her away. I shrugged my shoulders but couldn't keep the smile from my lips. "Zackary Michael Kincaid," she scolded.

I made my way to the bar where Tyler and Chris were waiting. I ordered a Jim Beam on the rocks and let out a big sigh. "Do you think she's going to hate me for this?"

Chris patted me on the shoulder. "I doubt it. I surprised Tori by taking her to Vegas. We got married that night and kept it a secret for almost a year. It was the best thing I've ever done."

I took a sip of my whiskey. "So, you two were already married when I came to your wedding?" I had no idea. I only got invited because of Kyla, I hadn't known Chris or Tori that well.

"Fucker didn't even tell me until the night before." Tyler scowled. "You'd think being his best friend, I'd have known."

"We didn't tell anyone. Only my brother, and our dads knew. And that was by accident," Chris defended.

"Kyla knew," Tyler huffed. Then he tapped his own chest. "Best friend."

Chris rolled his eyes. "She guessed. We didn't tell her. Quit acting like a chick and get over it."

I cleared my throat. "If you two are done bantering, can we get back to me? Did you bring my tux?"

Chris smiled. "We got your back. Do you really think our girls would let us forget a single thing?"

I laughed. "Not really. Those two together are a force to be reckoned with."

"You have no idea." Tyler chuckled.

I followed the guys to a small dressing room where my tux waited. This wedding wasn't traditional, but it was better than a courtroom. Clarissa wouldn't have her dad walking her down the aisle and I didn't have a best man, because that spot was reserved for Wes. Clarissa and I were the only two in our wedding party, and I was fine with that.

Chapter 39
Rissa

"How could you two do this to me?" I asked wiping the tears from my eyes.

Tori kneeled before me where I sat on a white bench. "We're doing this for you, not to you. Zack wanted to do this for you. Don't be mad."

I sniffed back my tears. "I'm not mad. I'm overwhelmed. I can't believe he would do this for me."

Kyla joined Tori in front of me. "That man is so in love with you, and he wanted you to have a nice wedding. And that's what you're going to have."

Forty-five minutes later, my hair was curled and beautifully piled on top of my head with a few flowers. My makeup was flawless. "Are you ready for the dress?" Tori asked.

I nodded my head as she unzipped the garment bag that hung on a hook. I gasped. It was beautiful. "Thank you. I'm so happy I have friends like you."

Kyla slipped the dress off the hanger and the girls helped me into it. I turned and looked at myself in the full-length mirror. Delicate straps hung off my shoulders. The top was white satin, embellished with jewels that sat between my breasts and underneath them. The fabric ran over my full belly and hung perfectly down to the floor where it flowed out behind me. It was simple, but gorgeous.

"Don't you dare cry," Tori scolded me. "You'll ruin your makeup."

"I won't," I promised.

"Just one more thing," Kyla said. She went to her bag and pulled out a box. "Zack insisted you wear this." She pulled out the diamond pendant and earrings from Wes. She fastened the necklace around my neck, and I slipped the earrings in. "Now you're perfect."

"What about my feet?" I wiggled my toes into the carpet.

"We've got you covered. I hated wearing shoes when I was this big, so I got you these." Tori held up a pair of shimmery white slippers with jewels on them."

I laughed. "That's just up my alley right now. I love my heels, but I don't think my feet could take it. I don't even think my feet would fit into heels right now." I slipped my feet into the slippers. I looked at my friends. "Where are your dresses?"

"It's just you and Zack today. He said it didn't feel right without his brother here to be his best man," Kyla answered.

I twirled my ring. "If Wes hadn't died, Zack probably would have been his best man, not the other way around." I looked at the girls. "Do you think Wes is looking down at me and shaking his head? Do you think he's mad?"

"No way," Tori answered. "If Wes loved you as much as you say, he'd want you to be happy."

I nodded. Although I loved Zack more than anything, it didn't stop the guilt from occasionally creeping in.

"It's time," Kyla said, handing me a bouquet of white roses. We stepped into the hallway where Lou was waiting. Tori and Kyla scurried off to find their husbands.

Lou took my hand in his. "You look beautiful, Rissa. Would you do me the honor of letting me walk you in? Make an old man happy?"

I smiled at Lou. I'd known since I was eighteen that my dad would never walk me down the aisle. Lou wasn't trying to replace him, but he had been good to me and watched over me as if I were his daughter. "Nothing would make me happier," I said as I kissed him on the cheek.

Lou held out his arm for me and I threaded my arm through his. When we walked into the restaurant, everything had been cleared away on one side and chairs were lined up with a makeshift aisle. Up front was Zack who looked very handsome in his tuxedo. He was standing in front of an archway that was covered in red and white roses. The lights of the city lit up the sky behind him.

Lou took me down the aisle, and all eyes were on me. When we got to the front, Lou kissed my cheek and sat down beside Catherine. I didn't know she was in town, but then again, I didn't know I was having a wedding.

Zack took my hand and pulled me close to him. "You look beautiful, sweetheart. You take my breath away."

"You look pretty good, yourself. I love you in a tux. It's sexy," I whispered.

"Are you mad about this?" he asked nervously.

"Nope. I love that you did this for us."

I saw the relief wash over his face.

Chase stepped up behind us. "Are you two ready?"

I eyed him, the question obvious on my face.

Chase chuckled and leaned into my ear. "I got ordained online. I assure you, it's all perfectly legal.

I wasn't worried about legal. Zack and I had been legally married in New York. I was just surprised that Zack would trust him with something this big. I touched his hand with mine, "We're ready."

Chase stepped to the front and addressed our guests, "We are gathered here today to bear witness to the love that Clarissa and Zackary share for each other." I giggled. No one ever called him Zackary. It all seemed so formal. He said a few more words and then turned everything over to Zack.

Tori stepped forward to hold my flowers as Zack took my hands in his. "Clarissa, I knew from the first time I saw you sitting on that bench, that you were someone special. Your strength and beauty lured me in from the beginning. The way we started may not have been traditional, but it's our story and I wouldn't trade it for anything. When we first started dating, you asked me to make you a promise. I promised not to tattoo your heart. I know I broke that promise to you, and I can't feel bad about it. You tattooed my heart a long time ago, but more than that, you've tattooed my soul."

He put my hand on his heart. "This is where you live. You're so much a part of me that I can't imagine spending a single day away from you. So, I'm going to make you a different promise, one I fully intend to keep. I promise to be the best husband and father I can be." He rested his hands on my stomach. "This is the life I want. I will always love you, support your dreams, and catch you when you fall. I'll give you the very best of me every day for the rest of our lives together."

I wiped at my eyes. "Wow," I whispered. "I don't know what to say. I wasn't prepared for this."

"You don't have to say anything," he assured me.

"Yes, I do." I swallowed down the lump in my throat. "Zack, thank you for making this such a special day for us. When we first got together, I was sad and lost and broken. You blazed into my life without permission, you were so pushy and persistent. But you were also kind and generous and loving. You saved me in so many ways. You showed me how to love again without being afraid. And now, you're my husband and I know you're going to be a spectacular daddy to our little girl. She's so lucky I found you. I hope that you have the same type of relationship with her as I had with my own daddy. I'm so happy to be sharing this life with you. And, Zack..."

"Yes, sweetheart?" He smiled down on me.

"You not only tattooed my heart, but my soul as well. And I'm glad you did, because without you I'd still be lost. With you my life is complete."

Chase cleared his throat and swallowed down the lump in his throat. "Well, I don't know that I have to say much more. Shall we get on with this?"

We both nodded. As we exchanged vows, Zack slid a diamond encrusted wedding band onto my finger, and I slid a simple band onto his. Sharing this in front of our friends, was one of the most important moments of my life. I smiled as I thought about the people I'd lost. I hoped they were looking down on us and smiling too.

Chapter 40
Zack

My mom stayed after our wedding. She didn't want to miss the birth of her first grandchild. Clarissa's old room had been turned into a nursery for our daughter. The bed was still in there, so my mom had a place to sleep, but she was actively looking to buy a condo close by. Secretly, I was glad she hadn't moved out yet. My mom watched over Clarissa like a hawk, tending to her every need. I also knew we were going to need some help when the baby arrived. Neither one of us had a clue how to take care of a baby, but we'd learn fast.

Clarissa sat up in bed and rubbed her hand over her stomach. She leaned against the headboard and let out a big sigh.

"Are you all right?" I asked.

"I don't know. I can't get comfortable. I feel like she's trying to kick her way out of me."

I sat up next to her and put my hand over hers. "Are you having contractions?"

"I don't think so. I'm just really uncomfortable." She grimaced. "I think I'm going to get up and walk around a bit." Clarissa got up and slipped her robe over her pajamas. "Go back to sleep. I'll be fine."

I was worried about my girl constantly. There was no way I would fall back asleep until she crawled back in bed with me. I heard the shower turn on and relaxed a bit. Maybe a warm shower would make her feel better.

I had just started to drift off when the light flicked on, "Zack."

I sat up and rubbed my eyes. "What's wrong, sweetheart?"

She put one hand on her stomach and the other on her back. "I think we need to go to the hospital. My water broke and I'm definitely having contractions," she said calmly.

"Shit!" I threw back the covers and jumped out of bed. "I'll go get my mom."

Clarissa grabbed my arm as I was about to run out the door. "Don't you think you should put some pants on?"

I looked down and realized I was naked. "Probably a good idea." I snagged a pair of boxer briefs from the drawer and stumbled into my jeans. I kissed her on the head. "Get dressed."

I woke my mom and left her to get dressed, then I called Doc Peterson. We were all out of the house within five minutes. Clarissa sat next to me holding her stomach and I could tell she was having another contraction. She bit her lip and growled. "Hold on, sweetheart. We're almost there." I grabbed her hand and squeezed it.

"Take deep breaths, Rissa," my mom coached. "It'll help. I did this three times, trust me."

We pulled up to the emergency entrance. My mom and Clarissa went in while I parked the car. I ran back into the hospital and looked around for my wife. She was being put in a wheelchair. I rushed to her side. "I'm her husband," I announced.

"We're getting her into a room right away," the nurse told me.

I reached for Clarissa's hand, and she squeezed hard. "It fucking hurts," she growled.

We got settled into a room and Clarissa was hooked to a fetal monitor. I watched the steady beat of my daughter's heart, while my mom sat on the other side of Clarissa and held her hand.

Clarissa wiped the tears from her face. "I'm sad that Wes is missing this. He was so excited. But I'm glad you're here with me, Zack. Don't leave, okay?"

I don't know where she thought I would go. "I'm not going anywhere," I promised. I was getting this moment with Clarissa that was supposed to belong to my brother. It was bittersweet.

Doc Peterson came in followed by a nurse rolling an ultrasound machine. "How are we doing, Rissa?"

"Not great," she gritted out. "When do I get the drugs?"

I laughed. For a woman who I'd never seen drink, she was awfully anxious.

"What are you laughing about?" she glared at me.

"Nothing, sweetheart. You're just so damn cute."

Doc Peterson pulled the sheet down and exposed Clarissa's belly. "I want to do a quick ultrasound." He put the gel on her stomach and rubbed the wand over it. He stared at the screen without saying a word. He wiped her off and pulled her gown back down. "I want to see how far you're dilated." He did a quick exam and snapped off his gloves. "We've got a problem."

Clarissa and I looked at each other and then back to Doc Peterson. "What's wrong?" I asked.

"The baby is breech. Seeing as you're already in labor, we need to do an emergency C-section. If we don't, the umbilical cord could wrap around the baby's neck. I'm not willing to take that chance."

I could see the panic on Clarissa's face. I leaned in and kissed her head. "It'll be okay."

"I'm scared," she whispered. "You can't leave me."

I looked at Doc Peterson. "Can I still be with her?"

He shook his head. "It's too late for a spinal. She'll have to be under general anesthesia, which means you can't be there."

I didn't like what he was telling me, but I trusted him to do what was best for my wife. Clarissa was rolled away quickly. I held her hand as long as they let me. When I had to let go and my fingers slipped through hers, she cried out for me. There was nothing I could do but wait.

This was not what we had planned or expected.

♫♪♫♪

My mom and I had been sitting in the waiting room for over an hour. She should have been out of surgery by now. "What's taking so long?" I asked.

My mom patted my knee. "Be patient. These things take time, honey."

A few minutes later, a nurse came to get me. My mom squeezed my hand before I followed the nurse. "Do you want to meet your daughter?" she asked.

"Yes. This waiting has been killing me. Where is my wife?" I needed to see Clarissa. Until then, I wouldn't stop worrying.

The nurse patted me on the arm. "She's fine. She's just taking a little longer than usual to come out of the anesthesia. You'll see her soon."

I let out a breath of relief. I don't know what I would have done if something had happened to her. Another nurse headed our way carrying a little bundle wrapped in a pink blanket. She placed Alexandria in my arms. "She's beautiful, Mr. Kincaid."

I stared down at the miracle in my arms. My heart split wide open. If there was such a thing as love at first sight, this was it. She was beautiful. She had a little tiny nose that reminded me of Clarissa. She had soft blond hair sticking up from her head. Then Alexandria opened her eyes. They were green, just like Wes's. "You're going to be a looker, aren't you?" I cooed.

I stood in the nursery rocking my daughter and just staring at her. Every moment I spent with her, I fell a little bit more in love.

A nurse approached me. "They moved your wife into a room. She's still out of it, but you're welcome to sit with her."

I followed the nurse down the hall, holding Alexandria tight. I went into Clarissa's room and sat in the chair next to her bed. I picked up her hand and kissed the back of it. "You did good, sweetheart. I can't wait for you to meet our daughter."

Chapter 41
Rissa

I could feel someone holding my hand. Thank God Zack was here. I struggled to open my eyes. The room was bright. Too bright.

"Wake up, Rissa."

I knew that voice and it didn't belong to Zack. "Wes?"

"I'm right here, baby. I've been waiting for you." He ran his fingers over my hand.

"Am I dead?" I asked.

He chuckled. "No, baby, you're not dead."

"How are you here?" I asked. My eyes focused on his handsome face. "I've missed you so much." I used my other hand to wipe away my tears. I never thought I'd see him again and here he was, holding my hand.

"I came to help you through this. You're so strong, Rissa." He kissed my lips and they tingled from his touch. "I don't have long."

"What if I want to come with you?" I asked. Leaving Zack would hurt, but all I ever wanted was to be with Wes. He was my first real love.

"You can't," he said. "You're needed here. You have our daughter to raise."

I felt my stomach and the bump was gone. "Is she okay?"

"She's just fine and she's beautiful. You did a good job, Rissa."

"We did a good job," I corrected. "Why did you leave me? Why didn't you stay with me?" I cried. I needed answers from him. I needed to know the truth.

"Oh, Rissa, I never wanted to leave you. I was weak, and I regret that every day." He squeezed my hand and lifted it to his lips, placing soft kisses along the back of it.

"You left me alone," I accused.

"I never left you alone," he said. "I watched you every day. I watched how strong you became. I watched you learn how to fly without me. You've

259

finally found your voice and it's beautiful. You're going to be more than I ever was and you're going to be a fantastic mom."

He'd been watching me? He had to know that Zack and I were together. "Are you mad at me?"

"How could I ever be mad at you?" he asked.

The tears leaked from my eyes. "Because of Zack."

"Rissa, don't you know? I sent Zack to you. I told you, I didn't leave you alone. I sent you him. I knew no one would ever love you or care for you the way I did except my brother. He was my gift to you. I know he'll take care of you and our daughter better than I ever could."

The tears poured down my cheeks. "I still love you, Wes."

"I love you too, baby."

"I'll always love you. You being gone doesn't change that," I cried.

"I know. And I know you love Zack too. It's okay, Rissa. It's the way it's supposed to be. You're supposed to be happy." He looked over my shoulder and nodded.

I looked but couldn't see anything.

"It's time for me to go, Rissa."

He placed another kiss on my lips and started to back away. His fingers slipped from mine. I reached out for him. "Don't go! Please stay!"

He shook his head. "I can't. I love you, baby."

"I love you!" I yelled. "I'll always love you." He faded away into nothingness. "Come back! Don't leave me again!" I cried.

"I'll never leave you," his voice whispered.

Then he was gone. I couldn't see him, and I couldn't hear him. I'd lost him all over again.

♫♪♫♪

I could feel someone holding my hand, running their fingers over the back of it. I struggled to open my eyes. Zack's face came into focus.

"Welcome back, sweetheart." His soft voice filled my ears.

I looked around the room for a sign that Wes was here. There was nothing. "How long was I out?" I asked groggily.

"Not too long, but you were crying."

I wiped at my cheeks. "I was?"

"Yeah, I think you were dreaming," he said.

Was it possible that it was a dream? Something I made up in my mind? I wouldn't believe it. "I wasn't dreaming," I said.

"No?" he asked gently. He picked up my hand and kissed my palm.

I shook my head. "No. I saw Wes."

Zack smiled at me. "Oh yeah? What did he say?"

I don't think that Zack believed me, but I believed me and that was what mattered. "He said he sent you to me. He said he isn't mad at me for being with you. He wants us to be together and be happy. You were my gift from him."

He chuckled. "I think he got it wrong. You were a gift sent to me. Would you like to meet our daughter?"

I smiled. "Yes." She should have been my first thought, but seeing Wes made me forget everything else. Zack lifted our daughter out of the bassinet next to my bed and cradled her to his chest. He kissed her on the head and then placed her in my waiting arms.

I pulled the blanket away from her little face. She let out a big yawn and opened her eyes. They were bright green.

"She has Wes's eyes," Zack said.

I ran my hand along the side of Zack's cheek. "She has her daddy's eyes. I want her to have both her daddies' names. What do you think of Alexandria Michaela?"

Zack beamed. "You want her to have my middle name?"

I nodded.

"Alexandria Michaela Kincaid," he said trying it out. "I think it's a mouthful, but it's a strong name."

I looked down on our daughter. "She'll be fierce if her daddy doesn't spoil her too much."

Zack kissed me on the forehead. "I have every intention of spoiling her. I'll spend the rest of my life spoiling both my girls. I love you both so much."

I uncovered Alexandria's little hands. Zack held his finger up and she grasped it tightly, making him smile. "I think I'm the luckiest man alive."

I smiled at Zack. "Thank you for loving us."

"Loving the both of you is the easiest thing I've ever done," he said. "My mom is in the waiting room. I think she's going crazy out there alone. Can I get her?"

"Of course. Alexandria needs to meet her grandma." I snuggled my baby close as Zack left. "You're the luckiest little girl, do you know that? You have two daddies that love you very much. You may never know the daddy that made you, but I have no doubt he'll be watching over you every single day. You'll never be alone sweet girl."

A soft white feather drifted down from nowhere and landed on Alexandria's blanket. I picked it off and held it in the palm of my hand. I was sure it was a sign that we had our very own angel. "Thank you, Wes. Thank you for watching over us and sending us Zack."

Epilogue
Zack

I was holding my squirmy four-month-old daughter in my arms, watching my wife through the window. Clarissa had headphones on, singing into the mic like a pro.

We returned to LA a month ago and met with Mr. Riley, the music exec who had originally turned Clarissa down. I waited outside in the reception area with our daughter while Daniel, Clarissa and Mr. Riley talked. Twenty minutes later, Rissa flew out the door and into my arms. They had signed her for a three album deal.

Now we were back, and the hard work began.

I took a month leave from Forever Inked and left Layla in charge. My friend, Draven, had moved into the apartment above the shop and was a huge asset. His tattooing was second to none. I just wondered how he and Layla would get along.

I bought us a house in the next town over. Shelby Township had some beautiful homes that afforded us privacy without being too far from work. I never thought I'd want a house, but when Alexandria came along it became obvious quite quickly that above a tattoo parlor was not the place to raise my daughter. Plus, I had plans to grow our family.

My mom finalized her divorce from Malcolm and moved permanently to Michigan. Once she saw Alexandria, her heart was stolen, and she couldn't stay away. Since she and my father had been married for thirty years, my mom walked away with a nice little chunk of change. Enough for her to buy a condo and never have to work another day in her life. But she liked to stay busy, so she spent a lot of time helping Clarissa with our daughter and helping Lou out at the bar. She was an expert at promotions and record keeping. Lou and my mom started to casually date and I couldn't have been happier for them. Although, seeing her in jeans and concert tees was something I had to get used to.

263

I watched my wife do what she did best. Make music. She had worked tirelessly to write songs. Everything she did, was a product of her own talent. The label assigned her a band to work with that complemented her, and they rocked it.

While we'd been here, Clarissa did a few promotional gigs and photo shoots. They were anxious to release her first album called *Broken Wings*, born from the original song she sang for Mr. Riley.

I watched Clarissa as she finished her last song for the day. She removed her headphones and stepped out of the studio. "How'd I do?" It was always the first question she asked.

"Amazing."

Clarissa reached out and took our daughter into her arms. "Did you watch mommy? Are you going to be a singer just like her?" Clarissa asked Alexandria.

Alexandria babbled and drooled but looked at her mom with pride.

Clarissa leaned over and kissed me. "How about we get out of here? I think the beach is calling our name."

"Sweetheart, I couldn't agree more."

We went back to the hotel to change and then started towards the coast. It didn't take long before the ocean was on our left as we drove up the Pacific Coast Highway.

"God, it's so beautiful here," Clarissa said. "I've never been to the beach before. I can't wait to put Alexandria's toes in the sand." Clarissa's hair blew in the breeze and her smile was huge.

"I can't wait to see my wife in that new bikini you've been hiding from me." I smirked at her. I drove past Santa Monica and up to Malibu. It was less crowded and not so touristy. I checked my GPS and followed the route to our destination.

We pulled up in front of a condo complex and Clarissa squinted her eyes at me. "What are we doing here? Do you know someone who lives here?"

I shrugged. "I might." I opened the door and took our daughter from her car seat. I held out my other hand for Clarissa to take. We walked around the back on a cobblestone path as I was instructed.

The real estate agent was waiting on the deck that led out to the beach. She held out her hand to me. "It's nice to finally meet you, Mr. Kincaid."

I shook her hand. "It's Zack, and this is my wife, Clarissa. And this little pumpkin here is Alexandria."

"It's nice to meet you, Clarissa." The woman shook Clarissa's hand.

The look of confusion on my wife's face was priceless. "What's going on, Zack?"

"Well, I was thinking that we might be spending a lot of time in LA. How would you like to have a condo on the beach instead of staying in a hotel when we're here?"

"Are you serious?" she asked, the shock evident on her pretty face. Then she leaned closer so only I could hear her. "We can't afford this."

I winked at her. "Actually, we can. We'll have our own beach," I said motioning out to the ocean in front of us, "and privacy. We can come here on vacation or when you're recording. Want to go inside and look around?"

Clarissa tried to mask her excitement with indifference. "If you want to."

"Come on. Let's take a look." We followed behind the real estate agent. It was gorgeous inside with huge sliding doors that opened to the beach. It had four bedrooms, which meant my mom could come here, and we had room to grow. The master bedroom had its own sliding door leading to the beach. It also had a private bath with a jacuzzi tub. "Do you like it?" I asked.

Clarissa's eyes went wide. "What's not to like? I love it, but are you sure we can afford this?"

"Yes, I'm sure." I laughed.

"Can I talk to you outside for a moment?" she said pulling me out the sliding door and onto the deck. "I feel weird asking you this, but we've never discussed it," she whispered. "Exactly how much money do you have?"

I leaned down and whispered the amount in her ear.

"Oh. My. God. I mean, I knew you had money, but I had no idea it was that much. I can't even fathom how much money that is," she said quietly.

"It's enough that we can buy this condo and never have to work another day of our lives if we don't want to. It's enough to take care of our children, their children, and their grandchildren."

"No wonder your father hated me so much. He really did think I was after your money," she said.

"Malcolm hated you because he's an arrogant asshole. Sooo... about the condo?"

Clarissa took Alexandria from my arms and held her up. "What do you think, baby girl? Do you like it here? Do you want to play on the beach with mamma and daddy?"

Alexandria started giggling like crazy, her little hands reaching out towards the ocean. "I think that's a yes, Daddy."

"Good. Let's go sign the paperwork," I said leading her back inside.

We spent the day on the beach, enjoying the cheese and fruit platter the real estate agent left us. Clarissa held our daughter up so the waves just touched her tiny feet. Alexandria squealed with delight. I snuck up behind them and lifted both my girls into the air.

"Zack! What are you doing?" Clarissa giggled.

Hearing both of them laugh was better than any song I'd ever heard. "Creating memories," I said. "I don't ever want to waste a single moment with you. I love my girls. You're my whole world."

"And what if our next one is a boy?"

"Are you trying to tell me something, Mrs. Kincaid?" I asked. "Are you pregnant?"

"Oh hell, no. Not yet. But you do want more, don't you?"

"You bet your sweet little ass I do. Which, I might add, looks mighty fine in this bikini. So fine, that we might have to go inside to do a little practicing."

"I might be up for that." She smirked at me, and I put her down on the sand. She hoisted our daughter in one arm and placed her other hand on my chest. "But seriously, Zack, thank you for this life you've given us. I keep thinking this is a dream. I love you so much."

"It's not a dream, sweetheart. It's destiny. I'm thankful every day that you came into my life. I didn't know how empty it was before, until you were in it. I love that we can have a simple life back in Michigan and be able to come here to live on the beach. I love your smile. I love your laugh. I love the sweet little things you do for me. I love your eyes and I love your body. I love your heart and that you gave me the gift of this sweet little girl. I love everything about you, Mrs. Clarissa Lynne Kincaid."

"Forever?" she asked.

"Forever and ever, sweetheart. You'll always be the best thing that ever happened to me."

Another Epilogue
Rissa

I'd finally made it! I got the music career I dreamed of and the family I desperately wanted.

Audrey had been right about so many things. Zack stood by my side through all the craziness of my new career. He was the perfect husband and an even better father to our daughter.

I was financially able to support myself, but I didn't have to. Although Zack had more money than I could fathom, we took care of each other. I knew now his intention had never been to buy my love. His devotion to me ran much deeper. It gave him pleasure to spoil me rotten. Once I realized that, I gave in and let him. He wasn't frivolous or showy, but I wanted for nothing. And underneath it all, he was still the tatted up, broody guy with a huge heart I first fell in love with.

Balancing a family and a music career wasn't easy. I was lucky Zack had his own business and could take time off to travel with me. I don't know what I would have done without him by my side, supporting me every step of the way.

Since Daniel was Bobby's agent as well as mine, he planned a tour for us. I opened for Bobby many nights and we sang a few duets during his show. But being that I was a mom, which Daniel understood, he gave me the luxury of choosing which shows I would sing at and which I would pass on.

Yes, a music career was what I always wanted, but I also had a husband and a daughter. They were more important than anything. I wouldn't give up one for the other. Balance was the key.

I wrote a song, just for Zack and me. Even if guitar wasn't Zack's first love, he was damn good at it. And his voice… it charmed the heart of every woman in America. I couldn't let him stand on the sidelines when he had a gift to share with the world. Tonight, we were sharing our song with twenty-

268

thousand people. We sat on the stage and stared into each other's eyes, then let the magic begin, alternating versus and coming together on the chorus:

I hated myself,
I pushed you away.
You were everything I needed,
I wanted you to stay.

We'd argue and we'd fight,
We lost precious time.
All our words were wasted,
I wanted you to be mine.

We were so lost, so broken and alone.
But we begged each other to stay.
We took a chance on love,
We saved each other in every way.

Each day I spend with you is a gift,
You make me complete, you make me whole.
You were an angel sent from up above,
You haven't just tattooed my heart, you've tattooed my soul.

Without you I was lost at sea,
Drowning in a pool of tears.
You rescued me from the chaos,
You silenced all my crazy fears.

We wanted to be together,
All we needed was a little shove.
I love having you in my arms,
We fit together like a hand in a glove.

Each day I spend with you is a gift,
You make me complete, you make me whole.
You were an angel sent from up above,
You haven't just tattooed my heart, you've tattooed my soul.

My heart doesn't belong to me,

269

It belongs to you.
My soul is not my own,
It belongs to you.
You have all of me,
I have all of you.

You awakened my heart, you awakened my soul.
It can no longer sleep.
You captured my heart, you captured my soul.
It cannot be released.
You own my heart, you own my soul.
It's no longer mine.
You tattooed my heart, you tattooed my soul.
You have all of me, I have all of you,
Heart and soul for all of time.

We were lost to each other, because the gift we were given couldn't have been any greater. Zack and I belonged to each other. He captured my heart, and I gave him my soul. Forever and always, he owned all of me and I owned all of him… heart and soul for all of time.

If you have a few moments, I'd love to hear what you thought of **Tattooed Souls**, by leaving a quick review. I am so grateful for your support and of the thousands of books available, you chose to read mine.

Want More?

Keep reading to get a preview of Layla's sassy story in
Smoke and Mirrors.

Smoke and Mirrors

Chapter 1
Layla

Dangerous.

That's the first word that came to mind when I set my eyes upon my new co-worker.

Beautiful.

That's the next word my mind conjured up. I'd never thought of a man as beautiful before. Handsome? *Yes.* Cute? *Sure.* Freakin' hot? *Absolutely.* Beautiful? *Never.*

Draven was beautiful. Six foot-three, maybe four, with defined cheekbones that looked like they'd been sculpted from stone, long dark hair tied up in a knot at the back of his head, and those eyes… amber with flecks of green. I felt like they were piercing my soul, trying to penetrate the deepest parts of me. My eyes roamed him from head to toe, taking in the perfection of his body. He had muscles on top of his muscles. His black t-shirt hugged tight across his wide chest. Black ink covered his arms in intricate designs.

I clenched my thighs together. I was sure I could come just from staring at him.

Draven was dangerously beautiful.

I blinked, realizing our handshake had lingered too long. I quickly pulled my hand back and wiped my sweaty palm on my jeans. "Welcome to Forever Inked."

My voice was raspy and breathless to my own ears. I cursed myself for letting him have this effect on me. He was here to work, and I was going to be his boss for all intents and purposes. Zack, our owner, was leaving for

California with his wife, Rissa, for a month and he'd entrusted his beloved tattoo parlor to me in his absence.

"I'm happy to help. I owe Zack, so when he called, I couldn't say no."

The rough timbre of his voice vibrated through me from my head to my toes. I took a step back.

Straightening my spine, I led him to the empty studio that would be his. "This is your workspace. You can go ahead and get settled. I don't have you on the schedule until tomorrow, so there's no rush. If you need anything, my studio is right across from yours. I have an appointment in ten, so I need to get prepped. Are you good?" I asked, taking another step back.

He gave me a chin jerk. "I'm good." He eyed me up and down. "Are you good?"

I swallowed down the lump in my throat. "Perfect. Let me know if you need anything." I turned on my heel and strode through the door of my own studio, closing it behind me. I sagged against the door, counting down from five in my head. *Five, four, three, two… one.* I slowly let out the breath I was holding.

Dangerous. God help me.

I stopped dealing with dangerous men years ago. I'd gone to extremes to avoid them. I'd created a new life for myself. I was happy. Perhaps a little lonely, but safe. I'd take lonely over a dangerous man any day, no matter how beautiful he was.

I was perfectly happy. Some would say I was running, but I was living, and I'd come to appreciate that more than a normal person should.

I just didn't know how I was going to avoid Draven since I had to work with him every day. Not even God was going to be able to help me with this one.

Chapter 2
Draven

I chuckled to myself as her door shut. That was interesting.

As a matter of fact, I knew my time here was going to be very interesting. My new "boss" was curvy as hell, all tits and ass wrapped in tight jeans and a t-shirt that showed just a hint of cleavage. Layla's inky black hair fell halfway down her back and begged to have my hand wrapped around it as she screamed out my name. I didn't miss the way her perfectly drawn, dark-lined cat eyes had roamed over my body or the way she had clenched her thighs together.

I wouldn't be here long, but Layla could entertain me while I was.

Why Zack had moved to this tiny town when he could have gone anywhere, was beyond me. Utica, Michigan was nothing like New York. The only thing it provided for me was a reprieve from my family, something Zack and I had in common. But Michigan? For Christ's sake, he could have chosen something a little more enticing. Miami? New Orleans? Los Angeles? Nope. Utica. I'd never even heard of it before he called. I came anyway because I owed him and needed an escape.

A knock sounded on my doorframe and Chase, one of my other new co-workers, stuck his head in. "You all unpacked?"

"Getting there," I answered. "What's up?"

"We're all heading over to The Locker around eight. Rissa's doing her last show before she becomes famous. It's sort of a good luck and bon voyage thing."

"That's Zack's girl, right?" I hadn't met the new Mrs. Kincaid yet, but she was the whole reason I was here. Apparently, Rissa was going to LA to record her first album.

Chase shook his head. "Zack stole her from me. I was this close," he said holding up his fingers, "from sealing the deal with her."

Zack appeared out of nowhere and clapped Chase on the shoulder. "You never stood a chance, asshole. But keep dreaming." He then turned to me.

"You should come. I'll introduce you to some people and it'll give you chance to bond with Layla and Chase. I want you to feel comfortable here."

I had no desire to go out but couldn't turn down the invitation without looking like an asshole. "Yeah, I'll be there."

"Cool," Zack said. "I need to know you guys are okay before I leave. I've never left for more than a week before and it's putting me a little on edge."

Chase crossed his arms over his chest. "Despite you stealing the beautiful Rissa from me, I've still got you covered. You know we won't let anything happen to your business while you're gone. All you need to do is soak up the sun and take care of my girl." He smirked.

"*My* girl," Zack growled.

Chase waved him off. "Same difference."

"*Not* the same difference. Not even close," Zack retorted.

"Now, now boys, play nice." I checked out the blond walking toward us holding a baby in her arms. She tucked one hand under the bundle and extended her other to me. "You must be Draven. I'm Rissa and this little girl is Alexandria."

I shook her hand. "Nice to meet you." I knew instantly why Chase teased Zack. "How do you always find the hottest chick around?" I asked him.

Zack wrapped his arm around Rissa's waist and kissed her on the head. "I'd say it was luck, but with this one I'm pretty sure it was destiny."

I'd forgotten how smooth he was. Zack had always been a ladies' man. He'd hit the jackpot with Rissa.

"Are you coming to my show tonight?" Rissa asked. "A lot of our clients will be there, and it will be good for them to put a face with a name."

"Yeah, I'm coming. What time should I be there? I want to get some unpacking done upstairs." I turned to Zack. "Thanks for the apartment, man. It's pretty cool that all I have to do is go up the stairs and I'm home."

Zack rubbed the back of his neck. "Moving out was bittersweet, I loved that apartment. But once Alexandria was born, it wasn't really practical for us anymore. On the upside, we've got a huge house to fill with kids."

Rissa rolled her eyes. "Let's get used to having one first, then we'll talk about more." Rissa handed Zack their daughter and leaned in to give me a hug. "We're glad you're here. Meet us around eight or so. The Locker is just down the street. You can't miss it."

After putting most of my things away in the apartment and setting up my studio, I was ready for a stiff drink. Chase and Layla had already left, so I locked the shop and headed down the street. There was a line outside the door, and I walked right to the front of it. Zack assured me I was on the list and wouldn't have to wait. Sure enough, once I gave him my name, I was ushered right in.

I went to the bar and ordered a vodka straight up. I wasn't sure I was going to fit in here. I'd stay the required month, no longer. Everyone had been nice so far, but it wasn't New York.

Zack clapped me on the shoulder. "You're here. We've got a table up front."

He led me to a table with Chase and Layla. She was busy texting on her phone. Layla let out a huff and set her phone down. "Oh, hey," she acknowledged me and pushed back from the table. "I need a drink. Anybody want anything?"

"Have Lou put it on my tab," Zack told her.

She squinted at him with her hands on her hips. "You think I won't take you up on that, but I will."

He laughed. "I know you will. Go get your drink on."

"Damn right, I will." She winked, turned on her high heels and strode off to the bar.

"She's feisty. What's her story?" I asked.

"She's a lot of bark, not a whole lot of bite," Chase answered. "She's more like a kitten than a pit bull. Unless you piss her off, then all bets are off. I'd stay on her good side if I were you," he advised.

I nodded my understanding. I hoped her good side was on her back, because that's where I planned to have her. I'd have her purring in no time. "She have a boyfriend?"

Chase and Zack gave each other a knowing look. "Don't go wading in those waters man, it's not safe," Chase answered.

"I've known Layla for almost five years, and I've never seen her with anyone serious," Zack admitted. "She keeps her personal life very private."

"So, no boyfriend?"

Zack shook his head, "Not for lack of guys trying. She gets hit on all the time, but ninety-nine percent of the time, she goes home alone. Actually," he mused, "I've got no fucking idea what she does."

"Same," Chase confirmed. "She's an enigma."

Just then, Layla returned with her drink. "Don't go using big words you can't spell."

"I can spell it," Chase retorted. "I-N... I-N-I-G-A... fuck! Who cares if I can spell it? I know what it means."

Layla threw her head back and laughed. "Sure you do." She reached over and ruffled his hair.

Chase swatted her hand away. "Enough with the hair. It takes a lot of work to look this good."

She rolled her eyes. "Yeah. You've got that *I just rolled out of bed and don't give a fuck* look mastered."

"Welcome to my life," Zack sighed. "I swear these two were brother and sister in a past life."

"I can handle it. Got one of each, it ain't nothing new," I assured him.

Layla flipped me off across the table. Feisty... and I loved it! I wanted nothing more than to grab that finger and suck it into my mouth, if for no other reason than to see how she reacted. I was *that* guy. A total asshole that pushed limits and crossed boundaries. All for my own entertainment.

"Jesus Christ, Layla! Can you at least pretend to be on your best behavior on Draven's first day here?"

She held her hand to her ample chest. "My bad! I promise I'll be on my best behavior while you're gone, Zack. I don't want you to worry. I'll be a total professional. Cross my heart."

I put my hand on his shoulder. "Don't sweat it, man. I don't get offended that easily. I have a feeling Layla and I are going to get along just fine. No worries."

Layla gave me a hard stare across the table. I didn't know what her problem was, but I was pretty sure if she could shoot flames from those green eyes, I'd be toast by now. Little did she know that she'd already started a fire within me. A curiosity. I wouldn't be happy until I solved the puzzle that was her.

Returning her stare, I refused to back down. "Isn't that right, Layla? Zack's got nothing to worry about."

"Absolutely nothing," she deadpanned.

Want to read more about the Forever Inked crew? Check out the rest of the Forever Inked Novels.

Books 1~ Tattooed Hearts: Tattooed Duet #1 (Zack & Rissa)
Book 2~ Tattooed Souls: Tattooed Duet #2 (Zack & Rissa)
Book 3~ Smoke and Mirrors (Draven & Layla)
Book 4~ Regret and Redemption (Chase & Maggie)
Book 5~ Sin and Salvation (Eli & Roxy)

Song List on Spotify

Tattooed Souls.

My Immortal~ Evanescence
A Little Bit Stronger~ Sara Evans
Baby Come Back~ Player
It's Not Over~ Chris Daughtry
On Bended Knee~ Boyz II Men
Collide~ Kid Rock
Tattoo~ Jordin Sparks

Listen and Enjoy!

Acknowledgments

Thank you for choosing to read ***Tattooed Souls***. After writing the "Hearts Series", all I heard from readers was that they loved Zack. I mean, who wouldn't love to have a man like him? I loved Zack too and knew that he needed his own story. But Zack and Rissa's story couldn't be told in a single book, hence the "Tattooed Duet" was born.

To my husband~ I could have never done this without your love and support. Thank you for putting up with my endless hours of writing, all the take-out dinners, and my hounding of you to read and offer input. I know I've made you crazy, but you were a trooper through it all! Thank you for believing in me!

To Amy, Kristy, Ari, and Denise~ You girls are the best beta readers anyone could ask for! You've supported my journey and spent endless hours reading and rereading. Your suggestions, critiques, and encouragement helped me in ways you'll never understand. Thank you for listening to my obsession day after day!

To Linda~ Thank you for the endless hours you spent proofreading. After reading the book several times myself, I still missed errors. Your expertise and constructive criticism helped me to make this book so much better. I could never thank you enough for all your help!

To Jill~ You've been a great friend! I wasn't very specific about what I wanted for this cover. Between our two creative brains we came up with something amazing. Thank you for the beautiful cover of ***Tattooed Souls***… I absolutely love it!

To my readers~ Thank you for supporting me in this journey. Please spread the word and leave a quick review on Amazon, if you have enjoyed this book. Without you, writing would still be a dream.

About the Author

Sabrina Wagner lives in Sterling Heights, Michigan. She writes sweet, sassy, sexy romance novels featuring alpha males and the strong women who challenge them.

Sabrina believes that true friends should be treasured, a woman's strength is forged by the fire of affliction, and everyone deserves a happy ending. She enjoys spending time with her family, walking on the beach, cuddling her kittens, and great books. Sabrina is a hopeless romantic and knows all too well that life is full of twists and turns, but the bumpy road is what leads to our true destination.

Want to be the first to learn book news, updates and more?
Sign up for my Newsletter.

https://www.subscribepage.com/sabrinawagnernewsletter

Want to know about my new releases and upcoming sales?
Stay connected on:

Facebook~Instagram~Twitter~TikTok
Goodreads~BookBub~Amazon

I'd love to hear from you.
Visit my website to connect with me.

www.sabrinawagnerauthor.com

Made in the USA
Monee, IL
28 February 2023

28575904R00164